Finding ⌐

A modern mystery, an ancient disappearance.

By
James Penhaligon

Dedication:

As always, this is for Ingrid. Ninaku penda sana!

The Author.

James Penhaligon *is a retired medical doctor & consultant psychiatrist in the United Kingdom. He is the author of* **'Speak Swahili, Dammit!',** *an autobiography of growing up as an expatriate child deep in the bush in Tanganyika, now Tanzania. This book has excellent press reviews around the world, and over 500 Amazon reader reviews in the USA & UK, with average reader rating of 4.5 out of 5 stars. These reviews may be seen on Amazon Books UK, and Amazon.com (USA).*

One

We was betray'd. It wer Jon Hicks, a fellowe Cornish free trad'r, or smuggl'r t' th' rev'nue men, who set th' trap an' stood witniss aginst me t' th' crown. I knowd not why, but be warn'd: jealousy, evin unjustf'd, maks demons o' men. Ignatius Myghal Tregurtha, September 10, 1790.

Heated air bent the horizon and shimmered the hills. My eyes ached, and sunglasses didn't help. It was hard to focus in the glare, risky at speed. The corrugations made a washboard, and the wheels bounced, spun and spat stones. The Land Rover skidded on loose shale, almost barreling into the boulders on the roadside. A red dust trail billowed behind.

When I got home, I'd gulp an icy beer. I glanced at the torn package. The book had come at last. The drive to Windhoek took three hours each way. I tasted dust, and the armpits of my shirt were dark with sweat.

On a rocky rise, a solitary black-backed jackal stood immobile as a statue, his head framed between two boulders, pointed ears cocked, the wisdom of the wild in his unblinking eyes, as he watched my roaring, stone-scattering progress. His wavering image in the heated air lent him an unearthly appearance, like a San-Bushman cave painting. The San believe these creatures, with their sly, sinister wisdom, are the greatest tricksters in creation, and even lions can't match their cunning.

My name is Tobias Vingoe. I was once a doctor at Royal Cornwall Hospital in Truro, before it gave me up and I moved here to Namibia.

—

I had no responsibility or relationship with anyone now, except Chiko, my wickedly outspoken partner and friend. My life was better. Though I still had to earn a living, I breathed that most precious thing – freedom.

I lived in a remote place, with just one person for company. I socialised with safari guests, but that was business. If they thought I was a tough, hard man, so be it. Nobody wanted to go into the desert with a wimp. Chiko was the only person in Namibia who really knew me.

I changed down as I neared the house.

Had somebody painted the wall? Used to be sandy like the earth. Now it was green. I blinked and my eyelids scratched like emery boards. Closer, I saw it was a caravan. Attached was a dusty Toyota Land Cruiser.

I slithered the Rover to a halt inches from the door, heaved myself out and climbed the wooden steps. The last unannounced visitors came in a Mercedes. Chiko called them *Wabenzis*, the tribe of Merc drivers. These weren't *Wabenzis*. Would Chiko call them *Wa-Toyota*? I wondered if they were the ones who phoned about viewing the solar eclipse from the desert. No, it wasn't due till the twenty seventh of February. Today was only the sixteenth. Whatever, my book would have to wait.

Through the kitchen door, I saw a tall man and a slim girl drinking beer in the lounge. People didn't ask out there. I took a bottle of *Windhoek* from the fridge and poured an icy stream down the sand dune in my throat. They stood as I joined them.

'Egon Neumann,' he said.

Clipped German pronunciation.

Neu–Mann, New-Man. I shook his hand. It was warm and clammy.

—

His blond hair hung over his forehead and his pale blue eyes avoided contact. He was thirtyish and chubby round the waist. An office type.

'Pleased to meet you,' he said.

'Tobias Vingoe.'

'Angelika,' she said, stepping forward. She was tall, with auburn hair parted on her forehead and hanging to her shoulders, high cheekbones, a long neck, a small mole high on one cheek, and freckles. Her eyes were a brighter shade of his. She put out a slim hand.

'We need help,' Egon said. He had a tic in one eyelid. 'But this mustn't go further.'

'A secret? Are you going to tell me?'

'Put it this way - it must stay in confidence,' she said.

'Okay.'

'We're told you're the best guide —'

'Oh, let me explain, I'll do it better,' said Angelika, elbowing Egon aside.

'Don't take your anger out on me!' he uttered tersely.

'We came to you on advice —'

'Who?'

'A friend,' she grinned mysteriously. We sat down in awkward silence. They hadn't come for Bushman art, nor the eclipse. A pity, because showing ancient human relics was my favourite thing. But no, that wasn't why this feuding couple had come.

Many clients wanted to 'experience the Namib', had no idea how tough it was off-road. Most didn't anticipate the heat, the bone-shaking ride, the dust, the rocky outcrops, the gulleys, the axle-deep sand drifts, the treacherous shale.

Nor did they even ponder that, exhausted by the end, you had to come back the same way.

I glanced at Angelika.

—

Had I walked in on a conjugal row? She smiled a lot, though dust discoloured her clothes and streaked her face.

'Sorry,' I said, 'I'm hot, tired, famished. You staying the night?' They nodded, her eyes glinting, his staring at the ceiling.

'There's only single beds.'

'That's fine,' she laughed, 'he's my brother.' She appraised me through half-closed eyelids, distantly reminding me of someone. I glanced at the book I'd dropped, still half-wrapped, on the coffee table.

I called Chiko. He was sixty-something, a San Bushmen. Most of his people had been forced to abandon their ancient lifestyle. His San name, *Tchi:xo*, meant 'unlucky'. He owed it to his father falling and breaking a leg on the day he was born. Chiko was cautious with strangers, and who could blame him? Ten years ago, he'd been shot and nearly killed. A police inquiry blamed an Owambo guard toting a British rifle on a German farm. A United Nations hit - job.

He padded up barefoot.

He was barely five foot, with short, tightly curled grey hair, and a face as wrinkled as old brown paper.

There are two Chikos. The one I knew and love, and the one others see.

With me, he's the consummate comedian, forever competing in ingenious tricks and ribald insults. With them, he's cautious and guarded. Strangers think he's a servant, but it isn't true.

Business is competition, winning and losing.

To the San, that's selfish. They live by an age-old code of cooperation.

Everyone does their best according to their ability. Based on their needs, and not those abilities, the rewards are shared. It's that equality which marks them out as the only true socialists on the planet.

Chiko is a very unusual business partner. He leaves negotiations, finances and decisions to me. His contribution is as a superb desert-tracker, and his knowledge of the wilderness where his people wandered for millenia. That is why we have such a good reputation. Bushbuck, lions, elephants, ancient rock-paintings, we found them. We earned a living doing what we loved, but relished most our friendship and things we weren't paid for.

His other, self-imposed, role was mothering me. He insisted on cooking, cleaning and doing household chores, and no amount of protest deterred him. It took time to understand that, in his culture, looking after others was an overarching need.

'So this is Chiko!' Had she heard of him?

Chiko was beside me, looking up. If only he'd wear a new shirt. The one he had on was full of holes.

'Kai?' Khoisan or San for a friend, minus the click. Should have been '!Kai', but white people found it difficult. Here, people spoke Afrikaans, German, a few English words to fill gaps, Zulu when the mood took them, and the odd clicky San word. He was in visitor-mode. Not even his beloved *Polar* ice cream from the shop on the corner of the musically named Bach and Brahms streets in Windhoek would have melted in his mouth.

'Chiko, would you make some delicious food?' Flattery works best.

'Beslis, Kai,' Chiko said with an all-but toothless grin.

Afrikaans for 'certainly'.

What was tickling him? Something rude, no doubt. Only a single tombstone-like tooth remained in his mouth.

He strode away, and shortly came the sound of knife on chopping-board and the clang and clatter of pans. He wasn't a quiet chef.

I turned to my guests. 'How can I help?'

'We need you,' Egon said. His tic was back. 'Our uncle is missing in the Namib.'

'Two months,' Angelika nodded.

'He was our guardian,' Egon said. 'Till I was seven, and Angelika five, we lived with our father —'

'Let me explain,' she said, spreading her hands. 'Our mother died when I was born, father was all we had. He was a jeweller. In 1976, he came from Germany to South Africa, opened a jewellery store in Johannesburg —'

'In 1990, he went searching for diamonds,' Egon interrupted. Ah, I thought, you're after diamonds! Why come to me? Only *de Beers* or *Namdeb* deal in raw, uncut diamonds. Then I realised.

'You mean IDB?' IDB is *Illicit Diamond Buying*, but includes finding, buying, dealing, smuggling, selling or even smelling uncut diamonds without a licence. The diamond laws are strict in South Africa and Namibia. That's how the CSO or *Central Selling Organization*, and *Namdeb*, the Namibian diamond mining company, keep their monopoly.

'They call it that.' The tic belied his calm voice. There was a tingle in my chest. People don't even talk about IDB. It's risky business, even by association.

'Diamonds? In the Namib? Not *outside* the forbidden zone, the *Sperrgebiet?*'

Egon nodded, but still didn't look at me.

'Never heard such nonsense!'

Everyone knew the history.

In 1908, the German government of *Deutsch Südwest Afrika* created the *Sperrgebiet*, which spans the Atlantic 'Skeleton Coast' and stretches two hundred miles from the South African border at Oranjemund to north of Lüderitz Bay.

It covers ten thousand square miles, six times bigger than Cornwall, I often reminded myself, and is still forbidden to everyone except *DeBeers* or *Namdeb*.

'Yes, outside the *Sperrgebiet*,' Angelika sighed. Her agitation rose to her neck in a pink flush.

'Your father was crazy. If diamonds are found outside the *Sperrgebiet*, they'll extend its boundary.'

'Maybe. It cost him his life.' Egon's eyelid had settled again. 'In 1990 a man called Axel Schneider sold him an uncut diamond as big as pigeon's egg. Flawless, size of my fingernail, twenty carats before cutting.'

Diamond-fables! Like when diggers, karakul-sheep farmers, and dissolute drifters of uncertain occupation drink too many *Windhoeks* at Ma Erhardt's unlicensed *'Verliere Deine Beine'*, or 'Lose Your Legs' bar, otherwise known as 'The Legless Arms', on the road to Omaruru.

The biggest diamond ever found was the Cullinan stone. Maybe *that* was as big as a pigeon's egg.

'When I was seven,' Egon said, 'they were always on the phone. One day Schneider brought a map showing where the diamond was found. Dad didn't know who he got it from, but thought it was a guy called Ernst Mencken. They decided to make an expedition and check it out.'

'And died doing it,' Angelika added, pointing with a sunburnt arm at the window facing northwest, to the barren wastelands beyond.

Egon drained his glass and, for the first time, actually stared at me.

'We were looked after by our uncle, Dad's brother Rodolf, who took over the jewellery store.'

'Okay, but why did your uncle also go after so long?'

Egon put his hand in his pocket and withdrew an envelope. He took out and passed over a single yellowing page. It was written in German, which I understood.

Kaiserhoff Hotel
Windhoek
23.10.90

Dear Rodolf,

I hope you are all well and coping with Angelika and Egon. Windhoek is living up to its windy name. This note is to say Axel is here. In the morning we go north and, with luck, should be back in a week.

Wish me luck. I hope Axel's map is not another lie!
My love to the children.
Take care,
Karl.

I folded the letter and gave it back.

'1990, your father... you confuse me. You say your uncle's missing, then show me a twenty-seven-year-old letter from your father!'

'Coming to it, the letter was the last we heard.'

'Never saw him again?' Egon nodded.

'It was a mystery,' Angelika said. 'Then, after five weeks, Schneider returned from the desert on foot. He was nearly dead, badly sunburnt and thin as a skeleton.' She shook her head.

'There was a rumour he'd murdered our father, but he died before they could question him.'

'And your uncle went missing two months ago because…?

'Don't know,' said Angelika, 'but that's why we're here. I also have a special reason for choosing you.'

Two

I was just short of twenty-one on the second of February 1786. I awoke at four in the morning, washed and dressed in several layers with a seaman's oilskin over it all, for it was dark and bitter cold outside. When I left her the previous night, Morwenna said she had a premonition it was the last time she'd see me. She never liked my work, and if I had anything else I'd have given it up for her sake.

'Git a move on,' said big brother Jacca impatiently, making me burn my mouth with hot tea. 'We mus' go dreckly!' It was always *dreckly* with Jacca, nothing could ever wait.

We stamped our feet and rubbed our hands to keep warm on the corner until Daveth Eva and Morcom Jago collected us in the pony-cart. Just before six, we came to Mounts Bay in the dark, and sneaked our way round to Prussia Cove.

'Eyes good this mornin'?' Daveth asked. Why wouldn't they be?

''Ansome,' said I.

'Proper job, ye'll be needin' 'ey!'

We had to row out and retrieve twelve roped and weighted eight-and-a-quarter gallon ankers of French brandy. They'd been dropped off in the night and marked with a buoy by *Cormorant*, John Carter or the 'King of Prussia's' own twenty-ton fast lugger, which made the smuggling run from Morlaix for three years.

It was silent as a graveyard on the beach. With hindsight, *too* quiet. As we pushed the gig to the water, the grating of sand and pebbles split the silence like nails on rusty steel.

The first blush of day lit the horizon.

It was good timing, for, with my keen sight, I had to spot the buoy. We knew which way to row. We'd been here many times, and there was nothing amiss.

In West Cornwall, day dawns quickly once the first first rays of the sun break horizon over the sea. We'd gone less than half a league when I spotted our quarry. It was red and six inches wide.

'Buoy ahoy,' I shouted. It bobbed in the waves less than a cable away. We rowed to it, seized the mooring line with a boathook, and set to hauling up the cargo. It was heavy work and took all our strength. Finally, all twelve anker-casks were boarded.

It would be full daylight in less than half an hour, so we hurried for the shore. We'd stow the casks in a cave, to be carried up the tunnel to Angwin Hendra's house on the cliff. From there it would be collected by donkey wagon. In our business, secrecy was vital. Some of our goods, we knew, gained the tables of the richest and grandest in Cornwall, even those of the very revenue men who tried to catch us.

'A-barth Dyw!' shouted Morcom. In God's Name! Out of the darkness of the western bay, sailing towards the rising sun, burst a sixty-foot cutter, sails bulging in the onshore breeze, water rippling at the bow.

'It be th' cursit revenue!' A cold hand seized my heart.

Even as we watched, two eight-oared gigs shot out from the ship's sides. By law, revenue gigs were allowed eight oars apiece, local Cornish ones only four. The trap was well planned and cleverly sprung. No wonder, for the traitor Jon Hicks worked with us for years, and knew every detail of our operations.

Though the boys bent to the oars with all their might, it was a race we could not win.

In the bow of the nearest gig, a man fired a musket.

The ball sent up a small spume of water just feet away. There was no choice but to stop, and no time to throw the contraband overboard.

The cove, still cloaked in darkness, was barely two hundred yards distant.

'Swim fur it, me 'ansomes!' yelled Morcom, and my brothers and friends dove into the water. I wasn't a strong swimmer and didn't dare, specially not in the vicious cold of the channel in winter. It was still too dark for proper aim, but a second Brown Bess belched fire as it discharged at the swimmers.

The revenue men boarded and took me prisoner. One shoved the cold barrel of his flintlock pistol against my neck.

'Can't swim, eh?' He clouted me on the head with his free hand. In less time than it takes to sneeze, I'd gone from free to captive. A Turkish trader in Morlaix once told me you could not avoid your fate. It was *kismet*, he said, pre-ordained by Allah.

Thus, was I apprehended by the kings' revenue on the eighth day of February 1786, at Prussia Cove in Mount's Bay, between Porthleven and Penzance.

'Your skulduggery is over,' a revenue officer told me aboard the revenue ship, between cuffing my ear and poking me in the ribs with his pistol. 'This cursed business will be stamped out, even here in Cornwall!' Over three-quarters of the tea and half the spirits in England were smuggled. To us, it was a source of pride, to them a heinous crime.

'Now what is your name?' he growled.

'Ignatius Tregurtha.' I flinched as he raised his hand again.

'Talkin' t'me as t' an equal?' he grunted.

'I'll teach ye how to address yourn superiors! It goes like this,' he said, '*With humble submission, Sir, my name is Ignatius Tregurtha!*' he spat as his open palm impacted my cheek and knocked my head back. I would learn to speak humbly.

The sheriff committed me to gaol on a charge of smuggling. The cells in Bodmin were full, so I was taken to Launceston Castle. Though punched and cuffed senseless, and starved for days, and my right hand crushed between the wall and the butt of a Brown Bess, I did not betray my comrades.

'Who were the others?' they asked me over and over.

'Jowan Trelawney, Tomas Rowe, Awen Trenoweth and Yestin Hoskins,' made up names all. Another beating, more false names. Let the revenue men do as they will, I would not assist them. Finally, to my great relief, they realised they were wasting their time.

Six weeks I languished in gaol, in the cold and indescribable filth of human waste. After that unhappy time, I was moved to the even more demeaning and inhuman Bodmin gaol. When my trial was due, they took me to the holding cells beneath the assizes, there to await justice. How suddenly my world turned upside down! A great wall had fallen between me and my former life. I could never go back. I was alone, and all I knew and loved was gone.

The past haunted me. Sweet Morwenna, above all. How can I begin to tell of my agony at our cruel and sudden parting? I *felt* her presence, saw her smiling face, heard her laughter and even smelt her hair. But she was beyond reach.

Such was my pain that, in those early days, separation from my family and friends could hardly distress me more.

They say a dying man's life flashes before him.

It is not only a dying man.

In my misery I relived it all.

The 'great recovery', when under Carter's leadership we stole our seized cargo back from Customs House in Penzance, and the excise said they knew who led us because 'like an honest man, he took onlie what wer 'is own!' We must have spent a fortune celebrating in the *Admiral Benbow* pub in Penzance that night. A place I knew well from carrying brandy up the tunnel from the beach, and into the pub itself!

There was the time when John Trewavas' sons defended his house against the revenue.

'By thunder, I'll blow th' brains out of anie 'oo come furth'r',' the older son threatened, cocking his pistol, while the smuggled goods were spirited out the back door.

I could never forget the 'switch', when, hidden by a cliff from the pursuing revenue, we swapped our contraband-laden craft with a fisherman's, and the jubilation on the officers' faces turned to bewilderment when they apprehended a boatload of pilchards.

They were good times, but my crowning joy was Morwenna.

My holding-cell was one of many in two rows of a dark, narrow, arch-roofed passage where the stone walls dripped and glistened with wetness. It was a stinking dungeon, with little light or hope. It was the very opposite to the warmth and comfort of *Chy Velah*, or 'The House in the Valley', the blessed Penzance home where I'd lived my whole life.

I was locked in a space two foot by two, and six high. I sat in the dark on an iron-hard plank, my back thrust up against the cold, damp wall.

Before me was a door of iron-reinforced wood, with vertical slots making a high barred opening eighteen inches wide by twelve high. I couldn't straighten my legs or raise my feet. There were chains linked together round my wrists and ankles.

It was the coldest I'd ever been, and the mildew on the wall dripped water from above. Even if not locked in that cruel, freezing box, there could have been no escape. How I wished I could see dear green-eyed Morwenna!

There were others in the cells, and though several coughed consumptively, nobody talked. I ached from the hard plank. The stench of piss, shite and unwashed bodies was overwhelming. At first, I tried not to breathe. But I couldn't hold my breath, and had to taste the putrid air. The pain in my buttocks and cramps in my legs grew ever worse. When I moved, my knees came up painfully against the cruel, unyielding door.

A charge of Smuggling was sent to the gaoler and shown to me. Next day, after more agonising hours in a holding cell, I was brought to the bar to be arraigned. I waited an eternity, but at last footsteps sounded on the stone floor, and keys jingled. Was it for me, or another? A dull light flickered through the grill, then I heard heavy breathing. The gaoler was old, fat and in ailing health.

'Tregurtha Ignatius?' he shouted hoarsely, rapping on the door.

'I am here.' He inserted a key in the lock. Relief welled up. At last, I would be able to rest my backside and stretch the cramp out of my legs.

With a loud grating, the door swung open. I'd been in darkness so long, the yellow light of the gaoler's hurricane lamp dazzled me.

'On your pins,' he grated out between coughs. The stench offended even *his* nose and throat. I struggled to my feet, the chains drawing me up and leaving me stooping.

He fumbled for a key to loosen the chain between my ankles and wrists.

A sorry sight I was, and all because of betrayal. Now would be my trial. The evidence against me was insurmountable. The choice was between hanging and transportation. What would become of me? Would I ever see Morwenna again?

Three

'That's terrible, but I don't know if I can help.'

'You don't believe a word!' Angelika banged her glass on the coffee table as if to break it.

'Egon, we're wasting our time.'

'I didn't ask you to come.'

Chiko stood in the doorway, concern etched on his face. He hated unpleasantness.

'Let's go, Egon.' Angelika started to her feet.

'Calm down,' I said.

Suddenly the room began to tilt and spin, and my heart hammered in my chest. Beer and wine on an empty stomach, the long drive, the heat, the stress. Even worse was a sense of foreboding.

'You alright?' Angelika asked. My dizziness cleared slowly.

'Okay.'

'You're pale, sure you're okay?'

'Fine.' I was still queasy.

Chiko shook his head and went back into the kitchen.

'What happened then?' Angelika sat down, brushing hair from her face.

'Nothing. The papers tired of the story, everyone forgot except Angelika, Uncle Rodolf and me. He brought us up, never married. After Dad was declared dead in February 1992, he became our guardian.'

'But why did *he* go into the desert after all these years, why the twenty-seven-year delay?'

'Life —' Egon began.

'I heard about UFO's at that time,' Angelika interrupted, 'I thought he'd been taken.'

'Alien abduction?'

'Not funny!'

'No.'

'He wasn't taken by a flying saucer, they found his body in 1994.' Egon spoke like I was a backward child.

'Where?'

'Kaokoland.'

'How did they find it?' It's the remotest place, the least populated in Africa.

'Army exercise,' said Egon, 'they found a skeleton with clothes. Dental records proved it was him.'

'How did he die?'

'Couldn't tell, gnawed and chewed, not much left. We were sure he was murdered.'

'I see.' People died in the desert, not hard to do. I changed the subject.

'You also in the gem-trade?'

'Yes, after being round diamonds and rubies from small. I studied gem and diamond valuation, grading, cutting and polishing.' I turned to Angelika.

'You in the business?'

'Oh no, I'm an anthropologist.'

'Meaning?'

'I teach at university, do research.'

'What you teach?'

'About ancient people. Physical characteristics, environment, diet, culture, language, art.'

'Who you researching?'

'The San in the Kalahari, Namibia, Botswana.' An expert on the San! More direct than reading *Untold Mysteries of The San'* by Sven Johannsen, that redoubtable and famed explorer and writer about these parts in 1790. It was good to meet someone interested in the San in this uncaring day and age. There weren't a lot around.

The tattered copy of Johannsen's book on my bedroom shelf, a 'Historical Editions' reprint from 1921, was, apart from Chiko, and Laurens van der Post's 'Lost World of the Kalahari', published by Hogarth Press in 1958, my only source on the ancient ways of the San.

A haunting passage from van der Post came back to me: *The older I grew, the more I resented that I had come too late on the scene to know him in the flesh. For many years I could not accept that the door was closed for ever on the Bushman. I went on seeking for news and information on him as if preparing for the moment when the door would open and he would reappear in our midst. Indeed, I believe the first objective question I ever asked of life was: 'who, really, was the Bushman?'*

The sad truth was that, already in his day, the San had all but vanished from the Kalahari, driven out by settlers and farmers, and African tribes alike.

'You do that from Jo'burg?'

'No, I've got a varied job.'

'Far-flung.' Egon stretched his arms. 'She's away so much, we hardly meet.'

'Away?'

'Different places. I teach at the Universities of Botswana in Gaborone, Namibia in Windhoek, and Western Cape in Capetown. I keep flats in Gaborone and Windhoek, where I spend half my time, and stay over in a hotel in Cape Town.'

'What you teach about the San?'

'Oh, Khoisan language, history, how imported epidemics and loss of hunting grounds decimated them. Our project is about helping them build the capacity to survive.'

'A good thing. You seem to have packed a lot into your life. How old are you?'

'Wondered when you'd ask,' she said, 'I'm twenty-nine, Egon's thirty-one. You?'

'Thirty-six.'

'Old man,' she laughed.

'Don't forget it. You said you had another reason for choosing me?'

'We have a common friend.'

'Who?'

'Dr van Loon.'

'*Pik* van Loon?' The surgeon who saved Chiko's life after he was shot ten years ago. He was an exception, my only friend in Windhoek.

'Yes, Pik's a member of *!ga:wa* or 'Awaken', the foundation which helps the San with healthcare, education, employment and housing. I know him through my fieldwork. He thinks highly of you. When I told him about Uncle Rodolf, he said there was nobody better than you to help.'

'Hope he didn't exaggerate!'

'Look, three months ago, something happened which made us sit up,' Egon said.

'What?'

'We found the map.'

'Your father's map?'

'Yes.'

'Didn't he take it with him?'

'That's what we thought, but he didn't want to risk losing it, stored it in his head.' The tic was time-limited, I decided.

'Didn't he destroy the paper copy?'

'It has his writing on it. There are two lines crossing in the middle of the desert. At the intersection is a circle in pencil and Dad's writing - *hier sind diamanten* - here are diamonds.'

'Why did it take so long to find?'

'It was in a jacket pocket. When Dad died, Rodolf put his clothes in a trunk and it stayed there until three months ago.' Egon sat back and drained his glass.

'Are you saying Rodolf used it to search for diamonds?'

'Yes,' Angelika said.

'When?'

'He left Jo'burg two months ago,' Egon replied.

'That's where you started.'

'Look, something's happened to him!' Angelika's voice was strained.

'Not a flying saucer?'

'I wish you'd stop!' Angelika shook her head, making her hair twirl. She wrinkled her forehead when she was angry.

I shrugged. The Namib is more than a desert. It's a mysterious and forbidding place, where imaginations run wild.

'Why was there nothing in the papers about a missing man?'

'He didn't tell anyone he was going,' Angelika said. 'If the media splashed it, bad people could move in. He thought Schneider killed Dad.'

'Put it this way - he's the only family we have.'

'We need your help,' Egon's tic was back.

'Read Rider Haggard?'

'What?' Egon's eyebrows arched.

'African adventure fiction,' Angelika said.

'King Solomon's Mines, Africa, missing man, diamonds…a brother and sister persuade a guide to take them on a journey to look for a missing man —'

'What rubbish,' she interrupted, 'this has nothing to do with Rider Haggard!'

'No,' Egon said, 'this is not fiction.'

'Nor a movie!' Angelika added.

'Are you going to joke or listen?' Egon asked.

'Let me see the map!'

'Rodolf took it but I made a copy.'

It was an old folded road map of Namibia. A desolate seaboard to the west.

The Skeleton Coast, lay there, where for centuries half-drowned sailors struggled ashore from shipwrecks and perished from thirst. Through that bone-littered, ever-changing sea of sand, wound a thin tarred road from Upington in the North Cape to Windhoek and Swakopmund. It was marked in red. Lesser roads were plotted as dotted lines. There were isolated villages and towns, many with unpronounceable names.

The west and north were pale yellow, with hardly any distinguishing marks. In the far north, somewhere in the middle of the Kaokoland, or *Kunene Province* as it was called now, were two intersecting pencil lines, with *Hier sind diamanten* written in fountain pen.

I was reminded of a two-centuries-old Herero story that a white 'witch-man or *omuroi* with a singing accent' passed nearby in the company of Nama tribesmen on his way to the Kaokoland. It was a coincidence. Both they and I had a mystery about a lost relative, though Ignatius went missing over two hundred and twenty years ago.

Dusty thoughts ran through my mind. The Namib is the oldest desert on earth. Only the hardiest creatures survive. There are a few scattered herds of wildebeest and eland on the fringe, but just bleached white bones beyond. A cauldron by day, a vast arena where granite is burnt black by aeons of merciless sun. Here and there, craggy mountain ranges rise above wind-carved dunes.

It's hard to imagine what great forces once tore and twisted the landscape.

I turned the map over. The other side was blank.

'Was there anything on the back?'

'That's a copy. The original had *Ersprungen von ....
heute, 14de März 1990* on it,' Egon replied.

'Originated from ... today, 14th March 1990. The middle, space for one letter, is too smudged to read, so no idea who it could have been.'

'A James Bond movie,' I said.

'I'm sure the smudge hides the source.' He was ticking again.

'Look, will you take us?' Angelika's shoulders were straight, her hands on her knees.

'I can't make up my mind just like that. Chiko and I have to agree before we take a job. You can't come here and expect me to rush off into the desert on a wild guinea-fowl chase.' She looked at me quizzically.

'There's no geese out here!' A hint of a smile played on her lips.

'Any idea how tough the going is?' They were silent.

I glanced at Angelika. Did her studies include how dangerous the desert was?

'No-one to bury anyone who dies, no mourners, just vultures, with sharp beaks and no sense of humour, tearing at them before they're even dead.' Her expression didn't change. 'The Kaokoland is the worst!'

In the silence, I turned my gaze back to the map. They were protecting someone. The pencil marks intersected. One linked Kamanjab, Herero for *Pleasant Place Where Fat Cattle Graze*, to Opuwo, a Himba name meaning *The End*.

The other ran north-south.

The intersection was four hundred miles northwest of Karibib, in the most desolate part.

'It's the middle of nowhere, and I think your father was wrong about *diamanten*!' Even as I spoke, I couldn't suppress the thought: What if there really *are* diamonds?

'Are you frightened?' I glared at her.

'You think *I'm* scared?

'Are you?'

After a long pause, I heard myself speak.

'I'll have to discuss it with Chiko.'

The trap was well laid. Involving Pik van Loon was a master-stroke. A rivulet of sweat tickled the corner of my mouth. I licked my lips. Salty. My forehead itched. The rust-streaked rattly ceiling-fan stirred the sultry air like a hairdryer on 'hot'. Nobody spoke. The old wind-up clock on the iroko mantelpiece ticked out the seconds.

'You really want us to take you?'

'We do,' Egon said.

'To find your uncle or diamonds?'

'Our uncle,' Angelika said.

'Tell me first, why the caravan?'

'Somewhere to sleep.' Egon sighed, staring at the ceiling.

'Think they don't know it's ideal for hiding diamonds? Loose panels behind the fridge or cooker. In the ceiling space, false backs in cupboards…. If the police sniff a rat, like you two heading into the desert with a caravan, coming from, of all places, a *jewellery* shop, they'll…' They exchanged glances.

'You do realise you could get into trouble?'

'What are your charges?' he asked.

'*If* we go, two thousand Namibian Dollars, or a hundred and thirty US, per day, plus food and fuel.'

'That's fine,' Angelika said.

Chiko checked the food, turned the cooker down, and followed me outside. His office had no roof.

'Men lost in desert?' he asked. The question wasn't if they were, but what it meant for us. Though his English was limited, he had grasped the essentials.

'Their uncle and another man.'

'Diamonds?' There was a shrewd look in his eyes.

'Seems so, but the men are missing.'

'You want to go, *Kai*?' Chiko was unique. Telling stories, he was loquacious and elegant, with business, brief and to-the-point.

'Do *you* think we should?'

'We cannot abandon them, they will die!'

'You agree to go?'

'What do you think, *Kai*?' He shook his head. The question was pointless.

Four

I know little of the law, except it is harsh, and my future so hung on its tender mercy that the memory of my trial will never fade. Nor will the words of those who stood in judgement. Though men of letters may deride my rendition, I write as one who, parted from love and family, stood with my life at the fickle mercy of strangers.

I was tried at Bodmin Assizes on the thirty first of March 1786, six weeks after my arrest in Mounts Bay. My account is bound by the limits of memory. Of they who sat on the public benches, or played no part, I have little recall. The court being set, I was brought in chains. It was a small room with high windows, rows of wooden seating and a raised platform and bench, where sat the mighties.

After several minutes, when many present conversed, the clerk of the court instructed the cryer, who, in a loud voice, commanded silence. The clerk instructed that I, the prisoner, be brought to the bar.

'Hold up thy hand,' he said.

'With humble submission,' said I, remembering my sharp lesson about humble-speak after swearing to tell the truth, the whole truth and nothing but the truth on the Bible held by the usher, 'I have done no more than earn a living.'

'A living, prisoner? Do we not all have livings to make, and do we steal to gain it?' It was the crusty judge who spoke, he with a grey wig upon his head, for all the world a murdered fox.

'With humble submission m' Lud,' I said, 'I stand indicted for smuggling.' I held up my hands.

'I am a poor fisherman, and though I engaged in free trade, I have never hurt a soul.' He stared at me as at vermin.

'Smuggling,' he spat, 'no matter how humble your submission!' The colour rose in his face. 'Free trade, indeed! If thou wants counsel prisoner, chuse now.'

'I have no counsel m' Lud.'

'Have you witnesses to prove thy innocence?' He was struggling to keep a straight face. His Lordship was amused by his own humour.

'None, m' Lud.' Better brief answers, it seemed. Now spoke the king's counsel.

'My lords,' said he in a loud voice, 'I am concerned for the King against the prisoner at the bar. The law sayeth it must be by affidavit of another, not the prisoner.'

'With humble submission m' Lud,' I started again, 'I ask only mercy'. A hush fell in the court. The judge beckoned the clerk to the bench, and leaning close together they conversed in whispers. Finally, he straightened.

'Prisoner, art thou pleading guilty, for if ye are the prosecution would have dispensed with preparing charges and calling witnesses, and the court could have proceeded to sentence.' He glared at me. How could I have made a plea from my cell? I had no time to think, for he sighed and spoke again.

'We shall plead you innocent. Jailer, take the prisoner. Return him to the bar at nine o'clock in the morning, with his irons off.'

In my freezing, damp cell, I was tormented by memories of sweet, gentle Morwenna.

She was my third cousin, the daughter of father's older sister's son.

She was a year younger than me, but seemed older.

Her name means Maiden, and never was anyone better named.

She was pretty, with long brown hair and bright green eyes, and a charming wrinkle on her nose when she laughed.

She bided with her grandmother, her mother dying of consumption, and her father perishing a year later by falling down a shaft at Wheal Owles near St Just, 'wheal' the English for *hwel*, or 'mine' in Cornish.

Their house was a small terrace half a mile from ours, and I began to visit, taking her small gifts of silk cloth, French perfume, or other contraband things, for which she showed much gratitude. They were desperately poor.

In 1781 I was sixteen and in love. At first, my visits to Morwenna were infrequent, the demands of my employment taking me from Penzance, sometimes weeks at a time.

When we were together she said the prettiest things. One day we sat on a bench in her grandmother's back garden.

'Your eyes,' she said, 'are a beautiful blue.'

'Not as pretty as your green ones,' said I. And so proceeded the sweet talk of young love. My infatuation grew, and with it came jealousy. Morwenna was a comely maiden, and unless I secured her there was a risk some other may step in.

With that fear uppermost, within a year I asked if, when I could afford a cottage, she'd marry me. She threw her arms around my neck and wept with happiness. Though we kept it secret, we were promised to each other. I thought nobody and nothing could ever come between us.

—

So it was, between 1782 when I was seventeen, and 1786 when I was twenty-one, that being the year of my calamity, I pursued two things in life, Morwenna, and saving money to lease a cottage.

For four happy years, we made ever more expansive plans for the future and fell more and more deeply in love.

Now, as if divided by a revenue cutlass, we were rent asunder.

The next day, the first of April 1786, at nine o'clock in the morning, the court set, I was again brought thereto from the holding cell, with my chains removed. At least it was warm there. When at last there was silence, the clerk of the crown spoke.

'Jailer, bring Ignatius Tregurtha to the bar.' I was led forward.

'Ignatius Tregurtha, thou standest indicted in the duchy of Cornwall thus: that ye did engage in smuggling. Ye were captured by the revenue ship *Imperious*, which chanc'd upon ye and four others in Mounts Bay on the eighth of February.' *Chanced?* That was not by chance. It was done through treachery! His words broke into my thoughts.

'How plead'st thou, guilty or not guilty?'

'Not guilty, m'Lud,' said I, remembering the judge's admonition, and deciding not to make a statement of humility.

'Not guilty,' echoed the judge, 'the plea shall in record stand thus.'

'Who will ye be tried by?' asked the clerk.

'God and my country.'

'God send ye safe deliverance,' said the clerk.

He cleared his throat, then instructed the jurymen to be called.

'Prisoner, if thou have objections against any of the jury,' said the judge, 'ye may chuse twelve out of thirty-six.'

'Knowing none, M Lud,' I said, 'I shall be satisfied with they as are called.'

'Jurors look at the prisoner, prisoner look upon the jurors.'

The clerk addressed the judge. 'The jury is sworn,' he said.

Now it was the turn of the king's counsel. 'My Lords, we call our first witness. The Crown calls George Laity.' I recognized the tall man who stood up. He was one of the officers who arrested me.

'George Laity,' said the king's counsel, 'of the Royal Revenue, deposeth he, between five and six in the morning on the eighth of February 1786, did see the prisoner at the bar with four others in a gig rowing from the sea towards Prussia Cove.'

'What was the prisoner doing when the witness spied him?' asked the judge. George Laity cleared his throat and spoke.

'He wer steerin' th' smugglr's gig, m' Lud.'

'What happened then?' asked the judge.

'We was in two gigs o' eight oars, an' cut 'ey off fro' th' cove. Thomas Brine loosit a musket shot as warnin.'

'And then?'

Th' four rowers dived into th' sea an' swimmed away'.

'And the prisoner, whom ye identify as the man at the bar, what did he?'

'He wer th' only one as didn't swimmed off.' Now the judge turned to me.

'Prisoner, have ye any questions for George Laity?'

'None Lordship, I cannot deny he speaks true.'

'Dismiss the witness, call the next,' said he with the dead fox on his head.

'The Crown dismisses George Laity,' said the counsel, 'and calls Jon Hicks.'

I recognized the thin, bald man who stood. He was a free-trader like me, and sometimes stood in when one of our crew were otherwise engaged.

He was also the husband of Kerensa Hicks, a Penzance beauty rumoured to have a wandering eye.

I'd heard it said she lived up to her name, Cornish for 'Love', by giving hers freely. There was something new in Jon Hicks' pinched features when he glared at me. Loathing and hatred are difficult to hide. Only later was I to know he deemed me Kerensa's secret lover.

'I beg lordship ask the witness how he knows me —'

'Jon Hicks,' said the judge, 'look at the prisoner, knowest thou him?'

'I do,' said Hicks in his reedy voice, 'he be knowed fer a smuggler.'

'And you, Jon Hicks, what are you?' I cried. The judge turned on me angrily.

'Mister Hicks is not indicted, remember thy place!'

'Thank ee, ludship,' said the weasel.

'If the witness knows me to be a smuggler, he must be one himself!' I said against better judgement.

'Prisoner, I have already said the witness is not arraigned before this court!'

'I beg pardon, lordship.' The judge snorted and turned back to Hicks.

'He is known as a smuggler, you say?'

'He be so knowed.'

'How came ye to assist the revenue in his arrest?'

'I 'eard o' a landin' o' brandy at th' cove, an' went to a officer o' th' law.' And there it was. He admitted his treachery!

'Is he here today?'

'He is, m'Lud, an' gave witness afore me.'

'Do you mean the previous witness, George Laity?'

'I do m'Lud.' The judge turned to me.

'Prisoner, ye did not denie the evidence of the first witness. Hast thou heard the second?'

'Yes, Lordship, I have.' He stared at Hicks.

'Did ye accompany the revenue men in their ship, or in the gigs?'

'Nay, m'Lud. I only show'd 'ey th' place.'

'Ask why he betrayed me now, after so many years,' I said.

'Prisoner, know thy place,' spat the judge. 'I will disregard the question. Gentlemen for the Crown, we have no more questions of this witness. Have you others?' The king's counsel stood.

'My Lords we call no more witnesses. The crown rests its case.'

'Prisoner, have ye any witness to call in thy defence?' asked the judge, adjusting his slipping furry headdress.

'No, m'Lord.'

''Tis your right.'

'None, m'Lord.' There was no point.

'Council for the King,' said the judge, 'hast thou any observations?'

'Nothing my Lords, except he be guilty as charged.'

'Prisoner have ye any observations?'

'With Lordship's leave, I deny not the evidence,' I said. 'I ask for leniency, your honour, for I am a poor fisherman.'

'I did smuggle,' I said, causing murmurs.

'It was my only way to earn a living. As your Lordship knows, many have no choice.' His face reddened dangerously.

'Because so many rob his Majesty's revenue, ye must be made an example. Have ye any more to say?'

'No,' I said, regretting my remark.

'Prisoner, speak up if thou hast anything more,' he growled.

'With humble submission m' Lord, I said again, 'I have nothing more to say.' The Council for the Crown stood.

'My Lords, the Crown does not prosecute the prisoner for his character, but for the crime of smuggling.'

The judge brought down the gavel upon the bench.

'Jury hear to the charge against the prisoner at the bar, and the evidence against him. Ye have heard the depositions of the witnesses. Withdraw to consider if the prisoner be guilty or no.'

The jury withdrew, and I was chained and returned to my holding-cell. Within an hour, I was brought back to the bar. The clerk of the court instructed the jury and me to stand.

'How finds the jury, be the prisoner guilty or not guilty?' asked the judge.

'Guilty, m'Lud,' said the jury spokesman. My heart turned to lead, and I thought I may fall down from dizziness. The judge waited for the murmuring on the benches to subside, then addressed me.

'Ignatius Myghal Tregurtha, what cause have ye to shew why sentence of death should not be pronounced?'

I was numb. Death…? Would they really do that? Would I be hanged?

Others had been for smuggling, but that was with violent resistance against arrest, resulting in death or serious injury to officers. I hadn't resisted.

'I ask for mercy, m'Lord,' I croaked with a dry throat.

'Hast thou any further cause to show?'

'No m' Lord, I have nothing further.'

Then spoke the judge gruffly. 'Ignatius Tregurtha, thou art found guilty of smuggling. Ye have not denied the charge.' How could I have, with all the evidence against me?

'Within my jurisprudence,' the judge continued, 'I may sentence ye be taken to a place of execution on the gibbet at Fivelanes, there to be hanged by the neck until thou art Dead. Have ye anything to say before I pass sentence?'

My heart beat a tattoo of fear. I was to die horribly.

There were whispers and murmurs in the public seats. For or against me hanging, I could not tell. Jon Hicks grinned evilly and drew a dirty finger across his throat. When I spoke, my voice came from somewhere else.

'I plead mercy, Lordship,' I heard myself say. The judge reached under the bench. He withdrew his hand. In it rested a black cap.

Was my life to end on a cruel rope? I saw Morwenna's sweet face. Would she weep for me? Father and mother, my brothers, what would it do to them? John Carter himself, our dear King of Prussia, who had put bread on our table for so long, how he would hate to see me hanged for doing his service!

'Thy guilt established, I shall now pass sentence.'

The black cap rested in his hand. The decision to don it or not was his. My neck hung upon it.

Five

Chiko shook the little brass bell in the kitchen. He found it hilariously funny the first time he saw it, and asked why, if there's a tongue in your head, you need such a thing to summon anyone. I explained it was an ornament, not for use, but he decided henceforth to needlessly, and gleefully, ring it at odd times.

When we had no guests, it would shatter the silence and bring me running. I did it back, and nobody would have understood the clamour of the bell, mixed-language curses and peals of laughter. That he rang it meant he was over our guests' arrival. I could tell he was excited at the prospect of another desert expedition.

We sat at the table, and charged the wine glasses. There was a delicious aroma of mutton chops. I'd defy anyone to say there was a better cook than Chiko in Namibia. Amazing, considering he lived most of his life in stone-age conditions, scorching things like *leguaans* over fires.

A month ago, he showed me a cave near Usakos. On the wall was a painting of little stick-men pursuing a rhino with spears. Later, we sat eating and watching the sunset. I chewed on something akin to chicken, but tougher. When I asked, Chiko showed me the severed head of a green lizard. He was adaptable, one day stone-age, next day shops, fridge, saucepans, electric cooker, microwave. And the darned bell!

'Isn't Chiko going to eat?' Angelika asked.

'Later.' Though he cooked it so well, he didn't like European food, nor sitting at the table. He had his own ways and tastes.

No 'Great White Bwana' existed here.

It was the wonderful thing about our friendship – he didn't change to be like me, and I didn't try to be like him.

It was cultural democracy.

'Kan nie kak eet nie,' Chiko exclaimed. Afrikaans for can't eat crap. We laughed.

'He only eats mongongo nuts, *sadhza*, or cornmeal, and meat from anything which flies, crawls or slithers,' he said.

'Zu: hã,' Angelika whispered to Chiko, who recoiled in amused astonishment.

'What did you say?' He'd never heard a European speak Khoisan so well.

'Oh, I called him a dung-beetle-eater,' Angelika laughed, and even Egon managed a grin.

After supper, we went back to the lounge, where Chiko brought the last bottle of Cabernet Sauvignon and coffee. There was devilment in his eyes.

'‡gúä hã,' he breathed with several clicks at Angelika as he walked away.

'What's he say?' I wished I'd paid more attention to Chiko's lessons.

'I'm a dog-eater,' Angelika chortled, 'he's cheeky. Did you teach him?'

'Didn't need to, but I can see you two are going to keep us entertained.'

I shaved before bed and studied myself in the mirror. I was tall and young for my thirty-six years, in spite of small crows-feet around my eyes, which were the same deep ocean blue as my late mothers. I didn't consider myself handsome, though I'd been told I had 'chiselled' good looks. I suppose a chisel's better than a hatchet! Who came up with these terms anyway? People's faces aren't carved.

I was no Leonardo DiCaprio, more Jack Nicholson with a touch of Daniel Craig. My teeth were even, strong and white. I was lean and tanned, more confident-looking than nine years ago.

I could hardly believe we'd agreed to take them. I'd never mounted an expedition to trace what became of Ignatius. Now we were going to search for someone else. Little did I know how one search would spark the other. I climbed into bed and snapped out the light. But I couldn't sleep. I put the light back on, picked up the half-opened parcel and tore off the packaging.

At last, JC Curnow's book, *'Trials at Bodmin Assizes, and Transportation of Cornish Smugglers to Australia in the late 18th Century'* had arrived. It was just bad luck that they came the same day. Looking back, it was more than that. It was the biggest turning point in my life.

For over a year, I'd wanted a copy of the out-of-print tome about the fates of eighteenth-century Cornish smugglers. It was published in 1951 by Messrs Clark & Son, Historical Book Publishers, London. Given its age and limited print-run, there were few around. No dealer knew of it until a historical bookshop in London replied to an email to say they had a tatty copy. I would have spent the whole evening reading, but for the visitors.

The first chapter described the terrible poverty and suffering in eighteenth century Cornwall, which led to the boom in smuggling.

I'd been running on adrenaline for hours, but now the words blurred. I put the book down and turned on my side. My mind was out there, where the hot wind blew dry sand into dunes, and the sun burnt the rocks black.

There, where skeletons with bleached and crumbling bones tried to swallow the sky with gaping mouths.

As I drifted between wakefulness and sleep, I imagined Angelika smiling victoriously, nodding her head, auburn hair flying, eyes bright, slender hands raised in jubilation. Just when I didn't want it, sleep possessed me. Hard on its heels was something else.

A hawk soared high above the desert. Far below, fingers of craggy black rock pierced the sand to point at the pale blue sky. The aerial hunter wheeled away in a dive, his bright yellow eyes fixed on a distant quarry, his wings arched back, his talon-toed feet folded beneath his powerful body.

There was a small, grizzled man, his skin the colour of wrinkled brown paper. His dark eyes glinted in the sunshine as he stared at the plummeting bird. Beside him, smoking a crude wooden pipe, was a big-boned middle-aged European man with a blond beard and mahogany tan. He wore only a leather moochi, but there was something familiar about his face.

I awoke with a start and glanced at my luminous *Seiko* watch. Two o'clock. My dream was so graphic. It didn't have a dream's wooliness. Who were the men, particularly the white one with a beard?

I buried my face in the pillow. It was a combination of diamond-madness, a woman, too much alcohol, and Curnow's book. Yet it was eerie, in view of great-uncle Ignatius, for the visitors' father to leave his bones in the Namib. Whirling thoughts chased each other. I couldn't sleep.

I clicked the light on. There was something I should have done years ago in Cornwall. The *West Briton* newspaper has been in print since 1810, and they might dig up something.

Their archive has even older sources.

I switched on my laptop, opened Safari, and typed in *'West Briton'*. The email address was at the top of the homepage. I composed a letter.

January 5th, 2017

Dear Sir / Madam,

I hope you don't mind me asking if your newspaper archives have any information concerning my great uncle. His name was Ignatius Myghal Tregurtha, and he lived in Penzance. In 1786, at the age of twenty-one, he was tried for smuggling at Bodmin Assizes, and sentenced to transportation to New South Wales in Australia. I believe, from a letter he wrote home in 1790, that he and another convict jumped ship in the Cape of Good Hope in October 1787, and fled to the desert in what is today Namibia.

I am Cornish myself, and previously lived in Truro. I am researching my family history and would appreciate any help.

I know your paper didn't exist before 1810, which is over twenty years after the trial, but perhaps they printed something historical? I believe the Plymouth Gazette and Bath Chronicle covered Cornish news until 1810. They may have shared articles about Cornwall with your archives. Could you possibly look into this?

I hope to hear from you, and will gladly reimburse any costs.

I tapped the 'send' button. and it was done. On impulse, I typed 'Egon' into the search bar. German boy's name. Means *'Edge of the sword'*. I had a feeling he was more the dagger type, in the back. It was a quarter past three when I crawled back into bed and switched off the light.

At six thirty the sun burst through the bedroom window. Sudden, scorching, unarguable.

Water was cascading in the bathroom.

Only the thickness of a prefabricated wall away, one of them was showering. I thrust away the thought.

Why had we agreed? What had we let ourselves in for?

I swung my legs out of bed. I had a vision of Angelika glistening wet in the shower. The splashing stopped. The shower door opened and closed. The wooden house amplified every sound.

Breakfast was ready. Angelika and Egon sat at the table, and Chiko dished up fried eggs, breadfruit and tomato. Angelika smiled as I joined them.

Chiko said something in Khoisan, and Angelika laughed. Living with him was a continual comedy show. I never knew which language he was going to be rude in.

'What was that?'

'Hyena-people always hungry,' she translated. I laughed. Chiko always invoked hyenas for abuse or humour, or a mixture of both. Why that creature, I'd never worked out.

'That's what the desert does.' I was relieved it wasn't worse. She sampled the fried spiced breadfruit.

'Delicious,' she declared.

We ate hungrily. It was the air. Angelika was dressed in a yellow shirt and white shorts. They wouldn't stay white for long. At least she had *veldskoens* or sensible bush-shoes on her feet.

'Down to business!' I said as we sat in the lounge. 'We have to go to Windhoek first. See my tour agent, buy supplies. Your caravan and Toyota stay here.'

'We go in *that?*' Angelika asked, pointing derisively at my beloved Land Rover.

'That,' I exclaimed, 'is a tough machine.'

I faced them. 'Your choice, Land Rover or nothing!'

'It's got funny seats,' Egon said.

'*Cessna 180* plane.'

'Where you get them?' He had no tic this morning.

'Plane crash in the Kalahari. Write-off, but the pilot wasn't hurt. It was scrap, and nobody bothered to collect it.'

'Except you?' Angelika asked.

'With the owner's permission. Insurance paid him out.'

'You took the seats?' Egon glanced at me in a 'this is the man for us to go to such lengths' way.

'Yes.'

'Only seats?' Angelika asked, grinning.

'No.'

'What else?'

'Engine, which I sold, prop.'

'Anything else?' she asked.

'Altimeter.'

'What for?'

'Good maps have altitudes marked. A useful check. If you think you're at X and its altitude is two thousand feet, but the altimeter says a thousand, you're not there.'

'Clever,' Angelika said, 'no satnav?'

'Got a *Garmin*, but they only work in towns and main roads. Useless in the desert. My last one died of heat and dust.'

'My phone's got a GPS app.'

'GPS needs transmission towers, and there's none out there. Altimeter's are more reliable.'

'Okay.'

'Write a list so we can check what we haven't got.' I passed her a ballpoint.

Angelika sat in front, Chiko and Egon in the back.

The hundred and fifty miles on the tarred B2 to Okahandja and B1 to Windhoek took three hours. It was after eleven when we arrived.

We bought cold *Fantas* from a corner shop, then I went to tell my agent I wasn't available until further notice.

On my way back, I saw a rounded bald figure coming my way. It was Doktor Pik van Loon of Katatura hospital, Chiko's life-saving surgeon, who sent Egon and Angelika to them.

'Doktor Vingoe,' he said, beaming, 'how are you?

'Very well, you?'

'Not allowed to complain because I'm the blerry doctor.' His ample belly rolled when he laughed. 'But tell me, how is Chiko? Still working with you?'

'Chiko, he's great.'

'Happy to hear it.'

'Thanks to you he's still alive.'

'No, no, it wasn't his time to go,' Pik laughed.

'No, suppose not.' Modesty should have been Pik's middle name.

'You going on one of your trips?' Pik asked, observing my khaki outfit.

'You sent the customers to me —'

'Yes, bad business about Angelika Neumann's uncle, particularly after what happened to her father.' He shook his head. 'Every now and then, someone disappears out there.' He patted me affectionately on the shoulder.

'So, you're off to the Kaokoland?'

'Yes.' They'd told him everything.

'It's dangerous.' It was true. We'd taken others, but never so far off-road as the point on their map.

'Yes, I know. Oh yes, Angelika says you're a member of *!ga:wa*, the San organization.'

'A founding member. I wanted to talk to you about that – we need people!'

'Count me in, I'll get in touch.'

'Be careful my friend, Kaokoland is no joke, but you know that. Must rush, give my best wishes to Chiko and Angelika. She's quite a young lady, speaks better San than any white person I know.' He looked at his watch.

'I came to town to get something for the wife. She stays in Rehoboth and expects me to do all the blerry shopping. My uncle Sterkbooi says I'm hen-pecked.' He smiled, patted me again on the shoulder, and ambled on his way.

What a nice man. Sterkbooi, he'd said his uncle was called. Strange name. Means *'Strong boy'*.

It was after one when I steered the Land Rover back on to the B1 towards Okahandja. From there the road continued another hundred and forty miles to Otjiwarongo.

The temperature soared, and the sun dazzlingly shimmered the road. I thought I saw a brown hyena crouching on the edge of a sandstone boulder, but it was only a sculpture carved be the wind.

Six

The judge pondered for an eternity, then fixed me with a baleful stare. He placed the black cap on the bench. I exhaled a long-held breath, and there were subdued murmurs in the public seats. Relief, or disappointment, for, to many, public hangings were welcome entertainment. Almost, I wished he had donned the cap, for death would be preferable to life without Morwenna.

'Ignatius Tregurtha, thy guilt established, I pass not the ultimate sentence, but instead that ye be held in Launceston gaol until a convict ship be ready, and ye be transported to a penal colony for the rest of thy natural life. And God have mercy upon ye, and God have mercy upon ye!' I was to learn from other convicts that judges repeated themselves, lest God wasn't paying attention. With those words, my future was sealed.

Why don't you have mercy yourself, not leave it to God, I thought, while mixed feelings of regret, relief and fear overwhelmed me. In this perplexed state, I was re-chained and led away. Out of the corner of my eye, I saw Jon Hicks. He was crestfallen. The sentence was not the hanging he hoped for.

For fourteen months between the end of March 1786 and the tenth of May 1787, I was held in the abysmal squalor and discomfort of the filthy, cold and overcrowded gaol at Launceston. A fleet was being prepared to take convicts to New South Wales, it was rumoured, and I should go with it. Such were my prospects, to escape one hell for another. If I didn't die of heartbreak, and the wild sea didn't claim my life, then servitude in a foreign land would kill me soon enough.

From an early age, I suffered bouts of low mood. Mother told me I'd inherited a 'melancholic humour' from her family. Mother and Father worried about me and indulged my every whim. They encouraged me in all I wanted, hence I was allowed to continue school until thirteen.

It also explained why Father allowed me to refuse the apprenticeship he'd arranged with John Trewhella, clerk with the customs and excise in Market Strand, Falmouth. Strange it was, but father knew him as a customer for contraband, French brandy in particular.

He was a fat, bald man, obnoxious in his ways, not least spitting black tobacco-juice and missing the spitoon. When I realized the purpose of his visit was to size me up, I rebelled, and the hawking, spitting, fat, bald Trewhella did not find an apprentice in me.

By April 1778, I'd persuaded father to let me join him and my older brother Jacca in John Carter's free-trade business. I was big for my age, strong, and considered clever because I could write. An asset, Carter proclaimed when father introduced us in Mounts Bay. Little did I know this was a path which would, in time, bring great pain and suffering down upon me.

'To 'ey born into wealth, or 'oo 'ave 'onest employm'nt, th' word 'smuggler' is akin to 'robber' or 'thief,' father said. ''Ey do not face bleak, grindin' poverty, wi'out means o' support.'

It was true. In Cornwall, prospects were few. The tin mines were harsh and dangerous, the pay pitiful, and even such work was difficult to gain, for more men were willing to endure hell below ground than were needed. Indeed, you should have been born into a family of miners, the positions being hereditary, sons joining fathers at a young age.

49

Fishing required a boat, nets and tackle, and the sons of fishermen learnt the trade before they could walk. Some Cornish folk laboured for a pittance, generation to generation, on wealthy landowners' farms. There were few choices. No wonder so many turned to smuggling, particularly those who grew up in the homes of free traders.

'God hisself design'd Cornwall fer free trade, me 'ansum,' father said. Again, he was right, for the coast of the peninsula between the Atlantic and the channel is breached by innumerable bays, estuaries, and inlets. Hidden away are countless caves and caverns, big and small, with high cliffs shielding them from above. In places, dense groves of trees and bush so obscure cave mouths as to render them invisible from the sea. Without spies, the revenue men could never prevail, for we were more wiley, and better knew the coast. John Carter and his men were far too clever to fairly fall prey to the revenue!

I was a free trader at thirteen. I learnt fast to be useful, and by sixteen I was an old hand with many skills. I could handle a lugger's sails, and row a gig with the best of them. I had outstanding long-distance vision, much valued by the others, for I could spot marking buoys from far, even in bad weather. It saved time retrieving cargo from the sea. For a while, my life was charmed.

Incarceration in Launceston gaol brought on my worst melancholia. My heart ached for Morwenna. I found it difficult to rise in the morning. Perpetually hungry and cold, I lost weight, and my filthy clothes hung loose about me.

I began to wish for the numbing cloak of death, to pray for release.

If it was possible to succumb to the grave from misery alone, I would not have survived.

I had a burning need to write about what happened, so Morwenna and my family would know how much I missed them. But my right hand was horribly swollen, and I could not. There was a fellow convict called John Penrose, who could write, and whose wife bribed the guards to let her bring him pencils and paper. He kindly offered to take down my words, for which I was deeply grateful. His good wife would deliver the message to my family at *Chy Velah* in Penzance, and they would show it to Morwenna.

One day in February 1787, Daveth Eva, in the guise of a preacher called Denzel Pendragon from St Mawes, managed to
visit me. If I'd been a strong swimmer like him, I'd also have escaped capture!

He unfolded a piece of printed paper.

'John Carter sent it to ye, because ye can read.' He passed it to me. It was a page from the London Chronicle, quoting a parliamentary record in Hansard on the twenty third of January 1787. It was announced in Parliament, it read, that:

The American colonies illegally and illegitimately, but by the will of God only temporarily, lofte to this purpofe, Lord Sydney, home secretary and peer of the realm under our sovereign King George 111, may he long reign over uf, has agreed to send convictes to the colony of New South Wales forthwith. His Majefty has eftablish'd the neceffary funds from the treafury to provide for the transportation and appointed Arthur Phillip, RN, to command the first fleet, upon arrival to become the convicte colony's first governor.

The fleet of 11 ships tranſporting 1450 people, or thereabouts, of whom 773 are convictes, will depart Portsmouth on or about the thirteenth day of May 1778, under the command of Captain Arthur Phillip. The fleet will call at Plymouth to load Weſt-Country convictes, before proceeding to sea.

I returned the paper to Daveth, who secreted it back in his gown.

'What says it?' he asked.

'There's a convict fleet being readied.'

'Will 'ey take ye?'

'I think so.' Daveth leaned forward and squeezed my shoulder. He wasn't a man to dwell on bad things.

'Rememb'r this?' he asked, parting his hair to show me the old cutlass scar from a brawl with a sailor at the Ferryboat Inn at Helford. It ran left to right across the top of his head.

'I do.'

'Well, see this one.' He parted his hair front to back down the middle. There was an angry red scar running all the way.

'How'd you get it?'

'The revenue man's musket ball,' he said, 'giv'd me a second partin'.' A permanent one, by the scar.

'What think ye?' Two red scars crossing, that's what I thought.

'Bloody flag o' St George 'pon me loaf,' he laughed, 'th' bastards mark't me good!' Even there in that grim place, he kept his humour.

'There be somethin ye shoul' know,' he said before he left.

'What?'

'Why Jon Hicks betray'd us an' testified at your trial, stab me!'

The question had tortured me since the Assizes.

'Ye know 'bout his wife, Kerensa?'

It appeared Hicks had grounds for suspicion. One of her fancy men was Phineas Tregaskis, the owner of the Dolphin Tavern, where we sold much French brandy. I knew not about him and Kerensa on the day I took a cart with a barrel hidden under straw bales to his back door.

'Tregaskis,' said Daveth, 'wer stokin' Kerensa's fire, wen Hicks cam' 'ome early, t' spy 'ee climbin' down fro; 'er bedroom window.' What did this have to do with me?

'Hicks chas'd 'ee all th' way t' th' Dolphin Tavern. Upon seein your cart, Tregaskis 'id 'eeself uner th' straw in th' back. Wen Hicks roundit th' corner, ye wer th' only man in th' road. Ee 'adn't spied Tregaskis' face, an' thort it wer ye he wer chasin'.'

'How know you this?'

'Tregaskis, curse 'ee, boast'd in th' tavern.'

'Hicks blamed me, betrayed me to the revenue, and let me be sentenced to transportation?' I said, bewildered.

'Hicks wer not th' kind to ask questuns. If 'ee 'ad, ee'd have learned ye wern't th' guilty man. Wi-out evin betrayin' Tregaskis, ye coul 'ave prov'd what 'ee wer about. 'Ee did'n ask, nor tell ye why he cam runnin' up th' road. He jumpt t' th' wrong conclusun an' decid'd t' git even. 'Ee lackit 'th currage t' fight ye. No, he did th' mos wickit thing 'ee coul t' a free trader. He betray'd ye, an' all o' us!'

'I wish I could get even.' Daveth grinned wryly.

'No need.'

'What you mean?'

'Ye 'avn't 'eard?'

'Heard what? We get no news in here.'

'Ther wer an accident. Six days since, Jon Hicks fell off th' cliff t' Bedruthan Steps.' He waited for his words to sink in. 'It be a turribl' shame!'

Bedruthan steps, halfway along the north Cornish coast between Newquay and Padstow, named for the legendary giant Bedruthan who hurled down huge outcrops of rock, to form the tortuous stairway to the beach below. There are sheer cliffs on either side.

'You don' git away wi' betrayin' th' King o' Prussia!' growled Daveth. Though I wanted vengeance, I was shocked.

'No,' I said. I should have felt satisfaction at what happened, but didn't. The evil could not be undone, and Hicks' death didn't change it. Loss of liberty, livelihood and home, and fear of the future, changes a man. I did not celebrate the news of Hicks' terrible punishment.

'Poor Kerensa,' said I.

'Don' concern yesel wi' 'er', word is one o' 'er fancy men 'as aready mov'd in!'

'No, pr'aps I should concentrate on what's happening to me.'

'Ye will come back, I be sure, an' we'll be waitin' 'ere!'

If a guard had looked through the grate, he'd have seen tears streaming down Reverend Pendragon's face.

'Will you take a message to Morwenna?' I asked through my tears.

'What shall I tell she?'

'That I love her.'

I knew Morwenna would not be allowed to see me before I was taken from Cornwall forever. What would become of my darling?

Seven

The wild, arid country had hidden traces of the ancient San. Like the beautiful hidden rock paintings or ǂketens Chiko showed me.

Did Ignatius ever see such things? I wondered. All I knew from his old letter was that after escaping the ship he travelled to the Great Western Desert. The mystery came *after* 1790. It was as if the desert swallowed him whole. I wished he'd written more than just a single letter. In the seat beside me, Angelika dozed. She opened one eye.

'Okay?' I nodded.

'Pik sends his regards.'

'Bless him, he okay?'

'Said he was. Asked me to join the *!ga:wa* foundation.'

'Yes, he would, he's a strong defender of San rights. Will you join?'

'Why not?' Her eye closed.

It was poignant to think the San were already in decline in Ignatius' time. Now they were all but gone, the survivors thinly spread through the Kalahari, the pro-Namib, southern Angola and Botswana.

How much, if any, of the ancient and musical Bushman tongue did Ignatius learn, I wondered. If he lived among them, he had to communicate.

The growl of the engine, the rocking and muggy air in the Land Rover was numbing. Angelika had pulled her big white hat over her eyes and wedged herself between seat and door. I glanced over my shoulder. Chiko and Egon were also dozing. So much for enthusiasm, but I couldn't blame them. This was enough to put anyone to sleep.

The sun reflected and dazzled from feldspar and mica-bearing rock, quartz crystals, and so-called 'semi-precious stones' littering the sand. Only the dark glasses allowed me to keep my eyes open.

It was ten years since I had the first of my strange dreams. It was about my many-times-removed great uncle Ignatius Myghal Tregurtha. The tragedy which befell him mirrored the misery of my own life. Next day, I visited the Bodmin assizes and ruins of Launceston Gaol. I began to search out records of Cornish trials in the 1780's. Then an uncanny coincidence happened.

On my way home from Truro library, I bought a copy of the *West Briton*. The headline was 'Historical Discovery in Penzance'. On the twenty seventh of March 2008, builders refurbishing a seventeenth-century warehouse on the waterfront in Penzance found some trapdoors. They led into a labyrinth of narrow tunnels running uphill. One was three hundred yards long, all the way under Church Street and into the back of the *Admiral Benbow* pub.

Things they found dated the tunnels between 1740 and 1780, and the construction suggested they were dug by tin miners. The *Benbow* tunnel even had a spyhole for smugglers to check excise men weren't lying in wait within.

It was two hundred and twenty years ago, in 1787, when Ignatius was arrested in Mounts Bay, Penzance. I wondered if he personally lugged casks of French brandy up those tunnels. Strange, I thought, that the discovery came so many years later. Particularly after my dream and visits to the assizes and Launceston gaol.

'I'll show you,' said the landlord at the *Admiral Benbow*.

It was good for business in an institution steeped in Cornish history. He showed the way with a lantern-torch.

It was dark and dank and smelt of damp earth, and there wasn't much space for a man carrying a brandy keg to pass. The torchlight fell on wooden supporting lintels, and decaying bratticing boards lining the ceiling.

'Haunting, hey?' he said, 'forgotten world of hard times.' I could visualise sweating men, almost hear them curse as they bore their burdens up that dank, earthy tunnel.

It was extraordinary to think my old relative was one of John Carter's smugglers. He, the smuggler-chief famed as the 'King of Prussia', of Prussia Cove in Mounts Bay.

I was so intrigued that my own predicament took second place. The prospect of going back to work dragged me down. It would have to wait.

Six months later, I found myself on a Lufthansa flight, Gatwick-Stuttgart-Windhoek. Why Namibia? Because of an old letter written in pencil on rag-paper, inherited by a paternal uncle in Penzance. It came from his father and who-knew-who, all the way back to 1790. For two hundred and eleven years, the flimsy heirloom had baffled them. I had no reason to doubt the veracity of the letter.

The family legend went that a Tea Clipper called at Walvis Bay on the southwestern tip of Africa in 1790, and the skipper bore the letter to Cornwall. The writer was none other than Ignatius Myghal Tregurtha.

Eight

Yes, I was one of those, whose *'cleane recorde aforeto'* being accounted, escaped the gallows and were sentenced to transportation and indentured labour in the penal colony of New South Wales.

One guard at Launceston, an Exeter man called Willis, was, unlike the others, kind and considerate. He'd read much about naval matters, his own father a retired petty officer. He spoke like an educated man.

'You have a hard voyage ahead,' he said one day when we were allowed in the grounds. 'This is to be the first convict fleet to New South Wales, and the ships are privately contracted, because the Royal Navy may need theirs against France in the near future.'

'Privately contracted?'

'Yes, a payment per convict embarked, without condition of good health on delivery. It doesn't bode well for your treatment, and I'll warrant you'll wish yourselves back before you've gone a hundred leagues!'

Willis told us three of the ships were *Scarborough*, four hundred and twenty tons, *Neptune*, eight hundred and nine tons and *Surprise*, four hundred tons, all fitted out for convict transportation. Comfort was no priority. With my future lying in such details, they bored into my mind. The option of sending us to the Americas was no longer available since the Americans sent the British, their tax collectors and convicts, packing after the revolution of 1776. Eleven years earlier, I would have gone to Virginia. Willis was a ship-fancier who'd missed his vocation, and hearing I was a sailor took the opportunity to regale me with his maritime knowledge. In my state, even this distraction from missing Morwenna was welcome.

HMS Scarborough, he said, part of the first convict fleet which would sail to Australia, was a decrepit and barely seaworthy ship. He even knew she was launched on Clydeside in 1741, a three-masted, square-rigged ship of eighty-six feet on the waterline, twenty-three in the beam, and a draft of nine feet in full ballast.

'She's forty-six years old, and long seen better days. She's tired and worn out by the Atlantic, taking trinkets and cheap goods from Bristol to the west coast of West Africa, embarking slaves, transporting them to sugar plantations in the West Indies, then bringing sugar back to Bristol.' He grimaced. 'Sailors call it *Hell's Triangle*!'

Why, I thought, did the English deal so harshly with paltry smugglers, when they indulged in slavery?

Willis told us about several other ships in the convoy, but none sounded as bad as *Scarborough*.

On the fifteenth of May, I was taken, with six other wretches, to Plymouth in a stout wagon drawn by four horses. We sat on the floor, for there was no seat. Nor was there even straw to ease our discomfort. We were fettered in irons of slave-trade design, including a short rigid bar between the ankles, so we could only shuffle. Through the barred window at the back, we sadly watched a patch of blue Cornish sky for the last time. The sky which would stay over Morwenna's sweet head.

We endured five hours of jerking, bouncing discomfort before we arrived at Devonport. We were herded directly from the wagon, and as the fates decided, onto the hulk *HMS Scarborough*. There, with curses and cuffs, we were herded below.

On that floating relic, two hundred and seven convicts were confined in the orlop or third deck, in a space of forty-five by twenty feet.

Headroom between the roof beams was just five feet four inches.

In such a confined and overcrowded place, disease would spread unhindered.

Though we were allowed topside liberty in the hours between sunrise until sunset, it was with great difficulty and pain we climbed the companionway in our chains. Even then, we were under constant guard by armed soldiers.

We were allowed the use of a small piece of deck, where, under the guns of guards, we shuffled about in an attempt to exercise and breathe fresh air after the cloying stench of unwashed humanity, urine and faeces in our cramped quarters. Only women and children had buckets to relieve themselves. Men and boys had to go to the open heads over the lee side.

'Your chains will be removed for the voyage,' said the marine officer when we were herded on deck. 'But insolence or infractions will be punished by flogging. The captain also has jurisdiction for capital punishment!'

The threats were many. Our rations were allocated on the 'six upon four rule,' six convicts sharing the same food as four sailors. It was mainly salt beef and sea-biscuit, with the rare addition of a small portion of wine or lime-juice. Even this meagre allocation could be reduced, and often was.

The removal of our chains took several days, for they were riveted and had to be chiselled off. Most of us had running ulcers on our ankles, where the skin was rubbed away and corruption had set in.

Even in the worst of circumstances, good things come to pass. On my first unchained deck-liberty, one guard showed himself different to the others.

It had been drizzling all day in Devonport, and I slipped and fell heavily on the slippery deck.

A guard with a black patch over one eye and a deeply scarred, pock-marked cheek helped me up, and enquired if I was hurt.

'Do ye tayk care,' he said with a north Cornish drawl.

Peder Pengilly of Boscastle would have been handsome were it not for the patch and scar. He was a little short of forty, tall and slim, and his single eye, almost the same green as Morwenna's, was bright with intelligence. What was such a man doing as a convict ship guard? No matter, he was sent by the angels. Soon he would hold my future in his hands.

After we were driven below, the hatchways were secured with stout stanchions of elm. The exposed woodwork was closely covered with broad-headed nails, making it impossible to attack even with a bladed instrument. A sentry with a primed musket was posted day and night to watch the hatch.

'Escape is impossible,' were the concluding words to many wistful conversations.

In the evening of May the seventeenth 1787, I was on deck when *Scarborough* weighed anchor, her sails unfurled, and, with canvas bellying to the breeze, she slid from her mooring.

As she gained speed and approached the harbour-mouth, the larger ship *Neptune*, flagship of Fleet Commodore Phillip, *HMS Sirius* and eight other ships joined the fleet.

We rounded the headland, the clouds briefly parted, and the waning sunshine painted the gently rolling sea silver. It was a beautiful, poignant and haunting sight, which I will never forget.

'Git down thur, good fur nowt!' a marine yelled in a Yorkshire accent as he roughly thrust me towards the companionway.

Deck-time was over. As night fell the ship began to roll in the wash of the English Channel.

We sat on our sleeping-berths. These were fashioned from deal boards supported on wooden frames, and divided into sleeping compartments. 'Horse-breakfast' mattresses of hay-stuffed canvas bags covered them. Four convicts were squeezed together on a bed only six foot square.

Unlike me, many convicts had never been to sea. The ship's motion in the broken water of the Channel made them ill and filled them with terror. Many crossed themselves and offered up prayers for their souls.

Soon after, the sea freshened further, bringing confusion and panic. Some prayed out loud to God for salvation, others cursed and swore, while some, immobilized by fear, were quiet. It was impossible to rest in that bucking, heaving place.

Nobody could sleep, and hour by hour the weather grew wilder, the ship's motion more violent. The pitch and roll took on a rhythm, and a cacophony of groaning timbers accompanied it.

Waves crashing at the bows sent vibrations throughout the ship, which rose up and crashed back down with a booming thud. Several women and child convicts, and some of the men, were sea-sick. The reek of vomit soured the already putrid air.

"Eavenly fa-ver up above, will it niver stop rockin'?' a pale and wretched woman asked in working class London-speak, bracing herself with both hands on the low ceiling.

'Sorry to say, it won't,' I replied, whereupon the poor creature into tears.

It was the beginning of a voyage to last five months.

It was for Tenerife we sailed on the seventeenth of May.

We would stay there a week, then head for Rio de Janeiro in the Brasils. From there, we would re-cross the Atlantic to the Cape of Good Hope, before the last leg of our journey to Botany Bay in New South Wales. We were not expected to arrive before January 1788. If I could never return to Cornwall, would God grant me a way to bring Morwenna across the vast seas to me?

Soon the very thought of arrival was driven off by panic when we encountered the wildest of storms and were pursued by pirates in the treacherous Bay of Biscay.

Nine

Depression robbed me of self-esteem, girlfriend, ambition and career. Friends want happiness, not gloom and despondency. So I avoided them. I was tormented by where it would lead. I couldn't continue for long, feared a bad decision, like my mother. I never planned an exit, but the spectre haunted me. The misfortunes of Ignatius put my own life in perspective.

In the darkness of that time, desperation, alone, was my driver. Yet, if Ignatius survived the horrors of his time, why couldn't I? How long did he live after 1890, and how? That was the question. To me, it was overarching, as if the level of his fortitude would be a signpost to my own future. Did everything happen for a reason? Why else did I discover his letter, and dream about him, just when the smuggler's tunnels were found? An echo of drowning men and straws, but who'd snatch away the straws?

For ten years, I'd avoided reminders of my breakdown. That meant relationships. I kept to myself, and, with the exception of Chiko, was self-reliant.

My quest for traces of Ignatius was, over time, diverted and delayed. I had to earn a living. I met Chiko, and we became tourist guides immersed in our own little world. It was eerie that, only recently renewing my quest for Ignatius, I should get clients with a relative lost in the same desert.

The heat made me dozy, and the Landy drifted towards the side of the road. I straightened up and concentrated.

Chiko and Egon were fast asleep in the back, but Angelika was awake. Her hair was in a ponytail, exposing her pale, slender neck.

The engine growled. In the mirror, I saw Chiko stir and I broke the silence to say Dr van Loon had enquired after him. *'Hy is 'n wonderlike man,'* he said sleepily. A wonderful man.

Ahead, snaking into the Khaki hills, the road ran north. It was hot, the sun still beating from the west and glittering on the sand. I was used to the heat, and the growl of the engine relaxed me. Unlike Chiko, who was superstitious about motorised vehicles. To him, the roar of an engine meant a furious spirit was trapped inside. Explanation and persuasion were useless. Yet, despite his protestations, he suffered many journeys in the Landy.

I began to whistle.

'I have to admit,' Angelika said with a nod and a smile, 'these seats *are* comfortable.' They were dark blue, lightly built on aluminium frames, very supportive. The backrests moulded into the body.

'Like I said.' Small-talk was deflecting from the real matter on our minds.

'Where's the altitude-reader?'

'Altimeter, it's this thing'. It was on the dashboard. Round, three inches wide, with vertical graduations. The arrow showed our altitude was one thousand six hundred feet above sea level. Angelika stared at me. 'If all else fails, altitude is a fair guide where you are.'

'What's that?' she asked, changing the subject. She pointed at the storage bin in the door where JC Curnow's book protruded.

'Old book about Cornish smugglers.'

'How old?'

'Sixty-six years, just collected it, was going to read it.'

'Before we invaded your privacy?'

'Something like that.' She grimaced.

It was true, after all. 'Actually,' I said, 'when I saw your caravan I wondered if you'd come to see the eclipse from the desert.'

'Really?'

'No, too early, not due until the twenty seventh.' She stared out the window at the endless expanse of sand, rock and stunted brown bushes. After several minutes, she turned back.

'What kind of tree is that on the dune?' It was a big spreading one, more than sixty feet high.

'Mongongo tree.... as a San expert, shouldn't you know?'

'Maybe,' Angelika laughed, 'I study people, not trees.'

'When it rains, it has yellow flowers. Bushmen eat the fruit and nuts inside if they can beat the elephants to them. Elephants love mongongos, but can't digest the nuts in the middle. They go straight through, and the Bushmen pick them from the dung.'

'I know, and its yuck.' She made a face.

'They're protected by a shell.'

'Well that's okay then,' she grinned, 'you know a lot about these things.'

'Thank Chiko.'

'You're a medical doctor?'

'I was, but I'd rather not talk about it.' She fell silent and turned back to her window. I tightened my grip on the wheel, changed gear and shoved the accelerator down. The engine roared.

It was three o'clock when we passed a sign to Omaruru.

'Show me the way to Omaruru,' I sang to the tune of 'Amarillo'.

'You're mad,' she laughed.

'I agree,' growled Egon, stretching.

Opportunist, I mused.

'I hope you don't get lost,' Angelika said, ''cos I can't direct you.'

'Anthropology not teach you to find your way?' She didn't answer.

The sun lay low in the west, throwing shadows from distant hills over the arid bushveld. We'd skirted the edge of the desert. All the way it was rocky terrain, with thorn bushes crouching between boulders, and rare patches of grass, verdant green through the recent rain. This year they'd the highest rainfall in a quarter century.

We coasted the edge of a high escarpment, then descended to the sandy plain below. Thirty miles on, we pitched our tents under a camel-thorn tree. While we erected the tents, Chiko gathered twigs and kindled a fire.

I took a stroll in the veld. When I returned, Angelika had disappeared, leaving Chiko to stir the pot. He looked up from where he squatted with a wooden spoon in his hand.

'It is better here than in the house!'

'I hope this isn't a wild guinea-fowl chase,' I said, laughing at my friend's happy enthusiasm. There were no geese here.

'The woman,' Chiko said in Afrikaans, 'she is like a young gazelle.' I was in no mood for homilies. 'What is a lion without a mate?' he continued. He spat into the fire. 'Friend, you have been too long a hunter without a bow.'

Without a bow?

'Lie with her, let your arrow rise up!'

'Chiko, you meerkat,' I laughed, 'you talk in riddles and always bring bows and arrows into it.'

'I am not a *fokin* meerkat!'

'Who said it was fucking? Only you have *jigi-jigi* on your mind, and you look like a meerkat.' Chiko snorted.

'You must fire the arrows —'

'Stop, remember the lioness is the hunter.'

'You are the one who dreams of *jigi-jigi*.'

'No more,' I laughed. Who'd have predicted I'd come to the wilderness to relaunch my life as a tourist guide, amateur archaeologist and art lover, and my business partner, psychotherapist and confidante would hail from an ancient tribe of stone-age hunter-gatherers? 'You are my older brother,' I said, hugging him. He pulled away in feigned horror.

We ate from tin plates and washed down the stew with *Windhoeks* from the coolbox.

'I'm tired,' Egon said at last, rising and heading for our tent. Thank heavens, I thought. The way he listened but hardly said anything made me uncomfortable.

Not that conversation was needed in a place like this. When it was only us, Chiko and I enjoyed the silence, broken only be far-off giggles of wandering hyenas or the muted fluttering and scratching of insects.

Chiko was bedded down on the sand a little way off, and Angelika and I sat alone beside the crackling fire. There were smudges of dirt on her legs. I'd have to erect the shower contraption.

Angelika studied me. 'Can I ask something, or will you snap at me?'

'Depends.'

'Where does your surname, Vingoe, come from?'

'It's Cornish, Norman origin.'

'What does it mean?'

'*Vin-gout,* wine-taster.'

'Oh, how wonderful, what a great job!'

'Suppose so.'

'A Norman name in Cornwall, aren't you Celts?'

'1066 and all that. After the invasion, the Cornish made a deal. We welcomed the rule of one of William the Conqueror's Breton earls.'

'Just like that?'

'Better than *Sowsneks*, or Saxons, and the Breton language is almost pure Cornish.'

'Saxons are Germans,' she protested.

'I know, my mother's parents were German, though she was born in Namibia.'

'Really?'

'Yes, from Munich. They came here after the war. My mother was born in Windhoek in 1951, and went to Berlin to study art in 1970.'

'The old country.'

'She lived with relatives.'

'Your father?'

'Tank commander, British army of the Rhine.'

'Where are they now?'

'She's dead.'

'Oh, I'm sorry,' Angelika paused. 'Your father?'

'Lives with a woman in Spain.'

'You speak German?'

'Some.'

'From your mother?'

'Yes, but she died before I was fluent.'

'That's sad. Sorry….'

'I practice German with Owambos and Hereros.'

'Oh yes, a lot still talk German.'

'Old German learnt from early settlers.'

'Amazing, imperial German from the Kaiser's time, in Africa!'

We stared a long time in silence at embers of the dying fire.

'It's an incredible country,' I said at last. 'My several-time's-great uncle on my father's mother's side was called Ignatius Myghal Tregurtha....'

'Myghal?' she sniggered. I stared at her.

'I didn't mean...' she began, 'I thought you were joking —'

'Forget it. He was a smuggler, tried and sentenced to transportation to Australia in 1787. He jumped ship in Cape Town and fled out here. I think he lived out his life in the Namib, but I don't really know.'

'That's why you carry the Smuggler book around!'

'Did you look at it?'

'Yes,' she grinned, 'shouldn't I?'

'Time for bed.'

'There's something I need to tell you.'

'What?'

'Pik van Loon didn't only recommend you.'

'What else did he say?'

'He told us about an IDB case involving Emmanual Maharero.'

'Did he now?'

'Yes, Emmanual Maharero. You didn't report him for offering you stolen diamonds. You didn't buy them, but you never told on him either.'

Poor Emmanuel, great-great-grandson of the Herero leader Kamahero, reduced to labouring in the diamond fields at Oranjemund, who took a few small stones for himself.

When he tried to sell them to me, I said no thanks, but didn't call the police. I wasn't their eyes and ears, and I felt sorry for the poor man.

Then he was arrested and mentioned me, and I had to appear as a witness in his trial. Bureaucracy gone mad. I had to give up three days of my life for a crime nobody said I committed.

'Put it this way,' Angelika said, 'where illegal diamonds are involved, people don't talk, advertise or write a CV. There's nothing to go on —'

'What does the Emmanuel matter prove?'

'Oh, nothing… We had Pik's recommendation, but I wanted someone with a heart. The IDB business is full of self-serving rats and thieves.' I stared at her.

'Where there's little to rely on, you have to take that little.'

'Time for bed.' I got to my feet.

'I agree.' Angelika stood, stretching one leg at a time. 'Good night,' she said as she walked away.

I'd fallen in with a taciturn man with an inquisitive sister. She was making a study of me, why I couldn't imagine. Who was I, after all? The Cadac's gas flame threw her silhouette onto the fabric of her tent.

The light snuffed out and left me in darkness. The fire was dead. A breeze whispered through the gulleys and kopjies of the arid, sleeping veld. Somewhere not too far away a jackal wailed like a wounded dog, then a hyena broke into an insane high-pitched giggle. At a time like this, I could almost believe San superstitions about hyenas.

Chiko had poetically told me one of their stories. Imbued with evil spirits, hyenas take on human voices and speak to their victims.

'Come hither unto me,' whispereth the invisible !gwäi, hyena, to the young mother with her baby upon her hip, 'I am your husband and I lie hurt upon the ground.

'Tis surely her man's voice in pain she hears, and she goes at once, taking her infant into the dark night. Then sees she many glowing yellow eyes, and 'thou art come,' she hears, 'now shall we dine on thee!'

It was as spooky as hell!

I shivered, pulled my bush-jacket close and groped my way to my tent.

Egon's breathing told he was fast asleep. I fumbled for my torch and switched it on. I found Curnow's book in the yellow beam. Propping the torch on my pillow, I turned the cover. There was a foreword about the author's research, then a few pages about the state of things in late 18th century Cornwall.

I found a quotation from *Hansard*, the Westminster parliamentary journal, dated January twenty third, 1787. Congruent upon the American revolution, convicts could no longer be sent to America, and Lord Sydney, the home secretary, decided to send them to the antipodes. A fleet of eleven ships was assembled under the command of Captain Arthur Phillip, RN, who would be the convict colony's first governor. It would depart Portsmouth in May 1788, call at Plymouth to collect prisoners from the southwest, then sail for New South Wales.

A breeze ruffled the bottom of the tent. I wondered what tomorrow would bring. I wished I knew what Ignatius thought when he lived in the desert. My mind snapped back to the present.

Why was I even in this crazy venture? It took forever, but I finally drifted into a restless sleep. The kind populated by the strangest of dreams.

Ten

On the twenty-fifth of May, in that home of storms off *Cap Finistère* we call the Bay of Biscay, there was a sudden drop in atmospheric pressure. A sailor from young, I didn't need a barometer to know what was coming.

Shortly, a squall rushed down upon us, the advance herald of a full gale. *Scarborough* was soon separated from the fleet in screeching wind and thirty-foot swells.

By nightfall, the storm had grown to force ten, and towering waves broke over the ship. Every loose thing was battened down, and none but essential crew were allowed on deck. Swells as high as the topmast rushed at the bow, lifted it high, then surged under the ship with a roar. As each passed, we fell off a precipice, then impacted with a juddering crash and a cannon-shot boom.

Scarborough, judging from below by her twisting roll, flew only a reefed storm-sail. She groaned with the agony of tortured timber, and constantly seemed about to flounder as she corkscrewed through the screeching maelstrom.

In the dim light, retching and moans, prayers and curses, added to the hellish cacophony, and the foul air was further soured by the acrid stench of fresh vomit. Overhead echoed the pounding of boots on deck, and voices muffled by the screeching wind.

'Sea-anchor away o' the stern,' a loud voice bawled above the tempest. The loud rumble of a heavy chain running overboard followed. It went on for what seemed a long time, though it could only have been a few seconds before it ended abruptly.

As by the hand of Neptune himself, with groaning timbers and creaking loud enough to stop our hearts, the ship was bodily dragged back in her headlong plunge. A mighty struggle between the power of the wind and the sea pushing the ship, and the
Sea anchor hauling back with the weight of the same sea!

Trawling the heavy chain-and-canvas drogue, the crew kept *Scarborough*'s head to the mountainous seas, and hour after terrifying hour we rode the raging storm.

On deck, you could see the waves coming, brace yourself for the roll and pitch. In the darkness below, the lurching and plunging came without warning. We lay on our stinking, scratchy mattresses, for standing was impossible. I tried to splint myself against a beam, and the man lying next to me dug his nails painfully into my shoulder. Icy water flooded into the hold and drenched us every time a wave broke over the bow. Everything was wet and cold. We shivered and prayed for deliverance. The agony continued for two whole days and nights.

The morning of the twenty-sixth of May brought a change. The wind died to a whisper and the sea lay calm. *Scarborough* had been driven back a hundred leagues, a sailor said. Now, with not a breath of wind, she lay becalmed. It was a rare blessing, for at least we could briefly escape the hell of our accommodation.

'On deck!' the marine sergeant yelled through the companionway. Those who were not prostrated rushed to the ladder. The fresh air was sweeter than any I ever breathed.

An hour before sunset an infant breeze blew up from the north, and sail was made.

Suddenly a cry of 'sail-ho!' rang from the masthead, and there, less than three nautical miles off the port beam, heading our way, was a ship. It was a three-masted lugger, of a style I recognized. I had seen ships like her in Morlaix, and even on the Cornish coast.

A white flag with a bold black cross flew from her topmast.

The Breton *Kroaz Du*, the inverse of the white cross on a black background of the Cornish flag of St Piran, or *Baner Peran*.

'Tis French, wi' guns,' Peder Pengilly, the one-eyed Cornish guard said.

He always seemed to find me on deck.

'Breton,' I corrected him, 'I have seen such ships in Morlaix.' He gave me a knowing look. Many was the Cornishman who knew Morlaix as well as his home town, every one a free-trader.

The ship flew no *tricolor*, and this was not war, though France, lately in the throes of peasant food-riots and anti-monarchist unrest, was edging towards new hostilities with England. War or no, the stranger's intention was unmistakably belligerent. One does not charge down another ship unless you intend to attack. Watching, the captain and officers concluded she was a privateer.

The crew raised every spare rag of sail. Yet she closed with us, approaching in short time to within three miles. Her sleek lines, long bowsprit, four-sided lugsails and raked mizzen mast confirmed their worst fears. She was a Breton *Chasse-Marée*, or 'Tide Chaser', a fast, multi-gunned Corsair privateer, operating with impunity and not-too-covert French sanction, out of Morlaix and Roscoff in Brittany.

75

How many ships of that design were there? Eight, ten? There weren't more. Corsairs left vessels alone if they flew the *Baner Peran* or Cornish flag, but *Scarborough* was English. Was my friend Alban aboard?

The Bretons are not French any more than the Cornish are English. They are our closest cousins, and, were it not for the channel, we'd be united.

They speak Breton, which, though it differs in accent and has some French words, is the same as Cornish.

Indeed, while the use of our native language continues to decline at home, and many young only speak English, it's good to see no such decay in Brittany.

The folk in Roscoff and Morlaix are so like the Cornish, not only in language. They were most hospitable to me, and I was at home amongst them. It was in Morlaix I met Alban Kermarrec, whose name even sounds Cornish. He was my age, and, like me, followed his father into the free trade business, though that didn't fully describe it.

Alban crewed on a Morlaix-based *Chasse-Marée*, free-trading brandy, tea and silks to Cornwall. It could, if pursued, easily outrun the fleetest ships of the Royal Navy. Some *Chasse-Marées* were known to engage in piracy, seizing English merchant vessels in the North Atlantic, the channel and the North Sea when the opportunity arose. Such pirates were known as Corsairs. This, my clever friend Alban told me, came from the Latin 'cursus' or Breton 'course', as in coursing wild hares. Their quarries were ships.

'Are you a pirate?' I asked him once.

'Depends,' he replied with a wink and a grin. Then he changed the subject. I pressed him on one question.

'Have you killed anyone?'

'No, never,' he said, fixing me with a stare. His wide-open eyes told he spoke the truth. Smuggling, even piracy without wanton killing, is fine with me.

The bulky, overladen and poorly manned *Scarborough* couldn't hope to escape. Even at this distance, six gunports gaped ominously. When our pursuer closed to one and a half nautical miles, she fired her bow-chaser.

The ball skipped and bounced off the water, sending a spume skywards a hundred yards from *Scarborough's* stern.

How ironic, I thought, to be killed by Breton kinsfolk, while a prisoner to the English! I was beset with a confusion of fear and hope.

Scarborough may yet escape, for the sun was going down, and visibility fast decreasing. If we could stay ahead until dark, we may yet be lost to them.

Mixed emotions competed in my soul. I was on a ship under attack, to be battered and maybe sunk by cannon-fire. I should pray for escape into the gathering darkness. Yet the Bretons were like me, smugglers when not pursuing booty. If we were captured, I could better deal with them than the guards.

They'd set any Cornishman free, and if I returned to Brittany with them I could contrive to bring Morwenna across the channel to me. I wasn't sure how they would deal with Peder Pengilly, a Cornishman in the English navy, unless he could convince them he was pressed into service.

The privateer fired three more cannon shots, but none hit *Scarborough*. Night closed in so suddenly, it took pursuer and quarry by surprise. Loosing off several more frustrated cannonballs into the darkness, the Breton gave up his pursuit and turned upon a north-easterly course for Roscoff.

There would be no prize from *'Albion maudit'*, the accursed English, this time.

'We're away!' shouted a sailor. I was plunged into lingering regret. Was my only chance of salvation, or ever seeing Morwenna again, missed? But there was nothing I could have done to alter it. The fates were not on my side.

Late in the afternoon of the fourth of June 1787, *Scarborough*, battered and missing her mizzen mast, broken off in a squall off Lanzarote, limped into the bay at Tenerife, Spanish Canary Islands, a whole day after the rest of the fleet.

Next afternoon Peder Pengilly encountered me on deck.

'Th' skipper endur'd many ungenl'manly curses fro' Commodore Phillip,' he said, 'fer takin' too easterly a corse, an' riskin' th' loss o' 'is ship t' French pyrates.'

'Breton,' I corrected him with a laugh, 'no more French than we are English!'

'Ye'd know bettr'n I,' he said, winking his one eye.

'How did you lose the eye?' I'd wanted to know since I met him.

'Target-shootin' wi' a flintlock pistol, 'blowed up in m' face!' That explained the black pock marks on his scarred cheek. Exploding pistols are a nightmare, and he was lucky it wasn't worse.

'She was called *Alargh Anethek*,' he said, changing the subject.

'The ship which chased us?' The name meant 'Fabulous Swan' in Breton and Cornish.

'Yes, read it through the telescope.'

'Good name for a beautiful ship.'

'A swan with sharp teeth,' Peder laughed.

Repaired to the best of the island boatyard's ability, *Scarborough* and the fleet set sail again on the morning of the thirteenth of June, 1787. Our course was west, sou'west, before the easterly trades, towards the Brasils in South America.

Two weeks from Tenerife, the first cases of scurvy began, and several convicts were unable to rise from their squalid beds. In a squall one afternoon in July, a seaman fell reefing a topgallant sail and broke his neck.

In a Force-nine storm later that month, a poor young convict woman walking on deck tripped over a coiled rope and hit the guardrail with such force that she broke through and fell overboard.

In that raging tempest, *Scarborough* could not retrieve her from the thundering, foaming sea. Would they have tried in better weather, I wondered.

One afternoon, we were unexpectedly brought on deck to witness a hanging. A young wretch of a sailor, whose crime was stealing a pint of rum from the officers' store, was standing under a spar supporting the mainsail. One end of a rope was looped over it and the other around his neck. His hands were lashed behind his back.

A single marine beat a slow tattoo on his drum, and at the Captain's command three burly sailors pulled on the free end of the rope. The poor man was drawn up until his feet hung six feet above the deck. His face went purple as he struggled, and a dark patch declared he'd wet his trousers. His bowels loosened, and a sickening stench of warm shit wafted over the deck. It was the most horrible thing I ever witnessed. It was a long time before his body hung still.

Now we were herded below, with the terrible spectacle seared into our minds. There was no compassion on that accursed ship.

A scurvy victim died a week later, another the day after. Two of the marine detachment fell to fighting over cards, one fatally stabbing the other, and being 'put in irons'.

For a reason I didn't understand, he was, unlike the poor hanged sailor, to face court-martial at Botany Bay. Another scurvy victim died soon after.

Days later, a young Welsh convict of fifteen or thereabouts, well-muscled from digging coal in the Rhondda valley, cursed a guard, who responded by giving him a clout on the head.

In a temper, the boy seized his musket and wrenched it from him. Before the guard could react, he stepped back, cocked the hammer, and fired.

The guard, clutching his chest where bright blood spurted through his shirt, sank to his knees with a groan, then fell on his face. A second musket-shot rang out from the gantry, and the Welsh boy lay dead beside him. At least he wouldn't die 'a-stranglin' from the yardarm'.

We endured two months of hellish passage, great heat and extreme discomfort. The nights below were such that all we could do was pray to survive till morning, when we'd taste blessed fresh air again.

Bringing up the tail of the fleet, we arrived in Rio de Janeiro on the seventeenth of August, 1787. There we remained until the fourth of September, the crew making repairs to rigging, filling water casks and stocking up provisions. We were not allowed ashore.

I met Peder Pengilly on deck for the first time in days. His arm was in a sling, and he said he'd badly bruised and sprained his shoulder falling against a hatch in the last squall. He was lucky not to break any bones.

'Taint fair nor proper, navigatin' a movin' deck wi' one eye,' he laughed. We spoke for several minutes, then he was called away by an officer.

Peder had expressed sympathy for my plight, but could I trust him?

It was while we were lying at Rio I had made up my mind. I would try to escape from the death-ship in the Cape of Good Hope. Could I count on assistance from my one-eyed countryman?

Eleven

From 'Untold Mysteries of The San' by Sven Johannsen, 1790: *To the San, dreaming is not a product of the sleeping mind, but truly seeing the consciously un-seeable, hearing the un-hearable, on the wings of the _//gãũa, the immortal spirit of the dead.*

'How did you and Chiko become so close?' It was the end of another gruelling day. Egon, surly and almost mute, had gone to bed early, and Chiko was off on a wander. The desert was moonless, the only light from the flickering fire.

'A long story.'

'Are you keeping secrets?'

'Don't you have any?'

'Put it like this - I'll tell you if you tell me.' I laughed. A boy-girl 'I'll show you if you show me' game.

'I told you about my great uncle Ignatius, the smuggler sentenced to transportation, who jumped ship in Cape Town and fled to the desert.' She nodded.

'Nine years ago, an old German-speaking Herero farmworker told me his rural tribesmen still believe in *omurois*. They're witches who fly, perform evil deeds and ride people by night.'

'Oh yes, I know about *omurois*, Herero witches, not San.'

'The history-telling of the Herero is uncannily accurate. Many of their stories are confirmed by official records, like those of the German-Herero war of 1904 to 1907.'

'I know.'

'They still tell those old stories to their children.'

'And so so should, it's their culture!'

82

'The Herero told me there is one story, at least two hundred years old, about an *omuroi* with 'singing speech' who went past with a clan of demon-servants disguised as Nama tribesmen. *Omurois* were ghostly white, like the first Europeans. They hypnotised their victims by singing. When they tried to kill it, the witch screeched like a demon and disappeared in a puff of smoke. Exaggeration of terrified tribesmen.'

'Like 'pale-faces' to the Red Indians.'

'I wondered if, by any stretch, the 'singing speech' may have been old Cornish-English. When I came to Namibia, I had a stronger accent, and Hereros said I sang my words. I wondered if that's what the old people meant. Long shot. Could have been a Frenchman or Russian, for all I knew.'

'I watched Poldark,' Angelika laughed, 'and that old servant of Poldark's, Judd I think he was called, sang his curses.'

'You know what I mean, *"taint fair, 'taint friendly, 'taint gentlemany, 'taint proper!"* I wasn't as broad as Judd.'

'Not long after I head about the *omuroi*, I woke after a strange dream. I had been in a cold, dark, misty place, though the horizon was beginning to brighten. I was looking at a bay with lapping waves. I knew I'd seen it before. I heard sounds, the creak of oars in rowlocks, dripping of water and heavy breathing of men. Out of the darkness came a gig, a long, narrow boat. Four men were rowing, a fifth steering in the stern. Suddenly, so close together as to almost touch, came two longer gigs in pursuit. In the bow of the first, a man fired a musket. Then the mist cut off my view.'

'Graphic, they call dreams like that eidetic.'

'What?

'Imagery vividly experienced, clearly remembered. San elders describe such things after trances.'

'I suppose they do. *Eidetic?* Well, I couldn't forget it. It was Mounts Bay in Cornwall. I rowed and sailed there for years. Ignatius was captured in a gig there in 1787. That's what I must have seen!'

'Amazing. You know, there are scientists who believe we live in parallel universes, and that there is no such thing as time. San beliefs are similar, they think their ancestors are still alive, in a co-existing world, and can communicate by trance-travelling.'

'You don't think I'm mad?'

'No. The San aren't mad.' I looked up from the fire.

'I'm not San.'

'Nor me, but Westerners don't have exclusivity on wisdom.'

'Okay, if the San are right, Ignatius sent me a message, is that it?'

'I don't know, but I wouldn't rule it out. Anyway, this started with you telling me about Chiko…'

'The dream left me feeling something important was going to happen. I went for a drive on the road to Okahandja. That's an Otjiherero name meaning *where two rivers join to make a wide one.*'

'I'm impressed,' Angelika said, grinning.

'On the road between Karibib and Okahandja, I was waved down by two ragged San. In broken Afrikaans, they blurted out their brother had been shot and needed help.'

'All Bushmen are brothers!'

'It was a long story. Chiko was a poacher, though he denies it. There was a farm near them, where they raised Steenbok.

They'd been 'walking', when their brother was shot.

Someone saw them at a distance and fired a warning shot. It hit him in his side.'

'Some warning!'

'The kind you can't ignore. They ran, then he collapsed. Another shot ricocheted off a rock. At the risk of their lives, his friends picked him up carried him three miles to his hut. They laid him on his sleeping mat. He was very sick, they said, unconscious and hot, and his stomach was swollen like a *tsamma* melon.'

'Pik told me you ignored the speed limit in the hospital grounds.'

'He was in a coma. The bullet missed his vital organs, but, judging by the abdominal distension, perforated his bowel. We bundled him into the back of the Landy, then I drove like a demon to Katatura hospital in Windhoek. I never knew sixty miles could be so far. I pushed the Landy hard, not knowing if he was still alive. I'd either bring in a living man or a corpse. Stopping wouldn't change it.'

'And that's where you met Pik, in Katatura, a Herero name for *The place where nobody wants to live*.'

'I see I've got competition for place-names.'

'Oh, you'll win, I only know San names. Pik told me that one.'

'As you know, Pik's a Baster from Rehoboth, a trauma specialist trained in Cape Town. He gets plenty of practice in Katatura. I was glad to leave Chiko in his hands. His 'brothers' had to wait in the yard.'

'He said Chiko would have died if not for you.'

'Maybe.'

'But you met Chiko again.'

'After ten days, I got good news. He was well and was discharged. Two weeks later, he pitched up at my house.

He'd badgered Pik for my address. He said he owed his life to me, and had come to thank me. Now, dressed in rags and grinning like a cat with a gateau, he was at the door.'

'That's beautiful,' she said. She made a silhouette in the dying glow of the fire.

'What did you say?'

'I see you looking well….and also very tall. If you comment honestly on a Bushman's size, they turn away as if they don't hear you.'

'You learnt a lot.'

'I said I saw him coming from far off. I remembered it was the thing to say, and Chiko's reaction confirmed it. He said he was both well and tall, and drew himself up to his full five foot.'

'Endearing.'

'I said someone as tall as him could never arrive unexpected, which was why I saw him from miles off.'

'What did he say?'

'He said I spoke the truth, his tallness ensured he was seen. We've never looked back.'

'You've been together since?'

'Yes. We drank sweet tea and talked about our pasts. He wanted to know why I, not only a /hũ, but one from far away, was living alone. Where were my people?'

'The San ask questions which would be rude from anyone else.'

'It was refreshing. People speak so much hogwash, specially those who've been to university. They skirt round subjects, never say what they think. Drove me crazy at work, nobody saying they meant. They'd say 'I have concerns', code for 'I'm on your case.''

'True, but not Chiko?'

'He was honest, wouldn't recognise political correctness if it bit him on the bum, and didn't check every thought through an acceptability-filter. I was relaxed with him.'

'Did you tell him why you came to Namibia?'

'Yes.'

'Listening is more important than telling to the San.'

'He called my ex a Snake-woman, and spat when I said she left me'.

'//kyi-tââ gae!' she laughed. There was a suppressed chortle from the darkness. I made out Chiko's shadow. He'd come back and was bedding down on the sand.

'That's what he called her. He translated it to me, but you....?'

'I learnt a lot, good things, and how to swear.'

'I had a *Eureka* moment. There, in the eyes of this rag-wearing man, was understanding.'

'Which you'd been missing?'

'Suppose so. Chiko said it was good I'd come, because I'd lost my //gãũa! My *what?* I asked him.'

'Your soul. Did he tell you about himself?'

'You know how the San love telling stories?'

'It's a wonderful thing about them.'

'He was born near Ojikondo. More and more hunting grounds were fenced off, and his people were driven into drier, harder areas. He married at about thirty, and lost his wife in childbirth a year later. His son is thirty-something, born in the year of the worst drought they remember. Eight years before, he went with a group seeking a better life across the Rovuma in Angola. He hadn't seen him since.'

'Tragedy of the San!'

'True.'

'He didn't believe life was better in Angola, and stayed to care for his parents and what was left of the clan. They lived in hovels and scratched a living by adopting maize-growing, chicken-raising Nama ways. They augmented it by hunting and gathering, but the pickings were lean.'

'For all the San!'

'Do you, in your research, collect individual San life stories?'

'Look, they add up to a bigger story,' Angelika said, using her hands. 'How can you understand people if you don't know about their lives?'

'Is that why you're interested in Chiko?'

'Yes and no.'

'One day he got an idea from a passing Owambo. If he could work for the /hũ, which he pronounced Hu, without clicks, for my benefit, he could help the twelve people left in his family. The Owambo told him there were jobs washing dishes in Windhoek hotels.'

I put a piece of dry wood on the embers, and a yellow flame began to lick it. Angelika added another.

'He was washing pots and pans when a Baster chef began teaching him the basics of European cooking. After five years, there was nothing he couldn't cook. He also learnt Afrikaans.'

'Ah, that's why he speaks it so well!'

'In Windhoek, he missed his old life. Two years before, his mother died, ten months later his father. He absconded from his job, and went back to his mud hovel between Karibib and Okahandja. There wasn't any land worth hunting, but there were farms with deer and sheep.' She nodded.

'What would it mean to the Hu, who had many, if they hunted a few?' She nodded her understanding.

88

'Poaching was a word he didn't understand. That brings me to the day I found him.'

'Quite a story, no wonder you're close!'

'I had an idea. He'd worked in an alien world, learnt skills and language, but his longing for his people was too strong. What if he had a job where he could keep his freedom, use his skills, *and* support his people?'

'He could work for you!'

'We could work together. He leapt at the idea. So, nearly nine years ago, we started *NST* or Namib Safari Tours.'

'Does he get a salary?'

'Salary? No. He's my partner, not employee, even if he acts like one.'

'You mean…?'

'You know how little people are paid here?'

'Of course, that's why I ask.'

'Chiko gets half of everything.'

'That's amazing, very generous!'

'Generous? I wouldn't have a business without him. How would I, with no knowledge of the country, or anything to do with it, have even started? I fix the Land Rover, read the maps, talk to agents, make business arrangements, chase payments and so-on. He does the other things, which make us successful.'

'What does he do with his share?'

'Supports his people.'

'Doesn't he spend money on himself?'

'Almost nothing. Our living expenses come out of earnings. He refuses to live in the house. Prefers to sleep in the shed, says it's the best 'house' he's ever had.'

'I understand you better.'

'Well, you could say we are close.' I got to my feet.

I stared at her.

'We made a deal,' I reminded her, 'that you'll tell me about you!'

'Oh, I will,' she replied with a grimace, 'just not yet.'

Twelve

We sailed from Rio de Janeiro on the sixth of September. There is no choice with square-rigged ships, but to run before the wind. Leaving the coast of the Brasils astern, we were driven east towards the Cape of Good Hope by the westerly trade. More agony, more hell, for there was no comfort on that terrible hulk. There was only one blessing. Seven months and two days after my arrest on the second of February, my pain at parting from Morwenna was no longer so sharp.

At midday on the tenth day of October, we caught our only sight of land in six weeks. A lingering mist briefly cleared, and there, two leagues off the port bow, pounded by a ring of white surf, was a ghostly volcanic island.

'Tristan da Cunha,' said Peder Pengilly, staring at the distant island with his one eye, 'th' onlie land 'tween Africa an' th' Americas, wi' niver a soul 'pon it!' Rock-strewn mountains pierced low clouds, and jagged cliffs and outcrops of boulders towered over a broken shore. Far below, galloping rows of waves broke in angry explosions of white. I cannot imagine humans will ever make that bleak place their home. A minute later the island was swallowed in the swirling mist.

'I have to escape at Table Bay,' I said, throwing caution to the blustering wind. What would Peder say? It was his duty to report such murmurings. I waited an anxious time for his response, my heart a hard lump in my throat.

'I wer thinkin' o' that,' he said at last.

'I just can't go to New South Wales.'

'I'll help ye,' he said simply.

'Why?' I asked, delight and confusion vying for prominence.

'Many a tyme, 'th' lykes o' ye help't my famile in Boscastle. Ye be no crim'nal, but a good Cornishman, stab me!' There was a tear in the good man's eye.

With *Sirius*, *Scarborough* made up the tail of the fleet, and we arrived at Table Bay on the evening of the thirteenth of October 1787. The first boat to come alongside brought a red-coated officer from the shore garrison. Two weeks ago, a fast Royal Navy frigate had brought news of more peasant revolts in France. It was feared there would be a general uprising against the King. In our condition, we cared little about events half a world away.

Here, at the southern tip of Africa, the ships were to be revictualled, and repairs made, before we sailed for Botany Bay. It would take a month, and we would not depart before the twelfth of November. Within a single week at the Cape of Good Hope, eight convicts perished from fever and five escaped ashore. Of those, four were quickly apprehended by the Dutche, and it was said they were to be hanged from the yardarm for their trouble. A Cape it was, but of hopelessness, not good hope! I'd witnessed one hanging from *Scarborough*'s yardarm, and didn't wish to see another.

I could also strangle on the end of a rope, but my desire not to be aboard the stinking, rat-infested and scrofulous *Scarborough* when she sailed for New South Wales was greater than my fear.

One of the other three who shared a stinking, scratchy horsehair mattress with me was a good and friendly man called Sterkbooi, which means strong boy in the Dutche.

He was mixed race, he said, part Khoi, part Dutch, part isiXhosa, they being the blacks beyond the Fish River, whose name he pronounced with a drawn-out click. In time, I would hear much of this peculiar clicking.

'I came from here,' he said in Dutche-accented English. 'Three years ago, I was recruited to crew on a brig returning to Portsmouth from the Indian Ocean. There, they paid me off and left me to fend for myself. I stole a leg of roast mutton from a market stall, and was sentenced to transportation.'

'I was caught smuggling,' I said, 'but it seems we're in the same boat!' He laughed.

'Blerry floating wreck, more like' he said. 'I'm a Bastard,' he added.

'No, maybe they think so, but you aren't!'

'Yes I am, but not like you think. There are coloured people here in the Cape Colony who call themselves Bastards or Basters, and I am one. We are proud of it.'

His surname was Bogaert, which the way he said it sounded like buggered. I didn't tell him, for who is there would like to be known as a buggered Bastard?

In short time, we set to plotting our escape, though it was hard to talk without being overheard.

Peder Pengilly found me in the lee of a lifeboat.

'Tonight,' he said. 'ther'll niver be a better tyme.' I stared at the one-eyed angel for a long moment.

'Bless you, but there are two of us now!'

'Who be th' uther?' I told him about Sterkbooi, and the good man shrugged.

'What's 'ee to me?' he said, ''ee can go too if ye chuse.'

We were moored close to shore, and the water was said not to be as cold as in Cornwall.

Poor swimmer or no, I had to try.

Once before, my reticence had cost me my freedom, and now I'd rather drown than fail to regain it.

Sterkbooi told me it was better to avoid contact with white folk ashore, be they Dutche or other, for they were sure to arrest us. His people he said, being Bastards, had been moving north for some time, carving out their own farms, out of reach of the oppressive whites. His own family lived in the Khamiesberg, a Dutche name for somewhere on a hillside, in a mountain range in the North Cape. That was where we would go.

It was midnight when Peder called us. 'It be tyme,' he whispered, 'ye mus' go dreckly!' Most of the guards had overindulged in cheap Cape gin and were snoring noisily on deck. Others were below. He put something in my hand. Wrapped in an oilcloth was a small brass compass. It was a costly thing, worth several months of his wages, and I suspected he didn't have another. Such unexpected generosity moved me deeply.

'Thank you,' I whispered.

'May it guide ye wher ye want t' go.' I put it safely inside my shirt. We dropped with barely a splash over the side, hoping we wouldn't be spied by a sober guard.

The sea was shocking cold, and, poor swimmer as I am, I feared I would not keep my head above water. Sterkbooi swam close, quietly urging me to kick my legs and paddle like a puppy. Thirty, maybe forty yards it was, but I made progress, and the wharf loomed out of the dark.

I thanked both God and Sterkbooi when, after ten freezing minutes we clambered, shivering, onto the narrow beach. At first, we didn't notice the man standing in shadow on the edge of the pier.

It was only when he pissed on our heads that we saw him.

Somehow, we managed not to react or draw his attention. All he had to do was look down, and he'd see us.

After a long time, the wretched man put away his accursed organ, and his footsteps receded on the walkway. When we regained our breath, we washed in the salt water we'd so recently vacated. We bided almost an hour, crouching close to the wharf with chattering teeth until we were almost dry.

First thing was to get away from the bay, then all signs of civilization. Flitting between wooden buildings and across open spaces, we reached the limit of the settlement before sunrise. Ahead was a long walk, without food or supplies. We would have to scrounge or steal to survive, with the risk of running into Dutche soldiers, or armed civilians hunting convicts for reward.

'This place is full of men like that,' Sterkbooi said. I was overcome with trepidation.

Thirteen

I'd been drifting off, but now saw the glint of moonlight on a Bay. I was in the Namib desert, hundreds of miles from the sea, yet there lay a watery expanse, the moon iridescent on wavelets running onto a shingle beach. I could even smell the sea. Though it was changed, I knew it was Table Bay in Cape Town. The dark shape of the mountain in the background was unmistakable. The ocean terminal and cranes weren't there, and only low wooden buildings stood beside planked wharves. Tethered to them were square-rigged sailing ships, while others rode at anchor. The light of oil-lamps in the buildings and ships cast yellow pools of light on the water.

Three figures stood in shadow on the deck of an anchored ship. One clutched a long thing in his hands. It looked like a musket. He glanced around and made signs to the other two. They crept across the deck, then, without hesitating, climbed over the rail and dropped into the sea.

A rusty iron ladder on to a pier vibrated as someone began climbing from the water. A man's bearded head appeared. He looked around, stared right through me, then heaved himself up. He shook his long hair, sending drops of water flying.

The scene faded, then a light from the gloom illuminated the dark snout and eyes of a hyena.

Journey with me, great-nephew of /hũ-brother,' it said, *'you seek the white man who was brother to the San, whose spirit rests among the firmament. I have shown him to thee, and I bring you hither.'*

'What are you?' I whispered. If I was awake I'd reach for my gun.

But I wasn't. I was paralysed. My heart pounded like a hammer, my mouth was dry. The hyena spoke again.

'Know that I am,' it said. 'I am /num, healer and spirit-traveller. Harken to me.' The head expanded and dissipated into a panoramic vision. It was the Namib. It couldn't be anywhere else. There was a family of San. They were golden brown, the young with smooth complexions, the old deeply wrinkled. They were naked, except for small hide moochis concealing their genitals.

The camp lay in the lee of a huge rock. It was deeply fissured and burnt black. The sun was declining, casting a cool swathe of shade on the sand.

'The star stones of the valley,' said an elder to a group of naked children, 'will bring salvation to our people.' Though it was San, I understood.

I half woke, the images so vivid I didn't know which was the reality, my bed, the bay, the sailing ships, the swimmers, the talking hyena or the San. Why did I dream about Ignatius and the San in sequence? Why a hyena? I shivered. The !gwaī of Bushman mythology…! I was thinking of Angelika before I fell asleep. Could her San studies and my obsession with Ignatius have got tangled up?

In the early hours, my dream and strange imagery was still fresh. The voice had called me 'great-nephew of /hū-brother, the white man who was brother to the San.' I had a pounding headache.

I imagined someone was sitting on my sleeping bag, then saw it was true. It was an angel. No, Angelika was gazing into my face.

'You okay? I heard you groaning. What did you dream, who were you talking to?'

97

I glanced at my watch. Twenty past four.

'Don't know.' My dream was strange, but so was her interest. Was this insanity? My head pounded.

'Oh, you don't want to say.' She stood and turned. 'I boiled some water,' she said.

I rolled out of my sleeping bag. In the other bed, Egon snored softly. He was a deep sleeper if Angelika could hear me moan, and he didn't. I pulled on my shorts and stepped into my sandals. Where were the Panado? Local paracetamol. I didn't take painkillers often, but this headache was different. I stepped outside. It was still dark, the moon a pale disk above the horizon. I sucked in the cool air. The gas burner hissed and the smell of coffee reached me.

'Thanks,' I said as she passed me a steaming mug. My head ached unbearably.

'Sorry I woke you, but you were groaning, I thought you were in pain.'

Pale moonlight breached the cloud cover, and I saw her troubled expression.

'Bad headache.'

'Oh, there's a box of Panado in the cubbyhole.' She went to the Land Rover and came back with the tablets.

'Thank you.' I took two with the dregs of my coffee, then went back to bed.

Egon was still snoring. I turned one way then the other, but couldn't stop thinking about my dream. And Angelika. Would she tell me about herself? It took an hour for my pounding headache to ease.

Fourteen

The long, tortuous trudge north is hard to describe. One must do it to understand. It seems that, under the greatest stress, humans adapt and carry on. We slept in the day, hiding under rocky overhangs or amongst the scanty trees. At night, we found our slow way by moonlight. Sometimes the sky was cloudy, and there was no moon to light our way. We fell into gullies and tripped over rocks. I recalled the words of the old Turkish trader in Morlaix. Your fate can't be avoided, it's *Kismet!* So this was mine, to die of hunger and exhaustion, baked by the relentless sun of day, frozen by the pitiless cold of night.

I never knew the nagging pain of such hunger before. A wild animal scratched and tore at my stomach, my throat ached, and a throbbing pulse beat in my temple. It would have been a mercy to end the agony, to give up and die.

Though I be a sailor and had a compass, I was no navigator. Sterkbooi, fortunately, had an instinctive awareness of terrain and directions in his head. Along the way, he always managed to locate streams or pools of water, and sometimes wandering Griquas or San hunters, from whom we obtained little gifts of strange foods.

It took us more than three perilous weeks to reach the Khamiesberg. The daytime temperature was hotter than anything I had known, while at night, with only our clothes for bedding, we shivered in the biting cold, and arose stiff and aching in the morning. But the day finally came when Sterkbooi climbed to the top of a rocky hillock and pointed.

'My father's house!'

We had arrived, and not a minute too soon.

More than twenty people lived in the ramshackle collection of buildings he called his father's house. We came shortly after they had risen from their beds, and the sight of their long-lost relative caused much jubilation.

Sterkbooi and I were joyously welcomed by his large family, who'd never thought to see him again, and rejoiced, crying and shouting to Almighty God in Dutche, 'thank you for returning our lost son'.

The biggest building was his father's, he who was called Sterkbooi *die Ouder*, or Sterkbooi the Elder. He was the *Kaptein* of the clan.

He wore a fine square-cut grey beard, contrasting with the dark oak colour of his skin. Though he was thin and almost toothless, and more wizened than an old Cornish fisherman, he cut a gallant figure. His eyes shone with wisdom and knowledge, and it was this which most distinguished him.

Ouder, as he was called for short, clapped his hands and gave orders in a commanding voice.

'The prodigal son has returned from his wandering,' he proclaimed, 'let us rejoice!' I was to learn that Basters embrace the bible literally. There was much running to and fro. A young bullock, which I was tempted to call the fatted calf, was slaughtered, and a fire was kindled on the ground. The skinning and butchering were rapidly done, the carcass impaled on a skewer over the fire. The women fetched huge earthenware jars of frothing white liquid.

'African beer,' Sterkbooi said, 'fermented corn. We Basters have many white man's ways, but we keep the best African traditions.'

I couldn't recall if the feast after the prodigal son's return included beer.

Huge parsnip-shaped potatoes, which they called African, or 'sweet', potatoes, were placed in the ashes and tended by a young boy with a stick. An iron cauldron, half-filled with water, was hung over the fire. There was a pile of green leaves, alike to cabbage, on one side, which were to be boiled.

A long table of empty barrels supporting rough-cut planks was set outside, and homemade chairs were carried out from the hovels. With the family, ourselves and friends from the neighbourhood, there were more than thirty diners. Serving the food onto earthen plates, and bringing jars of African beer, were three family servants, two elderly Hottentot men and a slim girl of fairer complexion.

Ouder proposed a hundred toasts to his son's safe return, at which we all drank deeply of the sour, yeasty beer, which left a white ring around the mouth. The Basters looked like made-up clowns, and doubtless so did I.

It was almost twenty months since I last saw dear Morwenna, now being the last day of October 1787, and my arrest in February 1786. I never thought of other women, and I was assailed by guilt when the serving girl caught my eye. There was something about her. Nothing like sweet, pretty Morwenna, she who I'd promised to love forever. But Morwenna was an ocean away, and, even if the distance could be overcome, my status as an escaped convict would never be. What folly to make oaths of eternal love when you know not what the next day may bring!

'What is the girl's name?' I asked Sterkbooi, the heady brew lending me audacity.

It had too many of clicks of the tongue for me but sounded like Marana.

From that moment, try as I did, though beset by guilt over Morwenna, I couldn't get her out of my mind.

One morning I chanced to find her sitting on a log under a shady tree, drawing upon a piece of rag paper made from old cloth. Even here, in the Khamiesberg, such things were traded from travelling Griqua and European merchants.

At first it was not her drawing which caught my attention, but what she was using. In her hand was a thin black rod, like slate, partially wrapped in string. As she moved it about the paper, it left a dark grey line. It was a crude version of the lead pencils used in Cornwall. I stared so hard that she looked up.

'*Zwaarte lood,*' she said, smiling shyly. Just then Sterkbooi happened along and translated.

'Dutche for black lead, *bleiweiss* in German. They find it on the ground, next to the feldspar and quartz crystals, cut it up, and draw with it. Not soft like lead for bullets, not really lead at all, but good for drawing.' I took it from her hand and examined the black point. It was much like the tip of a Cornish pencil.

'Where can I get some?' I asked. It would be easier to use than a quill and inkpot, if I ever decided to write. I glanced at her paper. The image was unmistakably the face of Sterkbooi's father, Ouder. The maid was gifted.

One day, an uncle of Sterkbooi's on his mother's side rode up on a horse. He had been to the settlement at Table Bay and bore the most terrible news about the convict fleet, which had since sailed for New South Wales.

There had been a hue and cry when two more convicts, one a Cornish Smuggler and the other a halfbreed from the Cape, under armed guard, had escaped into the sea from *HMS Scarborough*.

Six guards were flogged for drunkenness, and one, who had only one eye, was tried, found guilty of complicity, and hanged from the yardarm.

It could be none other than poor Peder Pengilly. I wondered whether, if he'd anticipated the outcome, he would have assisted us. It was another very bitter pill to digest. Our gratitude to him, and sadness at the awful price he paid would never go away. Yet, in our circumstances, we could not let even such a terrible matter overwhelm us. When life is tenuous, you have to look to your own survival. Kismet had not favoured our gallant hero, but we had to live.

There is much to tell about our sojourn in the Khamiesberg. Sterkbooi and the others taught me to speak Dutche, saying I needed it lest I be recognised as English, and questions be asked. It was a prophecy, for I would learn the danger of speaking that language in this land and beyond. I let the 'English' pass, even though I am Cornish.

I was more and more enchanted by Marana. She didn't look at all like the Basters, which I prefer saying to Bastards. They are tall. and mainly of dark complexion. This, Sterkbooi said, was because most had only a little Dutche blood, the children often marrying blacks from one or other tribe. Still, they kept the Dutche tongue and bible and lived very much like the Dutche.

Marana was short, barely five foot, and slim, and had the complexion of a Spaniard or Portuguese.

Her face was almond shaped, and thick, glossy black hair hung down the sides of her head, framing it like a painting.

Her eyes were a darker green than Morwenna's and glistened like emeralds, her teeth were pearly white, and she had a most captivating smile.

'Tell me about this serving girl,' I asked Sterkbooi in poor Dutche. This is what he told me:

Fifteen years ago, near a place called Kakamas, fifty miles east of Upington in the North Cape, wandered a group of Griquas. They were of Khoisan or San stock, interbred with some Europeans and tribal Africans. They spoke Cape Dutche, but lived by hunting and gathering in the way of the San. They came into conflict with whites and Basters from the south, who settled on the land and drove them off with great violence.

One day Ouder was out riding, searching for wild game, when he came upon a terrible sight. More than fifty San and Griquas had been massacred on a hillside, men, women and children. He was about to ride away from the horrible scene when something moved.

It was a tiny little girl of three or four trying to get up from under the bloodied dead body of a white man with blond hair and beard. He was Dutche, a rare one who married a San. Ouder got off his horse and lifted her. She was crying, saying in Dutche he was her father, and they killed him and carried her mother away. The little one said her name was Mãr!ãnna. He took her home, where she was welcomed with Christian charity.

'She's eighteen or nineteen now,' Sterkbooi said.

I turned to look at Marana again. She was clearing the table and wiping with a cloth.

Her eyes met mine and she smiled shyly. I never saw a prettier one, nor so delicate a build.

There was something about the shape of her eyes which reminded me of the Chinese, be it ever so slight.

It was hard to think about what happened to her family, or that it was white men like me who did it.

Now is time to record the story of Malkop. He sneaked into our lives in a way most unusual and became as loving a friend as ever we could have. If it was up to me, I'd never have named even a little brute like him *Mad-Head*, for that is the meaning of Malkop in Dutche.

Sometime before Sterkbooi and I arrived at *die Ouder's* house in the Khamiesberg, one of the beautiful wild wolf-like animals they call *Jakkals*, or Jackal in English, met one of the Baster's tame girl dogs of dubious roots and morals, and courted with her. The result was half-bred Jackal dogs, and, no matter how pretty, they were drowned, for such half-breeds were known to be vicious.

An elderly uncle was a kindly sort and hid the small black boy with long gold ears, big yellow eyes and a black button nose, saying he was 'mixed', just like themselves, and no Bastard should be killed. Slowly, the furry and friendly strangeling made friends of everyone, even the cats and scraggly farm chickens, and the feared attacks and bites never happened.

It was as a joke the old man called him Malkop, for he was always chasing his tail, licking people's faces, or lying on his back displaying his privvies and making funny expressions with his lips and eyes. He was a born comedian, and laughter followed where he went.

When Sterkbooi and I arrived at Khamiesberg, the pup was five months old, and his protector had shortly been taken too ill to rise from bed.

A meeting had been held to discuss what to do with the strange pet who no longer had anyone to care for him.

The decision taken was that Malkop, though he was friendly, should join his sisters and brothers in the grave they'd been put to, because it was only the old man keeping him civil, and without him who knew what he might do to the children?

They were discussing it one night as we sat talking and drinking sour African beer, to which I'd taken a great liking. I couldn't help noticing the little scamp seemed to know what was being said, and kept himself very quiet, staying close to Marana's skirt, which he'd have gone under if he could.

'They want to kill the *Jakkals-hond*,' said Sterkbooi, 'because they is *gevaarlik*.' Dutche for dangerous.

'*Jakkals-hond?*'

'Jackal dog, dangerous!' He made biting gestures.

'But he seems tame to me,' said I, 'and he's fond of Marana.' Even as I looked down at him gazing up with big wide eyes, half his head hidden by her skirt, I couldn't see he was dangerous at all, stab me! The argument went one way, then the other. Finally, Ouder came to the rescue.

'You want him?'

'Yes.'

Marana nodded keenly. It was the first time we joined in a cause.

'Then he is yours, but it's your fault if he bites,' said Ouder to our great relief.

I was surprised and delighted one day, when Ouder presented me with a tattered book.

It was published in 1719, the title was *Robinson Crusoe,* and the author Daniel Defoe.

'Kan nie blerry Engels lees nie,' he said.

'I can't read blerry Eenglish!'

With nothing to read since Cornwall, I set to ravenously devouring the story of the castaway on a south sea island forging a life and surviving against the odds. It encouraged me, for wasn't I also cast away? Yet, unlike him, I had kind companions.

My life in Ouder's house was a comfort and luxury like I never thought to ever experience again. Little did I know, it would end with hardly a warning.

Fifteen

With the effortless flight of a dream, I found myself in the courtyard compound of a crudely-built wood and stone house, where people milled about. There was a sense of purpose in the air. Everyone wore crudely fashioned old-style European clothes with patches of leather and, except for one man, had dark skin. Most had beards. There were muskets on their backs, and powder-horns hanging from their waists. They were talking and shouting in old-fashioned Dutch. They were Basters, like Pik van Loon and his relatives in Rehoboth, the place once called !Anis.

'It's better we go soon *Witman*,' said a rangy fellow to a white man who reminded me of the cousin who had the old letter. *Witman* means white-man. Could it be Ignatius, after his escape from Scarborough?

The grey-bearded elder was speaking. Among the listeners was a golden-skinned young woman with high cheekbones.

'You should go with them,' Sterkbooi *die Ouder* said to her.

'*Kai,* wake up!' Chico's face was inches away, almost invisible in the dark, and his breath was warm on my cheek.

'What, Chiko, what's wrong?' I sat up, rubbing my eyes.

'*Ek is bang, Kai,*' I am afraid, brother. He was squatting next to my camp-bed. I never saw him so agaitated.

'Sit, Chiko, tell me why.'

'I dreamed of a spirit.' Oh no, I thought, this is not what I need.

A frightened, superstitious Chiko in the middle of the night! My eyes accommodated to the dark and I saw the terror on his face.

'Tell me,' I said, preparing to hear a saga. Prolixity and verbosity hardly do justice to his storytelling.

'I went to sleep beside that big rock…'

'Yes —'

'The stars shone and seemed to approach then recede. Then I heard it.'

'Heard what?'

'The voice of the spirit.' It was uncomfortably like my own dreams.

'What did it say?'

'It said, "*Tchi!xo*, son of my people, you come at last." I was afraid…I twisted in my blanket, rolled on my side. The voice spoke in San. "I am peace," it said. An old man's voice. "Do not be afraid, for we are one. I am a spirit, and mean no harm." It was as clear as if I was awake. "I have waited long," it said, "and knew you would come."' He drew a long breath.

'Then I saw a face, even though my eyes were closed. He came close, a much-wrinkled face like that of my grandfather. His eyes were brown, the eyes of my people!' Chiko shivered.

'I awoke shaking. Dreams of ancestors have meaning, *Kai*. The /*num* is real, I know it. Those with the /*num* travel by invisible string tied to the kudu into the world of the spirits.'

He stared into my eyes. 'They travel between the worlds of the living and the dead. You cannot hide from the /*num*, for it sees all. What does the spirit want of me, *Kai?*

He was done. What should I say? The dream was so like mine.

Superstitious dread welled up. His eyes were wide. He spoke again.

'Is it *Gao:na,* the creator, or //*Gauwa,* the deadly? Both use the /*num* to visit mortal men.'

We could not have dreamt in synchrony. Yet talk of creators and death-bringers, in that lonely place with pale moonlight breaching the black of night, the breeze ruffling the tent and a wide-eyed Chiko kneeling beside me, was something else. For his people, there was no divide between past and present, no frontier between life and death.

Get a grip, I told myself. There had been so much talk of death and diamonds. As for ancient Bushmen, we had explored many haunting old sites.

'Be calm, your ancestors would not harm you, they visit with love.' Chiko was as sensitive to his beliefs as to his stature.

'It must be *Gao:na,* not //*Gauwa,* who sent the spirit.'

'If what you say, *Kai,* is true…' He was still shivering, but even in the weak light, I saw his features relax.

'Go and sleep, Chiko. We shall talk more about this.' I wasn't going to mention my own dream. It would stir him up double.

At sunrise, I awoke to the aroma of coffee. I was dreamily wondering why Germans carry coffee to the ends of the earth to share it with Bushman spirits, when someone shook me. It was Angelika. I looked around. Egon's bed was empty.

'Coffee,' she said, 'careful, it's hot!' I sat up and took the mug. Some coffee spilt and burnt my hand. The tent flap was open and the sun was rising. She sat down on Egon's bed.

Outside, I heard Egon and Chiko packing.

'I better help.'

'Oh, give yourself a break, enjoy your coffee. What do you want for breakfast?'

'I could get used to this kind of service!'

Ja Baas,' Yes Boss, Angelika laughed in Afrikaans, 'wine and dancing girls later.' She left, swinging her auburn hair. She was as changeable as the Cornish weather.

When I emerged, they'd finished loading the Land Rover.

With one of my rare cigars between my teeth, I turned back onto the road.

The thin tar strip stretched north through a terrain of thornbush and rock. Green patches were ever less frequent, and there were no hardy sheep restlessly searching for food.

In an hour it was hot, and I donned my sunglasses against the glare. Angelika was wearing oversized blue ones. Sweat was running down her neck and staining her shirt.

There was a sign for Otjikondo. 'What does the name mean?'

'Place of The Red Cattle.'

'Impressive!'

Our attention was distracted by a Herero wedding party on the side of the road. A colourful sight in the blistering-hot semi-desert, so many people dressed in their finery, walking and singing in happy procession. The men wore dark suits with tailcoats, and the women were dressed in multi-coloured Victorian-era many-layered petticoats and embroidered, lacy dresses. Copied from the wives of German settlers in the late eighteen-hundreds.

'Amazing,' she said as the wedding party faded into the distance.

'Really are.' Ready to discuss anyone except herself.

We had lunch on the verandah of a rustic hotel in Otjikondo, then headed west to bypass Kamanjab. The intersection of the pencil lines on the map was a hundred miles further to the northwest.

'I want to show you something,' Egon said, surprising me. He hadn't spoken all morning. Judging by his tic, it was important.

'What?'

'This, hold out your hand.' He dropped something in my palm. Hard like a marble, smaller than a Smartie, cold, round and ice-white. I turned it to the sun and it caught the light, its facets flashing in several colours.'

'A cut diamond.'

'That's right, ten carats, clear, flawless.'

'Very pretty.'

'Any idea of value?' he asked with a rare smile.

'None.'

'Three hundred thousand American Dollars.' In my hand was more than we'd earned in nine years.

'This,' he continued, 'is small compared to what's out there!'

'The one Schneider sold our father was one and a half times the size, worth six times as much,' Angelika said.

'But you said —'

'That's the thing,' Egon interrupted, 'bigger, rarer, the price rockets. For example, add just point two of a carat to a perfect two carat high-grade stone, and it could double its value.' I gave the shiny thing back.

'Impressed?'

'Maybe.'

'Oh, you wonder if we care more about diamonds than Rodolf,' Angelika sighed.

'We'd better get going.' I got to my feet.

'I wonder where Chiko is.'

At four o'clock it was still very hot. A ruined stone fort faded into the backward distance. From here it was the Namib.

In my sleep, I'd heard the voice of an old man with a strong old-fashioned Cornish accent. *'It be not easy to be tryed an transport'd far from home, to go wher you 'ave niver bin, t' suff'r sadness, an' ne'er agayn cast eye 'pon yourn 'ome countrie.'* That was all I remembered, a dream about Ignatius. It was this place, being out here. It was driving me mad.

Sixteen

From 'Untold Mysteries of The San', by Sven Johannsen, 1790. *To the north of the Cape Colony, beyond Namaqualand and the Transgariep, on the far bank of the great River Gariep, lies a mysterious, enchanted and treacherous land.*

We'd been in the Khamiesberg six months, when Ouder came home most perturbed and agitated. He was always so calm, wise and thoughtful, but now his eyes were wide, his nostrils flaring, and his mouth set in a grimace.

'The Dutche and English have sent armed riders to hunt down criminals hiding among us Basters in the Khamiesberg.' He turned to Sterkbooi and I. 'If you stay, you are in mortal danger.'

'What should we do?' Sterkbooi asked.

'Take horses and food,' he said, 'and some servants, and flee north. Waste no time. Go over the land of the Namaqua to the Transgariep. Cross the big river, and keep going until you find sanctuary. There is a place called !Anis, where there are Basters. You will be safe among them.'

I didn't need persuasion after Launceston gaol, Bodmin Assizes, the awful ship *Scarborough* or the hanging of poor Peder Pengilly. I was delighted when Ouder said Marana could go too, for I had taken a shine to her. From her, I had obtained a fist-sized lump of the black lead she called *zwaarte lood*. I would make it into pencils, and practice my long-neglected writing on a wad of cotton-rag paper gifted by Ouder.

I was torn between the terror of recapture and something to look forward to, the company of Marana, the presence of whom almost banished my fears.

If I could in time get a letter to my family in Cornwall, so they knew I lived yet, I would be pleased to give them the news. Yet my heart still panged when I thought of Morwenna.

There was a horse for each man, plus Marana and two of Sterkbooi's women. Five of the men had new-looking English Brown Bess service muskets. Very modern, because they were the second model of that name, only made twenty-two years before in 1777. The marines on *Scarborough* used them to guard us.

When I asked Sterkbooi how they came by the muskets, he rubbed the side of his nose with a finger and winked.

'Don't ask,' he laughed. The Brown Bess is a handsome piece, with a forty-two-inch barrel, a half inch bore, a fine flintlock mechanism, and polished woodwork. With these on their backs, powder horns slung from their waists, and seated on horses, the Basters looked fearsome indeed.

Sterkbooi and I had different weapons, because, he said, they were better than the Bess. Ours were *Jaeger* flintlock muzzle-loading rifles. They had inscribed plaques on the barrel, with the year 1760 stamped on them, and the name and address of the maker, *WC Freund, Furstenau, Deutschland.* That's in Germany. Rifling is cutting spiral grooves on the inside of the barrel. It makes the shot spin, and increases accuracy up to two hundred, even three hundred yards. By comparison, the Brown Bess has a smoothbore barrel and isn't accurate beyond a hundred yards.

It didn't matter, because infantry tactics relied on fusillades of fire in the general direction of advancing massed infantry, against which it was difficult to miss *someone.*

In those days, sharpshooters with rifles accurate over long ranges were not yet commonly deployed on the battlefield, though I believe that has changed in recent times.

The *Jaegers* had carved walnut stocks and butts, and gilded brass parts. The locks were well crafted, with curved hammers and workmanlike flint-carriers. I never saw anything better made. By their condition, it was hard to believe they were twenty-seven years old.

'These beauties have never been used,' Sterkbooi said as I admired mine, answering my unspoken question.

'Beautiful,' I said. They were indeed.

'Why were they never used?'

'Let's just say they were seized by the British from a Dutche ship bound for Java. They were part of a consignment for the settlers.'

'But how did you get them?'

'Aha,' he said, rubbing the side of his nose again, 'now that would be telling!'

Sterkbooi took me shooting with the *Jaegers* several times before we left, and they are lovely if you know how to use them. I didn't know a gun could shoot so far or so accurate. In no time, I found I could hit a rabbit at an incredible hundred and fifty yards.

The men, rough though they were, were a companionable group, and together we made good speed for the far northern Cape and the river marking the frontier of that accursed country.

Word came to us on our way that armed white horsemen were indeed carrying out raids against deserters and renegade Basters, to either kill or take them to Cape Town in chains. I'd never shot another man, but I was ready to defend myself.

The territory we passed through after crossing the Gariep, the river they renamed *Orange* twenty years later, is a desert land they call the *Transgeriep*. Rock and sand to the horizon in all directions, dazzling, blistering heat, mountain upon barren mountain, ravine after ravine, and scarcely any water. There were eight of us, all mounted on horses, or nine if I include Malkop. He needs including, seeing how like a person he was.

Malkop struggled to keep up, and Marana stopped and picked him up. He being still small and his legs short, he couldn't pace with the horses. It was amusing to see a baby jackal, for he looked like one, riding on a girl's lap upon a horse, looking for all the world like he was smiling.

At this time, I began a habit which would serve me well. With a splinter of black lead and Ouder's cotton paper, I began noting down bearings I took from my compass, with a guess of how long we followed them. With these, I constructed the crudest of maps, with little lines showing progress.

'Map-makers would laugh at you,' Sterkbooi giggled, slapping me on the back.

I rode my horse close to Marana's, caring lest she have difficulty. But she sat her saddle better than me, having grown up with horses among the Griqua and Basters.

Indeed, she rode with the style only a born horse-woman could, like Lady Robartes, who I once saw riding near her mansion in Lanhydrock. I already knew I was in love, and wondrously magical was the feeling. My feelings for poor Morwenna were never like this. How fickle is the affection of youth! I watched Marana's dainty figure and beautiful face with bursting passion, and she blushed at my attention.

117

'You like the woman,' said Sterkbooi when we sat by the fire one night, 'and she likes you. So, take her into your bed.'

'Never would I take a woman without asking,' I said, causing him to laugh and say I was a coward and should learn the ways of Africa, where they did things differently. He had two women of his own with us, and left another behind, because she was 'too old'. Strange, seeing how he proclaimed his Christianity. We were still discoursing when Marana appeared bearing food.

'You discuss me like a cow to buy and sell!' she said in Dutche. I wished the ground would open and swallow me.

'I didn't mean —'

'What *do* you mean?' I'd never seen her frown before.

'I —'

'You talk *about* me, but not *to* me!' She put the plates of food on a boulder, and placed her small hands on her hips. Out of the corner of my eye, I saw Sterkbooi sneak away. Set me up, I thought, then leave me to face the wrath!

'What should I say?' My voice came out unnaturally high.

'What you *feel!* What I felt? The truth? Here, now?

'I like you,' I said.

'Like, is that it, you *like* me and talk with Sterkbooi about taking me to bed?'

'Not *like* —'

'*What?*' I'd never been caught out like this.

'I *love* you,' I blurted.

'You love me?

'From the day I met you!' She let her arms fall.

'I know *Liefje,*' she whispered.

It was the first time she called me that. *Lief* is the Dutche for love, *Liefje* for loved one or darling.

'You do?'

'I is want to be your woman,' she said in broken English, the first time I heard her speak it. I was struck dumb. I never thought a girl would be so forthright. I was to learn the San don't waste time on frivolity, and Marana had taken after her San mother.

I put a hand on her waist, the other on her shoulder, and pulled her to me. She tilted her head and I saw light specks in her green eyes.

'You—'

Her lips, soft as the satin-cloth we smuggled from Roskoff so long ago, parted as I kissed them. She smelled of rose petals, and tasted of wild honey. Her arms wrapped around my neck and she pressed her body into mine. My breath came in gasps, my heart pounded, and I tingled all over. I thought I loved Morwenna, but it was never like this.

We kissed a long time, until we were breathless and dizzy.

'I is love you,' she whispered, 'from the first day!'

And so came a living angel came into my life, to make it worthwhile, to justify my banishment, to give me meaning and cause, and fill the terrible void and emptiness which had blighted me.

That very night, she moved her mat and blanket beside mine, and Sterkbooi, being our leader, stood us by the campfire and solemnly pronounced us man and wife. This was a rough and ready country.

We trekked into wilder and ever more hostile regions, my crude map gaining ever more lines. Two things kept us going.

The need to put distance between us and the Dutche, who'd take us back to Cape Town and deliver us to the English, and the need for water and food. Where there was water, there was wild game, and we made good use of our muskets, Sterkbooi and I proving to all that *Jaeger* rifles are better than a Brown Bess.

If I thought the territory we travelled was desolate, I could not imagine what lay ahead. Nothing could contrast so starkly with the gently rolling, well watered hills and valleys of my dear Cornwall.

Seventeen

Next day at five a sandstorm blew in from the west. It wasn't as dense as some, but visibility was down to ten yards and howling, driving wind buffeted the Land Rover. These storms stripped paint off cars, and mine showed bare aluminium in many places. The flying sand stung my arm, and I closed the window.

'We'll have to wait it out,' I said.

'How long?' Angelika was vainly trying to see out her window.

'Can be over in half an hour, or blow for hours.'

We sat it out in the Land Rover. It grew dark in ten minutes, though sunset was a long time off. By six, the storm abated and we made camp. Sand had piled against the Land Rover. The wheels were half-buried and we couldn't open the doors on one side. I dug it away with my folding shovel.

'It will make our search more difficult,' I said, straightening my aching back. 'If there *were* any tyre tracks, they're gone now.'

'Would there have been any?' Egon asked.

'The wind blows them away on the sand, but Chiko finds tyre traces where it's stony—'

'We have to leave the tarred road,' Chiko interrupted, 'those we seek do not live on it.' Once again, I was struck by his simple wisdom.

We bumped over ground covered by storm-driven sand. The terrain was rough, stones and rocks lurking inches below. The Namib, the oldest desert on earth, the slyest, most treacherous stretch of ruin, gave us an unworldly vista.

Rare stunted trees threw shadows over a magnificent desolation of reddened sky and endlessly receding earth. It brought a feeling of peace, wild beauty and eternity.

Exhausted by six in the evening on the third day, we struck camp beside a gigantic, lonely baobab tree. Its trunk was thirty feet round, and branches resembling roots or octopus- tentacles beckoned at the sky.

'There's a San legend that the baobab annoyed the creator god *Gao:na*, so he plucked it from the ground and planted it upside down,' Angelika said.

'Maybe true.'

'Bushman Gods,' Egon exclaimed, 'what next?' I ignored him, though my patience was running thin.

'I'll help Chiko with the fire.' Angelika was tired, hot and dirty, yet she refused to succumb. What was so bad to make her unwilling to talk about her past? While Chiko and Angelika attended to the fire, a surly Egon and I pitched the tents. This was only the third day.

I erected my home-made shower. Four aluminium poles tied together, suspending a five-litre water-bottle. You had to stand under and tip. I measured a litre of water into the bottle. If you were careful, you could soap yourself and rinse off. I faced away while Angelika stripped and washed.

For three more days, we zig-zagged across more than two hundred square miles of desert, much of it blanketed in fine sand. The satnav didn't recognise the names of the rare Himba villages. Egon and I argued over the maps. The one showing the *diamanten* and my latest roadmap were difficult to reconcile. Tempers danced like spilt milk on a hotplate.

Our clothes were stained with dust and sweat.

Angelika remained cheerful, Egon spoke little, and brooded, and Chiko's eyes had a faraway look.

It was late afternoon when Chiko tapped me on the shoulder and spoke in Afrikaans. He was pointing at a rise of sandstone and granite a mile west, the direction towards which the still white-hot sun orb was declining.

Just over there, high on the rocky outcrop, he knew of an ancient Bushman painting. I was relieved to see some of his old enthusiasm. I glanced at Angelika then Egon. They were expressionless, hot, grim.

'What you doing?' Angelika shouted above the engine's roar.

'You showed me a diamond, I'm going to show you art!'

After ten minutes weaving between black granite piercing the desert floor like giant dinosaur teeth, we pulled up in a cloud of dust at the base of the outcrop.

Chiko pointed. I looked, but saw only rocks.

'Where, Chiko?'

'There, under that round rock,' he said. Then I saw it. A huge boulder twelve feet wide protruded from the steep wall halfway up. The sun cast shadows. Shielding my eyes, I stared and saw a darker one. A cave.

'Coming?' I asked Angelika and Egon.

'Climb up there to see an old Bushman painting?' he asked.

'Don't bother!'

'I'll come,' Angelika broke in, smiling and nodding.

'I'm not coming,' he said. It was on the tip of my tongue to say I'd die of disappointment.

'Suit yourself.'

Chiko was already climbing, following a slanting gouge in the rockface.

We climbed in single file, the sun burning our faces, sweat pouring into our eyes. Angelika was fit, and her shorts revealed shapely thighs and calves. She'd tied her shirt up at the waist, showing a flat belly and the curve of her breasts. She went ahead, and I was hard put to keep up. Chiko disappeared.

Two minutes later, we stood on a narrow ledge before a gaping cave mouth. It looked smaller from below, but was fully ten feet wide and five high.

We ducked to enter. At first, we couldn't see. After a minute, we made out we were in a wide space. In spite of the low entrance, the ceiling was twenty feet above our heads. Chiko stood by the wall on the left. It was smooth sandstone. On it was something which made me catch my breath.

It was three feet long by two high. There was a big animal in the middle. In ochre-red and white pigment, it was unmistakably a kudu bull. It was galloping with that remarkable illusion of movement in San art. It was framed between a low grey sky and deep brown earth. The figures pursuing it were indefinite and ghostly. Men, a hunt in the after-world, or spirits presiding over an earthly hunt?

'The great kudu charges!' Chiko exclaimed in San.

'*A:kn,*' Angelika exclaimed, '*kaika!*'

'What?'

'Beautiful!' She patted Chiko on his shoulder and he beamed, his solitary tooth white against the darkness.

'Lovely, great skill,' she added in Afrikaans for Chiko's sake.

'The kudu has mystical meaning, it fills bellies, and transports men to the world of the ancestors.' Chiko nodded.

'The twisted horns show dexterity and wisdom in the air, and the strength they lend to the worthy.'

Did Ignatius see these beautiful things, I wondered, did he even know about them?

I took photographs with my pocket camera, then we returned to the entrance and descended to an impatiently waiting Egon.

'Enjoy yourselves?' Not interested if not on his agenda.

'It was wonderful,' Angelika said, 'you don't know what you missed!'

One day Chiko found a waterhole. It was a ditch at the bottom of a gulley. A fault let water seep up from underground.

'Thank heavens,' I said, 'we've used half our water.'

'I hope we can drink it,' Angelika said. Chiko made a comment in clicky San as she wrinkled her nose.

'What's that?' I asked. If it killed me, I'd learn more of his beautiful language.

'White people too fussy!'

Chiko scooped up a mugful and drank. We filled our canisters and continued our search under a raging sky.

'I heard about a man,' I said, 'with de Beers at Oranjemund, sieving the beach for diamonds. You can't sneak them out by swallowing them, because they X-Ray you when you leave. He came up with a plan. He smuggled in Helium in Carbon Dioxide cylinders for soda-water. Everyone in Oranjemund picks up diamonds. They handle them every day. But when they leave they throw them away, 'cos there's no way to get them out.'

'Bet they hide them in their cars,' Egon said. It took talk of diamonds to rouse him.

'No. When you arrive they take away your car and give you a company one. When you leave, they swap them back. The company car never leaves the zone.'

'Helium,' Angelika said, 'he had Helium?'

'His friend was waiting in the desert east of the barrier, armed with a radio receiver. Our chap filled six balloons with gas, fitted packets of stones and transponders to them, and let them fly one night when the wind blew east.

'I see.' Angelika's nose was burnt pink.

'The wind changed and blew them back. By then they were too high, and popped.'

'Couldn't control altitude,' Egon said.

'No. They were back over his house when they began to fall. They landed on his and two neighbour's roofs, in the gardens, in the driveways. Torn bits of balloon-rubber with bags of diamonds and radio-transponders, in brightly-coloured heaps. He was waiting for news on his radio, and was shocked when the police came.'

'Oh, poor man,' Angelika sighed.

'Yes, more than circumstantial evidence. He got five years, but died of a heart attack in jail.'

'Is there a moral?' Angelika was staring at me.

'Sure, diamonds are dangerous, and what goes up comes down.'

'But he was unlucky,' Egon said.

'Others were unlucky too.'

'Oh yes?' He was curious, too curious.

'Tell us,' Angelika said.

'One bloke thought he had a good plan. He figured they have safety rules when they do X-Rays. Radiation damages gonads. That's why dentists and hospitals put lead-lined aprons over your groin.'

126

'Aha,' said Egon.

'He thought hey, what a good idea to cut a hole in the back of my scrotum, put diamonds in, then sew it up.' Angelika winced.

By his expression, Egon wanted to know. So interested, I thought, about sewing diamonds in scrotums!

'Went septic.'

'So that's it,' Egon said.

'He needed an antibiotic. But he could hardly waltz into the company doc and say "hey, my testicles are rotting...", could he? The doc would see what he'd done, and wham, he'd be behind bars before he could say 'cut off me bollocks'. So, he pretended he had gonorrhoea. A burning discharge. But the doc insisted on an examination and a specimen.'

'Oops,' said Angelika.

'He bolted. It was either that or kill the doc, steal the antibiotics and evade the nurse....'

'Poor guy,' Angelika sighed.

'Yes, lots like that, half-baked plans. He not only went to chookie, but lost his lunchbox!' Egon crossed his legs.

'They had to amputate his testicles. And here's the moral: too much ambition could cost you.'

'Ambition....,' Angelika said, shaking her head.

'I want to find uncle Rodolf, that's the only point of all this. If I can find out more about the ancient San, that's a plus, but I am not after diamonds!' I stared at her, then back at Egon. He looked away.

We saw it when we were ready to stop. The sun was closing with the western horizon. It was like that.

All day high noon, heat pouring down, bodies sweating, skin itching.

Suddenly, as if at the call of a siren, the sun went down and cool breezes blew.

Long shadows lanced out from rocky outcrops to make zebra-stripes across the valley.

The Rover growled and squeaked as it clawed along the uneven surface of shale and sand.

'What's that?' Angelika asked, shattering the somnolence. She pointed through the dust-steaked window.

'Kai.' Chiko leaned forward and tugged at my collar. 'Can you see it?' I looked where he pointed. It was just visible in the dwindling light. The sandstorm had been here. There was a half-buried tent on the edge of a sand dune, uphill half a mile to the left.

Eighteen

From 'Untold Mysteries of The San' by Sven Johannsen, 1790: *When first you gaze upon the devastation of the great western desert, you see it as very hell come down to earth. To your eye, nothing lives, nothing moves, save the shimmer of the scorched air over the endless expanse of pale sand and sun-blackened rock. Yet even here, in this least hospitable place, the San, like the desert falcons, are able to make their traverses in their endless struggle to survive.'

The land south of the Gariep, which marks the northern border of the Cape, is hot and dry, and vegetation is sparse. But it does not compare to the other side. No wonder so few have crossed into this sun-blasted country, for 'tis terrible to behold. The huge waste stretches mile upon endless mile to the horizon on all sides, without water, plants, shade or shelter.

What is it you draw every day, *liefje?*' Marana asked, peering at my map. Looking at it, I doubted it would show me the way back.

'A record of our direction,' I said, taking her hand, 'to know where we are.'

'You don't need such a thing,' she laughed, her eyes sparkling with humour, 'you read it in the sky, the hills, you smell it in the wind, you see it in the stars.'

'Maybe *you* do, my love.' I kissed her sweet lips.

More than three months after crossing the river, and weaving our way over deep sand, around barren mountains and along ragged gorges, we arrived exhausted in the place the Namas call !Anis. This was where Ouder recommended we should seek sanctuary.

My first sight of !Anis plunged me into deep melancholy, for there was little to commend it. The name means smoke, for steam rises from hot springs there. It was well named, I decided, for such a devil of a place. My only comfort was dear Marana, whose love and understanding alone sustained me in the first days in that bleak place.

The Namas at !Anis are a Khoikhoi people, like their cousins in the Cape, and also the San. Perhaps it was because some of their people married Basters that our party was kindly received.

One good thing is the river the Namas call Oanab. After only a few days, I appreciated the wisdom of Ouder's advice. Barren though the place looked at first, close to the water the soil nurtured lush plants, and the isolation promised freedom from persecution. It was no Eden, but we were cured of our appetite for further travel.

'We'll stay here,' Sterkbooi announced, and none of us was sorry. Sterkbooi negotiated with the Namas that we may bide beside the river, and we set to building a settlement.

Our huts were of rock and sand, the roofs of leaves and grass. Marana chose a piece of riverbank, where we built our home, round and ten feet across. It was all we needed, and our doorway looked on the river.

Small she may have been, but she surpassed me in energy, collecting and piling rocks for the walls, fitting them together, gathering dead branches to frame the roof, cutting grass and leaves to thatch it. In less than a week, our home was built.

Now Marana went with the Nama women to gather reeds from the riverbanks. After drying them, she wove sleeping mats, baskets and other useful things.

Her skill and nimbleness filled me with pride. How fortunate I was, in this alien land, to have the love of this girl-woman!

From the Namas, we bought scrawny chickens, and they gave us plants called *manioc* to put in the ground, which produced leaves with the taste of spinach. They had thin trunks and huge tuber roots in the earth, which were dried and ground into flour. The bread it made was tasteless but filling. The most amazing thing was the cut-off plant, stuck back into the ground, quickly grew more nutritious leaves and another tuber. It was the staple of many tribes, Sterkbooi told me.

In return for these treasures, we hunted wild game and gave the Namas meat. They were much taken by our muskets.

It transpired my friend Sterkbooi was a crafty man of business. 'The Namas love nothing so much as guns,' he said, 'and that was before we came among them. When they see how easily we kill at a distance, they go wild for them.'

I'd been intrigued by a long canvas bundle on one of Sterkbooi's horses. Now he opened it. Wrapped in oiled brown paper within were eight brand-new *Brown Bess* muskets. Furious haggling took place, and the Namas parted with more plants, hides, earthenware pots, chickens and eggs than I could count. There was frenzied debate between them and Sterkbooi, of which I understood little.

Sterkbooi's genius had no limit. The Namas didn't know how to load or use muskets, nor how to obtain ammunition.

'I've said I'll train them,' he announced, 'supply them with powder and lead, repair the muskets when they break them.' He grinned wickedly.

'These people think you have to tug the trigger with all your might to give the bullet power. They miss the target by a mile and will soon wreck the locks!'

'Good for business,' I laughed.

As armourer, Sterkbooi said, he would travel to Walvis Bay, even back to the Cape, for supplies. From whom, he couldn't tell, he said, tapping the side of his nose with a finger and winking.

I hunted with Sterkbooi and two others and, though the area was dry and vegetation scarce, we found it well stocked with game. By now I was a crack-shot with my *Jaeger,* and I gained the respect of Baster and Nama alike. I pitied those with *Brown Besses,* for they didn't have as much success.

Malkop was a great helper in the hunt. He had a clever way of sneaking up on animals from downwind where they couldn't smell him, and driving them my way. It was instinct, but also cunning. I rewarded him with pieces of meat, and he beamed his toothy jackal smile. The Namas said he was a person in a past life, and Marana and I loved him dearly.

They were good days and happy times. One day Marana wore a strange smile.

'*Liefje,* I am with child,' she said.

'You —'

'We're going to have a baby!' She took my hands and my heart leapt.

'A baby?'

'Yes!'

'What wonderful news,' I laughed, 'I am so happy, my darling!' Our kiss was warm and long.

We were going to be a family. I couldn't wait to tell Sterkbooi, who jumped about with excitement, and proposed a feast.

Basters and Namas joined in jolly mood, and food and African beer came forward in great supply.

That night, overcome by coming fatherhood, and the effects of too much beer, I took a sliver of black lead and a piece of Ouder's paper, and, sitting on a log at a rough table, wrote to my family in Cornwall. Our time in the Khamiesberg, on our long trek north, and since we'd been at !Anis added up to almost three years. It was high time I told my family I was alive. It was already May of 1790.

I began in the Cornish language.

Care dâma, s/ʒira brodar ve, (Dearest mother, father, brothers) I began, before adding 'cousins', all Cornish being 'cousins'. *Dew boʒ geno* (God be with you). I continued in English, for that was the medium of my schooling.

I assured them I was yet living, and apologised for the pain I'd caused. I did not mention any of them being smugglers, lest my letter falls into wrong hands, and my words incriminate them. I told them of my suffering on *HMS Scarborough*, hoping John Penrose's wife had delivered my dictated letter, wherein I told of my pitiful conditions in gaol.

I told them of my escape in the Cape of Good Hope, my flight with a friend to the Khamiesberg, and how we were forced to flee across the great river Gariep into the northern desert lands, where I now bided.

If, perchance, my letter should fall into the hands of my persecutors, they were welcome to search for me in this vast, trackless land. I made sure not to mention the name of !Anis.

I wrote that I hoped to get my letter to the coast, and prayed it would be taken to Cornwall by a Christian sailor.

I promised to write again, and wished them health and prosperity.

Why did I not send a special message to Morwenna, mention Marana, or say I was to be a father? Somehow, though I was lost to her, I could not, even now, break Morwenna's heart. What good would it do? Better she thought I forgot her, or anything except I found love with another. Was I right? I have often wondered. Life presents the strangest, saddest, riddles.

'What is it you write, *liefje*?' Marana asked, standing behind me with her hands on my shoulders.

'To tell my family in Cornwall I am alive, and very, very happy,' I said, not untruthfully.

'That is good, my love,' she said. She didn't ask if I mentioned her, for which I was exceedingly grateful, stab me!

'You miss them?'

'Very much,' I said, 'but I am blessed to be with you!' She bent and kissed me.

For the first time in so long, I had committed words to paper. I never knew I would miss the habit so much. From now on, I would exert a little energy most days to making notes about my life. Writing was my link to the past. Would anyone ever read it, I wondered. Or would this letter, and the one I dictated to John Penrose in Launceston gaol, be my only epitaph? Would anyone remember me?

'I'm going to Walvis Bay for powder and lead,' Sterkbooi said one day. 'There is a harbour there. I'll give your letter to the captain of any ship going to England, and pay him to post it there.'

I didn't know it would not be long before my old fears returned with a vengeance.

Nineteen

It was a light-tan colour, almost invisible against the backdrop of a stage grown grand in the red glow of the dying sun. I veered towards it, changed down as the incline steepened, and engaged four-wheel drive. The Rover whined, and in the rearview mirror I saw Chiko flinch. I was dangerously goading the engine-spirit.

'Is this the place on the map?' Angelika shouted.

'Satnav's got no signal, but it's close,' I yelled above the engine noise. There were rocks and boulders everywhere. It was like driving without tyres. My arms ached as I held the juddering wheel. We neared the tent and saw it was half buried in sand. On the other side, also covered in sand, was a brown Jeep *Wagoneer*. The colours of tent and vehicle couldn't have been better chosen for camouflage.

I killed the engine and it clicked metallically. I glanced at Chiko, who grimaced. How could I officially explain my business partner's beliefs?

'Rodolf?' Egon nodded. Angelika averted her eyes, her face drained of blood. Nobody breathed. We approached the tent together, and I pulled the flap open. There was no one inside. A bedroll and sleeping bag lay on either side, and there were scattered objects, including empty water bottles, pots, a pair of binoculars, bits of clothing and a couple of books half-buried in sand. There were no footprints. The tent had been abandoned some time. The sandstorm was five days ago. The lack of prints meant no-one had been here since.

'Empty,' I sighed. Angelika was silent, her face white. Egon showed no emotion. We left the tent and examined the Jeep.

Apart from sand burying its wheels and reaching the doors, we couldn't see anything wrong. Egon opened the front passenger door and looked in the glovebox. He pulled out what looked like a logbook or manual, and a smaller book, which he examined in the light of his torch. At last, he straightened.

'It's Rodolf's diary, it's in German and the writing's difficult to read.' He held it up. A dark blue pocket diary.

'Let's look at it when we've made camp,' I said, 'it's already dark, and getting darker.'

'But where are they?' Angelika asked, sitting down heavily on a rock. She covered her face with her hands.

'Don't panic,' I said, 'or jump to conclusions.'

'What do you think?' Egon asked. It was the most animated I'd seen him.

'We should look for something, clues, anything. They must have gone before the sandstorm, or they'd have left footprints.' I glanced round. The marching shadows from the western hills had reached us. 'Let's pitch our tents while we can.' After a long pause, Angelika got to her feet.

'Where's Egon?' she said. I hadn't seen him leave.

'Having another look in the tent, I guess. Let's pitch camp away from here.'

We found a flat spot thirty yards off. In half an hour the tents were up, and it was dark. We kindled a fire, but nobody wanted to eat. Egon came back and sat studying the diary in torchlight. I couldn't see if he had a tic.

'What does it say?' Angelika asked.

'Their engine broke down,' he said. 'Six days ago, Rodolf wrote that the engine seized.'

'If it was the water pump, the temperature gauge wouldn't pick it up,' I thought aloud.

'What's that?' she asked.

'Pumps water round the engine to cool it, but also to the temperature gauge. If it fails, the engine overheats but you don't see it.'

'Isn't that stupid?' Egon said. 'What's the point?'

'Ask the Jeep.'

'Okay, so they were stuck,' Angelika sighed, 'but where are they now?'

'There's nothing more.'

'Was anything written *after* that?'

'Nothing.'

'Anything about the diamond map?'

'Rodolf knew something was wrong because they didn't find any.'

'Because there are no diamonds outside the *Sperrgebiet*.'

'Well, Rodolf was sure there were, though not exactly here.'

'What?' said Angelika.

'It was a lie.'

'Who lied?'

'The one who found the first diamond, who gave it to Schneider, who sold it to Dad.'

'Who?' Angelika asked, 'don't draw it out.' They knew things I didn't.

'Whoever gave Dad that map, marked the wrong place.'

'Who?

'It must be the smudge on the back of the original map, where Dad wrote *Ersprungen von* - whoever - *heute, 14de März 1958*,' Egon said. 'It could be any letter of the alphabet.'

'You thought Schneider got the map from Ernst Mencken,' Angelika said, 'then you seem to have forgotten.'

She clapped her hands to focus his attention. 'Was the smudge done on purpose? Was it M for Mencken or E for Ernst?'

'Maybe,' said Egon. His eyelid twitched furiously.

'Du hast doch gedacht, und mir nicht gesagt?' She'd forgotten I understood German.

'You thought so, and didn't tell me?' she asked again, 'you knew?'

'It was only a hunch. Who did we know that dealt in uncut stones, how many friends did Schneider have?'

'Why didn't you say so at Tobias' house? Why are you so cagey, Egon?'

'Angelika,' he spat, 'you haven't been the same since Phil!' It had a dramatic effect on her. She blanched and turned away.

'I still don't know if the map came from Mencken,' he said, 'but now, seeing the diary, I think it was misleading, which would explain the same thing happening to Rodolf and Dad.'

'How do you know it was wrongly marked?'

'It's obvious…, see any diamonds?'

'You're hiding something!'

'This is going nowhere,' I said. Out of the corner of my eye, I saw Chiko. He retreated, shaking his head, behind the Land Rover.

'We'll talk about it later,' Egon agreed, 'just accept the map is wrong.' There was a hard set to his mouth, and his eyelid ticked. Angelika's fists were tightly bunched.

Though I hadn't taken to him, my opinion of Egon soured further.

If I had to type him, I'd say he was a clever, overweight banker with a heart of flint. What else had he found?

'I wonder if it *was* Mencken,' Angelika said.

She was calmer now. I couldn't stop speculating about Egon's comment. Phil…. boyfriend, lover?

'If it was,' Egon said, 'he didn't want to give the location. There must've been something he didn't want found.

'Diamonds?' I asked.

'No, something which would put him deep in it.'

'Like?'

'Dead bodies.'

'Hell,' I exclaimed, 'more corpses!'

'Who knows?' Egon said. 'In 1990 Schneider blackmailed someone into drawing a map. He must have had something on him, but whoever it was bought time by marking the wrong place. It may have been Mencken, but I really don't know.'

'Surely he knew he'd be found out?'

'Maybe he hoped Schneider would die out here, digging for nothing. That would keep his secret safe.'

'If so, it worked,' I said, 'get rid of the blackmailer.' Egon gave me a curious look.

'And Dad,' Angelika sighed, 'our father too!'

'All for nothing,' Egon added, shaking his head.

'Did Mencken know, in 1990, your father would go with Schneider?'

'Don't think so, he was an associate, not a friend, and Dad didn't like him. He only knew him through the *Deutsche Gesellschaft*, the German club in Braamfontein.'

'Look, after Dad went missing,' Angelika said, 'Mencken vanished.' She stared out the window.

'The last we knew, he went to Cape Town,' Egon said. Controlling her anger, she cut her eyes at Egon.

'Nursing his conscience, maybe?'

'If he had one,' I said. Egon grimaced and shrugged his shoulders.

'If it *was* him,' he continued, 'then he knew where the diamonds were. But here were Rodolf and his friend Keller on the marked spot, supposed to be a sandy valley, where there's no valley in twenty miles.'

'Rodolf write that?'

'Yes. He was still convinced diamonds were around. The map was drawn before satnavs, and you can't rely on them anyway. They drew up a grid, did a search. Rodolf wrote that Keller wanted to confront Mencken, torture him even.'

'Then the Jeep's engine seized…'

'Exactly.'

'I see,' I said, 'and Mencken's in hiding. Why didn't you tell me this before? You wanted me to help, but kept me in the dark.'

'I didn't know.' Angelika glared at Egon.

'Perhaps you didn't…. I'm just here to see you don't get lost,' I said.

Why had the two men abandoned their tent, where did they go? I looked around at the blackness of the desert and shivered. It was getting cold.

'Anything about why they left their tent?'

'No, nothing more.'

'Let's sleep on it. In the morning, we'll examine the jeep and decide what to do.'

'I'm going for a walk,' Egon said.

'See you later.' We watched him go in silence.

'They fight like two *ratels*,' Chiko whispered as I passed him on the way to the tent.

The fierce and vicious honey badger. I laughed. I had an image of those two rearing up against one another, red in tooth and claw.

I lay awake a long time.

I heard Egon come in and lie down, and his breathing soon told he was asleep.

After an interval, there was a rustle at the tent flap, and a soft voice spoke in the darkness.

'Tobias.'

'Yes?' I whispered, not to wake Egon.

'Come with me.' The flap rustled again. I struggled out of my sleeping bag. Pale moonlight made a patchwork of grey and black on the rocky ground.

Holding a finger to her lips, she took my hand and tugged. Her hand was cool, soft, and slender. The desert was deadly quiet.

I made out the shape of Chiko sleeping beside a big rock. Angelika tugged, and we entered her tent.

'It's Egon,' she whispered.

'What..?

'Up to no-good.'

'What do you mean?' She was still holding my hand.

'Look, you know what the row was about?'

'Vaguely.'

'He's been cagey from the outset. Things I sensed…'

'He didn't tell you about Mencken, but I can't see…'

'He should have. A small omission, but I know him, and he's hiding something. Don't ask, I just know it!'

'And..?' I didn't know where this was going.

'Remember he went for a walk?'

'Yes…'

'I followed him. He went towards Rodolf's tent, then stopped halfway. He was fumbling with something. He turned…I think he saw me.'

'He *saw* you?'

'Not sure. I couldn't make him out properly, but he dropped what he was holding, like he was caught out.'

'What you mean?'

'He stamped on it, kicked it into the sand.'

'The thing he dropped?' She nodded.

'He got rid of it!'

'I have to find it. Will you help?'

'How, when —'

'Now, while he's asleep.' What had I got us in to? First, it was them and us, now I, if not Chiko, was in the middle. She released my hand, bent and retrieved a torch from her camp-bed.

'You mean search for what he dropped?'

'Exactly. You coming?' She took my hand again and tugged. I allowed myself to be led outside.

'Who's Phil?' I whispered, unable to stop myself. She stopped in mid-stride.

'Nothing to do with you!'

'Don't be upset,' I whispered, 'can't help hearing you arguing —'

'Sorry, I know it's difficult. I'll tell you about Phil, but not now.'

We crossed the space between the tents and tiptoed in the direction of Rodolf's campsite. We'd gone halfway, when Angelika let my hand go and switched on her torch.

'It was around here.' She shone the beam on the ground. There were footprints in the sand. We'd all walked both ways here. How did she think we'd find anything? It couldn't have been very big, for Egon to bury it with his foot.

'Somewhere here.' She got down on her knees, and began probing the sand.

I knelt down and, using my hands like shovels, began to prod under the surface.

Would I have agreed to this trip if I'd thought I'd end up on my knees, digging desert sand with bare hands in the middle of the night?

There was nothing. I crawled a yard forward and carried on. Nothing there either.

I swept from side to side under the sand. Like bloody windscreen wipers! Angelika was three yards away, moving slowly. Something tickled the back of my hand. A scrunched-up piece of paper or cardboard.

'Got something!' She straightened and directed the torch at my hands.

'Paper,' she said. I unravelled it carefully. It was half the size of a postcard.

'Let me see!' There was writing. She craned her neck.

'What's it say?' I asked.

'Oh, difficult to read, looks like an address. No name, just an address.'

'Where?' She squinted and bent closer.

'Bishop's Court, Cape Town.'

'Whose address?'

'Not so much whose address, as *why* he buried it!'

'What do you think he's up to?'

'I thought there was something from the outset, that Egon wasn't telling me everything. Last night he couldn't look at me. I *knew* he was hiding something.'

'You watched him, followed him…'

'Yes.'

'I sensed it too.'

'You did?'

'He's your brother, business partner. You're part owner ......'

'That's why it's so hard, not the business, but my brother!'

I touched her shoulder, and she put her head against me. She wore only a cotton nightdress, and her body was soft and warm against me. We stood for half a minute, then I drew away.

'I *bet* it's Mencken's address!' she said, turning to face me. Her torch, still in her hand, lit it up.

'Mencken'address? Why? Cape Town?'

'Yes, that's where he went.'

'Why would Egon….?'

'He's lying about Mencken, mentioning him, then forgetting.'

'Yes —'

'He knows more, doesn't want me to know…'

'Seems so. But if that's Mencken's address, how does it help?'

'Look, the fact he disappeared means he's changed his name.'

'Logical if he didn't want to be found.'

'That's it, nobody can find him.'

'Unless you have his address….'

'Egon doesn't want him found. I think that's why he came in the first place!'

'You mean not because of Rodolf?'

'Perhaps he thought Rodolf had something which could lead us to Mencken, and he didn't want that.'

'Why?'

'That's the question. 'The address must've been with the diary, but he didn't show us.

'Then got rid of it. Why?'

'I'm going to find out if it kills me,' she said.

It was difficult explaining to Chiko what had happened, but when I was done he demonstrated, yet again, his ability to grasp the essentials and put it into a few words.

'He is like the jackal,' he said, 'he knows more and keeps secrets. He is a bad man, *Kai!*'

Twenty

'You have one with a tail in front,' laughed the fat Nama midwife, passing me the squawking bundle.

I was paralysed with fear when Marana told me the baby was coming. From the size of her belly, I feared it wouldn't be born without killing her. Instead of me reassuring her, *she* had to comfort *me*.

'It is normal, my love,' she gasped through gritted teeth, 'it is how women have always given birth!' Just then Sterkbooi poked his head in the doorway.

'It has begun,' he said. He left, and returned two minutes later with the midwife.

'This is women's business,' he said, taking me by the arm and guiding me out. 'You and I will do men's work!'

'What you mean?'

'We will drink beer in the sun, and fortify ourselves!'

Thus it was when, three hours later, we were called by the midwife's young assistant, I was in the haze of alcohol intoxication. Marana was sitting up in the bed, and no longer in pain. She smiled and raised her lips for me to kiss.

'My darling, you've done it!' I whispered.

I have never known love to spring up so immediate, deep and abiding, scrub me with barnacles, as when I stared at the wrinkled little face of my newborn son. I'd never imagined my child would be quarter Dutche and quarter San Bushman, and I wondered what the future would hold for him.

We called him Pengilly Gert Tregurtha, after Peder Pengilly, the Cornish guard who helped us escape and paid with his life, and Marana's Dutche father.

Through the perpetuation of his name, poor Peder's martyrdom would never be forgotten.

It was fitting, because but for him I'd never have met Marana, or had a son. It was a name our son could be proud to bear.

Marana recovered soon, and, though we were poor, we could not have been happier. She told me her mother, Hama, was of the San Bushmen from this side the Gariep River, the great northwestern country known as the *Transgariep*.

'Hama was six or seven years old when a drought drove her family to cross the river into the Cape for food,' Marana said. 'It was nearly fifty seasons ago!'

'Some days to the south they came upon grazing sheep. Using their hunting skills, they killed two, for they had not eaten in many days.'

'While they were sleeping off their feast, the horsemen came,' she said.

'They had never seen horses, and thought they were devils sent by the death god //*Gauwa*. Riding upon their backs were demons with white skins, beards and magic sticks which roared and inflicted terrible wounds from a distance. Many died, and others hid among the rocks and gulleys. Some were taken as slaves. One was a young girl, my mother, Hama.' What evil white men performed in this land!

Hama's captors were Dutche, most brutal to their slaves, and she was taken to be a servant in a Dutche family house. They had a son called Gert, two years older than her. He was different to the others and was kind to Hama.

'By the time they grew up,' Marana said, 'Hama and Gert were very close, and his parents tried to separate them by sending her to a distant farm.

147

On hearing what they had done, Gert took his horse and rode to her.' She smiled her beautiful smile.

'They ran away together and found acceptance among the Griquas near a place called Kakamas. Gert was a good husband, and my father.' So that was how she came to have a European father!

'Then came the second massacre,'she continued, 'fifteen seasons ago my father was killed and my mother carried off by the Dutche, for the second time in her life. It is only because Ouder rescued me that I am alive today!'

'You never saw your mother again?'

'No.' She wiped a tear from her eye. 'I don't even know where they took her!'

Marana owed her life to Ouder for pulling her out from under her dead father and giving her a home and sanctuary. Like her mother before, she came to be a servant in a house. Only this was a Baster one.

'They treated me with kindness.'

Ever since I knew Marana, she spoke of where her mother's tribe came from, and how the survivors of the first massacre eventually recrossed the Gariep River to rejoin their people. She even taught me some of the language, which she spoke almost as well as Dutche, for she'd made an opportunity to practice with any San crossing the Khamiesberg. All this I knew, and that her mother's people came from the far north of this *Transgariep*.

We lived five years at !Anis, and good they were. Pengilly grew into a sturdy boy of four. He was strong and clever and looked like his mother, with a hint of me.

I sang old Cornish smuggler's songs to him, in the broad accent of my native Penwith, entrancing both he and Marana.

Hush m' littl' uglin', daddy's gone a-smugglin'.
'e 'as gone t Roscoff o' th' Mevagissey Maid,
a sloop o' nin'ty tons, wi' ten brass carrigge guns,
t' teach th' king some manners an' 'spect fer 'onest trade.

Sleep m' joy an' sorrow, daddy'll come amorrow,
bringin' 'baccy, tea an' snuff, an' brandy 'ome fro' France.
'e'll bring th' goodes ashore while th' old collectrs snore,
an' th' black dragooners gambl' in th' dens of ol' Penzance.

Rock-a-bye m' honey, fer Daddy's makin' money,
you shal be a genl'manf an' sail wi' privateers,
wi' silver cup in yourn sack, blue coat 'pon yore back,
an' diamonds 'pon yore fingrbones, an' gold rings in yourn ears.

Sterkbooi brought back more than guns and munitions from Walvis Bay and the North Cape. He carried news of world events, from which we were so far removed. I have never known a man with such memory for detail.

'You can be glad you're not living in France,' he said one day in 1793, 'terrible things are happening there.'

'How do you know?'

'I'm a clever Bastard,' he laughed. Not a buggered one, I sniggered, but I let him think I was amused by his joke.

I listened spellbound to what he had to tell. The expected revolution had finally come in France. The end-result of the troubles which plagued that country for so many years.

The King, queen and thousands of nobles had been beheaded on the guillotine, in the great reign of terror called *la Terreur*.

'I am definitely glad I don't live in France,' I said.

On the other hand, I was not a noble, I thought, and beheading revenue men and judges in Cornwall was not such a disagreeable idea.

I pictured the judge with the dead fox on his head waiting for the fall of the guillotine blade upon his scrawny neck.

Would the revolution cross the channel to Cornwall? I wondered if the turmoil had affected my Breton friend Alban Kermarrec. Was his father's *Chasse-Marée* still plying the waters of the English Channel?

'See, not so bad at !Anis,' Sterkbooi laughed.

In 1795, Sterkbooi again returned from the south to inform us that Britain had occupied the Cape of Good Hope, to prevent the French, who'd conquered Holland, and therefore owned its colonies, from using it as a staging post to invade India. There had been a battle at a place in the Cape called Muizenberg, where the English defeated the Dutche. Though the Dutche were not our friends, English ascendancy was cold comfort.

One day Marana came to me in a panic. 'A white man living with the Namas an hour's ride from here has been taken for bounty by the /*hũ*.' This meant bad white men. I was also a Hu, but a 'good' one like her father Gert. 'They will take you too,' she cried, 'we must leave this place and go north, where my mother's tribe wanders. We can live with them, where there are no Hu to pursue you!'

I could not argue with what she said. I needed no more lessons on the cruelty of the Hu!

Marana's grandparents had been killed before she was born, then her father murdered and her mother enslaved, all by white men.

I understood her fears, but was reluctant to give up the life we'd built with such sweat and sacrifice. It took hours to calm her. If we had to go, we'd go, I said.

Three months later I was hunting with Malkop two miles from home, on land where the trees gave out to grass.

I shot a small springbok, as they call them, and was butchering it. First, I noticed Malkop had disappeared, then three white men with long beards rode up and pointed their muskets at me.

'Who's you, where you from?' the nearest one gruffly demanded in Dutche-accented English. I kept my head and spoke back in Dutche. When they heard me, they lost interest and, taking me for a degenerate of their own, asked me in their language if I knew of any fugitives from justice. I shook my head. At that, they turned their horses and rode away cursing.

A minute later Malkop emerged. What a cunning creature. No doubt the riders would have shot him outright, for he so resembled a jackal, vermin to the likes of them. My curious four-footed friend was such an expert judging strangers!

Marana was making a most lifelike drawing of Malkop when we returned. When I told her what happened, she wrung her hands and lamented.

'They will take you in chains to the Cape, where you will be hanged,' she cried. That very night we made plans to flee north, out of reach of the cursed Hu. I never knew I could hate my own race so fiercely.

'It's a bad business,' Sterkbooi said, 'and a risk.'

He has also heard of those white hunters scouring the land for people like me. It was best if I did not stay!

After my near escape, I agreed.

Himself a Bastard, Sterkbooi said, he blended in and could take the risk, even though he'd also escaped the prison ship.

He stocked us with supplies, food, black powder, spare flints and lead. For me, he had a special gift, his twelve-inch hunting knife with a bone handle and fine steel blade.

He'd get another, he told me. I was even more delighted to receive a three-inch wad of his father's rag paper. Of the black lead, I had plenty.

'I hardly use it,' he said of the paper.

'I will employ it well,' I promised.

'It's strange,' Sterkbooi said, 'when I was young, Ouder told stories about men who disappeared in the great desert over the Gariep.'

'Well, I need to disappear.'

'The desert,' Sterkbooi said solemnly, 'will swallow you whole!'

Sterkbooi and two Basters from the Khamiesberg came with us as far as the place the Namas call AiGams, meaning *Hot Springs*. And so it was we travelled from 'Smoke' to 'Hot Springs'! We went on horses, but Sterkbooi told us we had to proceed from there on foot because the horses were worn out, and where we were headed was no good for them.

'There are horse-diseases there,' he said, 'which also kill donkeys. Sleeping sickness, African horse sickness and tick fever. Horses don't live long.'

We never saw the springs at AiGams, for there was urgency upon us to get as far as we could from the Hu.

From when we left !Anis, every time we changed direction I noted our bearing on my compass. Each night I transposed the details onto my crude map.

Were my drawings a waste of time? I thought they may be, yet it comforted to me, if only as a link to a happier life.

I was overcome at parting with Sterkbooi and his friends, for we'd been together more than six years.

There were tears on both sides as we watched them ride away.

In the heat, their images bent and twisted until they rode down the other side of the hill and out of sight. Before he went, Sterkbooi said he was sure we'd meet again, and he looked forward to that day. We'd endured much together, and a better friend I never had.

This was the first time since I escaped *Scarborough* I was so afraid. It was a nightmare to even think I may be taken back to those who treated me worse than a hound, and leave Marana and Pengilly to cope alone.

How would we survive in such a harsh country? Heavy of heart and filled with foreboding, Marana, Pengilly, Malkop and I began our laborious trudge north.

Still close to AiGams, we met a group of twelve Namas who had visited the !Anis area on their journey. They readily agreed for us to travel with them. This group of 'Hottentots', as the Basters called them, had been driven off their land in the Cape, and were heading north to find a new place to live.

We travelled ten miles a day, which doesn't seem much.

But in that country, with no roads and hard going all the way, it was difficult to keep up with the Namas. When Pengilly couldn't walk, I carried him.

The Namas could tell our direction by the sun, which I also learnt to do. I could lose my compass one day. They'd heard of a place called Okahandja where two rivers joined.

They wanted to settle on one of the riverbanks, they said, for they tired of filling goatskins with stinking water from muddy pools.

Crossing great flat plains of hot sand and rock, ringed by shimmering distant hills on all sides, we trudged towards the east in the glare of a vicious sun.

In the short time since we left !Anis, Pengilly had turned into a muscular, tanned little boy. Tireless as ever, he went ahead with Malkop to explore a hillock with gnarled trees on top, a rare sight in those parts. It was not unusual for them to do such things, and it caused us no concern. They'd disappeared from sight, and we assumed they were climbing the hill.

Suddenly there came the distant, but distinct sound of Malkop yelping and barking, and then, bringing us to a terrified halt, the bellowing roar of a lion. Everything seemed to stop, except the wild pounding of my heart. An earth-shaking roar boomed from a copse of half-dead acacias, and at that moment I believed Pengilly was lost. I turned just in time to catch Marana as she fell down in a swoon.

Twenty-one

I woke with a start. It came from the abandoned tent. Loud clattering and banging. Something big was moving around inside.

I grabbed the shotgun and took off barefoot at a run. The tent loomed in the moonlight and a low, dark shape dashed out. It was gone before I could level the gun. My heart pounded. I opened the flap with the barrel and peered inside. Running footsteps sounded, and Chiko appeared. Behind him came Angelika, barely visible in the glare of her torch.

'Shine here,' I said. One of the bedrolls had been dragged to the middle, and two cooking pots lay on their sides. I took the torch from Angelika's trembling hand. Her face was chalk- white. There were footprints on the sandy floor. Ours, and fresh hyena ones.

Hyaena brunnea, the Brown hyena, is a scavenger. With a bulky head, dirty-white mane, sloping brown black and pointy ears, he's smaller but tougher than other hyenas. He thrives in dry regions they dare not go. When cornered, he's a fearsome adversary, capable of biting off a man's leg, or even his face. Sometimes he doesn't even need to be cornered.

'Oh God, were they eaten by those things?'

'Can't say. Best go back to bed.' I gave her torch back. Just then Egon stumbled up.

'What —?'

'Hyena,' Angelika said.

'Oh, is that all?' I could have punched him in the face. What did *he* know about hyenas? I almost wished one would spring at him. He turned and ambled back into the darkness.

'What you going to do?' Her voice was strained.

'It won't be back.' I turned to Chiko, who stood like a statue in the dark. His eyes glinted and I knew what he was thinking. Hyenas are rare out there.

'They are the unclean servants of //Gauwa, the death God, they eat everything which is foul and rotten, except men, who they tear apart for pleasure,' he whispered.

'True, but they can't deal with this!' I held up the shotgun. Chiko wasn't impressed.

'Their evil is stronger,' he said.

In the morning, Angelika acted like nothing had happened. Chiko called me and pointed at the ground. There were fresh hyena tracks. They led away obliquely, then disappeared. No point following them.

Instead, taking the toolkit from the Land Rover, we examined the Jeep again. I opened the hood. There was a stink of burnt oil. I checked the central bolt on the flywheel and selected a socket spanner. With leverage from a lengthening bar, I tried to turn it, but it was stuck fast.

'Engine's solid.' Chiko's eyes bulged with dread.

'The wagon-spirit, the growling one killed it!' he whispered. 'It must have complained, but they didn't take heed!' I shrugged.

'Now what?' Angelika said.

'No point searching. We have no clue which way they went.'

'We can't abandon them!' Her hair flew as she shook her head.

'We don't even know if one or two left here.'

'What do you mean?' Egon asked. His eyelid ticked furiously.

'What if one died earlier, or one killed the other?'

'…and only one went off.…' Angelika thought aloud.

'Tell me where we should look,' I broke in. She squared her shoulders and stared, but no answer came. Just then, I noticed Chiko was gone. I looked around and made him out against the glare of the rising sun. A minute later, he disappeared behind a sand dune.

'It's pointless just hanging about. Whether we're searching or heading home, we have the same chance of finding anyone out here, and that's nil!'

'You're right,' Egon said, 'we may as well go.'

'We can tell the police when we get to a town,' I said.

'Whats the point? We don't know what happened, or even if they'll get out on foot.' Angelika gave him a sour look.

'Worried they'll ask what a Jo'burg Jeweller and an IDB dealer were doing here?'

'Look, if they make it out, or if they're dead, what difference? If they're alive they won't thank us, and if they're dead there's no point.'

'I didn't know you were so hard,' Angelika said, stressing the words. He looked away.

'We'll decide on the road,' I said, 'when Chiko gets back.'

It was half an hour before Chiko returned. My impatience was tempered with relief when I saw him.

'I saw you from a long way,' I shouted.

'I followed the tracks behind the dune,' Chiko said, 'but they ended in a rocky place.' Something in his eyes alerted me. It was his secretive look.

'Take us there.' He shrugged and began retracing his steps.

Angelika walked with me, and Egon followed.

The only marks on the sand were hyena prints and Chiko's footsteps, going and coming. The dune sloped upwards, then down again.

At the bottom were first a few small black rocks protruding through the sand, then others, growing bigger into the distance. Chiko was well ahead, when he turned and stopped left beside a towering boulder. As we approached, we heard loud, angry buzzing. Blowflies.

The sight and smell we encountered almost made me gag. Angelika went pale. I moved to catch her in case she fainted, but she waved me aside impatiently.

Two bodies lay on their backs. There were only torn rags left of their clothes, chunks of flesh had been ripped off their arms and legs, and their faces were unrecognisably torn and chewed. One's arms were raised with bunched fists as if fighting off the attack, but it was only the contraction of rigor mortis.

Fat black blowflies buzzed around exposed parts, but the flesh was too dry for them to feed. No doubt they'd laid their eggs before the sun and wind did its work. The eggs were maggots now.

The angry buzzing of the blowflies bored into my head. A funeral dirge by a choir of fat flying insects! Not only were they foul, they had *attitude!*

In the less mummified areas of armpit and groin, the foul little white things wormed about. Egon came up, but kept his distance, one hand covering his nose. Angelika stared like a statue. We retreated out of range of the buzzing flies and nauseating stench.

'//*Gauwa* the death-god!' Chiko's eyes were filled with dread.

'We have to cover them,' I said.

Angelika's eyes were blank, her face porcelain-white.

Egon seemed little affected.

Chiko and I gathered up rocks and, with our shirts as face masks, piled them over the bodies. Egon didn't offer to help.

'The hyenas won't get to them again,' I said to Angelika.

'Why did that one go in the tent, with bodies lying out here? Surely they had enough meat?' There was a shudder in her voice.

'Wanted something fresh!' It was only when she gagged that I regretted my lack of tact.

The conversation was stilted. After three hours, we joined the dirt road. It was hot and sticky. Angelika was exhausted, and Egon's silence was palpable. Chiko was expressionless. There were only two hours of daylight left, and I didn't feel up to driving further.

We camped on a sandy slope near the Otjikondo turnoff. I munched a few Marie biscuits and drank a mug of tea. Then I put up my tent, said goodnight and disappeared.

In the light of my torch, I turned the pages in *Trials at Bodmin Assizes and Transportation of Cornish Convicts to Australia in the late 18th Century*. It was better than dwelling on our grisly find. I looked at the index, where the chapters were listed with titles. Below was a list headed 'Trials and Convicts'. My heart quickened.

What if…? Under *T* were only four names. The third was Tregurtha – Ignatius! I turned the pages until I found it. *'Trial at Bodmin Assizes of Ignatius Tregurtha – record of Clerk of the Crown, March thirty first 1787.'*

In February 1786, during a crackdown on Cornish smugglers ordered by Whitehall, a smuggler's gig was apprehended by the revenue in Mounts Bay.

Four men escaped by swimming, but the fifth, Ignatius Tregurtha, was arrested.

He was charged and held at Launceston Castle awaiting trial at Bodmin Assizes.

I drifted off to sleep.

Next day we filled up in Otjikondo. I looked forward to a hot bath and cold beer. My thoughts were uncomfortable. What to do? We should tell the police, whether Egon wanted or not. But they'd ask questions, treat us as suspects. They only had two gears – forward and reverse.

Egon had a point. Perhaps we should bide our time, report it later. Nothing suggested murder. They'd died of thirst or were killed by hyenas. Maybe they hadn't left the tent voluntarily, but were dragged out.

Angelika stared at the parched countryside, the passing thornbushes and boulders. She didn't smile, shake or nod her head. I caught her gaze, but she averted her eyes.

I was worn out, and Karibib was still a hundred and fifty kilometres away. I drove on and didn't know I'd fallen asleep until Angelika prodded me. I was instantly awake, just in time to stop the Land Rover veering off the road.

'Thank goodness *you* stayed awake,' I said, 'that was close!' She smiled grimly.

'You've driven far enough for one day.'

There was no choice but to stop for the night. Egon was sullen, and the tension in the car was palpable.

Beside a rocky outcrop, a small group of half-naked people sat watching as we pitched our tents.

'Bergdamara, Damaras of the bergs, or mountains.'

'Who?' Angelika's eyes were bloodshot, her face streaked with dust.

'Another wiped-out tribe.' I was glad to talk of other things.

'They live in little groups, mostly in Damaraland and Namaqualand, but there's a few around here.' As we spoke, the watchers moved

There was a sharp crack as Chiko broke a piece of dry wood for the fire. The sun was sliding away and blessed coolness came on the evening breeze.

'Some people abuse them, call them *Klip-fokkers*, or 'stone-fuckers', because they hide out on rocky hills.'

'A good name,' said Egon. I glared at him.

'What happened to them?' Angelika ignored her brother's comment.

'*Hulle is bang,*' Chiko said, looking up from the fire. They are frightened.

'At the time of the German annexation in 1890,' I said, 'they were slaves to the Hottentots and Herero. Some joined the Bushmen to escape. They were afraid of strangers, still are. Note they didn't come down to say hello.'

'So scared, why?'

'The way they were treated. In 1889, a German settler described a group near Heunis. He called out a greeting, but they jumped up and fled up the hill like goats.'

'That frightened?'

'Yes, poor devils. They were once quite advanced. They mined, refined and made things out of copper.' Egon grunted and stalked off.

Angelika stared at me in the flickering firelight.

'You're an interesting man, Tobias.'

'Too talkative?' She shook her head.

'I don't suppose the Germans did the Bergdamaras any favours….'

'No, they didn't. They agreed to colonial rule, but the Germans massacred them with the Herero in the war of 1904.'

'Oh, that's dreadful, poor things!'

'Yes, not nice to be murdered.'

We continued our journey at first light.

Karibib is a one-street town like many in Namibia. It was rumoured to be distinguished by its farming and prostitution services, because the wives of one lot serve as the other.

I was relieved to be back. We stopped at OK Foods in *Hidipho Hamuntenya Street* for fresh food and beer. We took our time, enjoying the shop's air conditioning. Loaded with supplies, we drove home.

It was over. Leaving the dust-coated Rover, we went in and helped ourselves to bottles of *Windhoek*. In silence, we let the icy beers rejuvenate our parched throats. Angelika was desperate to shower, and left us. Egon drained his beer and went out to the caravan. Angelika had taken the inside shower, so I went outside.

Twenty-two

Malkop's yelps and ear-splitting lion roars came closer. Our four-footed protector was goading, yes goading, the monstrous cats, buying time for Pengilly while trying to lead the angry beasts into a trap. What difference, he must have thought, between springbok and lion? Did he know one swipe of a claw could tear out his bowels?

Our Nama companions ceased walking, and formed up in a cluster, their spears projecting like porcupine quills. Out of the dust emerged Pengilly.

For a five-year-old, he ran at great speed, his little feet churning up stones and dust. Malkop was behind him, stopping and turning to loudly snarl and bark every few yards, before fleeing again. In this way, he let Pengilly gain distance. I have never, before or since, seen an animal behave so nobly.

It was several seconds before two huge male lions burst out of the undergrowth. I frantically primed my *Jaeger*.

Pengilly and Malkop approached within thirty yards, when the Namas, moving as a body and emitting loud war cries, broke into a run towards them. For long seconds, the lions came on.

I fired, and my shot spurted sand in front of the leading one. The charging Namas obscured my line of sight as I reloaded. Suddenly, just as the boy and hound came abreast of the Nama phalanx, the lions veered off on another track.

Two minutes later, before I had time to calm down, there came the most awful, heartrending human scream, which will haunt me until I die.

'Oh God,' Marana cried. She'd seized Pengilly, but was staring in the direction of the scream.

Less than thirty yards away a young Nama woman, barely twenty years old, was on her knees with her hands raised to the sky, and from her throat came agonised wailing.

'What..?' I began.

'*Liefje*, a third lion took her baby,' Marana said.

I cannot describe the horror of that moment, or the aftermath. In all my life, boil me in oil, I never encountered its equal. Though they searched the bush for hours, the Namas never found the infant.

The event shocked us deeply. The lions had been sleeping in the shade of big rocks on the far side of the hill, when they were disturbed by the sound or scent of a small boy and his dog. To them, it must have seemed like two tasty morsels coming to their table. It was only Malkop's keen senses which alerted him to the danger, or it would have ended badly for Pengilly.

As it was, the lions were driven off, but not before another one seized an infant out of its mother's arms.

'Pengilly,' Marana said, 'you must never go so far away from us!'

'Sorry Mama,' he said, tears streaming from his eyes. Malkop stood with his forelegs on his little shoulders, and licked away the tears.

Our time in the relative comfort of !Anis had softened us. This was a hostile land, and it behoved us never to forget it.

From AiGams to Okahandja is only sixty miles, but it took a week to traverse.

At Okahandja there were Namas, two hundred or so, and a few Hereros farming manioc and beans along the river bank. But even here, the Hu had penetrated.

Some had guns and other manufactured things, and told us white traders came up from the Cape to sell goods.

It was no place for us, and Marana urged we go after a single day's rest. She told me the land was marked out in her head, and we'd find her family further north.

Now we headed in the direction which would take us to a small riverside Herero village called Otjandjomboimwe, which I shorten hereafter to Otja.

It was in the early evening near Otja, where the sight of me caused panic. It started when a small boy ran screaming to his mother for protection. She, looking for the cause of his disturbance, saw me and fainted. I tried to appease the frightened tribespeople, but several pointed and shouted *'Omuroi'*. As we made camp, the Namas told me that, to the Herero, an *omuroi* is a singing white witch who flies, performs evil deeds and rides people by night. It was most disagreeable to be called a witch!

'They'll remember you forever,' our Nama companions laughed. Little did they know the Hereros wouldn't only remember me. They would try to kill me that very night.

We sat by the fire and ate our meagre food. When it was time to rest, I sought a place to relieve myself. The moon was out, its light bathing the land, so I walked a long way, and found a hidden spot behind a clump of thornbushes.

I had just begun to loosen my belt when something whizzed past my ear like an angry hornet. If it hadn't clattered into a rock, I wouldn't have guessed it was an arrow. In the moonlight, I made a fine silhouette. I threw myself flat on the ground.

I lay still for long seconds.

If only I'd brought my rifle! Though I didn't make a sound, I feared my heartbeat would give me away. My thoughts whirled.

Who, in this desert land, wanted to kill me? I had been personally targeted. Watched from a hidden place, and ambushed as soon as I left camp. Who, why? I'd had no arguments. Then I remembered the Hereros' terror when they saw me. Was the fear of *omurois* so great that I had to be killed?

Just then I heard it. Heavy breathing, a metallic clink, and furtive footsteps in the sand. It was close and came closer.

I looked up and saw the shadows of two men, bent forward, carrying bows.

When there's no time to consider, the nimbleness of the mind can be surprising. Whether I was hunted as a witch or not, the element of surprise can work miracles.

I drew in a big breath, then, rising to my feet, let out an ungodly screech to make a witch proud. There were screams from the shadows and a flurry of running footsteps. Emboldened, I screamed again, with a volume I never knew I possessed.

By now the campsite was astir, and three Namas ran to investigate. I told them what had happened, and one cast about for the fallen arrow. He found it, and, raising it to the moonlight, pronounced it a Herero one.

Marana was thrown into a new panic, and it was difficult to calm her. 'It is because they think you're a witch?' she said. 'Imagine you ran away from !Anis because of the Hu, only to be killed as a witch!'

'Better you do not bide here,' one of the Namas said, 'for they will not give up until you are slain.'

'I agree,' said I with alacrity. I hugged Marana. 'We'll be away tomorrow,' I told her. She tried to protest.

'Tonight, I'll stay on guard with my rifle loaded.'

Next morning, I realised I'd fallen asleep sitting up, and dreamt of volleys of Herero arrows bringing down scores of broomstick-riding witches with powdered white faces and black capes.

'Het U sittend geslaap, Papa?' Pengilly was standing before me, a look of incredulity on his sunburned little face. Dutche for did you sleep sitting Dad? When he didn't speak that, it was San, and lately lots of Nama words.

'Yes, my darling, I was making sure the bad men don't come back.'

We were glad to join the Namas in breaking camp and getting away from that place.

It is always water which decides where you go in this sun-blasted, dry land. About fifty miles east of Okahandja, our Nama companions said north was best because it was easier and there was more water.

We walked as far as we could each day, but the going was hard, mostly up or down-hill, with rocks and stones tripping us every other step and the heat baking us alive. At night, we froze as much as we baked by day. We took turns to carry Pengilly when his little legs gave in, he being only five years old and unable to keep up.

I could tell more terrible things about that journey, but there's too much. To get to Otjiwarongo took eight days, and we had almost given up before we arrived among the Herero there.

The simple folk were kind and, though desperately poor, happily shared their meagre food. Fortunately, these Hereros, unlike the others, didn't see me as *omuroi*, for they had met Europeans before.

Even in this remote place, they said, white men sold them guns, and only the week before four had come on horseback. Didn't they know horses would sicken and die out there? I was shocked how white men seemed to cover even such small, far places.

We stayed a week, and Marana got to talking with an old mixed Herero-San woman.

'I remember some wandering San,' the old one said, 'two seasons ago, and they told me they passed by Otjiwarongo.'

'I know that place-name from my mother,' Marana said. 'She was near there many times. There aren't many groups so far north…I wonder if those San aren't connected to my family.'

It would take ten days to walk there, all being well. We must go on, Marana said, for the further north we were, the closer to her people, and good care they'd take of us.

On our way north, we kept the sun on our right by morning, and our left after midday. If the Namas didn't dig up little dry-looking sticks to get the big water-filled tubers beneath, we'd have had nothing to drink. Marana remembered these miraculous plants from her early years and shaved off pieces of the bulbs to squeeze, whereupon water ran into her mouth. It was an old Bushman craft too, she said, showing me how to do it and giving Pengilly a drink.

I cut short the story of our trek from Otja to Otjiwarongo. By that time all the strange names were confusing me, and I couldn't tell one from another. More sand and rock and sun and thirst and hunger. At night, we were grateful for the blankets we had traded from the Namas, for it was fearful cold.

For victuals, we had a bag of some kind of cooking grain from the Hereros, which tasted foul.

It was a long ordeal, but after fourteen days we came to Otjiwarongo. Near here there were many streams and small rivers, and indeed the people had fat cattle grazing on green grass. They were mainly Herero, but some were Namas, who are Khokoi and related to the San.

The Hereros were uncommonly friendly and gave us shelter and food. The word *omuroi* was not said, for which I was exceedingly grateful.

The tribesmen were terrified of Malkop, and who could blame them? He looked more like his jackal father than his farm-hound mother. Hereros are fearful of hyenas, which are both fierce and dangerous, but they trust jackals even less. They believe these creatures are so cunning and sly, that even hyenas, though stronger, cannot match their guile and sorcery.

No wonder these superstitious people were uneasy with a jackal at our feet. It didn't help that he was always ready to growl and curl up his lip if he sensed trouble.

Pengilly ran around, pursued by Malkop, and the good beast kept a lookout for his protection. It was so funny to have a guard like him, sleeping with one ear up, teeth half-bared just in case. Thankfully, the wayward pair never went as far from us as the day of the lions!

'Watching Pengilly cavort with his friend one day, Marana turned to me.

'Malkop makes me feel safe,' she said.

'Me too,' I replied, 'but I wonder what his mother would think of her half-jackal offspring.'

'She'd be proud!'

'Het Malkop 'n Mama gehad?' Pengilly asked. Did Malkop have a mother?

'Everyone has a mother,' Marana said. A look of wonder lit his brown eyes.

'Like you and me?' he asked in Dutche.

'Just like you and me,' she said, hugging him and kissing his cheek.

'I thought he came from the sky!' We'd remind him of that for years.

One old Herero man knew of some San passing the village six months ago on their way north to Kamanjab. Marana was excited.

'They may be my mother's family,' she said, 'we must go on.'

Between fleeing my arrest and seeking Marana's family, we had become the most travelled fugitives in Africa!

There is little to tell of the walk from Otjiwarongo to Otjikondo, as differing from the other Journeys. The kind Namas, who'd been our companions all the way from AiGams, left us halfway, for they were going east. It was sad to part with these friends and guides of twenty days. Then it was only us and Malkop. Except for a brief interruption.

The Namas had been gone less than half an hour, and only ten minutes ago had disappeared from view behind a group of Acacia trees, when, shouting and screaming, they frantically raced each other back, three huge elephants in angry, trumpeting pursuit.

We needed no invitation to join the Namas' flight. Being at the back we were now in front, and led the way to the top of a small hill.

Fortunately, the elephants halted, trumpeted some more warnings, then ambled away.

On our second parting, the Namas took a more southerly route.

Our latest encounter with wild and dangerous animals reminded us the lands we were traversing were filled with danger, and we should keep our eyes and ears open at all times.

By now we'd learnt better to find our way, and Marana was confident. With toothy, grinning Malkop to warn us of danger, and my trusty *Jaeger* rifle, we had protection against wild animals, and we'd be safe if we kept away from white men, who even I now called the Hu.

Marana's mother had told her many times where she'd come from. Describing a place, she'd say 'The furthest blue mountain rises high, but the summit leans left towards the valley,' or 'Many tall trees stand among black rocks, where you would not expect them to be.' Such were her descriptions, but much more detailed.

Like all San, she spoke of such things with intricate thoroughness. Hearing so much about the land, many times over, Marana, who'd never seen it, knew it for her own memory. To me, it was almost supernatural, for to Marana things and places she'd never seen were familiar. It would stand us in good stead in the perilous days ahead.

Twenty-three

We were in the lounge when Egon surprised us.

'Time to go home,' he said. I felt a pang in my chest. Angelika would leave too. Nothing more had been said, and Egon had been sullen since we came back. Angelika looked up from Curnow's book. I had been strangely pleased when she asked to look at it.

'Nothing more to do here,' he added.

'Giving up on diamonds?'

'Yep. There are none, as Father and Rodolf found out.'

'We have to tell the police, the sooner the better.'

'It won't make any difference if we don't.'

'Don't imagine it can be kept secret, or that I'll agree,' I said.

'You didn't ring the police when we got in mobile-range, or drive to the first cop-shop,' Egon said. Angelika, all the while, looking fresh and clean from a shower, listened in silence. She put the book down.

'They're dead,' and nothing can change that. We didn't kill them, or break the law.' His eyelid ticked furiously.

'Illicit diamonds aren't legal —'

'What diamonds? We didn't find any.'

'No, but —'

'We didn't!'

'Not even legal to look for them,' I said.

'It may be illegal in the *Sperrgebiet*, but we haven't been there.'

'No, but —'

'There are no buts, they're dead. They won't be more-dead if we keep quiet.'

'But – ' Angelika began.

'We haven't done anything illegal unless not reporting a death at your first opportunity is a crime.' He grimaced as he stood.

'I've got a jewellery business to run. It's been left too long. We leave tomorrow.'

'I don't know if I want to.' She was examining her fingernails. Egon stalked off.

'You staying?' I asked.

'If I can. I need time to think.' I didn't expect the lurch my heart gave, but I tried to hide it.

'You're welcome,' I said. She smiled, showing even white teeth.

The pressing thought came back. I should ring the police. Try to explain why I came home and didn't call them. There would be an inquest, questions. It could take months, and what would happen? But the longer left, the more suspicious.

'A stranger was here!' Chiko had snuck up as silently. 'What?'

'While we were away a hyena-snake, was here!' I laughed. Hyena-snake was one of his favourite terms of abuse, and the recent hyena scare had brought them to mind. I got to my feet and followed him outside. Chiko's searches always began there.

'See?' he said. He was on all fours next to the concrete paving by the steps. His finger pointed at the edge of a slab. My vision cleared and I made out fine prints in the dust.

'Voetspoere,' he said. Footprints. 'There are others.' He led me back into the kitchen and pointed at a smudge on the table.

'What is it?'

'Footprint of Hyena-snake,' said Chiko.

'Isn't that you? You don't wear shoes and look like a hyena.'

'Not I,' spat Chiko, 'and I cleaned before we went.'

'Okay, but are there others? There wasn't anything worth stealing in the house.

'It worries me, it was a ghost!'

'Chiko,' I sighed, 'you're too suspicious. Those people weren't killed by an engine-spirit, and nothing's missing.'

'Whatever you say.'

I put his worries aside when I found Angelika alone in the lounge.

'There's something I need to explain,' she said.

'Oh yes? Not about diamonds, I hope.'

'No, not about diamonds themselves. What I want to say is I never dealt in illicit diamonds. But it doesn't change one thing: the diamonds saved the jewellery shop, and whether we wanted it or not, paid for our upbringing.'

'And…?'

'Even if we aren't charged, what will they say about the shop, its assets, the property?'

'You think they'll take it away?'

'Oh, if they decide it was illegally earned, we'll be punished.' I stared at her a long time.

'That why your brother's not keen about the police?'

'Yes.' She stared out the window. 'He's dishonest and secretive, and I wish I knew why, but it doesn't mean we should tell the police.'

'I'll think about it, but why is he in such a hurry now?'

'I wish I knew.'

I went to bed in a muddle. People had died out there.

Then there was Angelika's tie to her brother, who I didn't trust at all. Who was Phil, and what was he to Angelika?

There were my recurring dreams, the hyena footprints in the dust, Chiko's certainty that something had been in the house.

If I wasn't careful…but what was this? Why was *Trials at Bodmin Assizes and Transportation of Cornish Smugglers to Australia in the late 18th Century* open on my bedside table? I'd put it on the shelf when Angelika gave it back. Why was it open?

I glanced and saw it was on pages 187-188. The chapter entitled *'Cornish transportees taken to Plymouth to meet the first convict fleet to New South Wales, 1787.'*

Someone was playing games. Either that, or it had accidentally fallen off the shelf, and accidentally opened there. I wouldn't tell Chiko or Angelika, or mention Chiko's hyena footprints to her.

I lay in next morning. The interior stud walls of my house were poorly soundproofed, which was why I overheard the conversation in the lounge.

'I'd like to know,' Angelika said, 'what you are going to do. Where are you going?'

'Jo'burg, where else?'

'Oh, just like that? I know you, Egon, and I know you were hoping to find diamonds, not only uncle Rodolf. Are you sure you're not going back to look for them?'

'They don't exist. It was a lie. Tobias is right, there are no diamonds outside the Sperrgebiet.'

'So why would anyone lie?'

'I don't know. Maybe to add mystique and obscure the real source of diamonds like the one Dad bought from Schneider.'

'What about Mencken?' I held my breath.

'I don't know anything about Mencken, or if he had anything to do with the bloody map.'

'So, you're giving up on diamonds, and going home?'

'You never ran the shop. You don't know how much it takes. I've been away too long.'

'Egon,' she said angrily, 'I know about your trips to Botswana. That time I bumped into you in Gaborone, you hadn't come to see me, and you never explained why you were there!'

'Not your business.'

'Okay. I hope you know what you're doing. I'm staying a while, then I'll go back to Windhoek.'

'You getting over Phil, soft on Tobias?' I held my breath again.

'Nothing to do with you!' Was that yes, I wondered with a pounding heart.

'It's your decision.' Footsteps sounded, the front door opened and closed.

I got up and opened the curtains. The sun was boring down, the temperature rising fast. What was that on the ledge outside the window? Scratches in the dust.

I looked closer. Definite marks. Were they hyena footprints? Looked like those on the kitchen table. My gaze wandered to the inside windowsill. Two dusty prints on the varnished wood. Prints outside and in.... how could it get through a closed window?

In the heat, a cold shiver ran up and down my spine. It wasn't imagination – the prints were there. The *!gwãĩ* or hyena-visitor in my dream, the one in Rodolf's tent, Chiko's eerily similar nightmare, the hyena-chewed corpses, the footprints in the garden.

Those on the kitchen table, now these… What would Chiko say about them, and the book falling open at that place? I wouldn't tell him.

Maybe, I also mused, with Egon out of the way, I'd find out who Phil was. And if she was really going 'soft' on me!

Twenty-four

A week and eighty miles past Otkikondo we met some Himbas. They were twenty, travelling northwest towards the Otjihipa mountains, where flowed a great river. They told Marana there were San hunting in those hills and valleys.

The desert walking was the same. It was a long and exhausting struggle going northwest and took us three weeks to reach Opuwo, more remote and isolated than anywhere I'd ever been. It seemed like the end of the world.

Otjinjangwe was next, and then we came to the mountains of the Otjihipa. It was dry, rocky and unbearably hot in the mountains, but there were little rivers and waterfalls in narrow valleys in between, and in those places Himbas lived and grew their crops.

We reached a village nestling on flat ground at the foot of a big rounded hill flanked by two smaller, narrower hills. Here we were made welcome, and invited to share their food.

The Himbas are not big eaters of meat, having it only two or three times a month, and living mostly on vegetables and fruits. These they had in great abundance. They had *manioc* like we planted in !Anis, several varieties of broad beans I had never seen, and the same long sweet African potatoes we'd eaten in the Khamiesberg. Then there were wild fruits and berries too numerous to list. They balanced their existence between simple farming, gathering, and occasional hunts.

To repay the tribe for their kindness, I went hunting and shot a fat oribi, which the young men carried back to the village in jubilation.

That night there was much celebration and feasting.

'You will always be welcome among us,' said an elder with his mouth full of roasted meat.

While they survived on other foods, a stomach full of fresh meat was a boon indeed.

Biding with the Himbas was a completely toothless old woman, whose father was Himba, and mother San. Her name sounded, without the clicks, like Anya. She had never forgotten the San language, imparted to her on her mother's breast. When she discovered Marana spoke Khoisan, her joy was complete.

I could not prise the two apart. Sitting on big rocks outside a crude mud and thatch hut, they conversed for hours at a time, in that high-pitched, clicking speech of the San Bushman. Later, Marana recounted what they had discussed.

It may not be the biggest coincidence, when you are near where your extended family live, to find a close relative, but what Marana said gave me gooseflesh.

Toothless Anya was no other than a twice-removed cousin.

'Well shoot me with with shite from a cannon!' I said. Marana looked at me questioningly.

'What's a cannon, *liefje?*'

'My mother,' said Anya before I could answer, 'was the daughter of your mother's mother's brother. She married and settled here with my father, a Himba warrior.' Not only that, but she knew where in the Otjihipa mountains the family group could be found.

Marana's instincts had finally brought us to the brink of reunion with her long-lost people. She was overjoyed.

Next day, for Marana refused to tarry, we went, taking Anya's directions, in search of the family.

The mountainous terrain was not easy to travel.

We could only follow a valley-floor so far, before it ended in a steep slope, or an un-climbable precipice, forcing us to turn back and search out another way.

Sometimes we climbed easier slopes, and other times the valleys extended far enough to take us a long way.

We did not find her clan that day, and sheltered for the night in a cave. Next morning, we resumed our search at first light.

It was a big black hawk we spotted first. He was circling high above the escarpment we had just scaled. He had a great wingspan, an off-white body, and black head. His pointed wings were slate-grey, with light streaks and black tips. His tail was long and narrow, ending in black with a white band.

'What does he see?' Marana asked under her breath. Such birds, she explained, are celestial messengers to the San.

The magnificent creature looked as if he was painted there, so elegantly suspended between sky and earth. We watched him as, minutely changing the angle of a few wing feathers, he narrowed the radius of his majestic swoop. What *did* he see?

Straining our eyes in the harsh sunlight, we made out movement on the ground. Marana started.

'It's my people!' she yelled. I stared hard, but couldn't see anyone. Pengilly, Malkop and I scrambled down the escarpment after Marana.

Big stones rolled underfoot and we risked losing our footing, but in a few hazardous minutes we reached a sandy, rock-strewn plain.

I never saw Marana so excited as she raced across the sand. Then, in the distance, shimmering shapes materialized in the dazzling light.

They were San hunters, young men of a family of twenty-three camped nearby. They were golden brown with smooth complexions. The wrinkles would come, caused by the sun and inheritance.

They reached the camp, chattering and clicking. They were naked, with the bodies of children.

Marana hailed them, and they stopped. In minutes, we reached them, and she engaged in joyful greeting. They stared at me in surprise, but Marana said something to reassure them. For once, Malkop didn't growl or expose his teeth, and though perplexed by our jackal companion, the young men were delighted to meet us.

Together we reached the clan sheltering in the lee of a massive rock. It was deeply fissured and burnt black. It cast a welcome swathe of shade. Meagre possessions lay on the ground. Buckskin-strung bows a metre long. Hollowed-out wooden quivers with reed-like arrows with stone tips smeared with deadly poison. A half dozen *tsamma* melons and a pile of mongongo nuts.

There were few cooking pots, for they had only simple recipes and roasted their food over a fire. The bones were left for the hawks and vultures, who, though not loved by the San, were also creatures of the creator-God *Gao:na,* and needed sustenance. There were few hyenas there, the pickings too lean.

The women had large buttocks. Only the young had smooth complexions and firm, pointy breasts.

We had found Marana's people at last.

Though delighted to see the daughter of one who was long gone from them, they were dismayed to hear their relatives had been massacred for hunting sheep.

They were suspicious of me, a Hu, and terrified by Malkop.

Yet they were warm people, and their suspicions soon passed, especially when Marana told them of my own persecution and Malkop's domesticity.

Within a day, the children were playing with Pengilly, and Malkop, grinning like a hyena and prancing with his tail wildly swinging, joined in the fun.

The San were twenty-three in all, being seven men of hunting age, two old men, and the rest women and children. They didn't build houses or huts, for they were continually on the move, following the game and gathering herbs, desert fruits and mongongo nuts.

'At last, I am among my mother's people,' Marana laughed joyfully. Her happiness was unbounded, and there was no end to excited chatter about this relation or that, the old woman who was a great aunt, the old man a great uncle, the child a cousin four times removed from Pengilly.

A group of hunter-gatherer nomads, they were stone-age, unchanged from their forebears. The land they travelled had sustenance for only the hardiest, never enough for long sojourns in one place. They followed the dwindling herds of oribi and kudu in their migrations.

From waterhole to tepid waterhole they were never far from the herds. When a kill was made, they gorged until they were unable to move. Then they went hungry. Between big kills, they snared small animals, dug porcupines out of their holes, and sometimes caught a *leguaan*.

When the herds migrated away, the Bushmen grew restless. They had to follow them across the wilderness to the hunting grounds beyond. Without fixed homes, and with few possessions, they travelled light.

We'd seen things strange and wonderful, but they were as nothing compared to what we would encounter. We wandered with the family for two years and were most content with the life we shared.

Everything I knew was turned inside out. These people had no money, no possessions. The absence of such things, rather than making life hard, made it inestimably better. For, instead of desiring wealth, they directed their energy and care to the welfare of the group.

Without even hearing of the Bible, they seemed to obey the commandments and the teachings of Christ better than we in the Christian world.

Our clothes turned to rags after a few months. We had no choice but to dress like our hosts.

'I look like a real San woman,' Marana laughed, topless and sporting a short kudu-skin skirt. To me, she was the perfection of womanhood. For myself and Pengilly, I contrived crude short trousers from uncured Springbok hide, using a bone needle, and twine of stripped tendon. These we held up with rawhide thongs.

I was something to behold, naked above the waist, long blond hair streaming down my back, and my beard down to my navel. Pengilly, clad in his rawhide shorts, brown and well-muscled, was the image of a miniature Robinson Crusoe.

There were no fixed shelters, and we slept in the open.

In the cold of night, we wrapped ourselves in skins. When dust-storms blew up, we took refuge in the lee of rocky outcrops. The San always knew when a storm was coming, for they had uncommon senses.

'A devil-stick!' yelled the frightened people at the report of my *Jaeger* rifle. To them, it was witchcraft, yet these kind people didn't say *I* was a witch!

After much explanation by Marana, they grew less fearful, and were delighted when I brought down wild game from a distance. My contribution to the larder was appreciated, though the young men's pride may have been a little hurt.

On Marana's advice, I only went shooting when the hunters failed.

To the astonishment of the family, I showed them how I could make fire without the labour of twirling a stick in a hole in a log. I put a little black powder in the pan of my *Jaeger*, put it next to the dry kindling, and pulled the trigger. Sparks flew and glowed where they fell, and I blew on them. In no time there was a flame, which I fed with sticks.

They were as amazed by this 'trick' as the one which brought down a galloping deer at two hundred yards.

'Where is Malkop?' Marana asked one day. He was nowhere to be seen, and we, especially Pengilly, were much distressed. The desert is unforgiving, and a tame animal is not equipped to survive it.

For two days, we fretted and worried, but on the evening of the second day he bounded into our midst, looking extremely proud of himself. Pengilly threw his arms around his beloved friend and wept with joy.

'Where have you been, you scoundrel?' I asked. He bared his teeth, lolled his tongue and grinned. There was no doubt the beast had a sense of humour!

An hour later a group of hunters returned, bearing a large deer they had killed, and chattering excitedly. Marana, like Pengilly and me, overjoyed by Malkop's safe return, translated what they were saying. Our jackal had distinguished himself, the San proclaimed, in two separate ways.

Since !Anis days, Malkop helped me in the hunt by outflanking and herding game into shooting range.

The way the San hunt is different. They use little bows, with arrows they dip in poison made from the bodies of rare desert beetles.

They stalk their quarry with great stealth, making sure they stay downwind so as not to startle it with a human scent. Their bows do not have great range, so they approach very close before shooting. The arrows themselves do little harm. The animal gallops off, and they pursue it. It can take many hours before the poison works. Finally, the quarry's muscles are paralysed, and it falls down. The hunters dispatch it, and the hunt is over.

'We were surprised,' the hunters laughed, 'when, instead of fleeing, a kudu ran towards us. We loosed our arrows as he came near, then we saw your jackal was chasing him.' Clever old Malkop had adapted his hunting style to theirs.

'When we began the chase, instead of allowing the deer to choose his own direction, your jackal harried and made him go back on himself, over and over, until, after only an hour, more from exhaustion than the effects of our poison, he collapsed just yards from us.'

They were overjoyed, and reversed their opinion of our four-footed friend. This, they told Marana with great glee, was only the first of our noble animal's accomplishments.

They'd told us he had twice distinguished himself.

'What was the second distinction?' she wanted to know.

'Ah,' they laughed gleefully, 'this was a salutary thing!' When the laughter subsided, one of the hunters stepped forward.

'On our way back, we ascended a small rise in the ground, and there in the scrubland below our eyes met a noble sight. Your noble beast had courted, and was gleefully mounting a wild female jackal.'

To the San, he was now not only a skilled hunter, but a great seducer. I know not if it was his farm-dog mother or his wild jackal father he took after in his amours, but one thing was certain.

Malkop was bent on diluting the purity of his wild jackal kin.

'What does *mounting* mean?' Pengilly asked.

'Kissing,' said Marana with a straight face.

'Oh, I thought it was *fiki-fiki*,' he said.

'Pengilly, *Liefje,* you must not say such things!'

It must have been a year after we joined the family when the elder called Xi addressed us.

'We will go south and visit an old uncle called Tátaba, who dwells in a cave in a deep valley. He gathers star-stones, and communes with departed spirits.'

Marana was excited. Her mother had told her a great uncle had become a recluse in a valley, and the description the San gave matched him.

In four days we came to the valley where Tátaba lived with his wife Xsara, or Zwara with a click, which I will henceforth write as Xsara, and gathered the star-stones called //*kweisa-!kau.*

'What are they?' I asked Marana.'

'I can't guess unless I see them,' she said, 'and even then, I may not know.'

We stood before the mouth of a large sandstone cave and called out a greeting. A bent and wizened old woman, wearing only a moochi, emerged from inside.

She recognised the family at once and was overcome with joy. She was Xsara, Tátaba's wife. He was out hunting for pretty stones.

Jokes about stones not satisfying hunger were translated by Marana.

Though Xsara tried not to stare, I could tell she was astounded by my appearance. Suntanned though I was, the colour of my skin, blond hair and blue eyes were difficult for her to apprehend.

Xara clapped and sang. By now I understood some words, and her song was one of warm, clicking welcome.

Later, everyone sat on the ground, chattering like a flock of birds. Gourds of cool water were brought, for there was a spring deep in the cave.

It was over an hour before Tátaba returned. He was greeted by the elder Xi and the others with great displays of emotion, and a dance in which, though stiff of joint, he gleefully joined. Never since Sterkbooi and I arrived at the Khamiesberg had I seen a reunion so rapturous.

I knew Tátaba was curious about me, but he made no sign. I had learnt that these people lived by a code, in which strangers are not made to feel uncomfortable.

After the dance, when the revellers reclined on the ground, Tátaba and Xsara came to sit beside us. The old man's dark eyes so bored into mine, he seemed to be reading my innermost thoughts.

'His name, Tátaba, means butterfly,' Marana told me, 'for it was his father's hope he would grow to be like that beautiful creature, able, through graceful flight, to move between the world of mortal men and that of the ancestors. It is because they are so much in that other realm, that butterflies are so seldom seen.' What a strange and curious person Tátaba was.

I think his father's hopes had come true.

He was spiritual in a way I cannot describe, and did indeed remind me of a butterfly.

Never in my life has another man so enchanted me.

I also couldn't wait to see his star-stones. It must have been the smuggler in me, for what else could they be but things of great value?

Twenty-five

Egon left early next morning. In spite of the tension between them, he urged Angelika to persuade me not to go to the police. He paid me from a roll of crisp Namibian Dollars, then, with barely a farewell, he left.

We watched the Toyota and caravan 'till they disappeared around the base of the hill. For minutes a cloud of dust hung above the road. It was seven thirty and the sun was, for once, obscured by low cloud.

I walked back to the house, leaving Angelika to watch the dust settle. I sat in the wicker chair beside the window and stared across the open country. In the distance, the *bobbejaan-kloof* or baboon-gorge beckoned. I'd spent many hours thinking there. Instinctively, I stood up and left by the back door.

I sat on the low granite cliff. The baboons weren't there today, and the pro-Namib was very still. For nine years until now, I'd carefully avoided stress. The desert, Chiko, the ancient art, and the fauna and flora of this wonderful land were balm for my soul. But I'd been away eight days, and it was time to get back to work. Yet I couldn't drive out the thought of people dying for diamonds.

It was ridiculous. De Beers exploited every diamond field in Southern Africa. They even dredged the seabed off the *Sperrgebiet* for marine diamonds. Could there *really* be diamonds outside the zone? What did the Bushman elder say in my dream? 'The star stones of the valley will bring salvation to our people.' I shuddered.

Yet maybe it wasn't madness. Angelika, and particularly her brother, hadn't told me everything, and Egon was hiding something.

Four deaths, and it wasn't over yet.

Not, I suspected, if Egon had his way. He'd given up too easily. It was as if he'd done what he came for, but I wasn't convinced.

If I really believed there were diamonds, did I want to look for them myself? No, I told myself. Yet there was the San storyteller. If diamonds were found, they could be used to buy land for the Bushmen. That was different, and there was a precedent.

In 1960, the South African government, working with the Rhenish Mission, bought up more than twenty huge farms to create a Damara homeland. The San needed such good fortune.

What if I had a properly marked map? Would I go looking? Would Angelika? I glanced at my watch. Eight-thirty. I'd had little sleep last night.

Angelika was waiting when I returned to the house.

'I've got something to show you.' She held out a piece of paper. I was tired and fed up.

'It's a letter to Mencken, assuming the address is his.'

'Is it wise. Maybe the address *isn't* his.'

'When we were small, we heard he was a big deal in the black-market diamond world. Also, Schneider, who died with our father, was his friend.'

'But Egon—'

'That's the thing, he said he didn't know, then went to great lengths to get rid of the address. Cape Town, where we know Mencken went.'

'Suggestive,' I conceded.

'Oh, I know I'm taking a chance, but how else can I find out what Egon's up to?'

'I don't know.'

'Read it.' She thrust the letter at me. At the top were my address and telephone number.

Dear Herr Mencken,

If you read this letter, then this address is yours. Egon hid it, but I found it. I am writing because he has been deceiving me. What is going on between you and my brother? I need to know! Please ring me urgently on the telephone number below.

Angelika Neumann

'To the point,' I said, 'no mention of Rodolf and his friend, or what happened to them?'

'No, my letter could be read by anyone.'

'True. I think it says enough. I wonder if he'll reply, or if that's even his address.'

'Shall I post it?' Angelika asked.

'May as well. It doesn't say anything incriminating.'

'Okay, I'll post it when we go to the village.' I left her and went to lie down.

I woke after one. Angelika had changed her mind and been to the post office in Karibib. Without asking, she'd borrowed my 1968 Volkswagen Beetle.

'Engine at the back makes it light in front, and it floats over bumps at fifty,' she said unabashedly. I grinned ruefully.

'Bloody cheek,' I said. Make free with my car! Yet I didn't really mind. The old thing needed a run. I was surprised she'd managed to start it after months of neglect in the garage, and didn't ask how she'd found the keys.

She'd set the table and prepared lunch. She had a way with Chiko, he being possessive about his kitchen.

'I posted my letter, and got this for you at the post office. It's from England.' It was a manilla envelope with stamps endorsed 'Truro'.

'Cornwall, not England!' She shrugged. I cut the envelope open with a knife.

There were four pages of old-fashioned print, and a covering letter headed 'West Briton, Truro, Cornwall'. It was dated ten days ago. In the dark ages, the West Briton. Still used post instead of e-mail.

Dear Dr Vingoe,

Your enquiry refers. It happens that the history of the Bodmin Assizes has long been of interest to me, as are all matters concerning Cornwall's past.

I contacted the archive keepers at both newspapers you mentioned, the Plymouth Gazette and Bath Chronicle. Sadly, they didn't find any old news relating to the matter and the person you are interested in. However, luck did not completely desert us, because I had better fortune with our own archives!

The attached is from our archives. It is a narration by the prisoner Ignatius Myghal Tregurtha on the twenty-first of February 1787, to a fellow-convict called John Penrose, who recorded his words, for Ignatius was injured in his right hand, and unable to write. Penrose died in the typhus outbreak in Launceston gaol of May to July 1787, and his wife infected on her visits to him, died just days afterwards. In 1810, when the West Briton came into existence, their son gifted the pages to our newspaper, a full twenty-three years after it was written!

It explained why Ignatius' dictation wasn't given to his family. Its purpose was frustrated by yet another tragedy! I continued reading.

There is something else. I managed to access HMS Scarborough's log from the National Archives, and checked the month of October 1787, when she was at anchor in Table Bay. Two convicts escaped overboard on the sixteenth, and indeed, one was Ignatius Myghal Tregurtha.

The date on the letter you mentioned was clearly accurate.

Several guards were flogged, and one, a Cornishman called Peder Pengilly, was hanged at the yardarm.

I hope this will be helpful in your research. Please do not concern yourself with costs. I would be delighted to hear if you are successful in your quest. Indeed, one of our reporters, who constantly looks for stories about old Cornwall, says he'd love to hear from you and would be interested in writing an article about your research in the West Briton.

With best wishes,
J Tregony, Librarian.
West Briton Archive

'Poor chap!' She was reading over my shoulder. It should have irritated me, but if it took her mind off recent events, that was good. I stood and extracted the four pages of old-fashioned print from Tregony's envelope.

'Read over my shoulder.'

'I already am!'

It was the record of the verbal account given by Ignatius Tregurtha in Bodmin gaol to fellow-prisoner John Penrose, after his trial and sentencing in 1787, given for publication in the *West Briton* in December 1810, and held in their Archives. It was written in old English, with strange spellings for many words.

Ignatius had suffered greatly after his arrest.

His right hand was badly hurt by the revenue men, so he was grateful to John Penrose for taking his dictation. The gaol in Launceston Castle was dreadful, but even worse were the dark, stinking, cramped holding cells in the dungeon at Bodmin Assizes. It was difficult to imagine the raw inhumanity of the time.

Unable to move or stand, chained at the wrists and ankles, Ignatius suffered physical and mental anguish.

At last, a personal account by him! It tallied well with *Trials at the Bodmin Assizes and Transportation of Cornish Smugglers to Australia in the late 18th Century.* Apart from that, and the single letter brought to Cornwall by the sea captain in 1790, it was the only other record of his fate.

'I don't understand old English,' Angelika said, shaking her head. 'The spelling's so—'

'Archaic,' I finished, 'let me tell you.'

'Thanks.'

At the end, she shook her head. 'Amazing, and so sad!'

'Tragic,' I said.

'He's important to you.'

'On my mind a long time.'

'You think he really ended up with the San?'

'Pretty sure. What I want to know is how, where and for how long. I can't accept that after his letter of 1790 he vanished off the face of the earth. There's much more to his story, and I want to know.'

'What will you do?'

'Wish I knew.'

'Same for me,' she sighed. 'Aren't we in a mess?'

Should I tell her about my dreams, I wondered.

'I'd like to find out what became of Ignatius,' I said. Like I hope you find out about Egon, I thought, and *I* learn who Phil is.

'I heard the name Ignatius before, but Myghal...' I hoped she didn't still find it funny, like the first time she heard his middle name.

'Cornish for Michael.'

'You can't forget him.'

She put a plate of ham, salad and local German *Schwarzbrot* on the table. She'd been to the shop too.

'No,' I replied, 'I can't.'

'I know,' she said, touching my hand. It wasn't an accident. I pulled back by reflex.

We ate in silence.

'I think I know why.'

'Why what?'

'Why Ignatius is so important to you.'

'You a therapist too?'

'No, but psychology is part of the study of people. I had a BA in it before I did my Masters and PhD in Anthropology.'

'So why do you think Ignatius is important to me?'

'I need more of your background.' She took my hand again, and led me over to the sofa.

'You told me about Chiko, what about you?' I stared at her.

'My mother drowned when I was ten.'

'How awful…how did she drown?'

'Swimming on a dangerous beach at Chapel Porth. Rip currents, no lifesavers.'

'Why did she —'

'I think it was suicide!'

'Was she depressed?'

'Think so.'

'Was there anything else?'

'Dad had an affair.'

'How did you find out?'

'Dad came to my school. Her body was recovered by a rescue lifeboat, and he identified her.'

'Oh, poor kid!'

'I should have noticed how pale she was, how cold her lips were when she kissed me goodbye.'

195

'You were only ten, you couldn't know.'

'Maybe, but I felt I let her down.'

'You never got over it.'

'No, I suppose not.'

'How terrible for you!'

'I can't even describe how I felt.'

'It's the worst thing to happen to a child,' Angelika said. 'My mother died when I was born. Very sad, but I never knew her.'

'I know, I'm sorry!'

'This is about you, not me.'

'At the funeral, I thought it was a trick, and she wasn't really in the coffin. I was sure she'd be there when I got home.'

'That's called denial.'

'I missed her terribly. Life with Dad was very different. He was an ex-regimental sergeant major w with the British Army on the Rhine. He was strict, had little patience.'

'Very hard for you.'

'I didn't want to go to school, and it got me in trouble. Many times, when he dropped me at the school gates, I waited for his car to disappear then made my way home, where I was locked out and spent the day huddled in the freezing shed.'

'You wanted to be alone?'

'Yes.'

'Isolation, it's normal in bereavement.' She tilted her head.

What happened then?

'One Saturday afternoon, he saw smoke in the garden.' She looked at me questioningly.

'He discovered I'd poured lawnmower petrol on my black suit, and set it alight.'

'Goodness!'

When he asked why, I said Mum wouldn't be dead if I got rid of it.'

'Magical thinking, making a bargain with God. Children blame themselves and think they can bring the dead person back. Quite common.'

'Is it?'

'Yes. What did your father do?'

'The fire made up his mind. He sent me to boarding school.'

'You must have felt rejected.'

'Yes. It was no fun with him, but….'

'Still rejection.'

'Yes. I was very unhappy at school.'

'Tell me how you felt.'

'Awful. I thought I was why she died. I didn't love her her enough. I wanted to join her.' My throat choked up.

'You've never really told anyone all this?'

'No, tried with my girlfriend, Roseanne, but she wasn't the kind to listen, always had something else on her mind.'

'Well, you survived, clearly, though you never got to the acceptance level.'

'What's 'acceptance'?'

'Put it this way, grieving people go through stages of denial and isolation, anger, bargaining, depression and then, unless the grief is abnormal, they reach a stage of resolution or acceptance.'

'Well, I suppose I didn't get there.'

'Think about it, Tobias.' She sat back. 'Only you can answer that question.' That was true. Who else would know if I ever got over it?

'You left Cornwall to come out here, and lived alone, obsessed by what happened to an ancient uncle. You have strange nightmares, it's not entirely normal.'

'No, I suppose it isn't.'

'Look, people with unbearable psychological stress subconsciously try to cope. Small children displace feelings onto a thing, like a comfort blanket or a toy.'

'I suppose they do.'

'Adults do it too, form attachments to 'transitional' or 'comfort' objects. It may be an old photograph or a family member, a piece of art made by a relative ..... even an old letter!'

'You mean Ignatius?'

'Well?' Ignatius *was* an obsession. Many people have missing relatives, but how many are as fixated?

'I need a drink.'

'Get me one too!'

'What happened between you and Roseanne?' she asked when I returned with a bottle of *Grand Cru* and two glasses.

'You won't say I'm mad and go skittling back to your brother?'

'Oh him? Never!'

'There's not much to tell.'

'Really?'

'Yes, really.'

'Well?'

'I graduated at twenty-three. Roseanne was my girlfriend, also a junior doctor in Truro. We moved in together, and, for a while, I thought I was happy.'

'But it didn't last — '

'No. It was good for two years, before I got depressed.'

'Thinking about your mum?'

'That was at the root of it. I'd had *my* memories for seventeen years, and they weren't going to fade away just like that.'

Just then Chiko appeared. He glanced at me, then Angelika, then back at me.

'Tea?' I know him too well. He knew he'd interrupted something.

'No Chiko, thank you.' He turned and slipped away.

'*Badly* depressed?' Angelika asked.

'Quite bad. I slept a lot. but was tired in the morning. I lost interest in everything. At work nobody noticed, but I began to doubt my dedication. After a few months, things went wrong.'

'Wrong?'

'I overslept and came in half an hour late, then did it again. I was rude to a nurse, who made a complaint. I argued over nothing with a radiographer.'

'You were distracted.'

'It came to a head with an old lady who broke her radius. A *Colles'* fracture. I wasn't thinking straight, didn't order an X-ray. She came back in agony a week later. My omission was noted by the consultant, and I lost my temper when he told me. I had to see the medical director, who expressed 'concerns' about my judgement and conduct. I was advised to take time off. Only it wasn't advice, but an order.'

'What did Roseanne say?'

'We were hardly talking. Things between us were moving to a final outcome or *dénouement*. It was difficult telling her.'

'What happened?'

'She left.'

'How did you feel?'

'Abandoned.'

'First your mother, then your father, then Roseanne.'

'I never saw it quite that way —'

'I'm sure you felt it. You were traumatised, depressed. In circumstances like that, rejection's the worst thing.'

'Suppose it is.'

'What about your job?'

'Couldn't bring myself to go back.'

'You were in a mess!'

'Yes, awful, really bad!'

'How old were you?'

'Twenty-seven.'

'What did you do?'

'Nothing for a couple of months.'

'Think of doing something?'

'What you mean?'

'To get out of your predicament.'

'I see what you mean. Yes, I thought about ending it.'

'Like your mother —'

'Like my mother! There didn't seem any point…'

'Somehow, you survived the crisis.' That was the word, it was *the* crisis of my life!

'One day, dozing in a chair, I had a strange dream.' It diverted me from self-pity and thoughts of suicide.

'It was about my great-great uncle Ignatius Myghal Tregurtha. I'd seen the letter he wrote in 1790, but the dream brought him alive to me!'

'He was one relative who, because he lived long ago, didn't leave you by dying, nor abandon you.'

'I started researching, looking through old court records, visiting the Bodmin assizes and the ruins of Launceston Gaol. Once I began, I couldn't stop. It seemed the only thing I was living for.'

'The court records wouldn't tell you what happened to him after 1790 —'

'No. I thought there'd be a comment by Ignatius about his intentions, but there wasn't one. I had very little to go on apart from his letter.'

'Curnow's book came a few days ago, now you've read Ignatius' dictation to John Penrose.'

'Exactly.'

'After you started your research, you never thought of killing yourself anymore?'

'No.'

'Makes sense. You came to Namibia to find what happened after 1790!'

We were silent for several drawn-out minutes.

'Thinking about it,' Angelika said finally, 'motivation is deep, often obscure, but I think that, looking for Ignatius, you were trying to re-connect with your mother and make up for your guilt as a child.'

Twenty-six

From 'Untold Mysteries of The San' by Sven Johannsen, 1790: *To the San the most important thing is balance, between them and the land, between members of the group, and between their need and the environment's ability to supply it. Balance is ordered by the god Gao:na, taught by spirits, and served by those who live.*

With Marana translating, Tátaba asked about my background. I could not match the colourful, mystical way the San recount their personal journeys, but told him I fled my people from far across the great sea, for they used me cruelly, and made me a slave. I told him of my flight from the south, of Sterkbooi and my Baster companions, my meeting with Marana, and how we came into the desert in search of her family. I could never safely return amongst my own people.

As I spoke, he listened intently, sometimes asking questions.

'But,' said he one time, 'this is confusing, because, like the ancestors, I know there are no lands across the water, for neither *Gao:na* himself, the creator-god of the eastern sky, nor *//Gauwa* the death-god, exist there, and where there are no gods there is no world.'

It puzzled him how I, a white man or Hu, came to be, and it hurt his head to wrestle with such thoughts.

'What is his name?' Tátaba asked Marana at length. To the San, a name is a precious thing, and should not be asked too soon.

'He is called Ignatius,' Marana replied. Tátaba rose to his feet. We had been talking for over an hour. He withdrew, saying something to Xsara and Tátaba, and disappeared inside his cave.

'The Butterfly has gone to consult the spirits of his ancestors,' Marana told me. I was disappointed because I was building up the courage to ask about the star-stones.

Xsara was walking our way when she suddenly stopped and uttered a string of sonorous clicks. As if by magic, two excited young San ran over, and dashed to the top of an outcrop of grey and black rock, stooping and clicking in delight as they struck at the ground with sticks.

'What on earth…?' I exclaimed, getting to my feet.

'*Agamas,*' Marana said, standing and pointing. *Agamas* are big lizards.

The action was over before we could advance a step. The gleeful young men came back, carrying the bloodied bodies of several agamas by their tails.

'Just like that….?'

'Good to eat,' Marana said, taking one and holding it up. It was six inches long, most of it tail, and had a small head and flattened body. The orange-red on the heads contrasted with the purple-blue on their backs. Xsara spoke, and Marana translated.

'They like rocky places, and this kind live in groups.'

'But how did she know they were there?' Marana translated my question, and Xsara pointed over my shoulder. In the distance, a solitary hawk soared high in the dazzling sky.

'*Torenvalk,*' Marana said. Dutche for Rock Kestrel, a desert raptor which loves Agamas. 'They were trying to get away from it, but Xsara saw him, then what he was after!'

If I needed a lesson why these remarkable people survive in such harsh conditions, here it was!

Only an hour later, a group returned carrying a fat porcupine they had dug from his lair. The quills would burn off on the fire, Marana said, and the meat would taste like wild pig.

With the *agamas* and porcupine added to the family's larder, I spent the rest of the afternoon listening to the conversation between the women. I was beginning to understand some San words and phrases.

Tátaba did not emerge for several hours, by which time it was sunset.

'I shall know the Hu as //*Ignï-tsãũ*, Brother Igni,' said Tátaba, addressing Marana, 'for I feel kinship with him, and that his destiny is linked with ours. Though he magically comes from nowhere-land, the spirits told me he is good. He, you and your child are welcome indeed!'

I was overcome at the kindness of the little old man, and seized his thin hand to shake it. He pulled away and stepped back. He was not ready to adopt the strange customs of the Hu!

Marana and Xsara took to each other like sisters. I never saw such a thing, for it seemed as if they had always known each other. I was much taken by Tátaba, who seemed to know much about me though we'd never met before. The San have uncanny abilities which white men could fain comprehend

A sandstone wall inside the cave was alive with colour, with charging animals pursued by stick-like hunters, unmistakable for San, spears brandishing and over-sized members projecting. It was a ≠*keten*, or wall-painting, of extraordinary beauty, and the artist was Xsara.

The colours, shaded from the sun, were unfaded by time.

A gigantic kudu or *!xãũ* in red ochre, fully two feet high, dwarfed the hunters and appeared to burst out of the rock.

I flinched instinctively to avoid the pounding legs and hooves, which, in the flickering flame, moved as if alive and magically propelled. Two *!kung* hunters were leaping for their lives. I sensed their terror.

'Tátaba and Xsara possess the */num*, or spirit-contact,' Marana told me, 'they are able to commune with the ancestors. Xsara's painting records what the spirits revealed to her in a trance.'

'What is this thing you use to draw?' Xsara asked another time, pointing at Marana's black lead pencil and tilting her head in confusion. 'Why do you draw on strange bark when there is so much good, firm rock?'

Pengilly appeared, dressed in his rawhide short trousers, and carrying a tiny San bow and a bark quiver of little arrows.

'Can I hunt *agamas* with my friends?' he asked. Behind him, two grinning young boys clutched similar bows.

'If you promise not to leave them, and don't go further than shouting distance,' Marana said. They ran off in delight.

Over the next days, speaking through Marana, Tátaba imparted many San beliefs. It was better to listen, before asking about his stones. One day he told how death came to be.

'The hare, who was a person then, argued with the moon,' he began. 'Moon said, just as he died and was reborn, so people would do. The hare's mother had died, and he said she wasn't going to come back. Moon offered to show Hare his own death and rebirth, but Hare refused to look.'

'Moon was angry, and hit Hare in the mouth, splitting his lip forever. Hare scratched Moon on the face, leaving scars.'

Tátaba shook his wise old head. 'Then Moon said to Hare he would no longer be human, but an animal to be hunted, killed and eaten by wild dogs. Ever since, hares have a split lip, and they, and all, mankind are mortal.'

There were many animal stories, passed down over thousands of years, for the San are an ancient people, steeped in the history of their ancestors, whose spirits they believe have never left them.

Their gods are all around in nature. They believe every morning *Gao:na,* their creator god, thrusts up the sun in the east, bringing life to the world. Then each night //*Gauwa*, his arch enemy and death-bringer, snatches it over the lip of the western sky. When this great struggle ends, so will the world.

Though we had seen the San dance themselves into a trance several times, we had not seen one as intense as that we witnessed now.

On our third day, a trance-dance was performed for healing the sick, but also for sacred reasons. The women gathered around the fire, and the men began to dance around them. They wore rattles of dried seed pods on their legs, lending loud percussion to each step.

The women sang and clapped, and fed the fire with sticks. Some hummed, others sang in rhythm. It was a most wonderful, un-worldly sound, like, Marana said, was heard for thousands of years.

The dancers slowly worked themselves into a frenzy, going faster and faster, around and around, stamping their feet and raising dust high.

It continued for several hours, then, close to exhaustion, three dancers went into a trance.

They sweated profusely, their pupils were widely dilated and staring, and their breathing heavy and rapid. Then they collapsed and convulsed with seizures.

'Are they sick?' Pengilly asked.

'No, darling,' Marana said.

'They go forth in spirit, heal the sick, travel to other places and times, and commune with the ancestors,' she said to me.

'Herbs induce the trances, but they don't talk about it.' She was right. About the substances used, they maintained great secrecy, to the point, even, when directly questioned, they answered 'what medicine can you possibly mean?' or 'why should we reveal what you do not need to know?'

One evening Tátaba sat on his haunches and told me the valley sands were blown here by winds from the high country, over time uncountable. His star stones, however, had come by other means. This was my opportunity.

'May I see some?' I asked through Marana. Tátaba rose wordlessly and went into the cave. He returned with an earthenware urn and tipped the contents into my hand. They were no less than uncut diamonds.

I'd come across such stones in Brittany. In the market in Morlaix, I watched a Persian merchant trade a few for a dozen casks of French brandy, though Musselmans aren't supposed to drink. I'd seen cut and polished diamonds too, in the rings of rich men's wives, and a fat priest in Penzance, who, though Catholicism was banned, adorned himself in their fashion.

I imagined how my old father, my brothers, Daveth Eva, Morcom Jago and all my free-trading friends would react to such things.

But what good were diamonds in the desert, there being no money, nor anything to buy? Even to a smuggler like me, they had no worth here.

Neither could I gather them to sell to the distant Hu. Yet I had changed.

The greatest wealth and pleasure surrounded me – my woman, our son, and the good folk we bided with. I had never thought this way before. Wealth, for its own sake, has no meaning. It is only to uplift those in need that it has value.

'The star-stones were not born of sand,' Marana said, breaking into my thoughts as she translated Tátaba's words. 'Though there is no river here, a great truth is clear. Unimaginable it may be, but in ancient times this place was no desert.' Tátaba's eyes glazed over, and he spoke as if from a distance. Marana whispered the translation in my ear.

'The spirits revealed to me that rivers once crossed this land, and lakes lay like pearls between the hills. Far away the patience of moving waters slowly gouged the star-stones from the rocks which bore them, and carried them away in the stream.' Marana and I nodded and remained silent.

My heart swelled with love for my pretty, loving woman, so attentive to my every need, who translated so diligently so I may understand.

'Thousands of years later, they lay at the bottom of a lake. Countless more years passed, and the waters fell. A long time ago, the last moisture evaporated, and sunlight touched the stones.'

'They reflected it back in all the hues of the rainbow. Only one thing was missing. The appreciation of humankind.'

Of all his diamonds, he was proudest of two exceptional stones.

One gave off a bluish reflection in the sun, the other a pale red. These he had named '*Blue Woman* and *Red Woman*.' They were things or rare beauty.

How I would have lusted after them just a few short years ago!

'These two star-stones are the soul of my beloved Xsara,' Tátaba said with a satisfied smile.

'Xi has decided the family should go west to hunt gemsbok and kudu,' Marana told me one day, 'but I think we should bide 'till they return.' I agreed readily, for I enjoyed this place and the company of the old man.

Thus, we lived over a month in the cave with our new friends.

Tátaba and Xsara had much knowledge of their people's history, in the Kaokoland and beyond. He knew Marana's mother's parents, and many of the group who crossed the Gariep River in the great drought. Indeed, he was her mother's second cousin, making him her third.

Every day, I helped Tátaba gather his diamonds. Through Marana, he revealed that the spirits, who dwelled in a world just like this, told him the stones would save his people one day. Someone special would use them to rescue the San in dark times.

The special one would be a man, a Hu, like me, and a descendant of my, yes *my*, family. How could he predict such a thing?

Yet, by the certainty in his voice, and the glint in his eye, I found, though I could not comprehend his belief, it was difficult to doubt him.

Marana and Xsara spent much time together, talking and gathering the nuts called mongongo, and big juicy *tsamma* melons which grow in the sand.

Sometimes they caught big lizards called *Iguanas*.

We roasted them on the fire, and they tasted much like chicken.

One day Marana led me to a place where a big boulder overhung a flat rockface on the hillside.

I was stunned at what she showed me. It was a painting of me, so lifelike that it made me catch my breath. I hadn't thought my beard was so long.

I heard Malkop breathing beside me. He was grinning from ear to ear, his mouth wide to expose his fangs, his tongue lolling on one side. I patted his great head. Stab me, but the blessed creature liked Marana's art!

'When did you do this?'

'While you and Tátaba searched for stones,' she said, 'do you like it, *liefje?*

'It's wonderful my darling!' Where had she learnt to paint so beautifully? I looked around and saw Xsara smiling and nodding her head. The gift was inherited, I realised.

The family returned from their hunt and rested just a day. Then we bid Tátaba and Xsara a tearful farewell, with promises to return, and departed for the faraway green mountains and valleys of the Otjihipa. I sensed our futures lay there.

Twenty-seven

My thoughts whirled as I lay on my bed. There was nothing new in what Angelika said, yet things fell into place. I wasn't unique. In similar circumstances, others shared the same feelings. I was comforted as I drifted off to sleep. My dream wasn't remotely connected.

There was a voice. *'He was known as the Shining One. From an early age, the /num was with him, and he travelled far in the world of the spirits. In the valley of the deep soft sands, he made a home in a cave and bided with his woman.'*

'He spent long days digging in the sands to gather up the stones which shine, for in time they will leave this place and bring salvation to our people. The stones he gathered were as the stars.' Then I saw two elderly San, a woman and a man.

'Many are the sky-stars you have gathered Tátaba,' said the woman with a number of clicks.

'Ai, Xsara,' he replied, *'and this day the sands have spoken like never before.'* He held something in his fist, then turned it over and opened his fingers.

'Indeed, both big and beautiful,' she laughed, clapping her hands.

'See white light comes from the soul of the sand-star, yet there is also blue when the sun strikes.'

'I see the blue, beloved one.'

'Hau,' he laughed in delight, *this one we shall call the Blue Woman!'* Xsara laughed with him. *'Red Woman and Blue Woman mirror your soul.'*

'I too have been busy, with my painting. Come into the cave and bring a flame-stick.' Tátaba followed, bending down to pick a burning numa root from the fire. It threw flickering light into the gloom, Xsara rounded the corner and stopped at the far wall.

The orange flames lit the rock, and he stepped back and flinched to avoid the galloping hooves of a great Kudu in red ochre and brown pigment. On either side, stick-like hunters were leaping aside.

She turned to him and smiled.

Now it was back outside. They were looking at the horizon, where forms were taking shape. People were coming.

They were San kinsmen. With them were two strangers, the tall bearded /hũ or white man I had seen, and one woman with fairer skin than the others. There was laughter in her eyes. Slim and girl-like, she rushed up to Tátaba and threw her arms around his neck.

'You come from the Otjihipa mountains in the north,' he said, smiling, *'and how are the Chimba people?'*

'We hunt freely, and they trouble us not.' Tátaba shook his head.

They led their visitors into the cave.

I was dressing when Chiko appeared with tea. Things had been strained between us. He hadn't rung the kitchen bell once since our return.

'Thanks, Chiko, you okay?'

'I saw the prints of the !gwãĩ on your windowsill,' he said.

'I don't want to talk about it,' I said, leaving him holding my tea. I was never offhand with Chiko, but couldn't face another discussion about a ghost hyena.

I found Angelika in the lounge. She looked stressed, no surprise after what she'd been through. She was waiting on her letter to Mencken. Had she had strange dreams too?

She put down a two-week-old copy of the *Namibian Sun* she'd been perusing.

'Where you been?' She flicked her hair from her face.

'Lying in. Have *you* had any experiences you can't explain?' She wrinkled her brow and squinted.

'You're joking, right?'

'Sorry, that's not what I mean…I mean, apart from Rodolf.'

'What do you mean, anything else?'

'Dreams, nightmares, anything unusual…'

'Oh… of course I've had nightmares, what do you expect?' She reminded me of the sudden gales which blow up in west Cornwall. The word tempestuous came to mind.

'I didn't mean —'

'Forget it,' she said, stalking off. I ate a sandwich, swallowed a cup of tea, and headed outside. In less than five minutes, I'd offended the only two people around.

I sat for nearly two hours trying to sort out my thoughts. Then, somewhere between the kloof or gap gouged in the rocky kopje or hill, something moved. It was only momentary, yet definite. I stared for several seconds. Nothing.

It moved again. Could be a tourmaline reflecting sunlight, a piece of mica or quartz. The country was full of it. Out the corner of my eye, I saw movement again. Not just the play of the sun. A dark shape between the rocks, one second there, then gone. A prowling hyena? Even here I had no peace. I may as well go back to the house, for all the good this was doing.

Twenty-eight

From 'Untold Mysteries of The San' by Sven Johannsen, 1790: *'Though they may not agree with that which another desires, or want it for themselves, the San, unique among peoples, will, when assured it is truly wanted by the other, be he or she San like they or of other race, lend everything in their power to achieve that end.'*

Recounting my life is a curious thing. Of momentous events, I write much. Then there are times when life slows down and nothing happens. There's no drive to write the mundane, even if it's a time of contentment. It was a happy life. I had Marana and Pengilly, the two people I loved, the friendship of the wonderful San, and our stalwart companion Malikop. What more could I ask for?

Gaps grew in my narrative. Weeks, months, even years went unrecorded. Peace, tranquillity and good living preclude terror, danger and risk. Yet, though we don't desire such things, they are the stimulus to the pen.

After existing so long with hunter-gatherers, we considered where to spend the rest of our lives. There could be no safe return to my people, or anywhere near any Hu. If Marana wished to continue wandering with her family, I would comply. She and Pengilly were my life. Yet, though Marana loved her people dearly, and would always want to see them, she was accustomed to a settled life.

'I want a home,' she said one day as we walked together on the sand, 'I miss our hut in !Anis, *liefje*.'

'Where?'

'There are places in the Otjihipa.'

'In the mountains?'

There are valleys watered by streams, flat land where seed can be planted, trees for timber and shade. We could sow beans, manioc and sweet potatoes, and get chickens from the Namas.'

'There's game to shoot in the mountains,' I thought aloud.

'I could find wild fruits and berries....'

'I love you!' I said, hugging and kissing her.

'Not as much as I love you!'

'It is good to be with you,' I told Xi, 'but we need a home in one place.' He pondered long.

'It would be best,' he said at last. 'Though you are welcome to travel with us, we know you cannot forever face the hardship of our wandering lives.' He was careful not to say we were a burden, though we knew it was true, for we struggled to keep up with these hardy people.

Barely a week after our decision, we came to a high place where thickly wooded slopes led down to a valley barely half a mile wide. At the bottom, a shallow stream or small river, as wide as the height of two men, gurgled over rounded boulders. On either side was a narrow strip of flat land.

'Is this a suitable place?' Xi asked in San, beckoning with his stick. By now I knew enough to understand. Marana and I exchanged glances. She could not hide the delight in her eyes.

'The best choice,' she answered, 'this is where we shall build our home!' My heart swelled with happiness to see her so pleased.

'Good,' said old Xi. He beamed in satisfaction.

'I have passed this way many times, and often wondered why those who settle have never taken it.'

'I hope you will visit us when you pass,' Marana said, 'for you will be welcome.'

'So it shall be.'

We descended between the trees until we reached a spot beside the stream. Pengilly was more excited than us. He had grown into a sturdy boy of almost seven years and was already as tall as the San hunters. He ran about, pursued by tail-wagging, grinning Malkop.

'We can build our hut here!' Pengilly proclaimed in San at a spot where a group of tall boulders huddled near the stream.

'These rocks almost make a wall,' he said. He was right. Four of them, five to six feet wide, no less than eight feet high, stood only feet apart. The gaps could be filled with mud mixed with grass from the slopes, and a solid, slightly rounded wall would be created. For other walls, we could start with rocks at the bottom, then build up with sun-dried mud-and-grass bricks. We could plaster and smoothe the whole with mud, which, with the stream so close, was easy to make.

We told Xi our intention, and he said the family would assist us to build, so long as we gave instruction, for they were not builders. We warmly welcomed the offer, and next day saw everyone, including the children and old people, joining in clearing and levelling the site of our new home. When it was done, we dug a pit by the stream, for mixing grass cuttings and mud for bricks.

The San had much to say about the strangeness of the 'cave' we were making. Much better, they said, to sleep beneath the stars and go where the spirits of the ancestors guided them.

Such things were declared by nature itself, in all its wonder.

It was better not to forsake the natural urge of humankind to wander, hunt and explore, or to abandon the natural order ordained by the creator-god *Gao:na*. Better not to remain in one place, and cut off the sky with a roof. It was something they could never comprehend.

Yet, despite their misgivings, these noble little people were of such generous character that they busily engaged in helping us do the thing they would never do for themselves.

Under Marana's guidance, for she had learned much of building in Ouder's house in the Khamiesberg, they stamped and twisted up to their knees in mud, until the ooze was mixed. Using a bucket they made from rawhide, they extracted it and put it into crude brick-frames made by me. They laboured long, sweating profusely, with never a grumble. They may not possess anything, but these people are generous and big-hearted like no others.

Within days, the first bricks were dried and hardened by the sun. The women and children gathered rocks and pounded them into the ground as a foundation. On this, with mud for mortar, we bridged the boulders. In a single day, a wall was complete. It was strange how a single, simple, construction changed the mood of that wild place.

Suddenly, where there had been nothing, there was the unmistakable evidence of human settlement.

Though there was no perimeter fence, no gardens of vegetables, nor chickens scratching in the dirt, a happy feeling of pride and ownership overtook us.

The San saw our delight, and, though our reasons were alien, celebrated with a dance around the fire. It was a huge one, fallen trees being so abundant in the Otjihipa.

The flames leapt high into the night sky, so bright that the moon and sun couldn't be seen.

After more than an hour of his foot-stamping, dust-raising dance, Xi went into a trance, fell down and convulsed. When he recovered, he told us he had good news from the spirits. We would be happy and thrive in our new home.

The building continued apace. In a fortnight, the hut was completed with a roof of wooden poles from the valley slopes, covered by a thick thatch of twine-bound bundles of elephant grass.

They had done what they promised, said Xi at last, and now it was time to leave us. Their sojourn here was the longest they'd made in many years.

'We shall miss you deeply, but cannot remain longer.' I took his hand and squeezed it. There are few people as kind as him.

They gathered their few possessions and assembled to go. There were tearful farewells between Marana and every one of them, this lady being a third cousin on her mother's side, that old man a great uncle. I, the white Hu who had come among them as a stranger, received a hug or friendly pat on the chest by every man, woman and child. Even Malkop, strangely subdued, was given parting greetings. Then, without a backward glance, for they believed it was ill to look back, they walked away in single file, climbed the slope, and were lost to sight. We were alone.

I turned to find Marana on her knees with her eyes closed and her hands clasped in prayer.

She was whispering thanks for our new home to *Gao:na*, the Creator-God of the San. Her reverence was something to behold. Marana was very close to her God.

Looking at her dainty form and the expression of infinite gratitude on her beautiful, girl-like face, I was overcome with emotion. I fell down beside her and thanked our Christian God.

Never in the pews of Gulval Parish church in Penzance had I felt so near to heaven. My heart swelled with peace and happiness.

Pengilly, seeing us kneeling on the ground, came to stand between us, and put his little arms around our necks. This was the African family Tregurtha, huddled together in worship and joy for our island of sanctuary in the midst of a vast, harsh country.

Malkop, his tail wagging with gusto, thrust his grinning face between Pengilly and me. Strange though our behaviour was, he would not be left out.

After the digging, pounding, chatter and laughter we had known, a silence like never before descended upon us. At first it was stunning how absolute it was, but in short time we began to hear things we hadn't noticed. Strange birds called from invisible places. From far away came the shrill bark of an African wild dog, and near at hand insects scratched and fluttered as they went about their routine.

We surveyed our estate. Apart from our hut and the stream, we had nothing. We hadn't cleared a place for a vegetable garden, erected a fence, or done anything to provide for ourselves. The San had left us a small provision of mongongo nuts, *tsamma* melons, and half a *dik-dik*, but it would not last long.

We rested three days. On the evening of the third, Marana snuggled against me as we sat on the ground. I held her tight against me, and we watched the sky together in our embrace.

The sun made a bright orange ball on the horizon, and was beginning to dip over the edge, casting a red glow in the sky and long shadows on the earth.

From far away an owl hooted hauntingly.

'Nothing lasts for all time,' Marana said. I put my arm round her.

'That's true, my love.'

'What would you do if I died?' I sat up.

'Why do you ask?'

'Just want to know…'

'Why are you thinking about dying?'

'It's so perfect, I might die of happiness!'

'You silly girl,' I said, kissing her cheek, 'people don't die of that!'

How I would have loved to abide with my wife and son in our new home! But there could be no rest, for we needed many things, without which we would not survive. Plants to grow in the ground, and scrawny chickens could be obtained from the Otjihipa Namas we had met before, and, by dint of my compass-log, I was confident I'd find them again. We'd go together, for we'd carry back the seeds and plants they gave us. Marana was doubtful about the compass.

We were interrupted by the high-pitched howls and barks of a nearby jackal, at which Malkop was excited to fever pitch. This jackal, for it had to be only one, had followed us here from the desert. We'd heard it many times. It was his girlfriend, Marana joked, as he jumped up at the door to be let out.

'If they do mounting, they must be married,' Pengilly said sagely, making us laugh until our bellies ached.

'How can you trust it?' she asked.

'The lady jackal?'

'No, your compass, *liefje*,' she said, 'I'd rather trust my senses.'

'Let us use both,' I said.

She nodded and shook her head at the same time. Marana was not easy to convince.

Taking our meagre supplies of food and six large calabashes of stream water, we set out on our journey early next morning.

We came to interminable gradients and descents, and though it was hot, it was as nothing compared to what we had endured in the shelter-less desert.

We found many streams to replenish our water, wash and refresh ourselves. Malkop, always the comedian, amused us by baring his teeth and barking at his reflection in still pools. We headed northwest, which, by my reckoning, was the direction of the Himba village. Marana seemed content with that. When we tired we found shade under trees, and rested.

On the third day, two hours after daybreak, we came to a place Marana recognised. There was a rounded hill ahead, flanked by two smaller, pointed ones.

'Their village is on the other side of the big hill,' she announced. Malkop tore ahead like he understood. He had inherited the supernatural navigational instinct of his jackal father. Why, I wondered, had I bothered with the compass.

The Namas remembered us, and began by lamenting their lack of fresh meat. They recalled the oribi I killed, and the feast which followed.

For people who mainly lived on vegetables, they were uncommonly fond of meat.

The screw on the hammer of my *Jaeger* rifle had loosened from the lock, and I had tightened it three times with the edge of a knife.

But the thread was worn, and it wouldn't serve much longer.

For now, I made do. I took the *Jaeger* and, accompanied by Pengilly, three young Nama boys and Malkop, set off to find a deer.

Halfway between the big round hill and the small one on the left side, about a mile from the village, we heard Malkop, who had gone off at a tangent, barking furiously.

There came the sound of hooves galloping on stony ground, then, from behind a copse of tall acacia trees barely twenty yards away, trailing dust and snorting, burst a fine Kudu bull with huge spiral horns. He saw me and veered right as I lifted rifle to my shoulder. I squeezed the trigger, and the Jaeger recoiled and belched fire.

The charging Kudu stumbled as if tripped, and fell heavily to the ground, his legs galloping in the air. My bullet had gone through his heart. We'd been hunting but a half hour, and had already gained our prize. With Malkop, my good eyesight and the *Jaeger*, we were formidable.

The kudu was three or four times as big as the oribi, and the ensuing feast and celebration exceeded the previous one by the same magnitude. The Namas declared they had never seen so much meat at one time.

They gave us grass baskets of sweet African potatoes, manioc plants and dried beans to eat and plant, more than we could possibly carry.

Twelve young chickens, only one a rooster, were brought in two impossibly small cages of woven twigs. Six young men would help us take the largesse home.

In the evening of the third day, we arrived back in our own valley. Our Nama porters rested for the night and departed in the morning.

Now was when I chose to tell Marana and Pengilly the bad news. The dismay and fear it brought to their eyes was pitiful.

Twenty-nine

'*Tu:I,*' I said to Chiko, 'I don't know what's going on!' He was pensive, quiet. He hadn't forgiven me for cutting him off. He was sitting cross-legged on the ground under the acacia tree, whittling a piece of wood. I sat on a big root beside him.

'I dreamed again, Kai,' he said without looking up, 'and I know you are also troubled by the spirits.'

'Me, Chiko?'

'I know, *Kai*, because there is a spirit whose name you know.' A pulse beat uncomfortably in my neck, and my mouth was dry. I hadn't told Chiko my dreams, lest it drive his superstitious mind to distraction.

'His name is Tátaba, the Butterfly.'

'How..?'

'I have seen your dreams!'

'You…?'

'I saw the star stones in the valley of deep sand. I heard the storytellers by the fire. I saw the ≠*keten* painted by Xsara and the hyena which struck such fear in you. I saw Igni and his woman Mãr!ãnna, she of the /*hũ* father and San mother. Indeed, I even saw their son Pengilly.'

Chiko knew my unworldly dreams. He couldn't possibly, but he did.

'You, like me, Kai, are troubled.'

'I am, Chiko, we're both going mad.'

'There is a way.'

'A Way?'

'There is a way to communicate with the spirits.' Communicate? Hadn't there been enough? I wanted no more communication.

'How?'

'It would be well not to waste words, for there are important matters.' His dark eyes bored into mine. In spite of the heat, a cold shiver travelled the length of my spine.

'The living spirit of Tátaba,' he said, 'says the star-stones will be the salvation of my people.' His eyes glinted. 'He prophesizes that an even more precious and healing treasure awaits you.' My mind reeled. Tátaba said the star stones would save his people. What could be *more* precious?

'I had another dream. Tátaba's spirit revealed a *!gɛitɘn* is coming to us.' San-Bushman for spirit-traveller, shaman or witchdoctor. 'He will bring a medicine, and you, *Kai*, only you, must drink it.' What, drink a Shaman's concoction? I opened my mouth, then shut it.

A flight of imagination, sorcery, barking madness. Yin-yang, positive-negative. On one hand, on the other hand, on the third hand…

'Why do I need this medicine Chiko, how will it help?'

'Tátaba revealed it will achieve a purpose. You will discover what you seek, in the mind of Ignatius or Igni.' The mind of Ignatius? Would the old man speak in another dream?

'*Kai*, the ancestors visit us through the /*num*.'

'If it's true they have come to us, why is it *me* who must drink the medicine?' By asking, I realized I'd accepted a *!gɛitɘn* was coming.

'The /*num* decides, not I.'

'If I drink it?'

'Mysteries will be made clear, *Kai*. You will be guided to the truth.'

I was being posed with an out-of-the-world decision, about something without a vocabulary.

What were the alternatives? There *was* no third hand, only yes or no, accept or refuse. A binary choice.

'Can I think about it, Chiko?'

'Don't think too long, *Kai*.'

I walked back to the house. It was surreal.

Three long days passed, and I saw little of Angelika.

Was a Bushman *!gɛitɔn* really going to walk out of the desert? Three times I asked Chiko when he was coming, and three times he shrugged.

'I will tell you when I know,' was all he said. Yet if the *!gɛitɔn* came with a potion, what was I going to do? Refuse it. It would only be a plant-based drug, hallucinogenic no doubt. It was ridiculous. I didn't want a drug-induced 'trip', and it might drive me off my head. Yet maybe I'd take it because of Chiko - he'd never allow me to come to harm. Could it really reveal something about Ignatius? Taking magic potions from witch doctors in the modern day!

From the garden and the kloof, I watched the horizon. Nothing moved, except a languid steenbok grazing on clumps of dry grass, a troop of baboons scouting for mischief, and a female cheetah with her best days behind her. I watched two hawks suspended on high thermals, and one, lower than the other, seemed to study me back.

The sun dimmed, and I thought it was a cloud. I looked up, but there were no clouds. I briefly glanced at the sun, and was blinded by its glare. I looked away, but even as I did the light grew dimmer. Then I remembered. Today was the twenty-seventh of February.

The solar eclipse was due from five in the afternoon until seven.

I glanced at my watch. It was a quarter past five.

I stole a quick look and saw a scooped-out shape on one side of the sun. The moon's transit had begun.

The light dimmed further, and looking at my watch I realised I'd been standing in growing darkness for twenty minutes.

'It is the sign!' Chiko whispered. The moon reached the middle of the sun, and a dazzling ring of light surrounded its dark shape. It sailed serenely on. In what seemed a few minutes, it travelled right across, leaving another round dent, then unmasking the sun back to its full glory and mastery of the sky.

'Perhaps, Chiko.' He was staring at me.

Angelika was sitting on the front step.

'Watch the eclipse?' she asked.

'Quick look, didn't have protective glasses. You?'

'No, I didn't either.' We weren't in the mood for chatter.

At three in the afternoon of the fourth day, someone approached. The air hummed with expectation. It was from the southeast. I went to the house for binoculars. When I got back Chiko was standing on a boulder, staring at the arid hills.

'He comes!' he whispered, 'as the sign foretold'. I focussed my binoculars and scanned the horizon. Nothing. Not even dust. Just unrelenting heat rippling the light over broken ground. I glanced at Chiko.

'He comes, Kai,' he said more loudly.

'Sure?'

'Sure as I am here.'

There *was* something out there. One of the hawks came back.

It was circling and descending two hundred yards away. Lower and lower it swooped, until it vanished behind a thornbush-covered sandy hillock, a miniature of the great dunes of the Skeleton Coast.

There was other-worldliness, unreality in the scene. It was somewhere between wakefulness and sleep, with fantasy and reality out of focus.

It was as if Chiko spoke from a distance.

'The !gɛitɘn is near!'

From behind the dune where the bird disappeared, emerged the strangest being. He was the embodiment of a desert-prophet. Golden-brown, deeply wrinkled, grey of hair, small and stooped, wearing no more than a rawhide moochi. He slowly advanced towards us. How did he get there? The hillock wasn't big, and I could see over it to the plain beyond. Except for the hawk, there was nothing there a minute ago.

He drew close, leaving no footsteps in the sand, and, though the sun cast our shadows on the ground, there was none where he walked.

Chiko clapped his hands.

'You were expected great one,' he proclaimed in sonorous, click-ridden San, 'we saw your sign in the sky before your tallness walked upon the ground.'

I was speechless, staring at the footstep-less, shadow-less little man, who, though his body was skeletal and stooped, had dark penetrating eyes.

The !gɛitɘn squatted on the ground and placed the upside-down shell of a small tortoise before him.

'I have been here before,' he said in San. With a start, I understood, like in my dreams. Staring at the old man, I knew with a jolt I'd seen him before. He was the image of Tátaba in my dream.

'I left my sign outside and within your home.'

My heart leapt. The hyena-prints, the open book!

He looked up at Chiko and addressed him in a thin, reedy voice, as from another place and time. It sounded like a monk's incantation, with clicks.

He made signs with emaciated arms and hands. There was a hint of a smile playing on Chiko's face, if only at the corners of his mouth.

'For the ages the San have roamed the territories between oceans west and east, from where the land ends on a flat mountain gazing over the southern sea, to where the anger and roar rises up from the plunging water of *Tokaleya Tonga*, the Smoke That Thunders.'

All the land between Table Mountain and Victoria Falls. He stared into my eyes and saw the effect of his words. I was overcome with superstitious dread. A wry smile played on the ancient face, and the old man spoke English with a Cornish accent.

'It be not easy to be tryed an transport'd far from home, to go wher you 'ave niver bin, t' suff'r sadness, an' ne'er agayn cast eye 'pon yourn 'ome countrie.'

The monologue stopped. The speaking was done, the effect achieved. He advanced and placed a cold, bony hand on my head. There was a flash like a strobe-light, and understanding flooded me. The spirits of the ancestors and Ignatius were watching. They had invoked *Gao:na* the creator to guide me.

He had medicine, to 'open channels to the spirits'. It would enable travel upon the invisible string of the sacred kudu to other times and places. There I would find answers.

At last, the old man ceased talking and placed the tortoise shell in my hand.

It was four inches long, three wide and two deep, with a surface pattern of brown and grey squares.

What had been beneath, where the tortoise once lived, was on top, ground to fit a dark wooden lid.

I opened it. Inside was a yellow-green liquid with a bitter-almond scent. I looked up. The old man was nowhere to be seen.

When Angelika said I was here to seek Ignatius, though I knew it, everything became clear. It was my driving purpose. Was this my chance? The strange vessel came to my lips as if on its own, and I tasted almonds, vinegar, mustard. Next, I'd swallowed it. I may have just taken a lethal dose of cyanide or foul poison from a desert beetle.

'We must return to the desert,' Chiko said, 'there is no other way!' Rising on a thermal current in the southeast was a solitary black hawk.

I returned to the house in a daze. I didn't *feel* poisoned, though how would I know? All I could do was wait. Either that or try to puke. No point. If I shouldn't have taken it, I shouldn't have taken it. The deed was done.

I was sleepy, and lay on my bed. I felt guilty for eluding Angelika, but I hadn't been in a state to share my turmoil. Or tell her I'd turned to paganism.

I picked up Curnow's book. It didn't open where I'd left my bookmark, but further on, at a new chapter on page 345. It was headed '*Cornish prisoners transported to Plymouth to meet first convict fleet to New South Wales, 15th May 1787*'. I hadn't got to this yet.

A minute ago, I was about to fall asleep. Now I was wide awake. Was this the effect of the potion? Was it the /*num* which opened the book at this place?

I'd seen the old man arrive from nowhere, walk without shadow or footsteps.

There's a rational scientific reason for a solar eclipse, but not for seeing a hawk turn into a *!gɛit9n*. I went back to Curnow's book and read.

Thirty

I had to go back to !Anis, alone. I was down to my last two ounces of black powder, the lead shot was almost used up, and my tobacco was finished. Without a working rifle, we couldn't live, not only because we needed meat, but protection in this wild place.

Had it only been munitions, I could have gone only as far as Okahandja, where the Namas had guns they'd traded from the Hu. If I could avoid capture and return to the Cape in chains, I could get my needs from them. Going there would require a wide detour to avoid the area of Otjandjomboimwe, where the Hereros called me *omuroi* and tried to murder me.

There would be risk enough between *omuroi*-hunting Herero and gun-trading, treacherous Hu.

But the hammer and lock on my trusty *Jaeger* rifle were coming apart, and there was only one person who could get it repaired. Sterkbooi was that one, and he was in !Anis. There was also another pressing matter. We'd run out of rag paper for my notes and Marana's drawings.

'Let us go together, *liefje*,' Marana pleaded.

'My love, it took two months to walk from !Anis to the Otjihipa. On my own, I can go faster, and more directly.' I showed her the pages showing the random directions we had travelled. 'If I'm alone, I can use my compass to cut out deviations. I can make shortcuts by going straight, and reach !Anis in less than a fortnight.' Marana shook her head.

'You'd trust your life to *that?*' she asked.

'Among my people, they make the difference between life and death on the ocean.'

She decided to take another tack.

'But if we are with you, you can still use it,' she said, 'and we will be safer together.'

'Pengilly is not yet eight years old, and cannot keep pace. He will slow us, and I do not, in any case, wish to risk your lives for no reason. You will be safer here, with Malkop to protect you. You and Pengilly can do things while I'm away. There's a chicken-run to build, manioc, sweet potatoes and beans to plant.'

The argument continued for hours. Marana was tearful one minute, angry the next, but I was unwavering in my determination. I had to go alone.

'Don't you care what could happen to *us* while you're gone?'

'Of *course* I care, but I'd worry more if you came with me!'

'What about Pengilly and me worrying about *you?*'

'I'm sorry, but it's the only thing to do.'

We'd made many devious turns on our journey to the Otjihipa. On a separate piece of paper, I plotted a direct course to Otjinjangwe, and thence to Opuwo. If there were impassable obstacles, I would go around them. Likewise, I would plot my course to Otjikondo, Otjiwarongo, Otjandjomboimwe or Otja, which I would skirt to avoid the omuroi-hunting Herero, and thence I would bypass Okahandja and AiGams before reaching !Anis.

'I have enough powder and shot to get meat on the way.'

'And what will you drink?'

'I will take as much water as I can carry,' I said, 'you have shown me which dry-looking sticks show where tubers lie beneath, which can be shaved and squeezed for water.'

She shrugged. It was an argument she could not win.

The die was cast, and there was no point delaying. I went out once more to hunt. Marana had learnt to cure and dry meat from the Basters at the Khamiesberg. There was just enough salt left for the purpose, and it was something else I'd get in !Anis.

I shot a wild boar on the hillside and carried it home. I would leave the butchering to Marana. It would keep her busy after I left. I wasn't ready for the flood of tears when I bid Marana and Pengilly farewell.

'Look after your mother,' I told Pengilly. He was wearing the new trousers and rough shirt Marana made from bright green cloth traded from the Namas. Mine, thankfully, were muted brown.

'I will,' he said, with tears streaming down his cheeks. Malkop, sitting next to him, issued a low growl. For once he wasn't grinning.

I copied the example of the San and didn't look back as I climbed the wooded slope behind our wild estate. Slung on one shoulder was my *Jaeger* rifle. On the other were two homemade deerskin containers, with more water than I could take in calabashes. On my back was a hide package of cooked sweet potato and manioc. It would only last two days, then I'd have to shoot, or find mongongo nuts and *tsamma* melons.

Malkop was more inclined to follow me than stay with Marana and Pengilly. I had to order him to go back from halfway up the hill. With his tail between his legs and head hung low, he reluctantly conceded, stopping every few yards to look over his shoulder with reproving eyes.

He didn't want to abandon me. Poor Malkop thought I was going hunting, and was hurt that I didn't want his help.

It had taken five days from Otjinjangwe to the Otjihipa Mountains fourteen months ago, but the course we'd taken, recorded in my lines, was anything but direct. It seemed the Himbas were guided by their souls, rather than planning a route. I asked them why they changed direction so often, and was told they cared more about the journey than the destination.

At last, I could draw a line, work out its direction, and follow it with my compass. In only two days, I recognised a footpath leading down to a stream. Otjinjange was nearby. I drank deeply and poured out the water I had not used. I refilled the deerskins, ate a *tsamma* melon and my last sweet potato, then struck out for Opuwo.

Next day, walking along a dry river bed, I spied three oribis. How they survived there, I did not know, but the nearest one met his fate from a well-aimed shot at two hundred yards. I butchered the carcass, used some precious powder to kindle a fire, and burnt ancient dried out wood from the river bed. Over this, I smoked and cooked the meat in the fashion of the San. I was careful not to eat too much, for you cannot walk far on a full stomach. I packed the rest of the meat in my food-hide and continued on my way until nightfall.

The distance from Otjinjangwe to Opuwo, on the northerly route north we'd taken with the Namas, was a hundred and fifty miles. My direct path reduced it greatly, and, calculating I covered twenty miles in a day, it was a mere eighty miles.

I soon recognised the surroundings of Opuwo.

It truly *is* the end of the world. I camped in a rare patch of thornbush and grass, and, for seven hours, slept the sleep of the exhausted.

I awoke in a state of blind terror.

Thirty-one

Angelika screamed. I woke with a start, jumped up and ran to her bedroom. She was sitting against the headboard, white and shaking.

'What is it?' I shouted, grasping her by the shoulders.

'Oh God, I saw a man being eaten by a vulture!'

'What?' I started. 'Tell me about it.'

'It was circling over the desert. It was huge, black with yellow eyes…'

I went cold. There was a passage in an another old book about the San:

'…the vulture commands deep respect and reverence. His soaring height and pinpoint vision make him the ultimate seer of creation. But that is not all, for he is clairvoyant and can foretell the future. He knows who death stalks. He comes early to the table, to devour not only the body but also the soul. The San cannot join the ancestors if they are eaten by vultures. That is why they must be buried.'

'…and a big curved beak, so ugly…' She shuddered. 'It walked up to the corpse and ripped off an ear!'

'Horrible.'

'Terrible things happened out there,' she whispered, 'and now….'

'Please stay!'

'Okay.' I sat down on her bed.

'Thank you.'

'Tell me about your nightmare.'

'It was so real, not like any other dream!' Her eyes were wide. 'He started high in the sky, then swooped down. It was the desert, hot, sunny, sand dunes.' She shook her head.

'He landed next to a gulley filled with rock and sand, and stared at me with his horrid yellow eyes.' She shuddered. 'He was huge. He turned as if he knew I saw him, and came towards me with that horrible walk. Halfway, he stopped beside something on the ground. It was a dead person, rotting like Uncle....' Her voice faltered. 'He grabbed one of the corpse's ears in his beak, braced his feet on the head, and tore it off!'

'Horrible.'

'You want me to stay?'

'Please!' I glanced at her. She only wore a thin cotton shift, like that night in the desert.

'Look, I don't mean...'

'Of course, you don't.'

'I won't attack you!' We burst out laughing. Why is sex, or the risk of it, always present between a man and woman? With a sigh, I switched off the light and lay down. The minutes slipped by. At length, her breathing told she was asleep.

I hadn't told her about the ǃgɛitǝn or recklessly drinking his potion. I hadn't even told her about my recent dreams or the hyena prints in the garden, on the kitchen table and my bedroom windowsill. Nor about Curnow's book eerily open at the chapter about Cornish transportees meeting the convict fleet in 1787.

I woke to find Angelika's outstretched arm on my chest. Who the hell is Phil, I asked myself, looking at her sleeping face. The events of the night flooded back. We could have become lovers. Her hair was awry. She was breathing softly like a child. It would be a pity to wake her, though the sun was shining through the gap in the curtains. I moved her arm carefully, then rose and returned to my room.

I thought hard as I lay on my bed.

I'd never have predicted I'd feel this way, but I couldn't get the image of her face out of my mind, the touch of her hand, the smell of her hair as I lay beside her, her arm around me when I awoke.

Suddenly I knew I had to tell her. I could no longer keep it all from her. My dreams about Ignatius and the ancestor-spirits, the *!gɛit9n*, the hyena prints in the house, the open book, the potion.

There was a choice. I could ask her to leave, and deal with my problems myself. Or I could confide in her, though I'd known her barely a fortnight.

I reached for Curnow's book. My need to know about Ignatius was ever more urgent. The potion, it was the potion!

I'd read about the sentencing on August first, 1876. Transportation. I turned over the page and read about the five-month voyage aboard the convict ship. The convoy's itinerary from *HMS Scarborough*'s log was supplied, with thanks to the National Museum of the Royal Navy, HM Naval Base Portsmouth.

Departed Portsmouth, May 13th, 1787.
Arrived Plymouth, May 15th, 1787.
Departed Plymouth, May 17th, 1787.
Arrived Tenerife, June 3rd, 1787.
Departed Tenerife, June 10th 1787.
Arrived Rio de Janeiro, August 7th, 1787.
Departed Rio de Janeiro, September 4th, 1787.
Arrived Table Bay, Cape Town, October 13th, 1787.
Departed Cape Town, November 12th, 1787.
Arrived Botany Bay, January 18th, 1788.

I read about a near escape from an armed Breton lugger, a great storm which broke the mizzen mast, repairs at Tenerife, the voyage to Rio, how they struck a course for the Cape, and the suffering and deaths among the prisoners.

It was on the evening of the thirteenth of October 1787, when the unhappy fleet arrived in Table Bay. Ignatius wrote that he escaped there. I'd dreamt about two men swimming ashore.

Ignatius' letter was dated September 1790, two and a half years after he sailed from Plymouth, and revealed he'd neither perished, nor gone to Botany Bay, but was alive in the great northern desert. After that single communication, he never contacted his family again.

I woke to the telephone ringing in the kitchen, but was too tired to answer it. I heard Angelika's muffled voice. I glanced at my watch. Nine thirty. I was still tired.

I woke again at midday, showered and dressed, and made myself some toast and a mug of coffee. I was sitting at the table when Angelika rushed in.

'I have something to tell you,' she said, sitting down. She looked distracted. Not still the nightmare, I hoped.

'What?'

'Oh, it *is* him, we were right.'

'Mencken?'

'Yes.'

'How do you know?'

'He rang.'

'This morning? I heard the phone about half past nine.'

'That was him. He got my letter.'

'He rang you?'

'Yes. Egon found out where he lives two years ago, and has been blackmailing him ever since, threatening to tell the police everything he knows.'

'You mean?

'Everything. About the diamonds Dad bought from Schneider, who was Mencken's friend, how Mencken drew that map, which proves the smudge was M for Mencken, which is incriminating in itself if it can be proved, and how Dad and Schneider died for their efforts. Everything. If the police knew all that, it wouldn't be difficult to prosecute.' She shook her head despondently.

'He must have made a lot of money over the years from his diamond dealing. They'd want to know where he got it. Once the squad's onto you, it's only a matter of time.'

'Yes, but he's had enough.'

'What you mean?'

'He's furious, wanted to know if I was in it with Egon.'

'Did he now?'

'Yes. I don't know if he believed I had no clue. He was sure I got his address from Egon.'

'Did you tell him how you got it?'

'Yes, but not sure he was convinced. He'd paid Egon over three hundred thousand US Dollars, and won't pay any more. He'd rather go down, and take Egon, and anybody else with him.'

'What proof has he got about Egon?'

'For a start, Mencken's no fool. He kept details of every payment he made, and even recorded Egon on a hidden recorder.' She sighed, then continued.

'He'd be arrested for Blackmail, to start with!'

'I see.'

'What would blackmailing an IDB dealer say about Egon, except he's in it himself?'

'You were right about him,' I said.

'But a blackmailer, all this time, and I never suspected…'

'Did he show he had money, spend a lot?'

'Not that I noticed.'

'He's very calculating, I'm afraid.'

'What should I do?' There were tears in her eyes.

'Not rush into anything, Egon's in Jo'burg, doesn't know what we know.'

'I don't dare think where he's gone or what he's doing!'

'What you mean?'

'I tried his cellphone, no answer, rang the shop and he isn't there.'

'Oh.'

'Only he knows,' Angelika said. 'I think he's gone to buy black-market diamonds in Botswana.' I bit my tongue. She didn't know I'd overheard their conversation about Botswana.

'Why there?'

'Corruption. If you have money, you can buy stolen diamonds!'

'But Egon….?'

'I hate to admit it, but he's been dealing in illegal diamonds for years. Him and Rodolf.' She opened her arms in admission. 'I didn't…' I nodded slowly. I believed her.

'Then, just a few weeks ago, I bumped into Egon in Gaborone. He hadn't said he was coming, and didn't explain. I'm sure he's got contacts there.'

'Well, at least Mencken's done a *mea culpa*, admits his part in all this. Isn't that taking a risk?'

'No, why would we tell on him, when we know what will happen to Egon, and us too?'

'It's almost too much, isn't it?' She nodded.

'You know I've had peculiar dreams?' I asked.

'Not surprised. In the desert, you moaned in your sleep.'

'There's things I should tell you.'

'Are there?'

As briefly as possible, I told her about my dreams. When I stopped speaking she was a long time silent.

'Mad?'

'No,' she said after a pause, 'I don't think you're mad.' She took my hand and squeezed. 'You are spiritually sensitive.'

'Me?'

'When we found the tent, I sensed something powerful – I never felt anything like it before. There *is* something in all this… look, remember when I spoke about parallel worlds?'

'You said that's what the San believe.'

'I think in your dreams you are seeing what is there, but others don't see.

'What are we going to do about you?'

We! If someone else said that, I'd run a mile.

What would she say when she heard about the *shaman's* potion? Would it be a step too far?

Angelika had connected my need to find Ignatius with the loss of my mother. It fanned the embers, and I abandoned caution with the potion.

Chiko's words echoed in my mind. 'You will discover what you seek, in the mind of Ignatius!' And the *!gɛitǝn* spoke Ignatius' words.

I was possessed when I drank the bitter liquid, then things became so much more intense. In one day, I'd read more about Ignatius than in the week before.

'Am I becoming a spirit-traveller?'

'Why else are you having the dreams?'

I had to go back into the desert. The Shaman spoke about the words of Ignatius. Then there was the prophecy of the star stones bringing salvation to the San. How was Ignatius connected?

Angelika watched me.

'There's more, isn't there?'

'Think so?'

'What is it?'

'You won't change your mind about my sanity?'

'Depends,' she laughed.

'Well,' I said, 'it's like this…'

I told her about the *!geit∂n* who came as a hawk, how he spoke of *//Gauwa* the destroyer-God and *Gao:na* the creator. How he knew the content of my dreams and quoted from Ignatius' letter. I described taking the potion, how not only Chiko, but *her* words influenced my action.

All the while, she listened, and when I faltered she encouraged me with a smile.

The diamonds in my dreams were there for a reason. They were meant to help the gatherer's people in wretched times.

They were connected to Ignatius. Chiko and my dreams, and the *!gεit∂n,* were part of a whole. It was something I'd have debunked only days ago.

'I have to go back!' I said.

As I half-expected, Angelika smiled. 'Kaokoland?' she asked.

'Yes.'

'Thought so! Your search for Ignatius pulled you out of depression. You can't give it up, or you might plunge back.'

'You're right.'

'I'm coming!' she said.

'*I* have to go,' I said, 'after all the strange things, my dreams, Chiko's, yours, the potion….'

'Me too, I'm coming with you!'

'Why?'

'I've never met anyone like you. You don't only connect with Ignatius, but with the San. I don't just mean Chiko. I study ancient people, but how can I reach the long-dead? There is no Western understanding. You have stumbled into something incredible.'

'So, you'll just take off with me, to God-knows-where?'

'I have to.'

'I don't even know where we'll go, the Kaokoland is huge.'

'I think you should trust your instincts, the *!gɛit9n*, your dreams, Ignatius himself, Chiko….'

'Just like that?'

'Heard of the universal unconscious?'

'Vaguely.'

'An unconsciousness beyond our own, an inherited link to the life of the ancestors. What they knew, their memories. Not very different to San beliefs.'

'You mean I have Ignatius' memories?'

'Why not?'

'So, you'll head off with a madman? Surely you think I'm round the bend?'

'There are things we don't understand. What you experienced is your reality, conscious or dreaming, nobody can say it isn't.'

'What about the bodies?'

'What difference if we tell the police later?'

'None, I suppose.'

'Okay, tell them later.'

'I agree.'

'Do you think,' Angelika said, 'the spirits and the !geitɔn will show you the way?'

'I hope so.'

'I've told you about me,' I said on impulse, 'but what about you, who is Phil?' She shifted in her seat.

'You know about my work —'

'Yes, but I still don't know who Phil is!' She grimaced and crossed her arms. 'Okay, I'll tell you.'

'Phil was my fiancée....' My heart lurched unpleasantly. 'He's a dentist in Jo'burg. Tall, handsome. We went out for three years, then I moved into his place in Randburg, at least when I wasn't in Gaborones, Windhoek or Capetown.'

I'd never felt such raw jealousy gnaw at my gut. I had no right to be jealous, but I couldn't help it. I groped for something to say.

'Must have been hard.'

'Yes, it was, 'I stayed there when I could, and he spent weekends with me. It was okay.'

'Happy couple,' I said, keeping my voice as calm as I could.

'We *were* happy, lived together over four years. I loved him.'

Loved! At least it was past-tense.

Yet the thought of her loving any stranger curdled my stomach. Her lip trembled and tears started from her eyes.

'What happened?'

'Ten months ago, I found out I was pregnant.' Ten months….? Where was the baby?

'I see,' was all I could say.

'I was mixed up. It wasn't planned. I decided not to tell him until I was certain, waited two months.' She sniffed and reached for a tissue.

'Then you told him….'

'I told him when he was in Windhoek.' She looked up, her eyes red.

'What did he say?'

'It's hard to describe!' Her mouth set in a grimace.

'He said it couldn't be his!'

'He didn't!'

'Yes, he did. I never saw him so furious. I must have been with someone else, I should go to the man who made me pregnant, he didn't want someone else's bastard!' She sobbed and rubbed her eyes on the back of her hand.

'Swine,' I said, relieved to vent my fury.

'He turned into a monster!'

'You poor —'

'I was never unfaithful!' Her voice broke and tears ran down her cheeks.

'What did you do?'

'What *was* there to do?'

'And the pregnancy?'

'After what he said, I took my car keys and ran out. I was crying, confused.'

'In shock.'

'I drove away out of town. I didn't care where. I never saw the lorry parked on the side of the road—'

'Oh no!'

'My tears and the sun blinded me, and I ran into the back of it!'

'Bloody hell! Were you injured?'

'Not so bad. Fractured humerus,' she said, stroking her arm, 'bruises, a gash on my leg, a black eye from the airbag….'

'Thank God!'

'That night in the hospital, I had a miscarriage!' There was nothing to say.

'It wasn't your fault,' I whispered, putting my arms around her.

'Oh, but it was! Not being jilted - that was Phil. But I killed my unborn baby!' She pulled away.

'Not on purpose….' I cut myself off. It was inane, meaningless.

'Later, I found out he was seeing another woman for over a year. The worst thing was Egon knew, and didn't tell me!'

'Hell,' I whispered, 'I don't know what to say.' Her brother was even worse than I thought.

'I promised myself I'd never trust Phil, Egon or any other man again,' she said, pulling away.

'Where's Phil now?'

'Jo'burg, with his girlfriend. I really don't know what I saw in him!'

'Do you still want to go back out there with me?' I asked, to change the subject.

'Try and stop me,' she sniffed.

Thirty-two

There was loud breathing and snuffling next to my head, and a dark shape moved against the pale light of dawn. I was never so quickly wide awake. The thing had an enormous head, and it was snuffling about. Suddenly I knew what it was. I lay, wrapped and pinioned in my hides, frozen with fear and unable to reach for the *Jaeger*, and not three feet away was a huge hyena.

With Marana's family in the desert, I had learnt about these creatures. They are both scavengers and fearsome hunters, and have been known to bite off the face of a sleeping man. I knew they hunted in packs. Where were the others? Was this my fate, my *kismet*, to be torn apart and devoured, here and now?

The shape moved towards my feet. There was silence, then louder snuffling and the sound of dragging. It had found the remains of my smoked oribi. If it would move away with it, just a few feet, it would give me the chance to grab my rifle. I slept with it loaded and primed.

The horizon lightened, and the hyena stood out better. He was huge, backing off with my meat in his fearsome jaws. I dared not breathe. He was six feet away, and stank of rotting meat and shite. I couldn't even turn my head.

He gorged on the meat. With my heart pounding in my ears, holding my breath, I twisted my left arm out from the skins and probed for the *Jaeger*. My fingers touched the cold steel of the lock. I closed them. Could I cock the rifle with my left hand? My thumb felt the curved hammer.

With a silent prayer, I pulled it back.

There was a loud click.

It did that since the screw wore loose.

The hyena stopped eating. His massive head turned my way. It is a second forever frozen in my memory.

The sun's first rays breached the horizon, and the menacing shape stood in clear silhouette. I had my hand on the stock, the wrong finger on the trigger. Would I have time to twist around, bring the rifle up? If I failed, it would be the last thing I did.

The devil-beast made my decision. I saw him clearly. His lip curled to reveal huge fangs, and he made a sound I hope to never hear again. I was used to the insane giggling of hyenas, but at a distance. This was a high-pitched scream, an alarm-call like no other. He crouched to leap.

It came up on its own. A *Jaeger* is a long and heavy rifle, and I could never raise and rotate it left-handed. As if by the strength of an invisible extra hand, it swung towards the hyena mid-leap. The retort mingled with an ungodly wail as the bullet thumped into his chest.

'Take that, you devil!' I yelled, rolling free of the hides. His huge jaws snapped as his head impacted the ground inches from me. I rose unsteadily to my feet.

The beast gurgled. His body convulsed, then he lay still. It was a heart-shot, and blood gushed from his wound.

Sunshine proclaimed the morning. It took a long time to gather my wits. I looked around, but there were no more hyenas. I reloaded the *Jaeger* and unsheathed my hunting knife, just in case.

From the San, I learnt that meat is meat, and every animal can be eaten. I had lost my fussiness in food. When I recovered, I butchered the hyena and smoke-cooked his flesh like I'd done with the oribi.

I had survived the jaws of death and replaced my pilfered larder.

From Otjikondo to Opuwo had taken us three weeks with the Namas, but my compass route cut the return journey to twelve days. I was relieved I'd brought big water skins, for, though the Nama's circuitous courses seemed wasteful, I cannot deny they know where to find water. The route I took was very dry.

Only once did I encounter a stream, and once a shallow, muddy pool among some rocks. Mostly, it was desert, with no vegetation, the scorching sun overhead, and the constant, unending need to walk.

I bypassed Otjikondo and camped beside some big boulders on the plain beyond. It took seven days to reach the area of Otjiwarongo, which I was careful to give a wide berth lest the gun-trading Hu seize me. I deviated even more to avoid Otjandjomboimwe, or Otja as I'd called it, not wishing to give the *omuroi*-hating Herero another chance to murder me.

When I reached the joining rivers at Okahandja, it was twenty days since I'd left my family in the Otjihipa mountains. In three days I reached AiGams, and was at last within striking distance of our old home at !Anis.

I was excited at the prospect of meeting the Basters again, especially Sterkbooi. After the hardship of travelling so far alone, I made an exception to my rule of bypassing settlements, and went down into the Nama village of AiGams. I was recognised by the Namas who had been so kind before. My food was finished, and the little water I had was stinking.

The hospitality of these simple-living people puts many to shame.

Not only was I made welcome, but the village chief, hearing I was headed for !Anis, instructed two young men to accompany me. Indeed, the chief said, it was opportune, for he wished to convey his desire for powder and shot to the tall gun dealer who dwelt there. Sterkbooi's market had expanded.

In three more days, I arrived at long last in !Anis, our home of five happy years. It had grown, with more huts and simple houses along the banks of the Oanab river. I was gleefully greeted by the Basters, especially three who had been with me on the flight across the river Gariep.

'Where is Sterkbooi,' I enquired.

'He will return from Walvis Bay tomorrow or next day, he is very busy with business.' The Namas were queuing up to buy his muskets, and using powder and lead in a way most prodigious, for it seemed they couldn't hit a barn door, if there was one, at three paces. They handled their new devices so poorly, too, that they were always breaking parts. So much so, that Sterkbooi had set up a repair-shop, and had acquired tools and spares.

For two days, I awaited his return impatiently. After my prodigious travels, it seemed only fair he would be here waiting for me!

When he arrived at noon on the third day, he came in fine style.

Thirty-three

'It is why the *!geitən* came,' Chiko said when I told him I had to go, 'it is the will of the */num*!'

'I know!'

At five next morning, I steered north for the second time in a fortnight. Angelika sat beside me, Chiko in the back, his fear of the engine-spirit dwarfed by anticipation. The spirits had spoken and could not to be denied. The presence of my *Walther* 9mm pistol in the glovebox comforted me. Driven by spirits, but a gun for safety!

We had between seven and eight hundred miles back to the Kaokoland, though exactly where in that vast territory we were headed only the */num* knew.

'What's wrong?'Angelika was staring at me.

I pointed at the Satnav. 'Much use that was once we left the main road,' I laughed, 'so it's spirits or nothing!' She rolled her eyes.

'Don't worry, I'll look after you.'

'Promise?' she said with a twinkle in her eye, causing my heart to leap.

The journey was uncomfortable, the heat worse than ever. From Karibib it was fifty miles to Omaruru on the tarmac C33. We reached it in an hour, and watched the sun rise over the eastern horizon as we bypassed the town on the way to Otjiwarongo.

After two hours skirting Omaruru, I turned left onto the C38 northwest towards Outjo, a Herero name meaning *Cone Shaped Hills*. Fifty miles later we passed through interspersed bushveld, savannah and woodland on the edge of the Ugab Valley. The milometer showed we'd covered two hundred and twelve miles in four and a half hours. It was ten thirty, and very hot.

We stopped on the roadside, ate Chiko's sandwiches and washed them down with tea brewed on a primus. An hour later, we struck out east-north-east on the C40 towards Kamanjab, a hundred and twenty miles away. It was over forty degrees Centigrade outside, the sun beating from a cloudless sky. Inside the Land Rover was a furnace. Too hot for conversation.

Package tourists come out in air-conditioned vehicles, stay in luxury accommodation at the Kamanjab or *Oppi Koppi* rest camp. In the middle of a desert, they enjoy the luxuries of modern city-dwellers. They briefly gaze at anything which moves or doesn't move, and take snapshots through the windows. The arid scrub, the rocky peaks and the limitless expanse of parched desert are, for them, just a fleeting view.

Angelika was dozing uncomfortably, Chiko snoring in the back. I struggled to concentrate on the road.

It was after three o'clock when we approached Kamanjab. We'd covered more than four hundred miles. There were still more than two hundred and fifty to go, of which a third was rough dirt to Marienfluss in north Kaokoland. In my dream, Tátaba had spoken to Marana, the slim white man's woman, of the Otjihipa Mountains.

The roadmap showed the mountains were thirty miles northwest of Marienfluss. I had a feeling it was a good place to be when the spirit-traveller or /*num* gave further instruction. I turned the Land Rover offroad, engaged four-wheel drive in low ratio, and headed for a small barren hill. There was a flat area at the base, ideal for camping. The rough ride woke Angelika and Chiko.

'Where are we?' she asked, stretching. Her hair hung damply, and her face was red.

'Twenty miles past Kamanjab, far enough for a day.'

I turned to Chiko. 'We have little to guide us,' I said, 'but in my dream Tátaba's visitors came from the Otjihipa. It can't be too far from where he lived.' Chiko nodded sagely. I pointed in the direction of Marienfluss, a Himba village close to the Mountains. 'I think we should go that way.'

'I'm out of my depth,' Angelika said 'you two are the ones who know.' I grimaced. Did we know or were we mad? *Folie à Deux* in French, madness of two. What about Chiko? Was this a case of *Folie à Troix?*

We started again at five in the morning, to beat the sunrise. The tarmac C35 ran west for half an hour before turning due north. In just over two hours we came to where the northern road ended in a sharp left turn west towards the Ovahimba village of Opuwo.

'The old Himba name for Opuwo was Otjihinamaparero,' I said. 'It means *They see the borehole and their water comes out.'*

'Yes Sir!' Angelika stifled a yawn. 'How do you remember such difficult names?'

An hour later, driving into blinding sunlight, we descended to the bottom of a decline, where a ramshackle town hunched among the most numerous and greenest trees we'd seen in many hours. The road bisected the dusty collection of concrete commercial buildings and traditional round Himba huts, then rose into the hills beyond.

On the sides, little groups of red-tinged, bare-breasted Himba women in short earth-coloured skirts and thick rope-like hair plaits sat making traditional ornaments and body-decorations.

'Why are they red?' Angelika asked as several Himba women jumped up to wave us down. Tourists meant money.

'It's *otjize* paste,' Chiko said, 'red ochre and animal fat. They think it's beautiful, and it protects their skin from sun and insects.'

'I see,' Angelika said, '*Ralph Lauren*, Himba style!'

'Each to his own,' I laughed, 'maybe you should give it a go.'

'Think I need it?' I didn't answer.

On the far side, both the tarmac and trees ended, and the road began to ascend into the hills. After a quarter of an hour, we pulled over.

From here the going would be slow, and parts gruelling. I rummaged in the travel pamphlets on the shelf and found what I was looking for, Driving Advice for Van Zyl's Pass. I glanced at it.

Rough debris track … extreme gradients…. only manageable downhill, east-west. Most attempts other direction failed… vehicles ruined all cases…not possible with trailer…. In Kaokoland…. rely only on yourself…travel in convoy. Take at least two vehicles. Reduce roof load… keep centre of gravity low… good offroad tyres with deep profiles… pressure upper range... Very important: Engage wheel hubs in front… stay in 4x4 mode. If equipped with diff locks, keep switched on. For steepest downhill passage stay in first low range gear…let vehicle crawl ahead slowly…. Foot off clutch! Stop in front of big holes, get out…. look how, where, to get through… fill holes with stones to avoid damage undercarriage… Pass only 10 kilometres long but can take 4 hours …

I'd call anyone who risked Van Zyl's pass without the backup of a second vehicle an idiot.

Even so, the old Landy was in great condition. There were two spare tyres and plenty of fuel. I'd done it up myself, could fix most things. We had lots of water.

And I'd driven in pretty rough places many times in Namibia.

Yet I was strangely anxious. Should I pray to God, I wondered, or would the */num* grant us passage?

'Tea,' Angelika said with a smile over my shoulder. I'd noticed her a moment ago, yet again reading over my shoulder.

'You're a spy,' I laughed, taking the steaming mug.

'Don't tell me we're going through that pass,' she said, 'sounds awful!'

'Let's talk about it.' I walked to where Chiko squatted on the ground. I unfolded the roadmap and crouched beside him. Angelika came too, but stood.

'Here,' I said, pointing at the thin yellow line representing the road, 'is where we are now. It will take at least four hours tomorrow to Etanga. From there to the Otjihipa mountains we have to use the pass.'

'We must go on, *Kai,*' Chiko said.

By twelve we passed through the tiny Himba settlement of Etanga, no more than a pinprick on that vast terrain of rock and sand. Conical thatched roofs topped little collections of round mud huts, surrounded by fences of thornbush and sticks. Even here, hand-made leather bags and trinkets hung on the roadside.

There was less vegetation. Here and there a strangled thornbush clung to life in a sandy place between boulders. A mile ahead was the entrance to the infamous pass.

I was shaken from my reverie when the juddering steering wheel suddenly jolted left. A hole, a boulder, I'd better check. We skidded on loose shale as I braked. No pothole, no rock.

Nothing. I studied the ground.

There wasn't any branch off the road, not even a track, but the ground descended gently into a narrow valley.

At the bottom were clumps of thornbush in the sand, but few rocks. What caused the wheel to twist in my hands?

The strip of low land receded to the west, to disappear behind two barren hills. This was the sort of trail Chiko and I took for rock-paintings. Before roads, they were the natural routes. A strange feeling overtook me. Was this the work of the spirits?

'I have a feeling we should go that way,' I said, pointing west.

'You have the /num, Kai,' Chiko replied. Angelika nodded uncertainly.

'I hope you know what you're doing.'

I turned off the road and down the slope. I sensed the ancients had come this way.

We ground our way over uneven stone and shale in low-ratio four-wheel drive, doing under ten miles an hour. I wrestled the wheel and Angelika and Chiko held onto the doorframes.

Four hours later we were exhausted by the teeth-jolting motion and soaring heat. The route became less and less passable, making us zigzag between rocks, gulleys and anthills. I pulled the Land Rover up beside a huge fissured boulder. It was after six o'clock, and my shoulders ached.

'Had enough for a day?'

'More than enough,' Angelika exhaled with a nod. Her face was streaked with dust, her shirt damp.

'Ver genoeg,' Chiko grunted. Far enough.

We pitched our tents, lit a fire and heated canned food.

Chiko ate with reluctance. It wouldn't be long, I knew, before he found other, Bushman, things to eat. He'd been quiet most of the trip.

The blood-red disc of the sun slid over the horizon, plunging the desert into darkness. Relief from the stifling heat wafted in on a cool, gentle breeze, breathing life back into our tired bodies. The only movement came from the dancing flames in the campfire.

A breathless silence surrounded us, then came the distant, high-pitched yelping of a jackal. Angelika moved closer.

'Jackals don't attack people in camps,' I said, 'they're more frightened of us than we of them.'

'That's good to hear.'

'They're not so bad. The San respect them for their cunning and kindness to each other.'

'Kindness?'

'They find Jackal skeletons with healed fractures. Unless others fed them, they'd have starved to death before the bones healed.'

'Isn't nature wonderful?'

'When it doesn't kill you!' She glanced at me curiously.

Thirty-four

He cut a dashing figure. He wore a fine square-cut beard, expensive clothes and a broad-rimmed hat with an ostrich feather on top. There had always been a strong resemblance between him and Ouder, his father, but now it was even more striking. Seeing him transported me back to the old days in the Khamiesberg.

Sterkbooi was mounted upon a bigger, nobler horse by far than the hacks we rode to this country. On either side, similarly bearded, dressed and mounted, was an assistant. All three had muskets on their backs. Sterkbooi's was still a Jaeger. Behind, drawn by four horses apiece, swayed two heavily loaded wagons.

He saw me from fifty yards and spurred his horse into a canter. As he pulled up, he leapt down and embraced me.

'Ignatius,' he cried, throwing his arms around me, 'I never thought to see you again!'

'I am here,' I replied, returning his embrace.

'How did you avoid capture, you scoundrel?' he laughed. 'Don't you know there's a price on your head?'

'Is there? I didn't know. I'm named, am I?'

'Yes, sorry to say. So am I, but I never gave them my real name.'

'How much?'

'A hundred pounds.'

'Goodness,' I said, 'they only offered two hundred for Dick Turpin!'

'Who's he?'

'Famous highwayman. The reward was offered in 1739, long time ago.'

'We're in good company, then, though I'm upset they only offered fifty pounds for Hansie Venter. You're a white man, while he's only a Baster, see?'

'Who's that?'

'Why, me! It's the name I gave when I was arrested in England.' He pulled away, chuckling, keeping his hands on my shoulders.

'You lied about your name?'

'Of *course*,' he laughed, 'why wouldn't I? But hey, good to see you, man! How are Marana and Pengilly? How's that *jakkals*, Malkop?'

His outriders dismounted, and one took his horse's reins. Sterkbooi steered me towards his house.

'They're all alive and well. Malkop wanted to come with me.' Sterkbooi laughed.

'That Jackal dog of yours is something else!'

'A great friend and helper,' I said. I'd tell him later how he diverted the lions from Pengilly.

'Can you believe It's been over ten years since we jumped ship?' he asked.

'Is it 1797 already?' It seemed like only two or three years.

'Yes, and so much has happened.'

'Here?'

'Yes, here, but also in the Cape and in Europe. Two years ago, the French army captured the Netherlands. It caused hell between the French and Dutche in the Cape. Then the English came and took over. Meantime, a French general called Bonaparte defeated the Austrian army in Italy, and took a hundred and fifty thousand prisoners. Then he marched on Vienna, and Austria sued for peace!' I stared at him in wonder. He should have been a history teacher.

'It's been a long time,' he laughed, clapping me on the shoulder, 'and we've got a lot to talk about.'

Just then we came to his front door. His house wasn't recognisable. It bore no resemblance to the building I'd last seen. That was a several-times expanded mud and thatch hut. It was gone, and in its place stood big house which, for a place like !Anis, was grand. It was built of stone and cement, with a fine tin roof.

We were welcomed at the front door by one of his two wives, who I remembered well. The third, he said, passed away in childbirth ten months after I left. Still, he had three healthy children and had recently replaced his deceased wife.

By the way Sterkbooi spoke, you'd think he was hard and heartless, but nothing could be further from the truth. He did it to hide his feelings, which would otherwise have overwhelmed him. I knew this from our travels, and the years we lived as neighbours. Sterkbooi didn't display emotions like sadness. I don't recall him displaying fear, either, at times of deadly peril. People like him are rare.

The children came running to meet their father. The new wife, a slim, shy Baster girl of nineteen or twenty, came forward shyly to greet us. She was heavily pregnant.

There was indeed a great deal to hear and tell. I told him of all the places we had been, and what we had done since we left !Anis, almost five years ago.

'Wandering the veld and desert with the San!' he exclaimed. 'I never thought it was in you.' He was delighted we'd finally found a place to call our own. 'A man has to settle somewhere.'

About himself, there was much to tell. As I knew, he supplied muskets and munitions to the Nama, from sources in Walvis Bay and the North Cape.

In the last three years, he had branched out into cured leather, sawn wooden planks, handsaws, hammers and nails, and food items like cornmeal and salt, which he bought at Walvis.

'I'm getting rich,' he chuckled, 'who'd have said?'

The African beer was brought, and we drank thirstily. I'd missed the sour, yeasty taste. We were very merry before the night was through.

!Anis had grown, and white men were frequently seen these days. You couldn't tell who may be a bounty hunter, or turn into one if the opportunity arose. The lure of easy money, too, could affect some Basters, many more of whom had come over the Gariep river from the Cape. It wasn't safe to bide there long.

I showed Sterkbooi the faulty lock on my *Jaeger* and was relieved that, among his spares, he had a new one.

'Happened to mine too,' he said, 'only fault in an otherwise perfect rifle. I'll give you two spare screws because the threads wear out.'

I spent a day looking around the old place. It was twice the size it used to be. Our old hut, now occupied by Sterkbooi's cousin and his family, had been extended, but remained a thatched mud hut. I thought of our happy times there and grieved that they had ended.

The next day I rode on one of Sterkbooi's new horses. He and his two assistants accompanied me as far as AiGams, on the first leg of my return to the Otjihipa. I described in detail how to find the valley where we'd built our new home.

'I shall visit you within a year,' he promised.

We parted reluctantly, and I watched the three men ride away, leading the horse I had ridden. In a leather pack on my back were powder and lead, the spare lock-screws, and a quantity of cotton-rag paper.

By now I was a skilled, if primitive, navigator. Keeping away from the bigger settlements and villages, I was guided by my compass and line-drawings, which, with notations and little drawings of noteworthy features, began to resemble a primitive map.

Our first journey to the Otjihipa mountains had taken over three months, and I had managed the return in twenty-five days. Now I made even better speed, for. I knew where to avoid obstacles and dead-ends.

After twenty-one days, I had bypassed Opuwo and Otjinjangwe, and in the dying rays of the sun stood at the top of the steep slope overlooking our valley. I had no sooner reached it than I heard Malkop's excited barking, and he bounded up the hill, tail swinging, ears awry, and toothy grin.

'Thank God you are safe!' Marana said as I embraced her. 'I was afraid you would never come back, *liefje.*'

My happiness was complete.

While I was away, they had done much, which they showed me with pride. A stout stockade of sticks and thornbushes ran around our hut. It would afford protection from marauding animals, and even now the chickens scratched about in the safety it afforded.

A vegetable garden had been planted in the rich soil, and irrigation channels cut from the stream. The manioc plants were growing well, and the sweet potatoes and beans had sent up fine leaves.

'Twice since you left,' Marana said, 'we went to the Himba village for food, and promised you'd pay them with meat when you came back.'

'You have made me a debtor,' I laughed. It was so good to be back with my dear woman and child. My life in this country was hard, yet I was blessed.

That evening we dined on boiled eggs and roasted manioc, and Marana gave me a calabash of beer she'd brewed herself. While not as good as that I'd had in !Anis, it was much improved from her previous efforts.

To sleep in the arms of the one you love is truly a blessing, and only when it happens no more do you truly realise it.

'Malkop has a family,' Marana said one day.

'Why?' I asked.

'Haven't you noticed? He carries off bones and bits of meat.'

'Where?'

'Into the bush. I think he's got a wife, like Pengilly said, maybe even puppies.'

'The devil!' I laughed.

Malkop was looking at me. His grin was wider than ever.

When we lay in bed that night, Marana snuggled close and held me very tight.

'Yesterday,' she whispered, not to wake Pengilly, 'I saw a black hawk.'

'They're all black, darling!'

'This one was blacker, *liefje*. It landed on the acacia tree by the stream.'

'Yes?'

'It's eyes were very bright, very yellow —'

'What's this about, my love?'

'It stared at me….'

'So?'

'If I ever die without telling you and Pengilly how much I love you —'

'Darling, you really must stop these awful thoughts,' I said, pulling her slender body to me. I kissed her on the mouth to stop her speaking.

Thirty-five

Disaster struck at noon. We were inching along a deep gorge which ascended to a wide escarpment. I steered the Land Rover out of a rut onto smoother ground. For the first time in two hours, I increased speed to twenty miles an hour, which, after the excruciating crawl, was a relief.

The surface was mainly sand, with half-buried boulders poking through in places. It wasn't difficult to steer here, and the ride was like satin compared to the gorge.

I was just congratulating myself when the vehicle lurched right with a loud grating noise and an ear-splitting bang. The Land Rover stopped dead, the front canted down to the right, the engine stalled and clicking metallically.

'What was *that?*' Angelika yelled, jolted out of her lethargy.

'Not good,' I breathed, switching off the ignition.

We listed at thirty degrees, the front axle buried in soft sand. I climbed out onto the slope. It was difficult walking at an angle, but I saw at once what had happened.

The wheel lay at forty-five degrees against a rock, like a dislocated, out-of-socket hip. The side shaft was broken, the steel shiny and jagged.

This wasn't something we could dig our way out of. I straightened my aching back.

Darn side shafts, the only weakness in a Land Rover! The rock I'd hit projected a foot above ground, but there was more under the sand.

Was this *meant* to happen, like the uninvited left lurch before the gorge?

Was the spirit-traveller or /*num* making us go where he chose? I'd driven without incident in places just as rough.

'Oh hell!' Angelika exclaimed. She'd come around from the other side, and was staring at the damage. 'How did it happen?'

'Side shaft's bust.'

'What we going to do?'

The Landy had hit lots of rocks before, harder, but the side shafts never broke.

'Why should the one thing happen which I can't fix?'

'It is the engine demon,' Chiko pronounced, peering at the wheel. 'It grumbled long, you should have heeded its suffering!' I laughed in spite of my rising panic. He put a different spin on things.

'Shit,' Angelika said, 'can you fix it?'

'No, we're stranded!' Angelika pulled out her *iPhone*. 'No signal.'

'Could have told you.'

'Oh God, it's what happened to Rodolf!' She had the same look after her vulture nightmare.

'Can we get out on foot….?'

'We're far off track.' I hesitated. Telling her what I thought would only make it worse. She stared at the desolation. Endless sand and rock shimmered and bent in the fierce sun.

'Read Charles Anderson, the early explorer?' she asked in a whisper.

'No.'

'He said the Namib was the worst place on earth. He preferred to die than be banished here.'

'We're not banished, just stranded.'

'No….' She bit her lip.

'We must start walking,' Chiko said, 'we cannot stay here!'

'We'd better get going,' I echoed.

'You mean ….?'

'We can't fix the wheel. If we head for Marienflus, we may just make it. Can't be more than thirty miles.'

'Are there people, water?'

'Himbas, a few Bushmen.'

We packed biscuits and water bottles in our satchels and put on our hats. Chiko tied a bottle round his waist. I took my Walther pistol and cartridges and the first aid bag, and slung the shotgun over my shoulder. I had the matches in my pocket.

Guided by the pocket compass and map, we set off to the northwest. It was the start of a nightmare.

Our position was extreme, and fear drove out all emotion. Without water, death comes quickly, and we couldn't carry a lot. I knew we'd never make it. Going back wasn't an option. We'd come too far. In my terror, I tried to reason. Maybe, just maybe, we'd find a water on the way. I clutched at that straw.

Walking was harder than Angelika imagined. There was no path, and obstacles lay in all directions. Where it was level, it was ankle deep in sand, which made every step a struggle, or sharp rocks tore at the soles of our shoes and twisted treacherously underfoot.

To make things worse, the terrain began to rise and fall like the sea, sometimes in a gradual slope, but steeper in other places. Here and there we skirted the high ground, shuffling through shoe-filling, energy-sapping sand. Sometimes we had to climb, for there was no way round. The sun was high in the west, and the heat sucked moisture and energy.

'I have to stop,' Angelika said at the top of a sandy slope. I was about to descend the other side but turned back.

'Five minutes. There's no shade, and we can't afford to cook in the sun.'

'I know,' she said, letting her legs fold under her. She wrestled the top off her water bottle and drank deeply.

'Careful, there's no more.'

'I need to pee!' She got up, half-walked and half-slid down the side of the dune. I turned the other way. A minute later, I heard her scream.

'Snake!' she yelled, struggling up the slope, holding her shorts up with one hand.

'What, where….?'

'It nearly bit me, just as I was getting up!'

I stared down the slope. There was a small patch of dark sand where she'd crouched, and near it lay a dried piece of *numa*-root.

'It's a dead plant,' I laughed, 'not a snake.' She pulled up the zip on her shorts and grimaced.

'Okay wise guy, it *could* have been a snake!'

Chiko went ahead, finding the best way. We followed, but Angelika, who, though young and fit, struggled to keep up. Every few minutes I waited for her to catch up.

That night Angelika and I huddled together against the sudden biting cold. It was strange, feeling her body against me. We were on a smooth sand-drift, more comfortable than shale and rock.

At first light, we breakfasted on two Marie biscuits and a mouthful of water, before checking the compass and setting off. We'd only been walking a day, and Angelika was limping from blisters on her feet.

We'd never make it unless we kept going.

We had covered maybe six miles since the disaster. At this rate, Marianflus would take forever. I let her limp on rather than force a stop. Chiko was making a brisk pace, opening a big gap.

By midday, Angelika was unable to go on. Her shoes had rubbed the skin off the top of her feet, and they were bleeding. I tore the sleeves from my shirt and bound them in strips. She winced as I helped her on with her boots.

Chiko's lead was growing. He was a hard pace-setter. After a half hour of watching Angelika struggle, I stopped.

'Let me carry you.'

'Oh no,' she shook her head vigorously, 'you can't!'

'No good punishing yourself until you're completely crippled. Then I'll have to carry you longer.' I dropped the shotgun on the sand. It was excess baggage, and I had the pistol.

She stopped walking and stared at me. I turned my back and bent, and she reluctantly climbed on. Chiko came and took our satchels.

'I'm sorry,' she whispered.

'It's my fault,' I replied, gasping. Carrying her was punishment for my foolishness. I prayed I wasn't taking her to her death. Sand and black rocky outcrops pointed needle-like at the pale sky which throbbed in the furnace of the sun.

Our water was down to three litres, the biscuits almost gone. We sat exhausted and thirsty at the top of yet another rise. Here the landscape was a dried-out sea, troughs of sand between rolling waves of black granite.

The sun slid down in the west, and a cool breeze eased our torture.

'I will find water,' Chiko said, shaking me out of a half-sleep. 'We cannot continue like this. I will return to guide you to it.' I looked at Angelika. She was rolled up like an infant.

'I go, *Kai*.'

'Take some water.'

'Keep it,' he said. 'May *Gao:na* protect you.' He pointed.

'Keep going that way, *Kai*, so I will know where to find you. You and your hyena-woman will not perish!' He grinned as he turned away. Following his instinct, he walked silently across the moonlit sands.

The first hint of dawn was tinting the eastern horizon. I was on my back on a thirty-degree slope. I shivered in the biting cold. Angelika murmured in her sleep.

When it was light enough to read, I unfolded the roadmap. Marienflus was marked by a dot fifty miles from the sea. Ten miles south was the Angolan border on the Kunene River. Its old Himba name was Otjinjange. Though I knew the meaning of many old place-names, I'd never deciphered that one.

Angelika stirred but didn't wake. Where was Chiko now, I wondered.

Thirty-six

Living with the San, we were used to rising before dawn to witness the birth of the sun, that great spectacle of nature. No wonder, when the great orb brought light and life to the desert, that, with the open sky as their roof, the San should thank the creator-god *Gao:na* for another day. That morning I noticed a pinkish hue in the east.

'Rain is coming,' I said.

'I feel it too.'

'Red sky in the morning, sailor take warning,' I said, pointing east.

'What's that?'

'Sailor's rhyme. Means bad weather.'

'Bad, rain is *bad?*'

'No, not here. Here it's only good,' I replied, putting my arms around her.

There was no cloud at daybreak, yet there was that brooding sense which comes before a storm. Soon clouds blew in from the west, great billowing, cotton-wool ones that we sailors call cumulus.

We employed ourselves digging, planting, harvesting, and collecting eggs from our Nama chickens. I'd repaid my debt to the villagers, and most of a smoked Thomson's gazelle hung in our hut. More cloud gathered as the day wore on, bringing a welcome respite from the heat.

At sunset, we lit the deer-fat tallow lamps I had fashioned from calabashes, as Marana called them, and waited for the downpour. For shedding water on our land, it was welcome indeed.

One learnt to appreciate the rain if only for the labour it saved in irrigation.

Indeed, our stream was running low and needed replenishment. We went to bed early.

It was a fierce tropical storm, preceded by rumbling from the west, then growing closer and louder. At first, there were distant flashes of lightning, briefly illuminating gaps in the deer-hide windows.

The lightning strike was a thing I hope to never see again. It was as shocking as it was unexpected. I don't know how much black powder, set off in a container, would make so loud a noise. Firing a ship's cannon next to your ear may compare.

We were shocked awake by the explosion, for that's what it was.

'What in the name of *Gao:na* was that?' Marana screamed, sitting up. In seconds, fierce orange flames engulfed our thatched roof, and choking black smoke poured down and filled the air. Malkop howled like a wild jackal, Marana whimpered, I yelped and Pengilly shrieked in terror.

I leapt out of bed, dragging Marana with me, and thrust her out the door.

Pengilly's bed was on the other side of the hut, cut off by falling bundles of fire. I ducked a big one, and found him paralysed with terror. Lifting him in my arms, I dashed across the smoke-filled inferno, and, seizing the Jaeger on the way, exited the hut. Malkop came close behind. We retreated from the searing heat. From sleeping in our beds, we were watching flames leaping high into the night sky.

I hadn't understood the power of lighting. If it caused a fire, I imagined it starting as a small one. Our roof was engulfed in seconds, and we had no ceiling between us and the flames.

Something was missing.

I couldn't place it until warm raindrops fell on my face.

That was it! The lightning came *before* the rain, not *with* it! Otherwise, the thatch would have been wet, and the fire wouldn't have spread so fast.

In only fifteen minutes our roof was consumed. The rain fell harder, and steam rose from the naked beams. Nobody was burnt. There was a great hissing as the fire was extinguished. Suddenly the rain stopped.

I groped my way inside. It stank of wet ash. Through our newly-opened roof, the stars appeared.

The rest of the night was most uncomfortable, for everything was sodden. Even in the worst disaster, one can be fortunate. Though the thatch was burnt off the roof, and the hut was inches deep in ash, the rain had prevented much more serious loss.

My most precious possession, the Jaeger, was safe, and the powder and lead were stored in an earthen pot buried in the floor. In our confused state, we didn't notice Malkop was missing.

When the sun rose, we surveyed the extent of the damage.

'Our bedding hides are covered with wet ash,' Marana lamented, 'and so is the Thomson's gazelle.' Indeed, the butchered animal hung like a wet grey rag on the wall. I looked around. Only the bedsteads, of stout poles, were undamaged.

While Marana and Pengilly cleaned up and washed the hides, I set to cutting new grass for the roof. We'd had a narrow escape.

I didn't know where to render up my thanks, to the Christian god, or to *Gao:na*, the great deity of the San, who they thank for all things good.

'When the lion strikes with blunt claws, it is *Gao:na* who has blunted them,' old Xi had said.

I was busy with the thatch when Pengilly, with Malkop prancing behind, came running down the slope with a pathetic bundle in his arms.

'Look what I found!' he shouted, 'it was lying in a clump of burnt grass.' It was an abandoned jackal puppy, newly born, with his fur singed off. Fortunately, his eyes weren't burnt, for they had not opened. He was making a pitiful mewing. What to do? Clearly, his mother had fled the fire. Was she Malkop's wife? Where were the rest of her litter?

While Pengilly went to search, Marana lay the pup on her lap and we contemplated what to do. Our minds were made up by an astonishing display from Malkop.

Standing on his hind legs, he began to lick the caked ash from the puppy's skin. He did it in long, gentle strokes, coating his tongue in grey, swallowing hard all the while.

'See, *liefje*?' Marana began, 'it's his baby, and he knows!'

After an hour, Pengilly came back in tears. He'd found two pups burnt to death by the grass-fire. To comfort him, but also for ourselves and Malkop, we decided to rear the waif. But how on earth were we going to feed him?

We needn't have worried. Standing just twenty yards away, staring forlornly at Malkop, was a fire-singed female jackal. Our family was growing.

It was at this time I set to using my notes to write my story. Marana cut more slivers of black lead and inserted them into hollow reeds from the stream.

They made excellent writing tools, every bit as good as pencils in Cornwall.

'Meeting you changed my life,' Marana said one day. We were harvesting green beans from the tall plants she'd led up the trellis fence I made with sticks.

'My life was changed too!'

'You and Pengilly are my world,' she said, looking up from the plants.

'I know, and I feel the same about you.'

'If I was dying,' she said softly, 'the last thing I'd say was how grateful I am for you and Pengilly.'

'Don't talk like that again!'

'But I must,' she said, 'you never know....'

'Darling,' I said, 'there is nothing to be gained by thinking these things!'

'*Liefje,* if ever I am unable to tell you, know that I love you with all my heart!'

'I know, my darling!'

Though we were content, we had to deal with many hardships and perils. I would have been grateful if those things, however hard, were all that would torment us.

Thirty-seven

I was flying, hurtling forward through space and backwards in time. There were galloping hooves above, and a pulling string around my waist. The earth loomed and rose in panorama. It was broken ground, and a life-and-death drama was playing out.

Clinging to the edge of a sandstone cliff, the *leguaan* stood immobile as a thing of stone. The only movement was the ripple of arterial pulse in his throat. Reptilian tail and clawed feet strained in immobility and indecision, his scaled head arched at forty-five degrees. Hooded eyes focused in the glaring light made vicious by a spiteful sun.

High on a morning wind wafting from the sea to the desert, there was also intelligence, a different, avian intelligence, for whom the morning light played another message. He was the seeker gifted with the freedom of flight, blessed with long black wings and eyes which could detect a mouse a mile away.

In a sudden blur, the *leguaan* shot along the sandstone cliff, missed his footing and plunged thirty foot onto a lower ledge. He regained his posture, a froth of blood blowing from his overheated nostrils, his hooded eyes scanning the sky for the circling danger. The odds had changed, his options diminished. He was detected. His leg was broken and there was no route from this ledge to flat ground.

I saw a man: Tátaba! His face was wizened and parchment brown, his dark eyes bright. When he moved, it was a fluid motion, as if he drifted across the sand. As the great black hawk turned in its descent, Tátaba closed the gap and was still.

A fallen vulture, a stranded *leguaan*. He would take his share after the hawk had eaten.

Black pupils were constricted against the morning glare, the yellow eyes half-covered by avian lids. The curved beak opened and closed. A shoulder muscle tightened, pulling one wing above the other, precipitating a swoop to the other side.

Tail feathers parted and fanned to create drag, the other wingtip lengthened to prevent spin. The speed of descent rose sharply, the whistling slipstream swept back the tiny feathers on the angular skull, and the hawk plunged towards the earth.

Tátaba stood motionless and waited.

Then I saw inside the cave, for time had passed. The aroma of roasting *leguaan* filled the air, and a fire near the entrance spat tongues of orange. Xsara turned the dripping reptile on its truss of thornbush branches.

Tátaba sat with his pretty stones. He had three in the palm of each hand, the dancing firelight reflected and exceeded in brightness in their glow. He smiled happily, and let the pebbles slip between his fingers into the clay pot. From the other pot, beside him, he withdrew the biggest one.

It sat in his palm. In the firelight, it glinted but did not play its blue-trick, that which it reserved only for the pure light of the sun. This was *tâa-qáe |kãũ*, the blue woman. I had seen it before.

'Hello,' Angelika said with a rueful smile.

'Hi. I wasn't sleeping.' Was it true? What was happening? Had the witchdoctor's potion transported me to a parallel world?

'You were in a trance.'

'I think I was.'

'It's the heat!'

The sun rose to become a searing-white ball as we continued our tired, painful trudge.

Rocky outcrops stood out black as coal from the yellow sand. The sand and rocks burnt through the soles of our shoes. Everywhere we looked wavered and shimmered in the blinding light.

Angelika stumbled along, eyes staring, mouth open to suck down dry air to aggravate her raging thirst. Our water was finished.

Her face was caked with dust. Her shirt was bedraggled and filthy, her shorts dirty and torn. Her hair hung loose, half covering the angry red skin of her face. She licked her cracked and swollen lips. She wouldn't last much longer. Thirst was driving us mad.

Would Chiko ever find us? Neither of us spoke. I knew Angelika's tongue, like mine, was dry as bark.

I found an outcrop of overhanging rock thirty feet high. Underneath was a three-foot patch of shade. I slumped down, exhausted, and Angelika collapsed beside me. She tried to speak, but only managed a croak. She slumped her head on her elbow and closed her eyes.

'What makes a desert great is somewhere there's a well,' I croaked.

'Who says?'

'Antoine de Saint-Exupéry, French author.'

'Who?'

'He wrote *Little Prince*.'

Angelika was exhausted. My thirst took over again. I imagined a big lake beside a snowy mountain. The gurgle of a brook. Splashing and laughing in the shallows. Drinking, drinking, drinking…

Vultures began circling. First, they were mere specks in the blinding sky.

Slowly, they spiralled closer, getting larger. One swooped lower than the others.

A Cape Vulture, buff body, naked black neck and head, scimitar-shaped beak.

He came to earth ten yards away and began an ungainly, ugly walk towards us. Two more prepared to land. Soon they'd form a 'wake', the ghastly term for a group of feeding vultures.

'It's the one in my nightmare!' Angelika gasped, twisting her head. I cocked my pistol.

'Let's see if your future-telling predicts this!' Cape Vultures look big with their plumage, but don't weigh more than twenty pounds. A nine-millimetre parabellum bullet is made for bigger things.

The crack of the *Walther* 9mm pierced the silence, and the undertaker-bird was hurled back in an explosion of blood and feathers. Two others which were landing flapped their huge wings in panic and rose back into the sky.

'What…?' Angelika croaked.

'Ever tried raw vulture?' I crawled over to it. Lying on its back, its wings were stretched out and its ugly head lay at an impossible angle. Blood spurted where the bullet had all-but severed its neck. I picked up the limp corpse in both hands. It was heavy, but I managed to knee-walk back to Angelika.

I never imagined vultures had so much blood. When you're as thirsty as we were, anything which runs is water. There was no choice. I didn't even think as I put my lips to the gaping wound. Warm, salty liquid gushed into my mouth and down my aching throat.

It was bliss.

I could have carried on drinking forever, but stopped myself.

'Drink!' I said with blood spattering from my lips and running down my chin, 'drink Angelika!'

I didn't need to tell her twice. Thirst like ours changes the squeamiest of people. She put her mouth on the gash and her Adam's apple bobbed as she swallowed.

We took turns drinking, streaking our faces red. I don't know how much blood a vulture has, but it was a lot. When it stopped running, I cut off pieces of feathered meat with my penknife. Hunger drove out distaste. The living, gnawing pains in our stomachs begged for relief.

Holding a bleeding chunk by the feathery side, I bit off a piece. It was chewy, it had a strong, wild taste, but it was wonderful. Angelika thrust a piece into her mouth. I never saw another person so famished.

'Funny,' I said, 'vulture thought he had us, but we eat him!'

'And drink him,' she managed to rasp.

With vulture blood, and stringy raw flesh filling our stomachs, we slept.

Thirty-eight

'Can we call the puppy Ash, and his mother Smokey?' Pengilly asked, cradling the pup. He was twelve years old, almost as tall as me, strong and mahogany-brown. He reminded me again of Robinson Crusoe.

Keeping a distance of just six yards, I could have sworn the bedraggled mother nodded her head. Marana squeezed my hand. It was her way of telling me she agreed.

'Why not?' I said. In a few weeks, their fur grew back. Soon, Ash turned into a beautiful young hound with big, haunting eyes. I say hound, because there was much of Malkop in him, making him only three-quarters Jackal. Smokey was slow to come close, but lured with bits of meat came a little nearer each day. Malkop assumed the strutting air of a contented family man.

Now began a time in our lives which, for many years, would be peaceful and happy. I have already reflected there is little to describe when peril and danger do not overwhelm. We planted and harvested, and hatched more chickens. I hunted, we extended our hut, and I built a lean-to for shade. Above all, our love, forged in the fire of our flight from the Cape, was mature, and our faith in one another was complete. Never has a man had a better companion and wife than I.

To Marana's delight, her family came by on their travels every year, bringing news and invitations to visit from Tátaba and Xsara. Six times, we journeyed to the valley of deep soft sands, where we enjoyed their joyful companionship.

Smokey never fully made the transition to family pet.

There was a distance her jackal instincts forced her to keep, and she never came nearer than ten yards. At that range she was comfortable, and no amount of coaxing could change it. I think the trauma of the fire had another effect, for though Malkop's amour for her never waned, she had no more puppies.

Ash grew into a fine specimen, very much in the mould of his father, in character as well as appearance. Malkop became first a mature, then an elderly gentleman. Though he still helped in the hunt for several years, he began to teach his son. One day he came hunting no more, and Ash assumed the role.

One day, when Malkop was fifteen years old and growing infirm, he lay beside us in the shade of the awning. Marana was cooking a rabbit on the fire. Suddenly, an ear-piercing jackal howl broke the silence.

'It's Smokey,' Marana shouted. I looked around, but she wasn't where she usually was. Now she stood fifty yards away, hackles raised, howling pitifully. Pengilly ran towards her, but she backed away, still howling, into a thicket. That's when he saw the mamba. It was six feet long, he said, dark brown in colour. Before he could react, it slithered into the undergrowth. Pengilly pursued Smokey, but she fled away.

With poor old Malkop following on stiff joints, we tracked her between the trees and rocks. She led us down the length of the valley, up the right-hand slope, down again, and up the other side. For nearly an hour, we tried to reach her. Only Malkop could get near. Finally, in a patch of dry grass, we found her lying. There was froth around her mouth, her tongue swollen and blue.

'She's dead,' Pengilly cried, lifting her limp body in his strong arms.

We carried her back reverently, and, with much sadness and tears, buried her beside our hut.

Malkop never recovered from his grief. Let nobody say animals don't know the meaning of love or grieve as we do at its loss! Though we tried our best to encourage him, he would not eat, and barely lapped water. It was a matter of only days before we buried him, with great sadness, beside the strange jackal wife he loved so dearly.

'Goodbye, and thank you, loyal old friend,' was all I could say by his graveside. I remembered the first time I saw him, that little bundle of frightened, big-eyed fur hiding under Marana's skirt. His personality and the sense of humour he undeniably possessed. His courage facing the lions that day, giving Pengilly time to escape. His love and loyalty to his wild wife and son, and the heartbreak which killed him so soon after she died.

What would they, who wanted to drown the little waif in the Khamiesberg, say now? I am haunted by the friendly ghost of that extraordinary creature-friend, and comforted by him in my dreams. From a continent alien to me and a different species, half wild though he was, he had become a faithful ally in all I did. A world which can make one such as he cannot be all bad.

'I love you Malkop,' Pengilly whispered, his voice breaking as he placed a bunch of wild hibiscus flowers on the grave.

'We all do,' Marana said, weeping uncontrollably. The lump in my throat prevented me from talking.

Ash became our only hound that day.For being Malkop's son, and so much like his father, he was already deeply loved. Poor hound lost both parents so close together, but we invested all our love for them in him.

We were never blessed with another child.

Suddenly, almost overnight, it seemed, Marana and I were no longer young. Pengilly had grown up and was a young man of over twenty. He became a crack shot with the *Jaeger* rifle, and a better hunter than I ever was. Ash found and drove the quarry towards him, and he unerringly brought it down with a single shot. Both Malkop and I had been replaced.

More years slipped by, sometimes with nothing to mark their passage, but Pengilly filling out, with more muscle and a thick black beard, and Marana and I beginning to feel our age. Unlike me, she retained her slim, youthful appearance.

One day, her wandering San family came again, with the sad news that Xi, whose age nobody knew, and who was expected to live forever, had died, and his eldest son, Xau, was the new leader. We mourned Xi, for he was a fine and kindly man.

During the visit, Pengilly became enchanted with a young girl called N!ai, pronounced with a loud click, and his feelings were reciprocated.

'He loves her,' Marana said, and I knew she was not wrong. Pengilly was over thirty by this time, and N!ai, though her birthdate was uncertain, about sixteen. The San do not mind differences in age, and her parents were delighted with the match, since, through Marana's mother, Pengilly was related to them. Two days later, we held a celebration, and the spirits were invoked to bring blessings on the couple.

When Marana's people departed, our family had grown to include Pengilly's young wife N!ai. The next day they began to dig foundations for their own hut, I set about making mud bricks, and Marana went to gather sticks and grass for the roof.

Looking back, this was a time of happiness.

We had the love of each other, a home, a strong, loyal son with a sweet young wife, and faithful, loveable Ash. We were safe from persecution and had no lack of food or comfort.

In the year 1816, nineteen years after my visit to !Anis, Sterkbooi came at last to the Otjihipa. Had he not informed me, I would no longer have known which year it was. With him were his two old assistants, known to us long ago as young men in the Khamiesberg. They had never undertaken such a journey on foot before, but could not bring horses so far north.

'Now I know how hard it was for you!' Sterkbooi said. It was a joyful reunion. He had news of grandchildren and an ever-expanding business. He had a real shop now, selling all manner of food and goods, as well as muskets and munitions, right in the middle of !Anis, which had grown to double the size since my visit.

Sterkbooi had news, old and new, of the Cape and Europe.

In 1803, the English had handed the Colony back to the Dutche under the 'Treaty of Amiens', whatever that was, then they re-occupied it in 1806, after beating the Dutche in the 'Battle of Blauberg'. In 1814, the Dutche formally ceded sovereignty to the British under the Convention of London.

While all this happened to the Cape, far away in Europe, in October 1805 the Royal Navy under Admiral Horatio Nelson had dealt a crushing defeat on a combined French and Spanish fleet off a place called Trafalgar on the southeastern coast of Spain.

It put an end, Sterkbooi said, to the French leader, Napoleon Bonaparte's, plan to invade England.

Such momentous events, and I didn't hear of them until so long after!

It was an ever-changing world, but my horizon had shrunk. I was glad that whoever ruled the Cape no longer concerned us.

He brought a roll of flower-patterned cotton cloth for Marana, more paper, powder and lead for me, and a wonderful gift for Pengilly, whose excitement could not be contained. It was in a leather rifle-bag.

It was the third model of the British *Baker* rifle, Sterkbooi said, based on the German *Jaeger*, but with many improvements. It had a long stock of beautifully carved English walnut, and an abundance of shiny brass fittings, including butt plate, escutcheon, side plate, and trigger guard. A sling was attached with iron fittings.

Sterkbooi pointed out the rifle's special features. The butt-waist was in the form of a pistol grip. The lock was of the same design as the Brown Bess, with the same swan's neck cock, and it was stamped with the word *TOWER* and a crown with the letters *GR* underneath. There was a flat lock plate, a raised pan cover, and a strong safety bolt. The barrel was thirty inches long, being only two and a half feet, and there was a folding backsight. The rifle fired a .653 carbine bullet, with a greased patch to grip the rifling in the barrel.

'Is it accurate?' I asked, 'with only a thirty-inch barrel?'

'Accurate?' Sterkbooi scoffed. 'You know there's been a war between England and the French in Spain?'

'How would I know?' I replied. He laughed.

'No, don't expect you keep up,' he said. 'Well, there has, and the English like to brag, don't they?'

287

'Do they?'

'They do. Hey, don't get upset, thought you were Cornish, or so you said many times!'

'So, what are they bragging about?' I asked.

'This rifle. The English officers tell their soldiers how lucky they are to be issued with the Baker, because it's so accurate. They don't mind if the servants hear, they talk, and that's why we know about their bragging.

'Come on, Sterkbooi, out with it,' I said, exasperated, *what* are they're saying? What do they say about the *Baker* rifle?'

'They say in a battle in 1809, at a place called Cacabella or Cacabelos, or something like that, in Spain, an English rifleman called Plunker or Plunket shot a French general called Colbert, or something, dead from six hundred yards, then shot his *aide-de-camp*!'

'Six hundred yards?' Surely it wasn't possible!

'Six hundred.'

'How do you remember all that?'

'Heard it ten times,' he laughed. 'Everyone wants one now.'

'I'm not surprised,' I replied. With that kind of accuracy, this gun could change your fortune.

'I suppose you also don't know about the Battle of Waterloo in 1815?' he asked, grinning. Of course, I didn't. How could I? Waterloo, he explained, was in the southern Netherlands.

'Last year?' I asked. So many battles, so many strange names, I couldn't keep up with him.

'They used these rifles and won the battle. The French emperor Napoleon Bonaparte has been sent into exile on St Helena.' An island in the middle of the Atlantic.

Peder Pengilly, our one-eyed Cornish guardian angel on *HMS Scarborough*, told me we sailed south of it between Rio de Janeiro and the Cape.

This beautiful piece was only manufactured a year ago, Sterkbooi said, and was stolen from a drunken soldier in Capetown. How far was the reach of my criminal friend?

Sterkbooi spent hours teaching Pengilly to shoot with his new gun. The valley resounded with gunfire, which echoed and echoed again from the hills and cliffs. We never saw our boy so thrilled.

After three days of feasting, drinking Marana's home-made beer and recuperating, Sterkbooi and his friends departed on their long return journey. Once again, it was with great sadness I watched them go.

N!ai and Pengilly had a baby girl, who they named Mara Hama, after Marana and her mother, and a year later a son, Ignatius Xi, after me and the late chief N!ai. We were a happy family. I cannot say the time was brief, yet it seems so looking back. If only it had lasted longer!

* * *

From 'Untold Mysteries of The San' by Sven Johannsen, 1790: *'Never mourn too long,' the San say. 'Life is but a circular path between this world and that of the spirits. Birth brings you here, death takes you back, and you are either here or there. What is wrong with that? Celebrate, it is wonder!'*

I take up my pencil in the withered hands of an old man, and in sadness.

I have not written in over twenty years, though my counting may be in error. Looking through my old pages, it strikes me I wrote too much about transient, immaterial matters, and not enough about the most important one, which is love. I lament I failed to appreciate it sufficiently.

The greatest sadness of my life, far worse even than the misfortune which took me from Cornwall to this so foreign land, befell me. It was that tragedy which caused me not to write so long, but now I feel compelled to record this before it is too late. It was several years after Sterkbooi's visit, when the heavens foretold the tragedy which was to strike us.

We were sitting outside, enjoying the cool breeze. Late that afternoon, clouds gathered and brought welcome relief after the heat of the day.

Now they parted, and the high sky was lit by a bright, furry ball of light with a long, wispy tail, tinged blue, purple and gold. The stars were outshone by its brightness.

It seemed to hang there without moving. Something similar was said to have appeared in the English sky before the Battle of Hastings. Many took it as an omen that the English would be defeated.

Over the next weeks, we saw it every day as it continued its blazing journey across the sky.

'It is an ill omen,' Marana said fearfully. I could not assuage her misgivings. The day came when we saw it no more. But it seems her fears were not misplaced.

She sickened. At first, it was only a cough, but it worsened over the days to become racking and painful. Living so far from people and crowded places, we were not used to contagions. At night, she developed shivers and sweats, like those I only saw in consumptives in Cornwall.

Though we did our best encouraging her to eat, she rapidly lost weight.

Though it broke my heart, I sensed there would be no happy outcome.

One morning, waking from a troubled, cough-wracked sleep, Marana whispered to me to bring Pengilly and N!ai, and sit close beside her, for she had something to say. She was so thin and childlike, but her dark eyes betrayed her suffering.

We gathered in misery around her, for we all could see the sign of approaching death.

'I am dying, my loves,' she whispered between bouts of pain-wracked coughing. Pengilly moved to protest, but I held his arm and he remained silent. She smiled sadly at him.

'Do not resist the will of Gao:na, my son,' she said, 'it will not change the future, which must be without me.'

Marana had ever clung to the San religion her mother taught her, about which she also learnt much from Xsara and Tátaba.

'No Mama, you cannot —' Pengilly burst out, tears streaming down his cheeks into his thick beard.

'Stop my son,' I said, 'your mother is weak, and wishes to talk.' He controlled himself with an effort. N!ai, also weeping, took his hand. At least he had her to comfort him, for which I was deeply grateful.

I looked down on the sweet face of Marana.

'I want to say…,' she began, then a fit of coughing overtook her, and bright blood shot from her mouth and nose. In just a few seconds, her head fell back, and my beautiful darling wife, Pengilly's loving mother, had left us and gone to the world of her San spirits.

She went so suddenly, without even the chance to tell us what she wanted to say. We had no time to tell her how much we loved her, or say goodbye. It came back to me then that she'd more than once spoken of leaving without being able to tell me she loved me.

We were stunned and directionless. We sat beside her a long time, without any words.

Hours passed, but my memory of them is obscure. All I know is I fell asleep holding her.

The love of my life was gone. I didn't think she'd ever die, as she had been never sick in all the years we were together. But she lay dead and cold in my arms in the morning. I cannot describe how Pengilly and I were taken by the blow upon us.

Next day we stood by her grave. In the heat of this land, the dead must be quickly removed from the living, for corruption of the body comes soon.

She had thought about death because a black hawk watched her with yellow eyes. Her words haunted me. *Liefje,* if ever I am unable to tell you, know I love you with all my heart!'

'What we going to do, Papa?' I turned to Pengilly. He was standing with N!ai, whose eyes were as swollen as his.

'I don't know, my darling,' was all I could say.

Harsh it was, but there was no choice but to live on, without the warmth and comfort of the best human being I had been blessed to know.

As if we were not sufficiently blighted already, a further disaster happened when hyenas ransacked the hut and made much destruction. Some of my records, I believe some twenty written sheets, which encompassed much of my life with Marana, were also lost.

After Marana died I had nothing left to interest me, though I loved Pengilly, N!ai, and little Mara Hama and Ignatius Xi dearly. I lived in my dreams, where a laughing, young Marana cavorted with grinning Malkop, and Pengilly, a baby again, chortled in delight. Awake, I carried on as best I could.

In truth, I was never so bereft, not even when I sat cramped in the holding cell as Bodmin Assizes, or huddled with three others on a horsehair mattress in the putrid hold of *Scarborough*.

The years flew by. Malkop's beloved son Ash died of old age and was replaced by first one, then another scraggy hound from our Nama neighbours. None grew so close as Ash or his father Malkop, the finest hound and animal friend I ever knew.

Though my life has not been easy, there are things for which I am deeply grateful. At the top of the list are Marana and Pengilly, but poor old Malkop holds a special place.

I was feeling my age. I decided I'd bide my last years with my old friend Tátaba in the valley. Marana and I had visited him and Xsara once each year, and sometimes stayed a month. He had lost his beloved Xsara, and was lonely like me. Pengilly accompanied me, and it took six days.

Tátaba was delighted to see us, and said the spirits foretold I'd be his last companion. Pengilly stayed three days, then went back to the homestead and N!ai.

Now sat Tátaba and I, and talked of lost love and days gone by. We comforted each other. He cursed the evil hyenas which stole my writing, saying they were *≠ketens* of great importance, though I secretly wondered if anyone, let alone a future relative, would ever read my work.

'For their safety, Brother Igni,' Tátaba said to me one day, 'I will show you where to hide your remaining *≠ketens* close to the star stones.'

Thirty-nine

I awoke with a tongue like sandpaper. Angelika was sleeping beside me. She looked near the end. Her lips were thick and red, her breathing laboured.

'Wake up, we must go on!' She opened her bloodshot eyes.

'Tobias,' she rasped.

'Yes?'

'If what I said is true that life and death merge into each other....'

'Yes?'

'I'm merging!' There was a gallows-grin on her face as she struggled to her feet. Her shorts were ragged and her legs burnt angry pink. The sun hung low in the west, casting long shadows over the plains. It was cooler, but our thirst and despair knew no respite. Angelika tried to keep up, limping on a badly swollen foot.

She walked in a trance, arms limp, a mechanical doll with little wind left. For a tortuous mile we pushed on, but when darkness fell we could go no further.

'I haven't had a wee the whole day!' Nor had I. We were dehydrated, and unless we got water soon, our kidneys would fail and we'd die.

'Sleep.' My mind was too dull for conversation. 'Chiko will come for us.'

When I opened my eyes, it was morning. An almost naked figure stood watching us. I was too stiff to move. Even being murdered was better than dying of thirst, I mused dully.

'*Kai!*'

'Chiko, you found us!'

Was it another hallucination, sent to torture me?

'Did you think I would forget the day you saved me, *Kai?*

I struggled to sit up. The glare from the rising sun made it difficult to focus.

'If not for you, I would not be here to save you,' he said, gaining solidity.

'Angelika,' I croaked, 'wake up, Chiko is here!'

'Whaaat…?' she mumbled, half asleep, 'are there more vultures—'

'Chiko's back!' I shook her by the shoulder. She opened her eyes. For a long moment, she grimaced in the glare. Then she saw him.

'Thank God!' she said in a dry, reedy voice.

It took a long time to re-orientate. We drank the water Chiko brought in his five-litre bottle. But water alone couldn't revive us. We lay down in the shade of a boulder.

We slept the whole day, waking several times to drink. I stirred as evening approached.

'How did you find us?'

'I watched the black birds of death, and they led me here. I feared I was too late.' He spat in the sand.

I got up, stretched my stiff limbs, and helped Angelika to stand. 'Can you walk?'

'Yes,' she said, biting her swollen lip. Was there any cream for her lip in the first aid box, I wondered. Where was it? I looked around. I must have dropped it, and the satnav, when I threw away the shotgun. I wouldn't tell her.

'I found water that way,' Chiko said, breaking into my thoughts and pointing.

'In the valley of yellow sands between the high country my people called Kxuuma, and the plains.'

I remembered the name from my dream.

'I walked two days, and Tátaba showed me the way. He guided me to a deep valley —'

'You found water?' Chiko grimaced and continued.

'He said I was of his tribe. I would find his star-stones and share them with our people. After he guided me to the valley, I saw a baboon, and used an old trick to catch him —'

'Rag in the hole?'

'I found a hole in a rock and put it in. Then I waited.'

'I know how you do it, Chiko.'

'When he held the cloth,' he continued unphased, 'his fist was too big to get out. I caught him and tied his legs with the cord from my waist, so he could only take small steps. He tried to run away, but kept tripping. After two hours, he got thirsty, and I followed him to a hill with a cave.'

'You found water?' Angelika croaked.

'A pool fed by a spring.'

'Take us,' Angelika rasped, take us there!'

'I will, but there is more than water. It is Tátaba's cave, I found his skeleton!'

'Is it far?' Angelika asked.

'No matter, we have no choice,' I said. I turned to Chiko.

'Let's go!'

The water bottle was half empty. Chiko led the way. The remains of his shorts resembled the *moochi* of ancient Bushmen. The stick in his hand was tipped with a bone arrowhead. Where did he get it?

Chiko walked with an easy stride, amazing for a man in his sixties. It was difficult to keep up.

At midnight the moon hung like a golden balloon, huge, round, yellow.

We wound our way slowly between outcrops of rock, keeping to the sandy patches between. There was no shadow, for the light came from overhead.

I watched Chiko's effortless stride, heard Angelika groan when she stumbled, and watched the moon swing away from the centre of the dark sky. We rested, cold and shivering, on the sand.

We walked and limped for two days. As morning approached on the third day, the moon lay low in the sky and the sun began to light the horizon. The oven was switching on again. The temperature soared. Soon we'd bake between stinging sky and smouldering earth.

In dazzling sunlight, black dragon-backs of rock pierced the yellow sand with sinister menace, daring us to climb their jagged peaks. We were insects trapped in a bottle. Everything faded from consciousness except sore bleeding feet and the old enemy thirst. Terrible, desperate thirst.

We turned into automatons. We could only watch our feet plough up sand and stones. It was hypnotic, detached. Thirst drove out all other sensation.

Suddenly Chiko's cry broke into our murky senses.

'*Kai*,' Chiko yelled, 'we are here!'

'Where?' Angelika asked dully.

I shaded my aching eyes. 'Here?'

'The cave, *Kai*, the cave I found with the baboon.'

'Oh, the baboon!' I gouged grit from my swollen eyes.

'Oh please,' Angelika moaned, 'if there's water, let's get it.' Her filthy shirt was torn and missing several buttons.

'Show us the water Chiko,' I croaked.

'In there, *Kai*,' he pointed at a stone wall at the base of a low cliff.

On one side was a gap where the piled-up stones had fallen on the ground.

The entrance to the cave was low and narrow. I pushed Angelika ahead, and she entered on all fours. I followed. Inside, we looked around, baffled. Though there was little light, we could see it was huge.

Chiko pointed left. There was a shimmer. We plunged deliriously down to the pool like half-crazed beasts. It was shallow and we fell on our knees and buried our faces in the water. It was rock-cool, wet and beautiful. We gulped and swallowed and choked.

Angelika lay down by the pool, the last of her energy spent. After a long time, she peeled off her clothes and washed. Seeing each other naked was as natural as drinking. At another time, in other circumstances, I'd gawk at a naked girl, be embarrassed at my own nakedness.

We attended to ourselves like preening cats. We were filthy, dust-and-sweat streaked, itchy and hot. We refreshed our bodies with handfuls of wonderful, cool water, splashed and submerged our faces.

When we were satisfied, we rinsed our filthy clothes. This was laundry, stone-age style. She read my thoughts.

'With your beard, you look like a caveman. Are you going to club me and drag me off by the hair?' Then we were laughing. There was a hysterical ring to it.

There was so much familiar here.

The rock formation, the big boulders in the sand, the cave. Suddenly I remembered the dream where I saw Ignatius. He was sitting on the boulder to the left of this very cave mouth, singing an old Cornish lullaby!

'What do you want?' I asked Chiko. 'Can't it wait?' I looked where he pointed.

He was holding a fire torch of dry numa roots in his other hand. I caught my breath. I approached the cave wall and gasped in wonder.

A beautiful painting in many colours covered it. San hunters pursuing animals, one a huge kudu. There was that grace and movement, a depiction of vigorous, robust and lusty life.

I'd seen this painting before. It was the work of Xsara. It was here, right here, I'd seen old Tátaba lovingly pouring star-stones from one hand into the other. Were they still here, in this cave, the diamonds in my dreams?

'I found the bones of Tátaba,' Chiko announced with a faraway look in his dark eyes, 'and buried him!'

'What?' I'd forgotten he mentioned a skeleton.

'It *was* Tátaba!' I couldn't doubt anymore. I'd also seen the old man, right here.

'Where did you bury him?'

'I cannot say. His grave must remain unknown.'

We put our clothes out to dry. I stared at her naked body without guilt, and she didn't avoid looking at me. It was innocent and child-like. When the chips were down modesty and bashfulness were luxuries we couldn't afford. Her recovery amazed me.

'If only I had a needle and cotton!'

'What for?'

'To mend my shorts.'

'I like them that way, your bum poking out.'

'So do the insects, but thanks for the backside compliment.'

Chiko looked amused.

These strange people, he seemed to think, are saved by my water and talk about her garments while they walk around naked. His manhood is still, like a sleeping snake, and she does not offer him her berry of delight.

All this I read in his twinkling eyes before he turned and walked away.

I glanced at the naked girl beside me. How often did people of the opposite sex, who were not intimate, sit together naked on the floor? She noticed my stare and coloured despite her sunburn.

'Tobias,' she said softly, putting her hand on my arm. I turned, but she averted her gaze by looking down.

'Yes?' I whispered.

'Nothing.'

'I love you,' I whispered.

'I know.'

She didn't move as my fingers gently touched her face. She leaned towards me with her eyes closed. Our kiss was long and tender, before she pulled away.

'I haven't been with anyone since Phillip.'

'I'm sorry, didn't mean to —'

'It's okay,' she whispered, taking my hand.

I awoke to find her lying on her side. Was this the beginning of something wonderful, or an embrace of the doomed? Something was missing. Even in the heat of our passion, she didn't say she loved me.

Next day we demolished more of the stone wall, and opened up the cave mouth. I stood rooted to the spot. It was exactly what I'd seen in my dreams.

If that was so, were Tátaba's diamonds somewhere in the cave? I went inside and walked around the walls.

The cave was huge, and there were many faults and narrow recesses cloaked in inky darkness. I used my hands, prodding into narrow crevices and irregularities, but there was nothing.

At the far end, a natural fault split one side of the cave into two narrow tunnels. One was wide enough to walk in to, but closed off after only three or four yards. The other was too narrow.

'There's no diamonds,' I told Angelika. 'It was just dreams.'

'No, there aren't,' she replied, 'I checked too.'

Later, sitting just inside the cave, I had an extraordinary experience. It was as if I saw, yet didn't. An awareness which was physically impossible, yet perceived.

The black mamba awoke from his midday sleep. He sensed an unfamiliar presence. Adrenalin poured into his bloodstream, preparing his muscular body for danger. The pupils of his hooded eyes dilated, drawing in the little light from the darkness. His slit-like reptilian mouth opened and closed, while his long forked tongue darted in and out. From the tip of his tail to his head he was at least seven-foot long.

His head was coffin-shaped, the inside of his mouth black as coal. His scaly back was brown, his belly dirty white. Without moving his head, he uncoiled his long body. He was deaf, but sensed vibrations. Something was moving, coming closer.

The sacs at the base of his tongue were filled with poison ready to squirt into the bloodstream of a foe. A small drop would paralyse the muscles of the throat, eyes and respiration. Only death would end the agony.

He lifted his head.

Sinuous muscles rippled with suppressed energy. If it came any closer, he would strike.

I was powerless to utter a word or warn of the danger. A voice was talking to me, but there was nobody there. It was Tátaba.

'Will the serpent not to strike,' he said in San. I was paralysed and couldn't move. I closed my eyes.

'Don't strike,' I whispered, 'don't strike!'

Angelika swept the floor with a handful of thornbushes. It was backbreaking work. But if we had to have a hard bed, at least it could be free of stones. She swept the pebbles into a corner, then straightened up.

Her foot came within six inches of the mamba's head. He stayed still like a thing of stone. She stood a moment, checking the floor in the half-darkness. Then she threw the thornbush into the corner and walked to the cave mouth where Chiko and I were. She seemed to wonder why I looked haunted.

The mamba sensed the widening range. The muscles of his back relaxed. Still, he held his head motionless and waited. After several minutes, he slithered across the swept floor into a narrow cleft on the other side.

Angelika sat beside me.

'So, what's up?' She had no idea she'd just avoided being bitten by the most poisonous of snakes.

'Nothing.' If she knew there were mambas, how close she'd been to one, she'd refuse to stay another minute. And how could I explain sensing the snake but not warning her?

'You're thinner,' I said.

'Crawly and slithery-thing diet.' They're not the only slithery things, I brooded.

Chiko was out on a lizard, or anything-which-moves, hunt. Angelika sat beside me.

'Are we going to get out of this?' she asked, putting her head on my shoulder.

'I hope so.'

In movies, women and men tossed together in dangerous places usually make passionate love, I thought, as if lovemaking would lessen their peril.

Angelika and I were lovers, but it didn't alter our predicament. Except make it worse, for now the thought of her dying was unbearable.

Just then Chiko came back.

'Have you brought something to eat?' Angelika asked.

'What's that?' I asked. Though Chiko had become more serious with me, he was always ready with witty answers for her. I wasn't surprised when he spoke in expletive San, with many loud clicks.

'He said I talk too much, and called me snake-tits!' Angelika laughed. 'What a cheek, snake-tits indeed!' She looked down at her breasts, which I reflected were perfect.

Chiko giggled delightedly. It was a relief to see this side of him again.

'Admit it's a good insult,' I laughed.

'I'll get even,' she said, then, changing the subject, 'the cave gets cold at night.'

'I'll get our clothes, they should be dry. Or do you want to carry on looking like an ape with snake tits?'

'Go and get…'

'Lost?'

'We are already,' she sighed, suddenly serious, 'and I'm hungry.' I fetched our clothes.

'My shorts have shrunk!'

'All the better.' Before she could answer, Chiko returned.

'I will cook these agamas, *Kai*.' Three purple and red six-inch lizards hung from his hand. Angelika shuddered.

Chiko dropped the agamas. Twirling a pointed stick furiously against another, he made a glow appear. He refused to use matches. Blowing hard on crushed bat droppings, he caused a thin tendril of smoke to appear, then a tiny flame. He added more droppings and dry numa roots.

Angelika tried not to look at the roasting reptile. She was so hungry, but a lizard?

'At least he didn't poison them,' she sighed, 'but they look disgusting.'

'No poison,' I agreed, biting through the crispy skin of a leg.

'How does it taste?' Her expression was between revulsion and hunger.

'Lovely,' I said. Chiko held out a steaming half-agama on a stick. She was too hungry to refuse. She chewed reluctantly but soon changed. Though it was stringy and tasted like rotten fowl, it was food. She closed her eyes when Chiko gleefully chomped on an eye.

I had another dream that night. It began like a replay.

'I am Tátaba, gatherer of the stone-ice, stars of the sands, the //*kweisa-!kau*. You know me well.'

I saw dark eyes fixed on me with strange intent. 'In your heart, which the /num reveals, you seek that which is more important than stones.'

'I do?' I heard myself ask as from a distance.

'It is the /hũ, the white man Ignatius, he who we named //Ignï-tsãũ or brother Igni, it is he whom you seek.'

It was true. I'd always known, but now I was sure.

Ignatius had filled my waking thoughts since I first heard about him.

'The /num has shown you much, and you have travelled with the spirits, but the word of Igni himself is at hand.' Like a candle blowing out, he faded away.

Forty

'We have to get help,' I said. Angelika, wearing only her ragged shorts, lay on her back on a flat rock. The early morning sun warmed her after the long cold hours of the night.

'I'm getting an all-over tan.'

'You are, but we need to get help.' I appreciated her being positive, but our situation was grim. How ironic, if my quest for Ignatius prevented my suicide in Cornwall, then killed us here!

'How are we going to do that?'

'I wish we had a radio transmitter, but even then, we don't have map coordinates.' Angelika turned on her side to face me. Her nose was peeling, but underneath she'd begun to tan.

'We don't even know where we are on a map, and I can't remember how we got here, let alone....' She sat up. 'It's hopeless, isn't it?' I didn't answer.

Chiko caught *leguaans* and bats, so we didn't starve. But it was no long-term diet. We'd been here five days, making it eight since we bust the Land Rover's side shaft. Good diet or no, we had regained some of our strength.

Chiko came up to me when I was alone.

'I must go back into the desert.'

'You are no longer young, it's not fair you should always be the one.'

'*Hau,*' he laughed, '*wie anders is daar?*' Who else is there? He was right. Old or not, he was a born tracker.

'If I stay, we die, all three of us. If I go, maybe I find help. The spirits will come to my aid, the /*num*, *Gao:na* the creator.' He stared into my eyes.

'Do you think anyone will come otherwise?'

'No.'

'Not so long ago,' said Chiko with a grin, 'you called me a meerkat. Well, they stand up on their back legs. If I climb a sand dune, with my great height I will see many miles!' I laughed. His great height!

Five minutes later, I couldn't find him. He wasn't in the cave, nor outside.

'Chiko's gone for help.'

'Won't he get lost? Tobias, are we going to die?'

'He won't,' I said, pulling her to me, 'he saved us before. There's plenty of water, and he left food.' I pointed at three dead *leguaans* and half a dozen bats piled beside the ashes of the fire. They were half-roasted, half-smoked, the best meat preservation in the San meat-preservation armoury.

'But, but… he'll die out there!'

I nodded. 'It's possible, but he has instincts to guide him.'

Angelika put her arms around my neck and kissed me on the lips. 'I didn't mean to get hysterical, Tobias.'

'You and me both,' I said, stroking her hair.

'I love you,' Angelika whispered in my ear.

'You love me?' She'd said it! I was afraid it was fear which made us lovers, that it would end if we were rescued. It was the pattern of my life – women, one way or another, always left me.

'I wouldn't tell you,' Angelika said, 'but if we're going to die I want you to know…' I hugged her and kissed her on the lips. They were warm and welcoming. I drew away after a moment.

'Isn't it our predicament? It can make you think all sorts of things. If we get out of here, you may feel different.'

'Oh, forget it,' Angelika spat, pulling away, 'it's just the predicament!' She turned and stalked into the cave.

'Sorry, I didn't mean…'

'It's okay,' she shouted over her shoulder. I shrugged. A pot easily boiled.

The late afternoon sun was less intense than before. With my back against the big rock, I dozed off. When I awoke, the shadows had grown long. While I could still see, I found some thin dry roots gathered by Chiko, and lit them as a torch. Then I went inside to find Angelika.

She wasn't there. I looked up and down the cave, but there was no sign of her. I called out her name, but there was no reply. My mouth went dry, and an icy hand gripped my heart. She wouldn't have gone off in a sulk, would she? I hadn't said anything terrible, or had I? Did I underestimate the effects of my words? What did I say? Maybe our predicament was drawing us together. What was so wrong with that? Did she think I only wanted her because of it?

Where had she gone? Did she creep past while I slept outside? Surely, she wasn't so reckless as to go off on her own? With rising panic, I checked again. She wasn't inside. I yelled her name outside, and my voice echoed from the sides of the valley. There was no reply.

How could I find her in the growing darkness? I wouldn't be able to see tracks. I found myself back outside. In a little while, there'd be no light. I tried to imagine her position. To go off like that, she was very angry, upset, or both.

Which direction had she gone? How long since she left? Instinctively, I went back the way Chiko first brought us.

The last light faded, and I stumbled in the dark.

For several minutes I was blind, but the rising moon began to throw pale light over the desert. My eyes adjusted, and I made out the shapes of big rocks. Steering between them, I walked on, calling her name.

I'd been searching for an hour when an invisible hyena giggled closeby. It sickened me with fear and dread. I'd left in a hurry, hadn't brought the pistol. Where was Angelika? Had I gone the wrong way? I tried not to think of the danger she was in. Was I too late? I hurried my pace, shouting her name at the top of my voice.

Two hours later, I began to lose hope. I had no clue where she'd gone, and I was exhausted. It occurred she may have returned to the cave. Not finding me, would she go out searching? We could both forever stagger uselessly about the desert.

With desperation and hope competing, I turned back towards the valley and the cave.

It was only through luck I found my way, and it was after midnight when, in a state of near-collapse, I arrived. Angelika still wasn't there. This nightmare was real. I wouldn't wake to find it wasn't true.

Forty-one

I awoke with a start. I'd been dreaming about Angelika sunbathing on the flat rock. Only one part was true, the morning sunshine was lancing into the cave mouth. I got to my feet and looked around, but Angelika wasn't there. How could I have slept, I asked myself. It was no excuse to be worn out. I should have kept searching.

I drank deeply, filled a water bottle, put my pistol in my belt and resumed my search. The sun shimmered the outlines of the hills and reflected dazzlingly from the white sand. Which way should I go? I tried to remember my mad search last night. It was in the dark, and I may have gone in circles. The morning sun was in the East. If I kept it on my right, I'd go north. The surrounding hills looked lower that way.

I trudged along the valley sands with the energy of fear. She'd taken no water, because both bottles were left behind. How long could she survive? If, I thought, fighting my nausea, the hyenas didn't get to her first! I imagined her surrounded by a pack of circling hyenas. The leader spoke. *'Thou art come,'* he rasped, *'now shall we dine on thee!'* I shuddered, and banished the thought from my mind.

Her words came back to haunt me. 'I think that, looking for Ignatius, you were trying to re-connect with your mother.' If only I hadn't been so stuck in my past! My mother died, true, and my life had never been the same. I'd felt abandoned by her death, rejected by my father, abandoned by Roseanne.

The memory of my mother's funeral came back, and with it the same empty, vacuous disbelief.

How would I deal with it if Angelika didn't come back, or if I found her dead?

How would I, self-obsessed idiot that I was, interpret *that?* Another abandonment? I looked at my watch. It was nine o'clock, and I'd been going this way for over an hour.

The ground rose and I began to ascend a hill.

Rocks of every size, some smooth and light coloured, others black and jagged, prevented a straight path. I walked on, my legs aching, my breathing ragged. Lying about and a meagre diet had done nothing for my fitness.

An hour and a half later I was exhausted, and stopped to look back. The view of the valley was panoramic. Two Cape vultures circled far below, but I could see no other living thing. Had they found her remains? There was no profit in that kind of thinking.

Where was Angelika? Was I going the wrong way? For all I knew, I could be heading further from her. Hopeless dejection overcame me, and I sat down heavily on a boulder.

I was desperately thirsty. I drank tepid water from the bottle, half-emptying it in a single go. With a headache pounding in both temples and into my neck, I retraced my steps. Going the other way, the sun was still on my right. Different leg muscles ached as I descended. I'd gone further than I thought.

Several times I stumbled, tripped over ledges or slipped on loose shale and sand. After exhausting the possibilities, I was letting my feet decide, and they were unerringly carrying me back to the cave.

It was after six as I came near, and the sun was hurtling down in the west.

———

A familiar smell assailed my nostrils. Smoke, something burning.

Could it be… what else could make that acrid smell? I quickened my pace. A small fire crackled, red and yellow before the cave mouth.

'Angelika!' I shouted, 'are you here?'

'I'm here.' She stepped out of the shadow.

'Thank God!' I was rooted to the spot.

'I came back.' Wooziness threatened to make me faint. She stepped forward to support me.

The haze cleared. Her face, very close, was burnt vivid pink. Her nose was tomato-red, her eyes skeletally deep.

'I didn't think, I was angry, I was upset, I just went, it was stupid…'

'I looked for you, I searched six hours last night, then went out early this morning. I thought I'd never find you —'

'I went up the hill where we get mongongo nuts, over the ridge…'

'How far?'

'Don't know. It was stupid, and I turned back. But I lost my way in the dark. I walked and walked, then lay down behind some rocks. I heard hyenas and other wild things and thought they were coming for me. When the sun came up, I went up the hill, and saw the valley. I was three, four miles away. I was walking in circles.'

'Please, Angelika, don't ever do that again.' Tears of relief streamed down my cheeks.

'Did you think….your mother, Roseanne….' There were tears in her eyes too. She turned her face away.

'Yes, I remembered what you said, realised how self-absorbed I've been.'

I hugged her close. 'I could have lost you!'

'I'm the one who came back, Tobias,' she whispered. 'I never wanted to leave!'

After a long time, we sat in the cave mouth.

'Just pray Chiko makes it,' I said, 'then we can make plans.'

'Plans?'

'For us.'

'You mean…?'

'I love you,' I said, 'I should have told you more.'

'I love you too, Tobias. Even though you were rude when we met. It took me time, but….' she was fighting not to cry.

Coming in from the scorching light, I could only make out shadows and darkness. 'The word of Igni is at hand,' echoed over and over in my mind. Another ear-worm. It must have come from one of my strange dreams, though I couldn't remember anything except those words in a thin, reedy voice.

Why did I dream such things? I'd been cynical about the supernatural.

In one dream, the voice said the /*num* would guide me. The spirit-guide. Guide me to what? The word of Igni…Ignatius? Was something hidden in the cave, something from Ignatius?

I'd checked for hiding places, and found none. But I hadn't properly searched the wider of the narrow tunnels at the back. Could something be hidden there? I got up, careful not to wake Angelika, and, taking the box of matches, left her.

The passage had just enough room for me to squeeze through.

The roof sloped down, meeting the floor ten feet in.

I lit a match, and, three feet from the floor, saw a narrow split in the rock. The kind of place someone could put things.

I lit another match, bent and peered into the gap. There was a pear-shaped object six inches high, half obscured by something light, like linen. I reached out, and it yielded to my fingers. A mat of sticky cobweb. The spider which made this was huge, I realised, withdrawing my hand.

Only baboon spiders make such a dense web.

Also known as the common tarantula, it grows up to four inches long and has thick, six-inch hairy legs resembling the fingers of a baboon. They hide under rocks, in clumps of grass, or any hidden, shady space. They have a toxic venom. The National Geographic quoted an ancient San parable:

Deadly be the lion and the elephant, the snake and the rhinoceros, but worse is he who strikes from the shadows, who warns not, and whose poison cannot be healed. He is the hairy-legged spider, servant of the death god //Gauwa. Ignore him not.

I was about to rise, when on impulse I reached into the cleft. To hell with cobwebs and spiders, what was the web covering? I prodded with my fingers. Cool, hard rock. I traced it down.

There was something there. With a pounding heart I lay on my belly and forced my fingers behind it. I pulled and, with a tearing sound, it came loose.

It was a long thin package wrapped in dried-out bark. No, leather. Untreated hide, that was it. It was eighteen inches long and eight wide.

I rose to my feet and examined it.

It seemed to be bellows, like those in old fireplaces.

Twine was wrapped round and round. I tugged and it parted in a shower of dust.

'What's that?' I hadn't seen her coming.

'Something in old leather, found it in a cleft.' I was trying to prise the edge of the leather apart where it overlapped. It was as hard as wood.

'Don't do that,' Angelika said, squatting down.

'How can I open it?'

'I heard about an old leather scroll, I think it was Egyptian.'

'Think this is a scroll?'

'Maybe, if that's leather, it might be.'

'The old Egyptian scroll was dried out, brittle…'

'What did they do?'

'They rehydrated it.'

'How?'

'If I remember, in a special way.

'Which was?'

'Dunno.'

'That's helpful,' I laughed.

'Put it like this, I imagine they used a vapourising chamber…. something like that.'

'Yes, would be, but we haven't got one —'

'You really want to open it?'

'I think we should, don't you?'

'Suppose so. What do you think's in it?'

'Haven't a clue.'

'I've got an idea.'

'Yes?'

'It's hot here, right?'

'That's no lie.'

'And we've got water.'

'So?'

'If we wrap it in dampened cloth and leave it in the shade, it might soften.'

'We haven't got cloth.'

'What about what's left of your shirt?'

'You're a genius!' I laughed, squeezing her hand, 'whatever would I do without you?' She turned her palms upwards and grinned.

Das weiss ich einfach nicht.' Angelika giggled. This I just don't know.

It was difficult to hold off and not tear the package open at once, but I'd seen the twine disintegrate.

What she suggested was only an act preparatory to opening the package.

It would take time if it worked at all. I'd have to wait to find out what was inside.

The package was less brittle. It had taken two days, and I'd re-dampened my shirt several times. I'd got used to living with a naked chest, and Angelika said it suited me.

Was it connected to Ignatius? Did it contain his words? Was this what the ghostly Tátaba meant when he said the word of Igni was at hand?

Next day it was pliable enough to prise the overlapping edges apart.

'Told you it would work,' Angelika said. I grinned. She was right, my wet shirt had done the trick. But had the dampening washed away any writing?

'Here goes!' I tugged the edges of the hide apart. It was still quite dry, but not brittle. With an effort, I managed to force it flat. When I took my hand away it curled up.

'Not vellum, it's a wad of paper.'

'It's old cotton or lint paper,' she said, 'made from rags before wood pulp.' She craned her neck. 'Is there any writing?' I couldn't see any. She bent closer.

'The sun's too bright, try in less light...' I edged backwards, keeping the roll flat. The glare lessened. I focused on the first yellowish sheet. I couldn't see any writing. It was the same with the next two. There was nothing on the papers, I decided with a sinking heart.

A bundle of blanks. I turned more sheets. Then I caught my breath.

'Can you see it?' Angelika said, 'writing!' It wasn't only writing.

The first three letters at the top leapt off the page. In big grey pencil letters, were the capitals *IMT*.

'Ignatius Myghal Tregurtha!' I exclaimed. There was writing below.

We began to read. Some words and parts of words were faded, but it was mostly tidy and regular.

'One of the other three,' it read, *'who shared a stinking grass bed with me, was a good and friendly man called Sterkbooi, which means strong boy in the Dutche... He was mixed race, he said, part Khoi, part Dutch, part isiXhosa...'*

I put down the wad and retreated to the coolness of the cave. Everything spun as I leaned against the wall.

'What's wrong?' I was shivering and covered in sweat. Angelika mopped my forehead with my still-damp shirt.

'Is it the writing?''

'Yes, it's like he's talking to us.'

'I know.'

'You need to eat,' she said, changing the subject. 'I'll get something.'

Two minutes later she brought cold roast *leguaan* and a water bottle filled from the pool. I ate and drank thirstily.

'Let's read,' she said, picking up some pages.

We moved back to the light.

Ignatius met Marana, the woman who was to become his partner, in the Khamiesberg. I'd heard her name, seen her in a dream! We read about their flight across the Gariep, or Orange river, how they fell in love, and arrived at !Anis. Angelika giggled.

'!Anis, not Anus,' I chided her with a punch on the shoulder.

Ignatius waxed eloquent in his praise for a fine Jaeger rifle, and a half-jackal scoundrel of a dog called Malkop.

It was three days since Chiko left. It was impossible to guess how far he'd gone. He'd started southwards, but this country didn't allow travel in a straight direction. Rocky outcrops, cliffs and deep gulleys always seemed to stand in your way.

Even the best can be overwhelmed. Would Chiko find water or *Tsamma* melons to quench his thirst? Food was easy, for he was expert finding crawling and slithering things. But, in that confused and broken country, would his sense of direction stop him heading even deeper into nowhere?

'Worried?' Angelika snuggled against my side. From the cave mouth, the view was dramatic. The granite hills in the east were trying to hold back the morning sun, but couldn't stop its adventurous rays breaching their summits. A thin orange rim conquered the heights and began to light the earth.

'Three days, I wonder how he's doing.'

'Can't have gone far in three days.'

'Far enough to die.' She sat up straight, eyes flashing.

'Aren't things bad enough without being a prophet of doom? We may not get out, but one thing I'm not letting go…'

'What?'

'Hope, Tobias, Hope! It's all we've got, unless you think we should also hit the road!'

'*What* road? No, you're right. I'll try to look on the bright side.'

'What bright side?'

'That one.' I pointed at the scorching sun.

'Oh, Tobias!' she giggled, and we burst into hysterical laughter. Eventually, with aching ribs, we lapsed into silence.

'Can you believe this pencil manuscript survived so many years?'

'Incredible, I wouldn't if I didn't see it. It was meant to happen, you were looking for him, and here he is in his own words!'

'Are you hungry?'

'Yes,' she said. 'This morning, I collected mongongo nuts and roasted them in the fire.' There were three lonely mongongo trees with hand-shaped leaves and yellow flowers growing on the escarpment above the cave. The nuts were like cashew-size, velvet-covered eggs. Roasted, they tasted like almonds. They were important in the San diet, and Chiko had been quick to find them.

'Thank you, what would I do without you?'

'Who knows?'

We ate hungrily and slaked our thirst with cool water. Then we went back to the cave mouth to read.

'He was a good writer, considering the times.'

'True, and his story is so….' I struggled for the right words.

'Touching.'

'That's it!' I put down the page we were reading. It was too hot. We retreated to the cool inside, and rested in the semi-darkness.

'Funny how nature provides respite from the elements even in the harshest country.' Angelika's eyes glinted in the low light.

'Go on.' She took my hand and rested her head on my shoulder.

'The cave and its water are the only reason we're not dead, why our bleached bones aren't lying out there. It was no accident. I saw the cave in my dreams, saw the old people, even Ignatius, sitting on that rock.'

'And Chiko just happens, in all these thousands of square miles,' Angelika said, 'to stumble on it, monkey or no monkey. What we're reading…. Even the biggest sceptic would surrender.'

She nodded. 'It was part of a plan!'

'A bad plan if, after all this, we die out here!'

'I'm trying to remember,' I said squeezing her hand, 'something I read. A river ran past the place which used to be called !Anis !' It was the Oanab. There's a Lake Oanab Resort there today, close to Rehoboth, which was founded by Basters. Their descendants are called Rehoboth Basters, and there's one we both know.'

'Pik van Loon?'

'Yes, he's from Rehoboth, or should I say !Anis?'

'It fits,' I breathed, 'proves Ignatius' story is true.'

'Did you doubt it?'

'No, but….'

'If we get out,' Angelika whispered kissing me on my cheek, 'you've solved your mystery.'

'It's incredible! The Great Baster Trek out of the Cape was in 1868, after a seventy-year trickle to !Anis. It would still be !Anis if Heinrich Kleinschmidt, the German missionary, didn't change it to *Rehoboth* after an ancient city on the Euphrates.'

We went back to to the pages and read about Ignatius and Marana building a hut on the banks of the Oanab, Sterkbooi trading firearms to the Namas, and the birth of Pengilly.

'It's beyond belief,' Angelika said. 'All that time ago, in such a harsh and foreign place, just making the best of it!'

'Amazing, to think Ignatius and his wife lived at Rehoboth.'

'You mean !Anis,' she corrected me with a grin.

'You've got an !Anis fixation!'

'I think you'll find that's you,' she laughed, getting to her feet.

'You haven't been eating,' she said sternly. 'I'm watching you!'

'It's the menu.'

'There's a choice today, grilled or smoked rat, grilled or smoked bat or grilled or smoked *leguaan*.' She threw her arms around my neck and gave me a sloppy kiss on the lips. 'That,' she said, 'is the starter.'

'I'll have two starters and leave out the main course.'

'Not allowed.' She walked back inside, her tongue darting in and out like a lizard. How long would her humour last if all reason for hope was snuffed out? What would be the last thing we said to each other?

Forty-two

This nightmare was different. Instead of seeing a great bird of prey in the sky, I saw through its eyes. It was like the youtube video filmed from a camera mounted on an Eagle's back. Far below, in the dazzle of a fierce sun, the trackless desert dunes curved and bent from horizon to horizon. At the bottom of one, a cairn of heaped up boulders broke the surface of the sand like gigantic pearls on a cosmic necklace.

But wait! The desert was *not* entirely trackless. There were human footprints going up the slope of a dune. The range shortened, then I was directly above the highest point. The prints continued over the brow, and down the other side. The great bird through which I saw swooped over the ridge, and came to where the tracks ended, and the maker lay crumpled like a rag on the sloping sand.

The creature landed smoothly. It had to be a vulture, judging by its ungainly walk. It inspected the naked body. The macerated face turned up to the sky had once been Chiko's. I awoke in a sweat.

It took a lot not to tell Angelika. She'd see it as prophecy, lose what little hope she had. It was better to distract ourselves with our strange manuscript. If we were going to die, nothing I could do would change it.

'The pencil is so pale in places.'

'I can't read more,' I said. Angelika got to her feet.

'After a bit,' she said, 'the sunshine dazzles, and you can't see.'

'And it's too dark inside.'

'Tell you what, remember where Chiko found those melon-things…'

'Tsamma melons.'

'Yeah wise-guy,' she laughed in a fake American drawl, 'I seed some when I got the mongongo nuts.'

'Okay, let's hunt melons.'

'You're useless hunting anything that can run,' she teased with a shake of her head.

It took an hour to reach the flat place beyond the escarpment, which, though less than a mile away, could only be reached by traversing a long, inclined gulley strewn with boulders. We found three watermelon-sized *tsammas*.

'It was there I tried to sleep that night,' Angelika said, pointing at an outcrop of rocks.

'Thank heavens you made it back.' I kissed her on the cheek.

'How can such big things as these grow in such a dry place?' she asked, changing the subject. 'How?'

'Deep roots, even then it's amazing.'

The return was downhill and took less than half the time. We cut up and gorged on a delicious melon. I took the others into the deepest part of the cave where they'd stay cool. It was almost completely dark as I bent to place them on the ground. Yet I sensed I was being watched. A tiny shaft of light filtered from outside, illuminating a square foot of floor two feet away, and I saw him. I'd seen one before, and read about them.

The scorpion's head had two eyes on top and five pairs along the sides. He was a granulated thick-tailed scorpion, known as *Parabuthus Granulatus*. He was five inches long and three across, with a dark yellow-brown body. His stinger, through which he injected lethal venom, was folded into the end of his up-curled tail.

Caught by surprise, he was watching me with all his eyes. I was rooted to the spot.

Being barefoot, stamping on him was out of the question. Suddenly he darted out of the light and disappeared behind a rock. I breathed again.

I went back to Angelika and, like the mamba or my avian vision of Chiko's corpse, didn't mention what I'd seen.

We read how Ignatius and his little family, fearing the bounty hunters, fled north from their !Anis home. Was there no end to his persecution?

Angelika was pensive and lacked her usual gaiety. Her shoulders drooped, her voice was strained, and there was tension in her eyes. We were too close for secrets.

'Worried?'

'You?'

'Two days ago, you told me not to be a prophet of doom, you said something about keeping up hope.'

'Yes, but…'

'You were right. I know Chiko, and he doesn't get lost.' The taste of dishonesty was bitter on my tongue, but I went on.

'Do you think all these things have happened just so we'll die here?'Angelika looked thoughtful. She was strong, fought her fear bravely, latched on to any hope.

'You really think…?'

'I know,' I said, wishing I really did.

'Okay…. here are two more pages ready for reading.'

'That's the spirit!' I took one and held it up.

'AiGams is the old Nama name for Windhoek. Tourist brochure.'

'Been useful.'

'Ignatius went through Windhoek.'

'AiGams,' she said with a grin.

After passing through AiGams, poor old Ignatius continued to Otjandjomboimwe, which he called Otja.

'I don't believe it!' Angelika raised her eyebrows.

'Don't believe what?'

'Otjandjomboimwe is the old name for Karibib!'

'Is that also from a tourist brochure?'

'Don't you see, he went through Karibib, where I live, before it even existed!'

We read on, then I whistled.

'It *was* Ignatius!'

'*What* was?' Angelika was parting her hair on her forehead.

'The *omuroi*.'

'Spooky,' she said, 'look, I've got goosebumps!'

'Me too!' I turned back to the page, and she leaned close. That night the Hereros tried to kill Ignatius.

'The places they went through, so....so connected, makes you feel close to them.' I looked up.

I was hungry. There was no meat, but there were roasted mongongo nuts and a *tsamma* melon in the cave.

'Let's eat.' Angelika went inside for food.

I almost called her back. The scorpion was in there. Yet, hadn't it always been? It hadn't stung us yet. I let her go, but imagined it crouching in the shadow of the crack between floor and wall, the tiny black beads of its many eyes watching Angelika's foot from inches away. As she bent to lift the melon, I imagined the thick tail-tip unfold, its deadly poison ready to be injected.

She came out of the cave.

Forty-three

'Sorry about these,' said Angelika, holding up two stuck pages.

'Can't help it.'

'Should we have waited 'till we're rescued, taken them to a laboratory, if ever we get out of here?' I looked up. It was bad enough being stranded, without setbacks.

'You're right,' I sighed, 'we had no choice, had to read them. Anyway, maybe a laboratory will be able to recover the writing. They use ultraviolet light, things like that. Even X-rays. If,' I added, 'we ever get to one!'

'They were layered in time sequence, weren't they?'

'Yup, oldest at the bottom. Ten unreadable pages out of sixty isn't so bad. The others okay?'

'Think so.'

'Let's read.'

She put the stuck pages down, and I took up another. Last thing, Ignatius was in Otjiwarongo. The stuck pages would leave a gap.

'Wow, they went past Otjikondo —'

'As we did,' said Angelika, 'it's like we followed them!'

'It's scary.'

The writing became too faint again.

'Leave that bit out,' Angelika wanted to know about Marana and her Bushman family. We read on.

'Tátaba, it's got to be Tátaba!' Angelika eyed me quizzically. 'Who I dreamed about, in the cave…'

'Very spooky. There's a theme, Marana's family persecuted by Europeans, and her determination to find her San family — '

'Yes, and Ignatius running from similar people…..
and me trying to find him…'

'Exactly!'

The writing faded again. Without the illegible parts
and missing pages, the story had jumped ahead.

'It must have been Tátaba in the cave, it can't be
anyone else!'

'The diamond gatherer in your dreams?'

'And Chiko's. But not any cave, Angelika, *this* cave!'.

That night I fell into a restless sleep.

Tátaba and Ignatius, both very old, sat on the rock
where I'd seen Ignatius before. 'Harken /*hũ* who seeks
Igni,' Tátaba said, addressing me in San.

'Igni and I long lost our beloved companions. In our
last days we bided together, here in the valley of the
cave and stones. The /*num* foretold your coming. It is
here his ≠*ketens* will speak to you!'

Looking older than before, resembling my
grandfather, or my father's father, Ignatius was
whittling wood. He wore a short cloak of Zebra skin.
His beard was long and snowy-white, his face deeply
tanned and wrinkled. He sang as he worked, a Cornish
smuggler's song.

Hush m' littl' uglin', daddy's gone a-smugglin'.
'e 'as gone t Roscoff o' th' Mevagissey Maid,
a sloop o' nin'ty tons, wi' ten brass carrigge guns,
t' teach th' king some manners an' 'spect fer 'onest trade.

Where was Mãr!ãnna, of the Dutch /*hũ* father and
San mother, who he called Marana? I hadn't seen her in
my dream.

She'd be two hundred and fifty years old, or more, by now. She'd died before Ignatius, that explained her absence when he was old. What of Malkop, the jackal-dog Ignatius loved so much?

Was it even Ignatius I saw, or a sleep-hallucination? Had the rock and sand recorded his image like a photograph? He began to sing again, his voice raspy with age.

> *Gawin' up Cambern 'ill, comin' dauwn,*
> *Gawin' up Cambern 'ill, comin' dauwn,*
> *Th' 'osses stood still, th' whils went aroun',*
> *Gawin' up Cambern 'ill, comin' dauwn.*
>
> *White stockans, white stockans, she wore,*
> *White stockans, white stockans, she wore,*
> *White stockans she wore, th' sayme as before.*
> *Gawin' up Cambern 'ill, comin' dauwn.*
>
> *I knowed 'er ol' fayther, ol' friend,*
> *I knowed 'er ol' fayther, ol' friend,*
> *I knowed 'er ol' man, 'ee plaid in th' band*
> *Gawin' up Cambern 'ill, comin' dauwn.*
>
> *I'ad 'er, I 'ad 'er, I 'ad 'er, I did,*
> *I'ad 'er, I 'ad 'er, I 'ad 'er, I did,*
> *I'ad 'er, I did, it cost me a quid,*
> *Gawin' up Cambern 'ill, comin' dauwn.*

Banished from home and the civilization of his time in this harsh and alien land, bereaved of the one he loved, in the twilight of life, he didn't despair.

I was ashamed of my weakness. When my life went wrong, I gave up.

Was this the ultimate message from Ignatius, that I should grow a spine?

There were only a few pages left, some stuck together.

After a breakfast of roasted mongongo nuts, we took up the free pages.

It was indeed Tátaba, and his wife Xsara, who they met in the sandy valley. Ignatius wrote about the star stones, which he recognised as diamonds.

The next sentence caused me to start.

'He told me the spirits revealed a special one would come, and he would be related to me.'

A tingle ran up my back, and my heart beat like a jackhammer. How did Tátaba predict *that?*

'What?'

'I saw Ignatius and Tataba again.'

'You look haunted!'

'They were right here, Tátaba with his diamonds, Ignatius singing.'

'I love you.' She put her hand on mine.

'I love you too.' She picked up the page she'd dropped.

'Not even a science fiction movie, or King Solomon's Mines, is as strange as this,' she said, recalling our first conversation.

'I know.'

'You always suspected something. You came to Namibia because of that old letter.'

'Then something made me drive into the desert and find Chiko.' Without him, we wouldn't be sitting here, or reading Ignatius' story.'

'Your dreams, the visions, the book you just happened to buy....'

'I was never a believer in anything supernatural, you know...'

'If you told me a month ago I'd see all this......'

'Me too, how little we know.'

'Strange,' she said, 'we're marooned, but I feel peaceful.'

'Me too.'

'Could it be Tátaba's spirit making us so tranquil?'

'And Ignatius.' She nodded. I leaned forward and kissed her.

'Look, we've got hardly any mongongos left,' she said, scowling, 'the *tsammas* are finished and the lizards are giving us a wide berth....'

'Yes, I know, we haven't seen an edible snake in days, they've buggered off.'

'Isn't it bad,' she laughed, 'when you're avoided by lizards and snakes?'

'We're socially unacceptable, even to them.'

'Shall we look at the last pages?' she asked. 'They were stuck, but I separated them. Only some parts are legible.'

We sat together.

'The writing's different,' she said, 'more scrawly.'

'You're right, I wonder...'

'He was older when he wrote this.'

'That would explain the change in his writing. Much older, I'd say.'

'Yes. But we may not have noticed the change if it happened gradually...'

'A jump of twenty-odd years,' Angelika said.

'I would've loved to read the missing parts, I wonder why he didn't rewrite them...'

'How did they live?' She looked around. 'He must have been too old to hunt.'

'Suppose so, far too old. They must have eaten grubs and scorpions, *leguaans* and lizards.'

There were only four pages left. I held one reverently in the dying light. If we were going to find out what finally became of Ignatius, it would be here.

After a break of twenty years, Ignatius took up his pencil again.

Once more, the writing became too faded to read. The second page was better.

'It's been an incredible experience for you,' Angelika whispered.

'You too.'

'Poor chap, never had much luck, did he?'

'He was happy with Marana. You can tell they were deeply in love.'

'At least he had that!'

'Like I have with you,' I whispered in her ear. I picked up the last of the writing. After a long time, I put it down.

'Two hundred years,' I said, 'seven generations. Some San have Cornish ancestry,'

'Maybe that's why.'

'Why what?'

'Why you are so attracted to them.'

'Who's superstitious now?'

'After everything, I thought you wouldn't use that word. But you could try to trace Ignatius' descendants.'

'What do you mean, how —'

'If we get out, we could put advertisements in the papers, ask if anyone knows the names Ignatius Tregurtha, Marana, Pengilly, N!ai, or Ignatius and Marana's grandchildren, Mara Hama and Ignatius Xi.'

She looked into my eyes. 'Families remember names,' she said

'You think — '

'You never know.'

From 'Untold Mysteries of The San' by Sven Johannsen, 1790: *When the San find the earthly remains of a fellow human they believe it is best not to grieve, but to bury them with dignity so they may join their ancestors. Then, without looking back, proceed on their way.'*

I can't leave Tátaba and I am too old for the long walk. Even if I could, I would not burden Pengilly, N!ai and their children. They are young and have their lives ahead. I am content to stay with my good friend, who is not going to live long.

My sight is fading, and I struggle to see. I have had more than my allotted time of three-score and ten years.

I am alone, for my brother Tátaba has yesterday gone to the land of his ancestors. Before he died he told me not to bury him, as the spirits said he should only be buried by a San, who would one day come to the cave and find his bones. So, with my heart breaking, I laid him out in the cave. I would never even know when my father died, yet this strange old man had been more than a father to me.

As a last gesture, I wrapped his most precious possessions in a piece of hide. They are the two great diamonds he called Blue Woman and Red Woman, which he told me were the mirror of his dear wife Xsara's soul. These I placed in his hand, to hold for eternity. How strange that once I would have given anything for such riches.

At least, I comfort myself, I could do this little thing for him, whereas with poor Peder Pengilly I could do nothing when he was hanged at the yardarm.

This is my last writing, and I shall put it with the others, in the cleft Tátaba showed me. Maybe it will lie there for all eternity, yet I feel it will be found one day, by the one the spirit foretold to Tátaba.

Peder Pengilly, the Cornish guard hanged after Ignatius and Sterkbooi escaped from Scarborough in 1787! Ignatius and Marana called their son after him. It was all true. Mr Tregony at the West Briton found the record of his execution in the National Archives. We read on.

If I bide here I shall perforce drink water, and die slow for there is no more food. It is my time to go, and I shall hasten it by walking towards the horizon. There are vultures circling, and I know they smell death. Marana believed they predicted the future, and knew for whom life had run its course Even now, it is a bitter thought that I shall never hear her sweet voice in this world again, or that most precious word she called me, liefje!

I hope one day my writings will be found, and my story told.

For me, there can be no greater joy than my blissful reunion with my darling Marana, she who rescued me from despair and abandonment, and brought such love and joy to me for so long.

If you read my words, you will know that for over forty years, when momentous events occurred in the world, when great wars raged across Europe, when kings and queens lost their thrones, when heads were severed on guillotines, when empires rose and fell, and no doubt many of my Cornish brothers perished in wars, it was here, in this remote dry land where I fought my own battles.

Here I found that greatest treasure, true and abiding love. For my darling Marana, Pengilly and his family, my beloved friend Sterkbooi, Tátaba and Xsara, old Xi and so many others whose lives I was so fortunate to share. In this list, I must include my stalwart four-footed friend, Malkop, without whom we would have perished long before we blossomed.

My enemies were not armies, but those who would hunt me down and hang me, those who would kill me as a witch, the fragility and tragedy of life itself, the cruelty of nature and time, the heat, the cold, the venomous snake and spider, the hyena and the lion, the flies and the dust. Along the way, I was blessed by love and friendship, without which I could not have prevailed. But my greatest enemy is my irredeemable longing for that which I had, which is lost.

I pray Tátaba's diamonds will bring comfort to his people one day.

Where were the diamonds? Were there any? Maybe they were allegorical or had some mystical, non-physical meaning. Perhaps 'diamonds' illustrated the value of Ignatius' words to me. I read the last two lines.

Though my arms are weak and tired, I shall gather rocks, and wall off the entrance lest wild animals disturb Tátaba's peace. I shall bid him farewell, and walk out there, where I know I will at last find my darling Marana.

'He built the stone wall we pulled down!' I whispered. Something done by his hands, which we'd undone! It was a strange feeling. And what about the 'most precious possession' Ignatius put in Tátaba's hand? Did Chiko find it with the skeleton?

'I'm lost for words.' Angelika sniffed and wiped her eyes with the back of her hand.

Ignatius' last sentence was in Cornish, the same as his letter of December 1789.

Ehaz ha sowena gen oll an collan ve Tereba nessa, gwro kelmy a hollan thewh ve benatugana. Health and prosperity, with all my heart. Until next time I bind my heart to you and may God bless you.

Below, in a scrawl, he signed his name. Angelika's eyes were red, her face streaked with tears. I couldn't cry. My emotions were too strong.

The chewed bodies we found near the abandoned tent haunted me. It had to be that which caused my nighmare about Chiko. I fervently hoped Ignatius was dead before the hyenas started crushing his bones.

That night as we huddled together in the cave, we heard the insane giggling of hyenas far out on the sands.

'*Hyaena brunnea,*' I whispered.

'Same as in Rodolf's tent?' There was a quaver in her voice.

'Yes.'

'Do you think…?' Angelika began, then stopped.

'Do I think Ignatius was eaten?'

'Yes, didn't mean to…'

'May as well face it, he must have been.'

'What about us?' she asked in a little voice. There was the glint of tears in her eyes, but she rubbed them away furiously.

'Wouldn't it be fate if we we're eaten by hyenas, while Egon gets rich buying diamonds in Botswana?'

'Not fair,' I said.

On impulse, next morning I walked out onto the flat plain of sand. Between two rocks, something glinted. I stooped and picked it from the sand. It was small, the size of a Smartie. Was it a diamond? Tátaba's words haunted me. He said the star-stones were swept here by water. I knew little about diamonds, except that those in the river mouth at Oranjemund were alluvial, washed there by water.

Diamonds found on the upstream riverbanks of the Orange River prove that the kimberlite rock which bears them is upriver, 'though it has never been located. Did ancient branches of the river carry them here, to lie undisturbed for millions of years at the bottom of a lake which evaporated?

I threw the stone away. On the way back, I thought I should have shown it to Angelika. Or should I? Maybe she'd want to find others, and expend energy she didn't have searching for them.

In the morning, Angelika took a walk around the base of the hill. She came to where a great boulder stuck out, overhanging a smooth rock face. Just then, the sun's rays lit up the recess, and she stepped back in astonishment.

'Tobias,' she yelled, 'come see this!' Shortly, I stood beside her. The painting was two-foot high and wide, a lifelike image of a long-haired, bearded European man. It was exactly what I'd seen in a dream, the face of a younger Ignatius Myghal Tregurtha.

'It's *you!*' she exclaimed. 'Unshaven!' My hand touched my beard automatically. It was six inches long, and my hair hung on my shoulders.

'Me? No, it's Ignatius, I've seen him in my dreams. It was painted by Marana.'

'If it's Ignatius, the similarity is scary.'

'Family resemblance.' The eyes in the image were alive, bored into mine.

'Is this really you, Ignatius?' I whispered, 'the you I came to find?' Angelika took my hand. She had no more words. For me, the chasm of two hundred years vanished. Here, faithfully depicted, Ignatius was alive, forever staring out at the barren wilderness of his exile.

'If we needed proof she loved him, here it is,' Angelika said. 'See the detail, the warmth!'

In the cave, I kneeled beside the pool. The water was still as glass, and my reflection stared back in the half-light. I was heavily bearded, and my eyes had the same intense stare.

'See, Mister Tobias Ignatius Myghal?' Angelika was staring at the pool. 'It's one face!'

'But....?'

'Believe in reincarnation?'

'Why?'

'You look like Ignatius, but that's not all.'

'What?'

'We've read his writing, can sense the kind of man he was. His personality comes through.'

'Yes ...'

'Like you!'

'Think so?'

'Yes. Silly, unfortunate, accident-prone, kind, modest, thoughtful, brave. Just like you, darling.' I took her in my arms and squeezed.

'In a way,' she murmured, turning her eyes up to mine, 'I think this whole thing was so important because you weren't only looking for your mother, but for yourself. I just hope we don't end up like Ignatius!' She turned her head away, not before I saw fresh tears welling in her eyes.

Forty-five

I don't know why I went into the cave. Maybe to briefly escape the heat outside. I stopped for a moment. I had a feeling my old friend the scorpion was watching me, and if I came closer it would sting.

'You coming?' Angelika yelled from outside. 'I've got food.'

'Coming!' I turned to go and the scorpion struck.

The sudden burning on the top of my foot was excruciating. I jumped backwards in agony and ran outside.

'What?' Angelika asked, surprised.

'Scorpion,' I gasped between gritted teeth. I threw myself down and grabbed my foot in both hands.

'A sting, what —'

'Scorpion.' Angelika fell on her knees.

'Here?' she asked, squinting and pointing. On the back of my foot was a tiny red mark. I recoiled as her finger brushed it.

'Don't touch it!'

'What can I do?'

'Don't know,' I said, rocking backwards and forwards.

'We need Antivenom, but haven't got any!'

'I know, I lost the first aid kit.' A knowing look crossed her eyes. That was why she hadn't found it.

'I'll wet a cloth, it'll cool it a bit.' She entered the cave cautiously. She tore the sleeve off her threadbare shirt and dipped it in the pool.

'Let me put it on,' she said as I pulled my foot away.

'No.'

'Look, I know it hurts, but we've got nothing else.'

I braced myself and let her wrap the cool cloth around my foot. I was surprised it wasn't worse when it touched the sting.

'Stone-age treatment for a doctor,' she said.

'Thank you.'

'What can we expect?'

'Not sure, different species, different effects.' The pain wasn't quite as agonising.

'How long does the poison take?'

'Pretty quick,' I said, 'ten minutes to an hour —'

'*What* effects?'

'Twitching, sweating, muscle cramps, weakness, salivation, headache, vomiting, paralysis, respiratory failure,' I reeled off through gritted teeth. That's what it says in the manual.'

'Oh God, how do you feel?'

'Pain.'

'Anything else?'

'Headache.' My mouth filled with spit, and I felt weak.

'Need to lie down,'

'Can you walk?'

I rose to my feet, and Angelika placed my arm over her shoulder. She led me to our sleeping place. I didn't think whether the scorpion was still there. I dripped with sweat, my legs were stiff and cramp, and my breath came in gasps. She helped me lie down. Suddenly my stomach heaved and I threw up, the bitter taste of half-digested mongongo nuts corrupting my mouth.

'Oh God,' she cried, tears starting from her eyes, 'you can't die, not after finding Ignatius. Don't leave me!' I couldn't talk. A steel band constricted my throat.

Spit dripped from the corners of my mouth, and I couldn't swallow.

My face twitched uncontrollably, and my whole body was numb. I began to retch again. I was dimly aware of Angelika wiping my face.

I was in hell. My stomach was empty, but the painful retching didn't stop. My skin tingled, and the muscle pains grew worse. The constriction in my throat threatened to suffocate me, and spit trickled out in a constant flow. I could barely breathe. Angelika's face was a smudge.

Something took her to the cave entrance. She shaded her eyes against the bright afternoon sun. There was a twirl of dust at the base of the southern escarpment. In places, the sand is talcum-fine and very light, and the slightest breeze can do it.

'Tobias,' she yelled, 'I think someone's coming!' I heard her, but couldn't answer.

'There's dust heading this way, wait, …. I think it's a vehicle!' She was silent a long time, then spoke again.

'Yes, it's a car!'

She scrambled into the cave and grabbed a pile of nama roots and Bushman grass. With one of our last matches, she lit some grass. Blowing gently, she fed more grass, then dry roots onto the flame. In a few minutes, she had a blaze.

'Smoke,' she shouted, 'I need smoke!' She rushed back inside, wet the remains of her shirt, and threw it on the fire. Steam rose, but no smoke. Seconds later, one corner burst into flames and thick smoke began to rise into the air.

'They've seen it!' she yelled, 'they've seen it!' She ran inside.

'Tobias, someone's coming, they're nearly here, they'll help you!'

Before the Nissan four-wheel-drive even stopped, a door opened and Chiko came running.

He saw Angelika and sensed something was wrong. He dashed into the cave. I saw him as a blur.

'*Doktor, Doktor,*' Chiko yelled as he ran back towards the truck. A big, portly man appeared. It was Pik van Loon.

'*Hy is baie siek,*' Chiko gasped. He is very sick.

'What happened?' Pik asked when they reached me.

'Scorpion,' Angelika said. He knelt down and looked at my swollen foot. Then he took my pulse. I retched painfully.

'When?'

'An hour.' Her knees threatened to give way. Chiko put out his arm for support.

'One of the *Buthidae* type,' Pik said.

'Can you do anything?' she asked.

'It's touch-and-go. Chiko, please get the green plastic box with a red cross on it. It's in the back.' Chiko was gone before he finished speaking.

'Antivenom?' Angelika asked.

'Yes. Polyvalent, mixed antivenom for three of the worst scorpions.' Chiko dashed back in with the box. Pik opened it, withdrew three vials, a syringe and needle. While he drew it up, Angelika wiped my face.

'Hold his arm,' Pik said, 'I need a vein.' She took my wildly twitching arm in both hands and held it still. Pik fastened a cuff. He found a vein and slowly injected the contents of the syringe. After two long minutes, he undid the cuff.

'He'll need more,' he said, 'another vial in an hour, then another....'

'Will it work?'

'All we can do is pray,' he replied.

343

'You love him, Angelika?' Pik surprised her.

'Yes,' she sniffed. In the midst of my torment, that single word marshalled me to fight for my life.

I began to improve. First, the painful muscle spasms eased, then the salivation stopped Gradually, my nausea went away and my stomach rested. My vision cleared. Angelika looked worn out. I touched her arm.

'Tobias!' she gasped, relief lighting her eyes, 'you're a bit better!'

'Injection!' intoned Pik van Loon, re-fastening the tourniquet.

After the second dose, the improvement was rapid. In an hour I could sit up.

'Not too quick,' said Pik, *'Jy is nog nie uit die bos nie.'* You're not out of the woods yet.

'You live,' Chiko proclaimed, grinning and touching my face. He hadn't died on that sand dune in my nightmare, and he hadn't let us down!

'The snake-woman did not need fire, *Kai,'* Chiko said, 'I know the valley.' Someone else joined the circle. He was a man of considerable years, white haired, dark and rangy.

'This is uncle Sterkbooi Bogaert,' Pik said. Sterkbooi Bogaert. I couldn't believe it. It was the same name as Ignatius's Baster friend, who he escaped *Scarborough* with, who took him to his home in the Khamiesberg....

Here, staring down at me, was a tall sinewy old man with a shock of white hair contrasting with his dark chiselled features, and he was called Sterkbooi Bogaert! Either the world was extremely strange, or I was stark-raving mad!

'Your name,' I whispered in Afrikaans, 'it's an old one, isn't it?'

'Baie oud,' he replied. Very old.

'It was the name of my great, great, great, and more greats, grandfather.'

'Who was the first one with the name?'

'He crossed the Orange or Gariep River from the Cape in 1788.' In my weakened state, it was too much. The world began to rotate, and I toppled over, senseless.

I awoke with my head cradled in Angelika's lap, and Pik bending anxiously over me.

'You're in bad shape, half-starved, bitten by a blerry scorpion. Plus, you've turned into Robinson Crusoe!' I touched my long beard.

'How did Chiko find you?' I asked, sitting up with Angelika's help.

'A long story,' he laughed. 'Chiko will tell you if you promise not to faint again.'

'It was a long walk, *Kai*. Six days, my only water from *tsamma* melons. For food, I dug a porcupine out if its den and killed it with a rock. Many times, I feared I would perish. Then yesterday evening, just before the sun went down, I climbed to the top of a hill. With my great height, I saw dust in the distance. It was coming towards me, but began to turn to one side. Luckily, there were clumps of Bushman grass, which I used to make fire.' I know it well, *Stipagrostis Ciliata*, the hardiest grass in the Namib.

'We saw the smoke, lucky we did!'

'What were you doing in the desert?' Angelika asked.

'Ask uncle Sterkbooi,' Pik laughed, putting an arm around his sinewy companion's shoulder. 'He is my mother's brother. He also lives in Rehoboth, our Baster town, and he's famous for knowing its history.' Pik raised his hand.

'Four nights ago, he came to my house and said he couldn't shake a bad feeling. I tried to calm him, but it didn't work. He said he'd known me since I was born. Had I ever seen him drunk?'

Pik shook his head and Sterkbooi nodded.

'He said he had a dream. He fell asleep in a chair and dreamt about an elderly Bushman lost in the Kaokoland. He was 'guided' to see me because I would cast light on the mystery.' Pik grimaced.

'How did he think I'd know about a Bushman in the desert? It was crazy. Then, because he said Kaokoland, I remembered my chat with you in Windhoek, when you said you were going. *You're* not a Bushman, but Chiko is!' Chiko grinned, his solitary tooth like a tombstone.

'Chiko's an old friend, and he goes where you go. What were the odds, what chance my uncle should dream about someone I knew being lost in the bloody Kaokoland?' Pik shook his bald head.

'I checked my diary. I'd seen you in Windhoek twenty-three days before.' There was wonder in his eyes.

'I wouldn't have gone along, but Sterkbooi said he saw a Bushman walking in the desert, far from any road, exhausted… What was I to do? I said I'd put an end to it. I rang directory in Windhoek, asked the operator for your Karibib number. Your phone rang and rang, no answer. Then Sterkbooi made me explain, and I told him about you and Chiko. He jumped on it. He was certain it was Chiko he dreamt about.'

'It was midnight, nothing could be done till next day. I told him we should tell the police, but he said they wouldn't believe us. They don't chase blerry dreams, hey?'

'You mean you….?'

'In the morning, we took the Nissan and drove north. We've been searching for four days.'

'And Chiko?' I asked.

'That was a near thing. He saw us in the distance and lit a fire. We didn't see the smoke at first, because we weren't looking that way. In fact, we were three miles off and headed away on a tangent, when I spotted it in the mirror.'

'Smoke?'

'Smoke. Lucky I'm on holiday, or my blerry ears would be smoking too when I go back to work!'

'It's the second time Chiko owes his life to you,' I said.

'Still wasn't his time to go.'

'A vulture like you could never die of a scorpion sting,' Chiko quipped in Afrikaans. He was back to himself.

'No more than a rock-lizard like you could from thirst,' I replied.

While Pik and Sterkbooi washed in the pool, I, feeling almost back to normal, stood outside with Angelika and Chiko, who had still not stopped beaming.

'What's that Chiko?' Angelika asked. He was holding something in a closed fist.

'*Dit was met Tátaba se geraamte—*' he began. This was with Tátaba's skeleton.

'Oh,' Angelika interrupted, 'what is it?'

'Don't be rude,' I said.

'Sorry Chiko,' Angelika said.

'…*gehou in die bene van sy hand,*' Chiko completed.

Held in the bones of his hand. I felt a tingle in my spine. Ignatius had written he'd placed something in Tátaba's dead hand.

'Scorpion-woman! Chiko clicked at Angelika in San. He hadn't forgotten her interruption.

Angelika laughed as she translated. I didn't laugh. My eyes were focused on what he was holding.

'They are special star-stones,' Chiko said, opening his hand. 'These are the finest of the stones of Tátaba, the Blue Woman and the Red Woman.' Angelika took them and turned to the sunlight.

'Goodness,' she breathed, 'Tobias, look at these. I've never seen anything so beautiful!'

'The mirror of Xsara's soul!' I remembered Ignatius' words. Angelika nodded in amazement.

'I found others, come, I will show you!' Angelika and I looked at each other. *Others…?* We followed him into the cave. Pik and Sterkbooi didn't look up from washing themselves.

Chiko took us to where the two narrow tunnels led off the back of the cave. It was in the wider one I'd found the manuscript. He stooped and entered the other. I followed, but it was too narrow for me to continue. He crawled into the darkness. Angelika came up against me.

'There may be more scorpions,' she whispered.

'Can't fit in there, anyway, let's wait here and hope there aren't.' It was a long, anxious time.

'He found more diamonds?' Angelika whispered. Something to do with the darkness, I realised, made her afraid to raise her voice.

'That's what he said.' Grating came from deep inside where Chiko had vanished. It sounded again, and again.

He was pushing something along the ground.

348

An ancient-looking earthenware pot eight inches high and six across came into view, Chiko's hands on either side. He squeezed through the gap, and, holding the pot in both hands, got to his feet.

'These,' Chiko said, offering it to me, 'are the star-stones of Tátaba!' It was too dark to look, so I took the pot and we made my way outside. Pik and Sterkbooi had finished their ablutions and were at the Nissan.

The sunlight hit the pot. Pebbles. Old sling-ammunition. No, too small. I probed with a finger. They chinked like marbles. With a racing pulse, I looked round for Angelika. She was craning her neck beside me.

'Oh Tobias, look, are they…?'

'What you think?' *She* was the expert.

'Diamonds!' She took a stone, rubbed it on her arm, licked it, and held it to the sunlight. Even I saw the flash of colours. She trembled. Behind her, Chiko, still dusting himself off, was beaming and nodding his head.

'He found them,' she whispered. 'They're worth a fortune!' That was the word I dreaded. *Fortune*… was she a fortune hunter after all, was everything between us an elaborate bluff?

'Are they the ones you dreamed of?' I nodded.

'Yes.'

'It's scary.'

'I know.' What I'm scared of is you, I thought. Will *you* change?

'How did you know they were there, Chiko?' I asked.

'The night before I left, the spirit of Tátaba told me he would show me,' Chiko said in Afrikaans.

'When I awoke, I had forgotten, but my legs and arms were scratched, and I was covered in dust. I had been somewhere, but didn't know where.' He smiled.

'I didn't remember until this morning, when it came back to me.'

'They couldn't have got into the pot on their own,' Angelika said 'you were never crazy, Tobias. And all those people didn't die for no reason... I'm scared!'

I put my hand on her shoulder, and she turned her face into me. Relief flooded through me. This wasn't the reaction of a mercenary.

'They aren't for us,' I said in Afrikaans, so Chiko would understand, 'you know that?'

'I know,' Angelika said, they never were....' My heart swelled. I hadn't built her up to see my edifice come crashing down. Chiko beamed.

'Can you imagine someone, today, collecting diamonds with no value for them, to put away for the benefit of others in the distant future?' I asked.

'No.'

A whirlwind of emotions threatened to overwhelm me. We'd found them, the diamonds gathered by Tátaba. Were they cursed, like those Egon and Angelika had been searching for, which killed their father and uncle?

I'd transited from cynic to believer. Both Chiko and I had seen and heard Tátaba in dreams, seen his diamonds. I'd heard his voice when I was awake.

Like Egon and Angelika said the day I met them, there really *were* diamonds outside the Sperrgebiet! Some were in the pot. Angelika's father, and Rodolf, and all the IDB men they'd spoken about had been right. My heart beat like a hammer. How would life be, with my beliefs annihilated?

Just then Pik looked up from the car.

'I brought something special,' he shouted, 'come see.' Angelika and I followed him to the back of the Nissan.

He opened the door, to reveal a Mobicool car refrigerator. He lifted the lid with a flourish.

'Doktor's special medicine!' he laughed, pulling out two frosty bottles of *Windhoek* lager. If there was anything I dreamed of, the sight of those bottles outdid it.

'Is it safe for him to drink?' Angelika asked.

'No harm from only one,' Pik flipped the tops off and handed the precious objects to us. I thrilled at the iciness of the glass, touched the dew running down the side, studied the green bottle like I'd never seen one before.

There was a sheaf of barley at the top centre on the bright green label. On one side was the word *'Since'*, and on the other *'1920'*. Around the outside it read *'Carefully brewed in the slow traditional way using natural ingredients only, malted barley, hops and water'*. On the metallic green wrapping around the neck were the words *'Premium Natural Lager'*.

We lifted the bottles to our mouths and drank. How much small things are taken for granted, until they are taken away!

'Chiko didn't want one,' Pik laughed, 'only drinks water!'

'This is the best beer I ever tasted,' Angelika laughed, before taking another big swig.

Forty-six

We bumped onto the main road. All the while, Sterkbooi sat silently, not taking part in the small talk. Suddenly, he spoke.

'We know about the diamonds,' he said. His words hit me like a punch in the stomach.

'What diamonds?' I meant to say, but 'how did you know?' came out instead.'

'The ones hidden in that old leather,' he said. Was there no end to this silent man's clairvoyance? I looked at Angelika, whose eyes were wide.

'Chiko told us,' Pik laughed, 'Sterkbooi isn't *that* good!'

'What do you want us to do?' Angelika asked hoarsely. My pulse beat uncomfortably in my neck, and my mouth was dry as Namib sand.

'Exactly what you were going to do,' said Sterkbooi. How did he know our plans?

'Not tell the police, the diamond squad?' I asked. Pik burst out laughing, and even Sterkbooi managed a wry grin.

'Never,' said Pik, 'they would disappear.' Sterkbooi nodded.

'No, help the San. Maybe, even, buy an MRI machine for my hospital!' My hand felt the hardness inside the folded hide. There was more than enough to build several hospitals.

'What's the name of the San charity?' I asked.

'!ga:wa,' said Angelika. At this, Chiko looked up and beamed.

'I think they're in for a change in fortune!' Angelika squeezed my hand so hard it hurt.

'I thought you were a good man, Tobias,' laughed Pik, 'and this proves it.'

Chiko joined his laughter, then, with the exception of Sterkbooi, we were all laughing.

On the last stretch to Windhoek, Angelika checked reception on her iPhone and found it was back.

'There's a voice message from Egon, must have rung me when we had no signal.' She listened for half a minute and frowned.

'What's he say?' I asked.

'Too much crackling.'

'That's Namibian morse-code,' laughed Pik.

'I wonder what he wanted.'

Home, at last, we took several days to rest and recover. We'd lost a lot of weight and were overwhelmed with physical and mental exhaustion.

I'd found Ignatius. I'd changed in a profound way. Life was so much more meaningful. To go through all I'd experienced, and not break, was astounding. I had, without realising it, conquered my fears and insecurities. It was one thing to survive due to the efforts of others, and I knew I wouldn't have made it without Chiko or Angelika. But I was surprised at my own forbearance.

'I wonder if Ignatius had any inkling that, after being a smuggler, his life out here would lead to a fortune in diamonds doing good two hundred years later,' I said.

'Couldn't have, life is so strange!'

There were other things. When we were marooned, I'd worried more about Angelika and Chiko than myself. I never imagined I'd put others before my own safety. To me, it was an insight into someone I hardly knew - myself. And, though I loved Chiko, I not only loved Angelika, but had learnt to accept her love.

Twenty-seven days ago, I'd never even met her.

I thought there'd never be another relationship for me. The Kaokoland changed everything. We survived, thanks to Chiko and the spirits of Tátaba and Ignatius, but I owed most to Angelika.

'What are you doing?' I asked. She was sitting at the table, wearing one of my shirts and busily typing on my laptop.

'Advertising for anyone who knows the names Tregurtha, Ignatius, Marana, Pengilly, N!ai, Mara, Hama, or Ignatius Xi.'

'Where?'

'Oh, all the papers in Namibia - get your debit card!'

'Yes Boss!' She hadn't lost her cheek. I gave it to her, and she entered the details.

'Add Sterkbooi Bogaert to the list of names.'

'Good idea. If not for the original Sterkbooi, Ignatius would never have survived long enough for you to trace.' A minute later she stood and stretched. 'I'm going for a walk.'

The telephone rang. It was Pik van Loon. I listened, and what I heard caused my heart to lurch. What should I do, I wondered.

I hung up and sat down to think. It was a shock, and I had no idea how to deal with it. On impulse, I fetched the keys for my Volkswagen Beetle and was shortly hurtling along the dirt road to Karibib. An hour and a half later, I was back. Just as I sat down, Angelika appeared.

'You did it,' she said, blissfully unaware of my news. She came up behind my chair and put her hands on my shoulders. She was barefoot, in a clean pair of shorts and a tee-shirt. She was thin but still lovely.

I put my arms around her waist, buried my face against her breast.

I had learnt to love, not the infatuation of teens and twenties, but deep love for another human being. Now I was about to break her heart.

'We've got a lot to do,' I said, stalling for time and taking her hands in mine.

'I know,' she said, nodding.

'I love you.'

'Oh, do you really?' Her blue eyes were wide with devilment.

'I do.' I pulled her to me. 'More than I can say. So, don't go scuttling off anywhere!'

'Will you never forget?' Angelika punched me on the arm.

'No,' I laughed, but it sounded hollow.

'I love you too, Tobias.' She nuzzled into my neck.

'Strange thing,' I said, hugging her tightly.

'What?'

'I almost miss our time in Tátaba's cave.' I was stalling for time, putting off the dreaded task before me.

'Me too. It was tough, the menu wasn't great, but I had you all to myself.' I tilted her head up and kissed her on the lips.

'Egon —' I began, coming directly to the terrible thing with which I was confronted.

'You know,' she interrupted, 'I've been thinking….'

'There's something I have to show you.' She looked up. 'You'll find out sooner or later.'

'What?'

'It's Egon. Pik rang while you were out walking. He told me it was in the paper.'

'What paper?'

'*The Namibian.*'

'What's in the paper?'

'It's about Egon,' I sighed, unfolding the newspaper on the table. 'I went to Karibib and got it. Had to see for myself. I'm so sorry…' She reached for it in alarm.

South African Resident Identified As deceased In Botswana Police Car Chase.

The man killed in a high-speed car accident near the Botswana-South Africa border crossing at Mashatu-Pont Drift on Tuesday has been identified as Mr Egon Alexander Neumann, a 38-year-old Johannesburg resident. Mr Neumann died of his injuries when his Toyota Landcruiser, pursued at speed by Botswana police, overturned on a corner. He was identified by his vehicle registration and documents in his possession, including his passport.

In a press conference at CID headquarters in Mmaraka Extension 1, Gaborone, Police spokesman Superintendent Simeon Kagiso today stated that Mr Neumann, the owner of a jewellery store in Johannesburg, had been under surveillance by plainclothes officers of the Botswana Diamond and Narcotic Squad, and had attempted to buy diamonds stolen from the Botswana Jwaneng mine.

Superintendent Kagiso issued a plea for the deceased's sister, Dr Angelika Neumann, who lectures part-time in the philosophy department at the University of Botswana in Gaborone, to urgently contact him on the following telephone number --- . He stressed that she was not suspected of any involvement in Mr Neumann's illicit diamond dealing.

From Our Gaborone Correspondent.

'Oh God!' Angelika cried, bursting into tears. I pulled her to me and kissed her. 'What's he gone and done *now?*' This was the first time I saw her really break down. She'd kept up her reserve through every nightmare.

'I'm so sorry!' I held her. I dreaded this moment ever since Pik told me the news. Breaking a thing like this to anyone wasn't easy, but to her.....

'I thought he left suddenly,' Angelika groaned, 'and he didn't put up any resistance to me staying. It was strange because he liked to get his way.'

'You said he may have gone to Botswana.'

'Oh, bloody hell!' Angelika sniffed. 'When he wasn't in Jo'burg, it should have confirmed it.' I gave her a tissue, and she blew her nose. 'I wonder what he wanted to say when he rang my cellphone in the car. Now I'll never know!'

'He was determined, one way or another, to get hold of diamonds,' I said, 'when one thing didn't work, he changed direction.'

'If he even believed there were diamonds in the Kaokoland. I think he only came to make sure we didn't find Mencken's address.'

'Maybe true,' I said.

'He had his Botswana contacts. No wonder he was in such a hurry. He didn't waste time.'

'And police informants were among them.'

'What a fool, he almost deserved to be caught,' she sobbed. 'He didn't take heed of those awful stories you told, your warnings about the risks!'

'Yes, they do always seem to come unstuck. To be honest, I thought my stories excited him.' She nodded.

Tears streamed down her face. My feelings were torn and confused. For Egon, I was sorry. But, for Angelika, this girl I loved so dearly, clinging to me and weeping uncontrollably, my heart broke. Vicarious grief, sorrow for the pain of another. My throat tightened and tears blurred my vision.

'The worst thing,' Angelika said, staring up at me with red eyes, 'is that I'm angry. I can never confront him with his lies about Mencken, hiding the address, his blackmail, and now this...!'

At the time, I never imagined my search for Ignatius would be ignited after Egon left us in Karibib. Strange, isn't it, how some people's real agenda can differ so widely from how it first appears? Yet the part he played was central to what happened. If he hadn't left Angelika with me, I wouldn't have confided in her, and we wouldn't have been together in the Kaokoland. I'd never have found the cave, the diamonds or Ignatius' manuscript. Nor would we be together now. *Kismet,* as Ignatius referred to the fates, is a fickle, capricious and unpredictable thing!

'What are we going to do?' I asked, wiping my eyes on the back of my hand.

'*We,* Tobias? No, you were dragged into this, not your problem.'

'We, your problem is mine!' I took a tissue from the box.

'You mean it Tobias?' She tried to smile.

'Of course!' I wiped my eyes.

'What should we do?'

'It's awful, but we have to call that police superintendent. It would be suspicious if we didn't.'

'What will I say?' I wished I could do it for her, but I couldn't. She could only do it on her own.

358

'It's standard procedure, contacting relatives when someone is killed. You're not under suspicion.'

'I never even worked with diamonds, I went to University when Egon started in the business.'

'I know. You're an academic, beyond suspicion.'

'Wouldn't be if they knew....'

'They won't. Anyway, they aren't stolen, and aren't for us.' Thank goodness, I thought, she isn't like her brother! *Late* brother, I corrected myself.

'It's best I ring now, don't put it off.'

It took half an hour to get through to Superintendent Simeon Kagiso at Botswana Police Headquarters. Angelika confirmed her identity and that Egon was her brother.

The Superintendent gave his condolences on behalf of the Botswana police, then asked if she knew about her brother's business affairs. She didn't. As an academic, she didn't have anything to do with jewellery, let alone diamonds.

She had no knowledge of the black-market diamond trade, and was surprised her brother engaged in it.

She was on holiday in Namibia, had just returned from a guided tour, which could be confirmed by Mr Tobias Vingoe of Namib Safari Tours, at whose home in Karibib she currently was. Her bank details were available, and they'd find the only deposits were her salary and expenses as lecturer and researcher.

He asked what arrangements she'd make for her brother's funeral, and gave her the contact number of the undertaker where his body was.

An officer from the Botswana FIA or *Financial Intelligence Agency* would be in touch about the bank details, but it was a formality.

He took down her contact numbers. With that, his responsibility ended.

'It's done,' she said as she replaced the receiver. Her face was strained, her eyes red from weeping. I took her in my arms.

'You're a brave girl!' In the short time I'd known her, she'd proved it over and over. Now she was facing her sadness with great dignity and self-control.

'Am I?'

'You know you are!' I hugged her close and kissed her lips.

'What about the bodies …?'

'I agree with one thing Egon said…' She was silent, and I waited several seconds before I spoke.

'They won't be any more-dead if we don't mention them.'

'No, they won't.'

'You okay?' I asked, holding her by the shoulders and staring into her eyes.

'I've got you, thank heavens!'

'And I've got you!'

When we told Chiko the news, he was, for once, lost for words. He grasped Angelika's hands and placed his forehead against hers for a whole minute. It was his way of condoling. Literally, a meeting of minds, an 'I'm with you' without words. He hadn't liked Egon, but he felt her pain.

Chiko stayed behind when we flew to Botswana.

Ten days later, we sat on the sofa.

Angelika was coping with her awful news courageously since we came back from Botswana, where she dealt with the formalities of her brother's death and funeral.

'Strange, isn't it' she said, 'Egon dead, trying to buy a fraction of what we've got, and us free as birds?'

'We're doing it for the poorest people on earth.'

'I know,' she replied, snuggling against me. 'I've been thinking about Egon. He was determined to stop me finding out he was blackmailing Mencken.'

'That's for sure.'

'It was *him* who smudged the 'M' on the back of the map. He knew who it was, and didn't want me to discover what he was up to. When Rodolf didn't come back, he must have thought the secret died with him.'

'Then you decided to search —'

'Exactly, and he thought he'd better go along. If Rodolf was alive, no problem, because he never discussed business, legal or illegal, with me.'

'But if he was dead —'

'And we found him, there might be something written down…..'

'Which might lead you to Mencken.'

'Then it would all come out.'

'You think his whole motivation was to keep you in the dark?'

'Yes. Whatever he was, Egon loved me. He never loved anyone else. He lost his mother when I was born, his father when he was young. He was never close to Rodolf, never had a girlfriend.'

'What you thought of him must have been very important…..'

'Maybe the most important thing to him. You must have noticed,' Angelika said, 'that he had a nervous tic in his eyelid.'

'One of the first things I noticed.'

'Until we started our first expedition, I never saw it before.'

'Nerves?'

'Tics are a sign of arousal. He was terrified.'

'That you'd stumble on the truth, expose his blackmail.'

'And, for him, even worse, that he'd been deceiving me.' We were silent for several minutes. Even Egon, I mused, though not easy to like, had a human side. He was a complex, difficult man, avaricious and friendless, but even in his black heart he loved somebody. Who was I, with all my failings, to judge others?

'What about Ignatius, now you've found him?'

'He needs to rest now, wherever he is. Spooky though, isn't it, that he and Marana and Sterkbooi lived for five years at !Anis, old Rehoboth, that Pengilly was born there, and that there's a Sterkbooi living there today!'

'Yes, very strange. But Ignatius needed you to find his writing, just like you needed to find it. Do you feel more settled?'

'I do, especially since I found you!'

'That's so sweet,' she said, kissing me on the cheek.

'Isn't it amazing? Ignatius' story kept you alive in Cornwall and brought you to Namibia. You found Chiko and a way to make a living. Then we met. Now you've found Ignatius, we've got each other, and a small matter of Tátaba's diamonds and landless San to deal with. I'm sure Chiko and Pik will advise us.'

'We'll do it. By any means, fair or foul!'

'There's nothing foul about helping those wonderful people,' she said, taking both my hands and squeezing. I squeezed back.

'Tea for the Hu and his snake-woman,' shouted Chiko in San, loudly ringing the kitchen bell.

He bustled into the room with a broad grin and two cups on a tray.

END

EPILOGUE

It was another beautiful sunny day in Windhoek. Sunlit purple Jacarandas and hanging bunches of golden shower danced to the tune of the gentle street breeze. I parked my beloved Land Rover, retrieved at great expense from the Kaokoland and sporting a new side shaft.

Chiko alighted, grinning broadly, for once persuaded to dress in a brand-new shirt, long trousers and sandals. He followed Angelika and me as we walked arm in arm into the grand entrance foyer of the New Africa Hotel.

Waiting for us were Pik van Loon and Sterkbooi Bogaert. Together, we followed the sign with the words 'Family Reunion'.

They were gathered in the big reception room. Thirty-three people in all, male and female, children and adults of different ages, varying in skin colour from very dark to very pale. They were a cross-section of modern Namibian society. As we entered, everyone broke into applause.

'These people,' Angelika whispered, 'are your family. They wouldn't be here if Ignatius and Sterkbooi hadn't jumped ship in Cape Town, or if you hadn't been so determined to find what happened to Ignatius.' I squeezed her hand.

'Or if *you* hadn't stuck with me through it all,' I said.

I looked at the expectant faces. She was right. These were the lasting progeny of three dispossessed peoples, San, Rehoboth Baster and Cornish, alive after more than two centuries. Never again would I feel so alone and abandoned. The first chink in that wall of indifference had been Chiko, then I found Angelika, and now, here in Africa, I had an extended family. What would Ignatius and Tátaba think?

Ω

Printed in Great Britain
by Amazon